HAZARDOUS DUTY

OTHER BOOKS AND AUDIO BOOKS
BY BETSY BRANNON GREEN:

HAGGERTY MYSTERIES

Hearts in Hiding

Until Proven Guilty

Above Suspicion

Silenced

Copycat

Poison

Double Cross

Backtrack

OTHER NOVELS

Never Look Back

Don't Close Your Eyes

Foul Play

Christmas in Haggerty

HAZARDOUS DUTY

a novel by

BETSY BRANNON GREEN

Covenant Communications, Inc.

Top Image: "Congressional Medal of Honor Displayed in the Capitol Building Tallahassee Florida" photography by Ilene McDonald. © 2007 Alamy Images. www. alamyimages.com.
Background Image: "Soldier Hiding Behind Leaves Wearing a Camouflage Helmet" photography by Nick Daly. © 2007 by Digital Vision/Getty Images. www.gettyimages.com.

Published by Covenant Communications, Inc.
American Fork, Utah

Printed in Canada
First Printing: September 2007

11 10 09 08 07 10 9 8 7 6 5 4 3 2 1

ISBN 978-1-59811-445-4

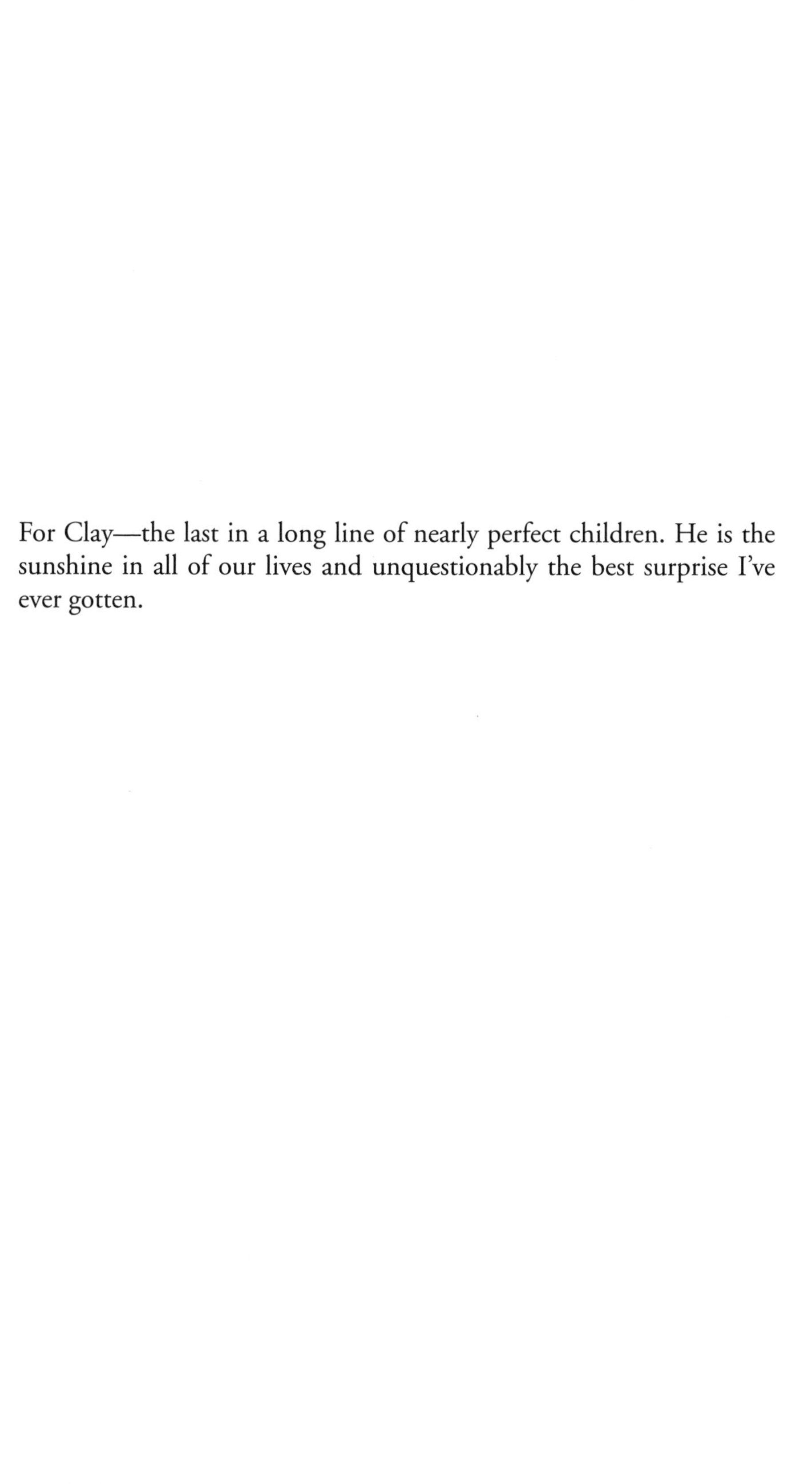

For Clay—the last in a long line of nearly perfect children. He is the sunshine in all of our lives and unquestionably the best surprise I've ever gotten.

ACKNOWLEDGMENTS

Thanks first and always to Butch. He not only helps me through the struggles of life—he makes life worth living. I couldn't accomplish anything without the support I receive from him and my children. They love me even when I'm at my worst (which is more often than I like to admit), and they encourage me when I think I'm unequal to a task (which is pretty much all the time).

I also appreciate the love and support I get from my extended family, friends, and faithful readers. Your comments, questions, and suggestions are invaluable. Thank you for trusting me with your time and for sharing my books with your friends. You'll never know how much I appreciate it when you take moments from your busy lives to e-mail me.

As always I owe a huge debt of gratitude to the people at Covenant, who consistently put out some of the best LDS fiction on the market. I am particularly grateful to my editor, Kirk Shaw, for all he does to bring out the best in my books and to Jessica Warner and the others in the art department for creating such wonderful covers. Special thanks also to Rachel Langlois for promoting me and my books so well. I'm proud to be associated with all of you!

PROLOGUE

From her position behind the cameraman, Savannah McLaughlin covertly checked the clock on the wall of the studio at Channel 7, the ABC affiliate for the Washington, DC metropolitan area. She needed to leave in fifteen minutes in order to pick up her daughter from school.

With growing anxiety, Savannah sidled over to her assistant, Lacie Fox, and whispered, "If we don't wrap this up soon, I'm going to be late getting Caroline."

Although Lacie was in her thirties, she could easily be mistaken for a teenager at first glance. Small and thin, she wore trendy clothes, applied makeup with a heavy hand, and changed her hair color often. Today the short, overprocessed tufts were burgundy—with a little of last week's platinum still visible in spots.

"Do you want me to go get her?" Lacie offered.

Savannah shook her head. "No, but you might have to do this commercial for me."

Lacie's eyes widened in horror, and Savannah laughed, earning herself a scowl from the cameraman.

"I'm just kidding." Savannah glanced toward the set where a poor-looking family was gathered around a fake fireplace. A couple of ragged stockings were strategically hung to designate the season, indicating that Christmas was being observed but not really celebrated. There were no gifts or tree. The whole spot was cliché and overly sentimental, and Savannah wished she wasn't a part of it.

"They've filmed that same shot from every possible angle," Savannah continued in her complaints. "Surely they've got enough footage by now!"

"Surely," Lacie agreed.

Savannah checked the clock again. Now she had ten minutes. Then a voice spoke behind her. "We're ready for you to add the crowning moment of this piece," the director said, and Savannah resisted the urge to roll her eyes. He turned to the cameraman. "Once Mrs. McLaughlin is in place, focus on her, but keep the family scene visible in the background."

The director rushed off as if he were directing an Oscar contender instead of a fifteen-second public service announcement.

"Go crown this thing, quick," Lacie teased. "So we can all get out of here."

Savannah picked her way carefully through the tangle of cable strewn along the studio floor. She ran a hand over her hair, although she already knew every professionally highlighted blonde strand was in its proper place. After taking a position in front of the camera, she gave the edge of her lavender suit jacket a tug. And when the red light flashed, she addressed the camera.

"I'm Savannah McLaughlin of the Child Advocacy Center," she said. "No child should live in a cold house. No child should ever go to bed hungry—especially not on Christmas Eve. I hope you'll join me in making this holiday season merrier for needy children by contributing to "Santa's Helpers." Donations are being accepted at all police and fire stations in the DC area. Remember, you *can* make a difference."

The light on the camera went out, and the director said, "Perfect as always."

Savannah smiled more from relief than the compliment. "Thanks." She turned and waved to Lacie. "I'm gone to get Caroline!"

"I'll be leaving in a few minutes myself," Lacie replied. "See you tomorrow."

Savannah left the studio and hurried down the hall toward the station's front entrance. She maneuvered through the revolving door and stepped from the cool lobby into the steamy August afternoon. During the short walk to her car she unbuttoned her jacket to allow a little air to circulate through her light silk blouse. She was in the process of unlocking her car when her cell phone rang. She opened the phone and pressed it to her ear as she slid into the car's sweltering interior.

"Hey," her boss, Doug Forton, greeted. "Lacie said the piece went great."

"The piece went *long,*" Savannah corrected. "I should have been out of there an hour ago."

Doug didn't seem concerned by the time she'd lost. "Think of all the underprivileged children you helped."

Savannah clenched her teeth together. Of course she was glad to do anything she could for poor children. But Doug was always volunteering her for things. She couldn't decide if he really wanted to earn the goodwill of local leaders or if he was just showing her off like a prize pony.

"How about dinner tonight?" he invited.

"Can't," she returned without stopping to consider her schedule.

"Why not?" Doug pressed.

She started the car and turned on the air conditioner as high as it would go. "I have a daughter."

"You can get a sitter," Doug cajoled.

"I'm away from Caroline all day. I won't leave her again at night." She backed out of her parking space and drove toward the parking lot's exit. "I'm going to let you go so I can concentrate on the traffic. Talk to you later." Without waiting for his response, Savannah disconnected the call and checked the clock on the dashboard. It was going to be close.

By the time she crossed Roosevelt Memorial Bridge and turned on to Constitution Avenue, Savannah started to relax. She was only a few minutes behind schedule—which was bad, but forgivable. She readjusted the air conditioner vents and tuned the radio to her favorite station. Then she smiled, anticipating the happy reunion with her daughter. It was the moment she most looked forward to every day.

Savannah was trying to decide whether they would go straight to the park, which she knew would be Caroline's preference, or if they should stop for a sandwich first, when she saw the red flashing lights. There was a car crash at the intersection half a block from the entrance to Epic School where Caroline was enrolled. Since Savannah hadn't been able to see the crash before she turned, she was now stuck in a hopeless tangle of traffic. She stared at the roof of Caroline's school, so close and yet so far away.

Anxious to do something constructive, she pulled out her cell phone and entered the school's number. Seconds later, the annoying tones of a busy signal pinged in her ear. She ground her teeth together in frustration. It seemed that when things went wrong, they *really* went wrong.

A horn honked behind her, and she realized that there was a two-foot gap between her car and the vehicle in front of her. She eased forward before dialing Lacie's cell number.

"Lacie Fox," her assistant answered promptly.

"There's a wreck on my side of the school, and I'm stuck in traffic," Savannah explained. "I'll never make it before car-line ends, but if you come from the other direction, you might be able to get there in time."

"On my way," Lacie promised and disconnected the call.

Savannah concentrated on the tail lights of the car in front of her, inching forward at a maddeningly slow pace. She had progressed maybe a foot when her cell phone rang. "This is Savannah McLaughlin," she said in her professional voice.

"Savannah, it's Lacie." The assistant sounded out of breath. "I've got a problem."

"What kind of problem?" Savannah struggled for patience.

"A flat tire," Lacie announced. "It will only take me a few minutes to change it, and then I can go and get Caroline."

"Never mind, I'll be there before you can change a tire and drive to the school. I've been trying to get through to the office to let them know I'll be a few minutes late, but I keep getting a busy signal. Maybe you can try too?"

"Will do," Lacie promised. "And say hi to the little princess for me."

Sirens heralded the arrival of ambulances, and Savannah felt guilty for her self-absorption. The people involved in the wreck had worse problems than she did. She turned up the radio and tried not to worry.

It took almost twenty minutes for Savannah to get past the wreckage, and she was nearly frantic by the time she drove her car through the gates of the brick fence that separated Caroline and the other students of Epic School from the rest of Washington, DC. She parked in front of the main entrance in flagrant disobedience of the several signs posted along the curb.

By the time she climbed the twenty-seven steps to the front door and rushed in to the lobby, she was perspiring and out of breath. The wooden bench, where children with tardy parents usually waited, was empty. Hoping that the principal hadn't called the police and reported her for negligence, Savannah hurried into the school office.

"I'm Savannah McLaughlin," she told the woman sitting at the reception desk.

The woman, obviously used to dealing with self-important Washington types, gave her a bland look. "And how can I help you?"

Savannah took a deep breath before she answered, "My daughter Caroline is a first grade student here. I'm late picking her up."

After glancing out at the empty bench in the lobby, the woman said, "One moment, please." She lifted the receiver from the console on her desk and spoke to another school employee. When she hung up the phone, she said, "Caroline was picked up fifteen minutes ago."

"That's impossible," Savannah replied. Then she started to second guess herself. It seemed unlikely that Lacie would have been able to get her tire fixed quickly enough, but . . .

"Who signed for Caroline?" she asked.

The receptionist sighed as if gathering this piece of information was a huge inconvenience, and Savannah began mentally composing a letter of complaint to the director. After another brief consultation, the woman informed Savannah, "According to the parent sign-out sheet, *you* picked up your daughter."

"Well the sign-out sheet is wrong, since clearly I don't have her," Savannah shot back.

At this point a middle-aged woman rushed in, and the receptionist said, "This is Mrs. Land, the head teacher for our first grade. Perhaps she can help you."

Savannah turned toward the teacher, grateful to have someone more cooperative to deal with. "I'm here to pick up my daughter," she told Mrs. Land. "And apparently she's been misplaced."

Mrs. Land looked tired and proportionately stressed after a day of dealing with precocious six-year-olds. She pointed to a clipboard in her hand and said, "Here's the sign-out sheet. Isn't that your signature?"

Savannah stared at her own name. It wasn't exactly her signature, but close. "No, I didn't write that," she said. "And I didn't pick up Caroline."

So far during the experience Savannah had been annoyed, confused, and even angry, but not really scared. However, when she saw the fear on the faces of Mrs. Land and the rude receptionist, her heart started to pound. The door to the director's office opened, and Mr. Segars himself walked out, looking grim.

Over the ringing in her ears, Savannah heard Mrs. Land explain the situation to Mr. Segars. The director instructed the receptionist to call the police. At that moment, Savannah was forced to accept that this was not a clerical error or an administrative mistake. Caroline, her child, her heart, and her reason for living, had been kidnapped. Then she felt herself falling and everything went black.

CHAPTER 1

Savannah McLaughlin stared dully out the window of her office at the sprawl of Washington, DC below. It had been late summer when Caroline had been abducted from one of the most secure and respected educational institutions in the area. Now multicolored leaves were falling from the trees that lined Constitution Avenue as autumn asserted its authority over nature.

Two months had gone by since that awful day that had changed her life forever. Two months without a ransom note or a demand of any kind. No one had seen or heard from Caroline. It was as if the child had disappeared from the face of the earth. Savannah closed her eyes and pictured her daughter's smiling face. Surely someone so beautiful and full of life couldn't just evaporate.

"Savannah," Lacie said from the doorway. "You need to go home and get some sleep."

"I can't sleep," Savannah whispered. "And I certainly can't go home."

"Well you can't go on like this," Lacie insisted.

Savannah ran her fingers through her unwashed hair. "I know."

Lacie came further into the office and stood by the window. "It's been almost two months, and statistically speaking . . ."

"There are always exceptions," Savannah pointed out.

"It's been too long," Lacie whispered.

Savannah glanced at the faxes and e-mails and bulletins stacked on her desk. "Maybe today someone will see her and call us . . ."

Lacie bowed her head, bringing her orange hair tufts directly into Savannah's line of sight. "It's time to accept reality and go on with your life."

"What life?" Savannah demanded. "What will I do if I stop searching for Caroline? Go back to my regular job looking for *other people's* children?"

Lacie leaned closer. "If you don't eat or sleep, you'll die. How will that help?"

Savannah put her face in her hands for a few seconds and collected what was left of her composure. Lacie was right—she wasn't thinking clearly. She opened her eyes and said, "Okay."

Lacie seemed relieved. "I know letting go is hard, but sometimes it's the only way."

Savannah shook her head. "I won't stop looking for Caroline. I *can't* do that. But I will try to take better care of myself."

"You're going to drive yourself crazy if you don't stop obsessing," Lacie warned. "You've already tried everything."

Savannah returned her gaze to the window as a desperate idea started to form. "No, Lacie," she corrected. "I haven't tried everything quite yet."

Lacie raised her hands in supplication. "What is left?"

Savannah licked her lips and forced the words out. "I have an old . . ." she searched for the right word and finally settled on ". . . *friend* who finds people for the Army. Maybe he could do the same for me."

Lacie looked astounded. "And why haven't you mentioned him before?"

Savannah considered this. "Our relationship is, well . . . complicated, and I'd contact him only as a last resort."

"We were down to last resorts a month ago," Lacie pointed out.

Savannah acknowledged this with a sad smile. "The real reason I didn't mention him is because I'm not sure he'll help me."

"What kind of *friend* would refuse to help you find your child?"

"I told you. Our relationship is complicated."

Lacie shrugged. "It's worth a try. But before you begin the next round, I'm going to take you home. You need rest and calories and a bath."

"Home," Savannah whispered.

"Don't worry," Lacie said. "I'll be there with you."

* * *

Sixty-three days after Caroline McLaughlin's kidnapping, Savannah sat in the reception area outside the office of Major General Nolan Steele, commanding officer for the U.S. Army Intelligence and Security Command in Fort Belvoir, Virginia. Although she was clean, her hair hadn't been tinted or trimmed in over two months, her nails were chewed to the quick, and her suit was a size too big.

Trying to forget about her less-than-optimum appearance, Savannah glanced up at the general's new secretary. The woman looked back with obvious disapproval. Years ago when Savannah had worked for General Steele, she too had been disdainful of friends and former employees who took advantage of their relationship with him for personal reasons. Now she understood how it felt to be desperate beyond pride, beyond shame.

The office door opened and General Steele walked out to greet her. He was an inspiring sight in full uniform. Tall with broad shoulders that looked equal to any task, he was just the kind of man the country needed in these perilous times.

"Savannah," he said, wrapping his arms around her in a gentle embrace. "Has there been any news about your daughter?"

She blinked back tears that were never far away. "No."

He released her and pointed toward his office. "Come in and have a seat."

She preceded him into the familiar room and settled into one of the leather chairs positioned in front of his desk. Instead of walking around the desk, he took the chair beside her.

Clasping her hands nervously in her lap, she said, "Thank you for seeing me on such short notice."

He waved this aside. "Nonsense, you're like family. I always have time for you." He crossed his legs and regarded her. "I've been following your situation, both on television and through official channels. From what I understand, there's been no ransom demand?"

Savannah resisted the urge to rub her temples where a headache was starting to form. This conversation was unavoidable, but the necessity didn't make it any easier.

"No," she confirmed. "The only communication I've received from the kidnapper is a card that was delivered on the day Caroline was kidnapped. I'm not at liberty to disclose the exact content, but it indicated that she'd been kidnapped to punish me."

"For what?" the general asked.

"I don't know," she told him honestly.

"Do you have many enemies?"

"None that I know of," she said. "The police and FBI assumed the motive was related to my job at the Child Advocacy Center, but they checked into every case I've handled since I've been there and found nothing." Savannah chose her next words carefully. "The authorities have worked very hard trying to find Caroline, and I'm not being critical of their efforts. But after two months, we don't know any more than we did on the day my daughter disappeared."

"That must be very frustrating," he said.

"It is," she agreed. "And every day I see a little less enthusiasm from the officers and agents assigned to the case. I understand that there have been no breaks, no leads, no progress, and they feel that their time might be better spent on other cases. And statistically speaking, Caroline's chances of survival are decreasing by the minute. So I feel that the time has come for me to take drastic action."

The general nodded. "How can I help?"

Tears stung her eyes again. He was making it so easy for her. "Since all the normal avenues of investigation seem to have been exhausted, I think it's time to try something abnormal."

"Abnormal?" he repeated.

"I need help from the person you trained to find people."

General Steele sat up straight in his chair as the seriousness of her request dawned on him. "I understand that you're feeling desperate," he told her. "But I think involving Dane would be most unwise."

"He's the only hope I have left."

General Steele shook his head. "He's not the same man you knew years ago. He was seriously wounded while in the Russian prison."

She nodded, remembering the last time she'd seen Dane—one of his legs in traction, his face swathed in bandages. It was heartbreaking to watch him lying there so helpless and in terrible pain. But before she could offer any sympathy, he'd stopped her with a malevolent look from the bloodshot eyes peering at her between layers of gauze. Now, years later and sitting in the general's office, she still shuddered at the memory.

"Is he terribly deformed?" she made herself ask.

"He has residual effects," the general replied vaguely. "The Army has placed him on limited duty, and he only takes cases he's interested in. I haven't been able to 'interest' him in anything for quite a while."

"He always liked a challenge," Savannah remarked. "And Caroline's kidnapping is certainly that."

The general looked pained as he said, "I hate to point this out, but you're the last person he'd want to help. And if revenge is the motive for your daughter's kidnapping, you'd be wiser to consider Dane a suspect than to ask for his help."

Savannah closed her eyes briefly, garnering her strength. "No matter how much he hates me, kidnapping helpless children is not Dane's style," she said with confidence. "He's an expert at locating and extracting people. He has contacts all over the world on both sides of the law. He's smart and relentless, and I'm hoping he won't be able to resist the chance to make me grovel."

There was sympathy in General Steele's eyes as he said, "I'd like to help you, Savannah. But what you're asking is impossible."

"Nothing is impossible," she insisted.

"Actually, some things are," the general disputed. "Dane can't take your case because he's in prison."

The unexpected obstacle took Savannah completely by surprise. "Prison?" she repeated.

"Dane was caught on the wrong side of the law, publicly this time, and there was nothing the Army could do. He was convicted and sentenced to three years at the Petersburg Federal Correctional Complex near Richmond."

Savannah processed the new information and decided that while inconvenient, this was not an insurmountable problem. "You can get him out," she told General Steele with certainty.

His eyebrows rose. "You overestimate my authority. I can't circumvent the law. Dane will have to serve his time. We are working to have his sentence reduced, but we have to go through legal channels, and that takes time . . ."

"Now," she interrupted. "I'm going to have to insist that you get him out *now.*"

The general had never been anything but kind to her, and she watched with sadness as his expression changed from sympathetic to guarded. "I've already explained that Dane's fate is beyond my control."

Savannah clutched her trembling fingers more firmly together and forced herself to say, "A few months ago, I found a disc Wes had hidden. It was labeled 'Operation Nick at Night.'"

General Steele paled noticeably, and Savannah knew her words had hit the desired mark.

"The disc contains the details of an operation that went tragically wrong in Nicaragua a few years ago. The names of all the participants are listed, the mission is explained, and the killing spree that resulted is carefully documented. There are even some pictures—probably taken with a cell phone. And the subsequent cover-up is described as well."

"I'll have to ask you to give me that disc," the general said, his voice cold.

"I will be glad to give it to you." He looked relieved, and she hated to dash his hopes. "As soon as my daughter is located and returned to me."

"You're trying to blackmail me?"

"I prefer to consider the disc as incentive," she amended.

The general frowned. "Possessing information like that can be very dangerous."

"Not nearly as dangerous as being held hostage by a kidnapper," she countered. "I'm sure you'll agree that it would be cheaper and much less embarrassing for the Army to arrange Dane's release from prison than to have the information on that disc made public."

His eyes were so cold she had to control a shiver. "Even if I can get him out, I can't guarantee that he will help you. No one can force Dane to do anything."

Savannah nodded. "I'll handle that part if you'll set up a visit for me at the prison."

"I can set up a visit," General Steele replied. "Whether he'll see you or not is another matter entirely."

"He'll see me." She had no doubt.

General Steele reached across his desk and picked up the phone. "I'll arrange for a visit and have my driver take you there."

"That's not necessary," Savannah said.

All traces of friendliness were gone as the general replied, "Oh, I think it is."

In spite of her disloyal behavior, she trusted him. So she nodded. "Thank you."

The general didn't respond.

She wanted to add an apology but was afraid it might be interpreted as a sign of weakness. So she stood and walked through the door into the waiting area beyond without a backward glance.

CHAPTER 2

Savannah was escorted to the officers' parking area by a stern lieutenant. He walked up to a black sedan and opened the back passenger door. Once she was settled into the backseat, he closed the door and climbed in behind the wheel.

As they merged in to westbound traffic and headed for Richmond, she pulled out her cell phone and called Lacie at the Child Advocacy Center. "I'm on my way to the Petersburg Federal Correctional Complex now," she told her assistant. "As it turns out, my friend is incarcerated there."

"That's bad," Lacie decided.

"But if I can talk Dane into helping me, the general will get him out."

"That's good."

"I suppose. But I can never ask the general for anything again. I've definitely burned my bridges with him."

"It couldn't be avoided," Lacie said. "Have you eaten today?"

Savannah thought for a minute. "No."

"I put a snack in your purse. Eat it now unless you want to faint when you see your old friend."

"If I thought it would convince him to help me, I'd give it a try," Savannah murmured as she searched her purse. There was a pack of cheese crackers and a Hershey bar.

"Eat the snack," Lacie advised again.

"Thanks, Lacie," Savannah replied. Then she disconnected the call.

While Savannah nibbled on a cracker, she leaned her head against the cool glass of the car's window, and the memories, held so long at bay, came back of their own accord.

* * *

She had met Wes and Dane on the same day nearly eight years earlier. It was also her first day as an official member of General Steele's staff. Fresh from William and Mary with a bachelor's degree in government, Savannah was nervous and excited and sure that she could single-handedly change the world.

When Savannah arrived at the personnel office that first morning, she found the general's personal secretary, Louise, waiting for her. Louise was a heavyset woman with light brown skin, cotton-white hair, and a no-nonsense attitude. After greeting Savannah with a firm handshake, she went about the business of getting the new employee settled.

The morning was a blur of forms to be filled out, rules to be kept, and endless hallways that all looked the same. By lunchtime Savannah had given up any hope of changing the world and just prayed that she'd be able to find her way back to Louise's desk when she left the cafeteria.

Savannah did make it back to Louise after lunch, with a minimum of wrong turns, but before she could enjoy her accomplishment, she was startled by the sound of shouting from the general's office. Savannah approached Louise and pointed at the door. "Do you think you should check on General Steele?"

Louise shook her head. "No, it's just a couple of delinquent majors here to get their weekly reprimand."

"There are majors under the general's command who get in trouble every week?" Savannah asked as the decibel level inside the office increased.

"Unfortunately," Louise confirmed. "They wreck cars and break laws and misappropriate taxpayer funds. But this time they've outdone themselves. They created an international incident in India."

Savannah stepped a little closer and whispered, "Do you think he'll court martial them?"

Louise sighed. "He should, no doubt about that. But since they lead the best extraction team in the Army, I expect he'll just yell at them for awhile and turn them loose on some other unsuspecting nation."

"What do they extract?"

"People," Louise clarified. "If the Army wants someone removed from wherever they are, they call in the Special Ops extraction team. The team finds whomever and removes them—whether the extractee wants to go or not."

"That can't be an easy job," Savannah murmured.

"It's not," Louise agreed. "The two of them are like evil geniuses—which is why the general puts up with them."

At this pronouncement, the door to the general's office had opened and two men stepped out. They were both strikingly handsome yet completely different—like opposite sides of a beautiful coin. One was tall and lean with blond hair and bright blue eyes. The other was shorter and compact with dark coloring and a mischievous smile. Neither man seemed fazed by the tongue-lashing they'd just received from a general. And both men zeroed in on Savannah the moment they saw her.

"You're new," the shorter one said.

Savannah glanced at his nametag. "Yes, Major Dane, I'm new."

"Are you a college intern?" the taller officer asked as he fixed her with a practiced smile.

"No, Major McLaughlin," Savannah read from his nametag. "I'm a college graduate and a paid employee. Today is my first day."

"Well, then you need someone to show you the ropes." Major Dane reinserted himself into the conversation. "And I'd be glad to do the honors."

"I saw her first," Major McLaughlin argued.

"That's just because you turned tail and ran out of the general's office the fastest," Major Dane contended. "But I *asked* first." He turned his attention back to Savannah. "Wouldn't you like to eat dinner with me tonight?"

Savannah had plenty of experience deflecting unwanted attention from men. And she was smart enough to realize that most of their interest in her was fueled by competition rather than genuine attraction.

"Dinner tonight is a good idea." Major McLaughlin stepped in front of his companion. "But go with me instead. I'm a better conversationalist and am considerably more charming."

"Both claims are flagrantly untrue," Major Dane countered. "Besides, you already have a date for tonight."

"So do you!" Major McLaughlin shot back.

"Now why don't you go on about your business and leave Savannah alone!" Louise interjected from her desk.

Savannah didn't appreciate the secretary's interference. She could take care of herself and wanted these two men to know it. "They aren't bothering me," Savannah said. Then she addressed the majors. "Thanks, but I don't need anyone to show me the ropes or pay for my meals."

"You heard her," Louise said with satisfaction. "She's not interested."

"Of course you don't *need* our help, Savannah." Major Dane changed tactics like the military genius he apparently was. "But it only makes sense to utilize all the available resources. I'm offering you a free meal with good company and a chance to learn about Fort Belvoir from someone who really knows. What sensible woman would refuse an offer like that?"

Savannah was mildly intrigued but still wary.

Major Dane saw her hesitation and reached up to put an arm around the shoulder of his taller companion. "We'll bring Wes along as a chaperone if that will make you more comfortable. And since he has a hefty trust fund, we'll even let him pay!"

Major McLaughlin smiled again. "My presence would guarantee that Dane behaves like a gentleman, and I'd be delighted to buy your dinner. But Dane will have to pay for his own food."

Louise stood and made shooing motions with her hands. "You two get out of here—go burn down an embassy or insult a diplomat or whatever is on your trouble-making agenda for today. She's got work to do and doesn't have time to fool with the likes of you."

Major McLaughlin looked offended. "We're decorated Army officers! We don't make trouble—we ensure domestic tranquility!"

Louise made a derisive sound.

Instead of defending himself, Major Dane used the insult as a bargaining tool. "We'll leave as soon as we find out what time she gets off work."

"Five o'clock," the secretary replied with obvious disapproval.

Major Dane grinned. "Perfect. We'll be back at five. You can come too, Louise," he invited generously. "It will be like a welcome to Fort Belvoir party."

"It's bad enough that I have to spend part of my working hours with you, and I'm definitely not going to waste my off-time in your company," Louise assured them.

Major Dane stepped closer to Savannah and whispered, "So are you up to the challenge?"

Savannah frowned. "After the way you've groveled, a refusal would be so embarrassing for you. So I guess I'll accept—out of pity."

She thought they might retract their invitation, but they didn't.

"Is that a yes?" Major Dane asked.

"Yes," Savannah confirmed.

"We'll come by to get you at five." Major McLaughlin started for the door, pulling his friend along with him.

"And your invitation still stands, Louise," Major Dane added over his shoulder, "if you change your mind."

"Change my mind indeed," Louise repeated disparagingly. Once the men were gone, she told Savannah, "You'd better think twice about getting involved with those two. Neither one of them has a lick of sense."

Throughout the rest of that first day on General Steele's staff, Louise had taken every opportunity to warn Savannah against any association with the two majors. Rather than discourage her, this continuous tirade stiffened Savannah's resolve to keep her appointment. If these officers were as dangerous as Louise claimed, backing down from them would be a monumental mistake. She had to show them from the start that she couldn't be intimidated.

Savannah didn't feel quite so confident when five o'clock arrived. It had been a long day, and she would have preferred to go back to her tiny little apartment and collapse on the couch. But she was not a coward, and she would not show fear. She had pulled a compact from her purse and was studying the reflection of one magnified eye when the majors arrived.

"You boys better behave yourselves tonight," the secretary said when she saw them.

Major Dane frowned at Louise. "I'm offended that you would think it necessary to say such a thing!"

The secretary shook her head in disgust. "It's impossible to offend you. Now I mean it. Act like a gentleman!"

"I'll keep him in line," Major McLaughlin promised.

Louise didn't look impressed. "Like you did in India?"

Major McLaughlin shrugged. "I'll be more vigilant tonight."

Major Dane drew himself up to his full height and extended his arm to Savannah. "May I escort you to dinner?" he asked with exaggerated chivalry.

Louise rolled her eyes.

Savannah laughed and put her hand through the crook of his elbow. "Sure."

Major McLaughlin took possession of her other arm. "I don't want Dane to get the idea that he's your only date tonight," he said as he tucked her arm around his.

Savannah lifted her elbows. "This clearly designates us as a threesome."

"Awkward." Major Dane led them toward the door. "But I'll deal with it until Savannah picks me."

"Or me," Major McLaughlin added, patting Savannah's hand.

As they walked, Major Dane announced that they were eating at the Poor Man's Grille, which he claimed he had chosen to fit his budget.

"I thought you said Major McLaughlin was paying," Savannah reminded him.

"Call me Wes," the major requested. "And Dane loves to harp on the fact that I inherited money—as if that's something to be ashamed of."

"Wes here is a full-fledged, card-carrying aristocrat. His real name is Westinghouse McLaughlin IV. Westinghouse—like the refrigerators," Major Dane clarified.

Wes laughed. "I was named after my great-great-grandfather, not a kitchen appliance."

"He's always been rich because of a trust fund from his grandfather, Westinghouse II," Major Dane added. "But while we were at West Point, his parents took an oath of poverty and signed all their money over to him, so now he's like one of the richest men in the world."

"Not even close," Wes contended in exasperation.

Savannah smiled at Wes before returning her attention to Major Dane. "If we're all going to be on a first-name basis here, you'll need to tell me yours."

She knew the warm look he gave her was calculated to make her heart beat faster. He tapped on his nametag. "Dane."

She frowned. "If Dane is your first name, then what's your last name?"

"Dane," he provided.

She narrowed her eyes. "Your name is Dane Dane?"

He winked. "No, just Dane. I'm like Cher—I only need one name."

Savannah narrowed her eyes at him. "Everyone has a first and last name legally," she told him. "I'll bet I could find out what yours is if I tried."

He shook his head. "Not with your security clearance."

"His first name is Christopher," Wes provided. Dane sent him a venomous look and Savannah had to laugh.

"I don't have a problem with calling you Dane. It suits you better," she decreed, and he rewarded her with another bone-melting smile. "So, are you?"

He raised an eyebrow. "Am I what?"

"A Dane?"

"I have no idea," he returned.

"I'll bet his parents could tell you," Wes contributed. "They do all kinds of genealogy because they're Mormons."

Nothing could have surprised Savannah more. In her preconceived notion of Mormons, they were clean-cut, moral to a fault, and dull as dishwater. Major Dane didn't meet any of these criteria. "Really?"

He shrugged. "Guilty."

"Don't hold it against the Mormons," Wes interrupted with a smile. "Dane isn't very churchy."

"Didn't anybody ever tell you that religion and politics aren't considered polite conversation?" Dane asked his friend.

"And making fun of somebody's name is?" Wes demanded.

Savannah decided to step in and attempt to restore peace. "Did your parents really name you Westinghouse?" she asked Wes.

Wes grimaced. "I'm the fourth person to be cursed with it. From what I understand, my parents wanted to break with tradition and name me something normal, but my grandfather insisted."

"The Westinghouse curse does help with getting into the right schools—like West Point," Dane pointed out.

Wes gave Savannah a long-suffering look. "Dane got in to West Point too."

"Your family name got you in. I had to make good grades," Dane said.

"He's also proud of being smarter than I am," Wes told her. "He mentions his grades almost as frequently as my money."

They seemed like an odd pair, and Savannah was curious. "How did you meet?"

"In a bar near West Point." Dane was happy to provide the information. "I was getting beaten to a pulp, and Wes stepped in to save me. If his timing hadn't been so good, my nose might have been broken or my lip split." Dane leaned closer to Savannah. "And then I wouldn't be so handsome."

"From that moment on we were best friends," Wes explained. "And for the next four years Dane picked fights constantly just to make me prove my loyalty."

Savannah was enjoying herself. "It's fortunate that Wes saved you from permanent deformity," she said to Dane.

"He's returned the favor enough times since then," Wes said.

"True," Dane agreed. Then he turned to Savannah. "Just in case you're wondering, I'm also the bigger hero."

Savannah laughed. "Really? Well what if I prefer the underdog?"

Dane pulled her a little closer. "Then I might want to amend my last statement."

She leaned back until there was a safe distance between herself and Dane. "Too late."

"I have a lake house near Lynchburg," Wes said. "Maybe you'd like to come there some weekend. We can swim in the lake or the pool." Wes winked at Savannah as he added, "Being rich does have its advantages."

For once Dane didn't look amused. "We've established that Wes is the richest and has the dumbest name. I'm the smartest, the bravest, and the most handsome . . ."

"Hey, I don't remember conceding the handsome part," Wes objected good-naturedly.

Dane ignored him. "The only thing left to find out is which one of us is most appealing to women. I guess we'll let Savannah decide that."

"Why do I have to choose?" she asked. "Can't we all just be friends?"

"Of course we can," Wes assured her. His sincere expression was comforting, and she felt herself relax. "Don't pay any attention to Dane. He's crazy."

Dane leaned close again and whispered, "Friendship is all well and good, but I have a feeling that the day will come when you will have to choose between us. Because being in love with two men at one time is just too complicated."

She felt a blush stain her cheeks. "I don't plan to fall in love with either of you."

"But you will," he promised.

* * *

Savannah opened her eyes and looked out the window of General Steele's car. It had started to rain, and as she watched the heavy drops hit the glass, she acknowledged that Dane had been right. Eventually she'd grown to love both men. Then there came a point when she had to choose between them. As a result of her decision, Wes was dead and Dane was her enemy. But Dane was the only hope she had of retrieving her daughter, so in spite of everything, she was going to beg for his help.

CHAPTER 3

General Steele's driver pulled up to the security checkpoint outside the Petersburg prison facility at one o'clock that afternoon. They were admitted promptly and directed to the visitor parking area. Once the car was parked, the driver remained seated, staring straight ahead. Savannah assumed he was going to wait for her but didn't really care. If he was gone when she returned, she'd call a cab.

She climbed out of the general's car and hurried up the steps of the administrative building. Thanks to the steady rain and the fact that she had no umbrella, she was uncomfortably damp by the time she reached the entrance. The air conditioning inside was working overtime and goose bumps puckered her skin.

"You're Savannah McLaughlin," the guard at the door said. "I've seen you on television." He was standing a little too close for comfort, and Savannah resisted the urge to step back.

"Yes." She glanced at his nametag. "Milton, I'm here to see a prisoner."

He nodded. "Dane. I'm supposed to take you up to meet him. You'll have to be searched first, though." His eyes dropped to her damp blouse. "I'd do it myself, but it's against the rules."

Savannah gave him a withering look. "I don't have much time. Could we hurry please?"

Milton laughed and led her down the hallway to a room marked PROCESSING. There he turned her over to a female guard. After a humiliating search, she rejoined Milton in the hall. He waved for her to follow him to an elevator. Once inside, she stood as far from him as the small space would allow.

When the elevator doors opened on the third floor, they got off and Milton guided her down another long hallway and finally stopped in front of a brown wooden door. With a sly smile over his shoulder, Milton opened the door and ushered her in.

Savannah had expected her reunion with Dane to take place in an interview room like the ones she'd seen on television—sterile and impersonal, with a thick Plexiglas divider to separate her from Dane in case he was of a mind to strangle her. But the room she was standing in looked more like an apartment. There was a living room with overstuffed furniture cozily arranged around a television, a small kitchen tucked in to the corner, and through an open door she could see a bedroom.

"Nice, huh?" Milton said.

"Very," she agreed.

"We call it the honeymoon suite," Milton informed her. The leer was back in his eyes and Savannah blanched.

He was aware of her discomfort and seemed to enjoy it. "Prisoners with good conduct get to use it when their wives or girlfriends visit."

"Where is Dane?" she asked.

"Anxious, aren't you?" Milton said with an unpleasant smile. "I'll be back with him in a minute." He waved at the room that now seemed anything but welcoming. "Make yourself at home."

After Milton left, Savannah took a deep breath and tried to calm her nerves. Soon she would see Dane again. She would learn the extent of his injuries, the depth of his hatred for her, and whether or not he would set his feelings aside to help her find Caroline.

She was pacing around the room while rehearsing the plea she'd prepared when the door behind her opened. She turned, expecting to see Milton, but instead Dane stepped into the room. He was unrestrained and unaccompanied, and all her carefully planned thoughts disappeared. She had prepared herself for this moment and didn't intend to stare, but she couldn't help it.

Instead of the crisply starched uniform that had been his daily attire at Fort Belvoir, Dane wore a bright orange prison jumpsuit. No longer required to keep his hair military-short, he'd let it grow until it curled gently around his ears. He was thinner, and as he walked into the room she noticed a slight limp, but otherwise he seemed physically sound.

"Dane," she whispered. Her relief must have shown on her face because his lips twisted into a sneer.

"What did you expect? A monster?"

She denied this with a shake of her head. "No."

He moved closer. "Well, I am. And if you're wise, you'll remember that."

Savannah squared her shoulders and said, "I need your help."

He sat down in a comfortable recliner. "So I understand." He pushed back and raised the footrest. Once he was settled, he regarded her with a bored expression.

"My daughter's been missing for over two months, and every day her situation becomes more precarious." She reached into her briefcase and pulled out the file she'd brought. "Here's most of the information I have. As soon as you're released, you can come to my office at the Child Advocacy Center in Washington, and I'll get you anything else you need."

Dane held up a hand. "Before I do any investigating, there's the matter of payment to be settled."

"I'll pay you whatever you want."

"Only someone who is very wealthy can make a statement like that," he said. "Lucky for you that you married well."

Savannah ignored the reference to her marriage. "How much do you want?"

"So I can name my price?" he verified.

She nodded.

"What if it's not money that I want?" His voice was so cold.

"In addition to money, I've arranged with General Steele to get you out of prison."

He waved it aside. "My release benefits you as much as it does me, so it doesn't count as part of my price." His hateful eyes studied her, lingering on her lips, and Savannah's mouth went dry. "I might require your soul as payment."

She pictured Caroline's face as she said, "I told you I'll pay any price."

He laughed, but it was a harsh, humorless sound. "Honestly, even if I had an interest in the case, I'm not sure I could take it since that would mean I'd have to see you on a regular basis. You used to be easy on the eyes, but you've really let yourself go."

Savannah fought back her humiliation and anger. He was toying with her, wasting time they could be using to find Caroline. But she had to tread carefully. If he refused to help, all was lost. She raised a hand to her wet hair. "I usually look a little better than I do at the moment. A tense discussion with General Steele, the long ride here, and a sudden rainstorm have taken their toll."

There was a flash of genuine amusement in his eyes, but it was gone so quickly she wondered if she'd imagined it. He studied her for a few more seconds and shook his head. "Even if you could improve your appearance, the answer is still no. I won't take your money or your soul in a hopeless cause. Your daughter is dead."

Although his words didn't surprise her, they still hurt. "I've come to grips with that possibility," she told him. "I believe that heaven exists, so if Caroline is there . . . I can live with that. What I can't live with is the alternative."

"Alternative?" he repeated.

She rubbed her hands up her arms to ward off the chilly air. "My first assignment with the Child Advocacy Center was a kidnapping case," she told him. "A seven-year-old boy was taken out of his own backyard. He was missing for several weeks before his body was discovered. His captor didn't kill him immediately. He was tortured first. The police found tapes of the child crying out for his parents, begging them to help him." She paused until her lips stopped trembling enough for her to continue. "That's what I can't live with—the possibility that Caroline is alive and afraid and waiting for me to come and save her."

She didn't try to hide her desperation, and finally he said, "I find it highly ironic that you've come to me to help you find Wes's child."

"You and Wes were closer than brothers at one time," she reminded him. "I don't believe feelings that strong can just disappear."

"I still have strong feelings for Wes, all right," he replied, and she wondered if she'd gone too far. Then he pointed at a chair across from him. "Sit down."

Obediently, she sat.

"The first step is to figure out why your daughter was kidnapped," he continued. "Money would be the logical motive, but there has been no ransom demand. All you've received from the kidnapper is one hate note, correct?"

She nodded.

"This note convinced the police that the motive was revenge against you."

"Yes."

"Apparently related to a case you worked on at the Child Advocacy Center."

"Most likely."

Dane frowned. "I agree that this is the best theory. If it's not the right theory, and your daughter *was* the random victim of a serial criminal, then hopefully her body will turn up soon so we won't waste too much time, and you'll have your closure or whatever it is people want these days."

Savannah knew Dane was being purposely callous and accepted this as part of the price for his cooperation.

"I think . . ." she began and then faltered.

"What?"

She didn't want to tell him. "You'll laugh."

"That's most unlikely," he returned. "I almost never laugh, unless women I find highly undesirable offer their souls to me."

Savannah ignored the jab. "I don't know that much about what happens to people after they die. But if Caroline were dead, I think she'd find a way to let me know I should stop looking."

Dane was regarding her with open skepticism. "So you can communicate with the dead?"

She shook her head, sorry that she had even brought up this particular subject. "No."

"You don't normally see ghosts or angels or the Ghost of Christmas Past?"

Savannah sat up a little straighter. "No."

"Has Wes visited you since his death?"

She looked down. "No."

"But you admit that he is definitely deceased."

She nodded. "Yes, but that's different."

"How?"

She couldn't explain. "I . . . I don't know. He wasn't my child."

Dane sighed as if he was dealing with a dimwit. "I'm sorry, but I can't accept your lack of heavenly visitations as evidence of your daughter's continued existence. Now, tell me why in the world I should take on this case."

"Because if you solve it and find my daughter, you will have done something no one else was able to do—not the Washington, DC police, not the FBI, not the private investigators I've hired."

"And why did you come to me for help?"

"You're the best. You can find people even if they don't want to be found," Savannah began. "I need someone with contacts and experience and . . ."

"A criminal mind," he supplied.

Since she didn't want to alienate him further, she decided not to respond to this directly. "I have to find Caroline, dead or alive. I believe you are the only person who can do that."

He surprised her by saying, "General Steele e-mailed me the police reports and newspaper accounts of your daughter's kidnapping. From what I can tell, the case has already been thoroughly investigated, and I'm not sure what more can be done."

"You can succeed where the others have failed. You can find Caroline."

"That remains to be seen." His tone was not encouraging.

Savannah's heart pounded. "So you'll take the case?"

"Sure," he fixed her with a cold look. "For old time's sake."

She wanted to thank him, but her lips were paralyzed.

"I do have some conditions, though."

"Of course."

"I want to be out of here by the end of the day."

Savannah nodded. "That shouldn't be a problem."

"And I won't work at your office in Washington under the nose of your lecherous boss."

She blinked—surprised that Dane was aware of Doug's romantic interest. "Okay."

"I want to be on my own turf," he continued. "So we'll set up at my cabin near Fredericksburg, Virginia. It's secluded and quiet and about an hour's drive from DC. We'll be close enough to investigate near the scene of the crime, but interruptions can be kept to a minimum."

Savannah wasn't going to argue such an unimportant point. "Whatever you think is best."

"I want computers," Dane continued his demands. "Top of the line stuff. And I want to reassemble my special ops team—or what's left of the men who were part of my team. Some of them have been discharged from the Army. I want them returned to active duty at full pay for a minimum of six months."

"Do you think it will take that long to find Caroline?" Savannah whispered.

"No, but I need to offer them that much money to make it worth their while."

Savannah extended her cell phone toward him. "Just let General Steele know what you need. He's promised to give you anything."

"The general has promised *anything*?" Dane asked.

Savannah blushed as she nodded.

"That's not like the general."

Savannah didn't know exactly how to explain. "I have some information . . ."

"You're blackmailing him!" Dane interrupted. "Well, well, well."

She thought she would die of shame, but she said, "I told you I would do whatever I have to in order to save Caroline."

His eyebrows arched and her blush deepened. "Yes, I remember that. Offering to sacrifice your soul was drastic enough, but your integrity too . . . Now I know you're serious."

She averted her eyes and stared at the small window while he made his phone call. Once he had things worked out with General Steele, he tossed the phone back into her lap.

"My final requirement is that you have to keep yourself accessible to me. You have to do whatever I tell you to, and you have to be completely honest with me."

Savannah nodded. She'd expected the groveling requirement.

"I presume you brought me a copy of the note the kidnapper sent you?"

She removed the copy from her purse and handed it to him. "It's printed in calligraphy on a heavy vellum paper according to the experts at the FBI," she told him. "No prints or trace DNA."

"So they didn't lick the envelope?"

"There was no envelope," Savannah said. "Just the card stuck in my mailbox. The mailman found it the next day when he was delivering the mail."

"Let the iniquity of his fathers be remembered with the LORD," Dane quoted. *"And let not the sin of his mother be blotted out."* He frowned at her. "Not from one of your fans, obviously."

"Obviously," she agreed.

He set the copy of the card aside. "Now describe the events leading up to the kidnapping."

"I thought you said you've read everything . . ."

"I want to hear it in your own words."

She took a deep breath and began. "The day of the kidnapping began like any other. We ate breakfast, then Caroline dressed for school and I dressed for work. I dropped her off at school fifteen minutes early so she'd have time to visit with her friends before class started."

Savannah wiped away the tears that leaked from her eyes. Everything had been fine then. If only . . .

Dane's harsh voice put an end to these pointless musings. "You didn't notice anyone watching you or following your car?"

"No."

"Anything at all unusual?" he persisted.

"Nothing. I went to the CAC and worked until noon. Then I left for a lunch appointment."

"With LuAnn Baxley from the Red Cross."

She knew she shouldn't be surprised by his knowledge of her movements, but she was. "Yes."

"You left the restaurant at 1:05 and went to the Channel 7 Studios where you participated in the filming of a public service announcement."

She nodded. "It ran long, and I was late leaving to pick up Caroline."

"Why did it run late?"

"I don't know—the director kept insisting on retakes."

"Did the police investigate the director?"

The thought had never occurred to Savannah, and she doubted the police had considered the egotistical director a suspect either. "No."

"Then he just moved to the top of my list. As you were leaving the studio, you talked to your boss, Doug Forton, who asked you out to dinner."

Savannah was both impressed and embarrassed. "Yes."

"But you didn't accept. Why?" he asked.

"I told him I didn't want to leave Caroline."

"And . . ." he prompted. "Remember that you've promised to be completely honest."

"He would like for our relationship to become more than professional, and I don't want to encourage him."

"Because . . ."

"Because I'm not interested in him romantically."

"I guess after you've been loved by the late, great Westinghouse McLaughlin, all other men pale in comparison."

This remark didn't deserve an answer, so she ignored it.

Dane waited long enough to be sure the silence was awkward before he said, "After you turned down your boss, then what?"

"A few blocks from Caroline's school there was a car crash that had traffic backed up."

"Convenient."

"Yes, the police thought so too. But they investigated the people involved and couldn't find anything suspicious."

"Then they didn't look hard enough," Dane predicted. "When you finally got to the school, what happened?"

"I parked in front and walked up to the office. There's a bench in the hall where children sit when their parents are late."

"And you knew this because you were late often?"

Savannah was offended. "I'm *never* late. I knew about the bench because Caroline had pointed it out to me."

"So you got to the school, finally, and your daughter wasn't sitting on the bench where she should have been since you were late?"

"Yes, I mean, no," Savannah stammered. "She wasn't sitting on the bench. So I went into the office."

"Then what?"

Savannah concentrated on the question, trying to remember the exact sequence of events. "I asked the receptionist where Caroline was. She called someone to check and told me that Caroline had already been picked up. While I was arguing that this couldn't possibly be true, the head teacher for the first grade came in. She showed me my name on the sign-out sheet."

"The police report says that your daughter's regular teacher was out sick, so a substitute was handling the distribution of children that afternoon."

"Yes," Savannah confirmed. "But the police questioned both the regular teacher and the substitute and didn't consider either one of them suspects."

"Which is why they haven't found your daughter," Dane told her. "That's too much coincidence. One or both of the teachers were involved."

Savannah found this possibility disturbing but his conviction reassuring.

"All the statements given by school personnel who were working on the car-line say that the woman who picked up your daughter looked exactly like you."

Savannah nodded. "She was driving a car just like mine and had her hair fixed the same and was even wearing the same color suit. She must have looked just like me. Otherwise Caroline wouldn't have gotten into the car with her."

Dane frowned. "Even identical twins can be distinguished by people who know them well. The kidnapper was very fortunate to find a woman who looked enough like you to fool your daughter."

"The imposter would only have to fool Caroline for a minute or so," Savannah pointed out. "Just long enough to get away from the school."

Dane was still frowning when he said, "It was very well planned and perfectly executed."

"Yes," Savannah agreed. "The police and the FBI remarked on that."

She braced herself, waiting for more painful questions about the kidnapping and the subsequent investigation, but instead he said, "Tell me about your life."

She tried to decline. "I'm sure you know everything already . . ."

"You promised to obey me."

This wasn't exactly true, but she didn't want to haggle over terminology. "Most of my cases at the CAC are simple ones—children who need better housing or can't afford adequate medical attention.

Things like that. But some of them are more complicated, like custody situations."

"Abuse cases?"

"A few."

"Do any of your current cases involve kidnappings?"

"No."

"How long has Wes been dead?"

Savannah swallowed hard and then said, "Two years."

"Any reason to think his death wasn't an accident?"

Savannah dropped her eyes to keep him from seeing her distress. "The insurance company wouldn't have paid the claim if they had doubts. Why do you ask?"

"I'm just wondering if Wes could be the one with the enemy. The note did mention the iniquity of the fathers as well as the sin of the mother."

She was still considering this when he continued.

"I want a list of every case you've worked on since you started with the Child Advocacy Center—even if you had a minor role, and even if it didn't seem like the outcome made anybody unhappy."

"A list has already been prepared, and both the police and FBI have investigated all of the cases."

"We'll do it again," Dane said. "Get me a copy. I want all your financial records for the past five years. Bank statements, stock transactions, pay stubs . . ."

She nodded. "The police and FBI have checked those too."

He raised an eyebrow. "Do you want me to do an investigation or not?"

"Yes, of course. I'll get you all the records."

"I also want your personal correspondence for, say, the past three years. I want birthday cards and Christmas cards and thank-you notes and invitations to parties. Everything."

"Okay."

"In addition, I want you to make a list of every person who had access to you, your daughter, your home, your car, your office, etc. That means teachers, doctors, coworkers, janitors, repairmen, exterminators—everyone."

Savannah was daunted. "That will be a very long list."

"And somewhere on that long list we might find the kidnapper." He reached into his pocket and pulled out an index card. "Here are directions to my cabin. Bring everything there tomorrow at noon."

Assuming that she was being dismissed, Savannah forced her nearly numb limbs into a standing position.

He frowned up at her. "Where are you going?"

"Home to get the information you'll need."

"Not yet," he told her. "If you leave now, I'll have to give up this suite. You stay until they come to tell me I'm being released."

With a sigh, Savannah sank back down into the chair as Dane reached for the remote control and turned on the television.

CHAPTER 4

They sat there for almost two hours—Dane watching ESPN and Savannah watching him. It was painful to be so close to him physically but so distant emotionally. She assumed his intention was to cause her pain. Conversely, her proximity didn't seem to bother him at all.

By the time the warden finally came for Dane, Savannah was exhausted, starving, and taut with anxiety. Dane didn't even give her a glance as he followed the warden from the honeymoon suite. With a weary sigh, Savannah stepped into the hallway and was relieved to find a female guard waiting for her instead of Milton. The guard searched her and then escorted her to the parking lot in front of the administration building. General Steele's car was just where she'd left it hours before.

Savannah climbed into the backseat and gave the driver the address to her Victorian-row house near Capitol Hill. It was possible that the driver had been instructed to shoot her and dump her body in a remote spot somewhere between the prison and Washington, DC, but at the moment she couldn't make herself care. On the outside chance that she would reach her home alive, she pulled out her cell phone and called Lacie.

Her assistant answered promptly. "So how did it go?"

In the dark recesses of General Steele's backseat, Savannah allowed herself a shudder. "I guess you'd say it was a success. Dane agreed to help me."

"How much is he charging?"

"He hasn't given me a *monetary* amount yet. He just asked for computer equipment and active duty pay for several men he's worked with in the past."

"Did he also require a pound of flesh?" Lacie asked.

"His only interest in me personally is that I provide myself as a willing victim for torture," Savannah said.

"You were counting on that," Lacie pointed out.

"Yes."

"And you can stand a little torture as long as he finds Caroline."

"True," Savannah agreed. "That's all that matters."

"Are you going to work from your office at the CAC? Doug has offered to provide any support personnel you might need."

"I appreciate Doug's desire to help," she said, although she really considered it more of an intrusion. "But Dane refuses to run his investigation from the CAC. He has a house in Virginia near Fredericksburg, and I'm supposed to report there tomorrow after collecting an unbelievable amount of data."

"What can I do to help?" Lacie offered.

Tears stung Savannah's eyes. "Thank you, Lacie."

"Hey, what are friends for?" the other woman asked.

Savannah cleared her throat to hide her emotion and then said, "He wants to see that list of every case I've ever worked on since I came to the CAC. Will you print off a copy of the one we gave the police?"

"That's a piece of cake," Lacie said.

"He also wants my financial records—they should still be in that box the police returned to me by my desk."

"I know right where it is," Lacie confirmed.

"And I have to bring every scrap of personal correspondence for the past three years—even Christmas cards."

Lacie laughed. "Some of that is on your computer here at the office. Do you want me to download the information onto your flash drive?"

"Please."

"Then I guess we'll have to go by your house to get the Christmas cards."

"Yes," Savannah agreed, although she couldn't bear to think about that task now. "Finally, he wants a list of everyone who's had access to me, Caroline, our house, the office, or my car."

Lacie whistled softly into Savannah's ear. "Wow, that's a tall order."

"Overwhelming," Savannah agreed.

"I'll download your correspondence and meet you at your house," Lacie suggested. She knew Savannah hated to be alone in the house she'd shared with Caroline, and Savannah was grateful for her discreet offer. "Then we can work on the list while we dig out your old cards and such."

"Fortunately I don't get that many," Savannah said. "A benefit of not having many friends."

"Way to look on the bright side."

"That's me . . . an optimist," Savannah said. "I'll see you there in a couple of hours."

After ending the call, Savannah ate the Hershey bar Lacie had packed for her and leaned her head against the back of the seat. She was so tired that she dozed off, despite her concern for her safety. She startled awake when the driver pulled up in front of her house. Lacie's car was already parked at the curb, and Savannah was relieved to see lights on inside. She thanked the driver, who nodded curtly in response. Then she climbed out of the car and hurried up the sidewalk. Lacie met her at the door.

"I downloaded all your correspondence—personal and business—for the last three years onto your flash drive. Then I made a copy of your financial records for Dane. I started a list of everyone who had access to you and Caroline, but I decided to wait on the Christmas card search until you got here."

Savannah put her briefcase on the antique table she and Caroline had bought at a flea market in Georgetown. "I don't know what I'd do without you."

"Let's hope you never find out." Lacie turned and headed toward the kitchen. "I got a ham and pineapple pizza."

Savannah forced a weary smile. "My favorite. Thanks. I'll eat some later. Right now I'd better start collecting that stuff Dane wants."

Lacie glanced over her shoulder and fixed Savannah with a firm look. "You'll eat first and look later. If you don't take care of yourself, you'll be no good to Caroline."

Savannah nodded and trailed after Lacie into the kitchen. "I know."

Lacie removed a plate from the cabinet and placed a large piece of pizza on it. Then she extended the plate toward Savannah. "I expect you to show your appreciation by eating every bite."

Savannah accepted the plate and took a bite of pizza. "According to the directions Dane gave me, Fredericksburg is about an hour's drive from Washington. He told me to be there at noon, so I hope I can collect the rest of the stuff he wants and complete the comprehensive list of people who had contact with us and be ready to leave here by eleven o'clock."

"We don't want to look too anxious to meet his demands," Lacie murmured. "Maybe we should leave at noon and get there an hour late."

"We?" Savannah said with her mouth full of pizza.

"I can't send you there alone," Lacie said simply. "I asked Doug for some time off, and he said to take all I need. So I'm coming with you."

This time tears filled Savannah's eyes and spilled on to her cheeks. "What about your mother?" she asked in concern.

Lacie's face lit up with happiness. "I've moved her to this fantastic assisted living place. It gives her the illusion of being independent when she's really closely supervised. They can give her the medical treatments she needs right there without transporting her to a hospital, and for a nominal fee, they'll provide a night nurse. So my mom's taken care of."

"I'll pay for the cost of the night nurse," Savannah offered. "It's the least I can do."

Lacie smiled. "We'll wait and see how much your 'friend' charges you to find Caroline. If there's any money left after he gets through with you, I'll take you up on that." Lacie pointed at the pizza on Savannah's plate. "Now finish eating so we can start searching for Christmas cards."

* * *

Savannah and Lacie worked well into the night collecting old cards and making lists. Finally Lacie insisted that they rest for a few hours. Even though Caroline's room was empty and available, neither woman suggested it as a possible place for Lacie to sleep. Instead, Lacie slept on the couch in the great room.

Savannah dozed for a while but never really managed to fall asleep. By the time Lacie woke up the next morning, Savannah had been hard at work for hours. It was nine-thirty when they finally completed the list of every contact they could possibly think of.

"I'm going to go see my mother and explain that I'll be out of town for a few days," Lacie said as she stood and yawned. "While I'm gone you can pack and make yourself presentable for your next confrontation with Dane."

Savannah groaned, but she didn't argue. After following Lacie to the door and locking it securely behind her, Savannah walked upstairs. In order to avoid an emotional meltdown, she carefully kept her eyes averted from both Caroline's room and Wes's office as she hurried into the master bedroom. She pulled out a suitcase and packed enough clothes to last her a few days. Then she took a shower and dressed in a pair of jeans, a soft white sweater, and a corduroy jacket, hoping to give the impression of casual professionalism.

Lacie returned precisely at eleven-thirty. But instead of driving the little Volkswagen beetle she'd owned since high school, Lacie was behind the wheel of a brand new SUV.

"Where did this come from?" Savannah asked as she carried her suitcase outside.

"Doug rented it for us," Lacie announced cheerfully. "Wasn't that nice?"

"Hmm," Savannah murmured.

"And he said that we are to consider everything we spend while we're in Fredericksburg a business expense."

Savannah frowned. "But this isn't a CAC case."

"He said it is now."

Savannah knew she should be grateful, but she was capable of paying her own expenses and would have preferred to drive her own car to Fredericksburg. And she really didn't want to be *more* indebted to Doug Forton.

"Doug says you never know what kind of terrain you'll have to deal with when you get out in the country, so an SUV is the best choice of vehicles. And this thing is equipped with OnStar in case we get lost."

Savannah couldn't argue either point, so she nodded. "That's good, I guess."

Lacie studied her closely. "You look tired. Why don't I drive and you can navigate."

Savannah put her suitcase in the back, walked around to the front passenger seat, and climbed in. She consulted first the map and then the index card Dane had given her. Seeing his neat, precise handwriting was a little unnerving, but she forced herself to concentrate. She directed Lacie to head south on I-395. The traffic was heavy as they passed through the busy industrial area. When they merged onto I-95, the traffic thinned.

"Take the Plank Road exit," she instructed Lacie when they saw a sign announcing Fredericksburg up ahead. "Then we'll be looking for the Blue and Gray Parkway, which will take us on in to Tylerton where Dane's house is."

They passed through Fredericksburg, a nice city with some impressive architecture and a rich history, but Savannah was too edgy to enjoy any of the scenery.

"We're going to turn right on Kings Highway," she told Lacie.

They watched for the signs together as they passed through the surprisingly rural area, and found the turns without difficulty. "Now we're looking for Rumford Road. There should be a golf course. We go around it and then turn on Creekside."

"There's the golf course." Lacie pointed to an impressive clubhouse framed by greens and sand traps. They circled the golf course and made a left onto Creekside.

"Now we're looking for a dirt road to our left about three miles down," Savannah told Lacie. "Dane says it's easy to miss."

Lacie watched the odometer and notified Savannah when they had gone the specified distance. Savannah was beginning to worry that they'd missed their turn when she saw a small opening in the dense foliage. Frowning, she pointed and asked, "Do you think that could be considered a road?"

Lacie stopped the SUV, backed up, and stared. "It's the right distance from the main road. I say we give it a try." With that, she plunged the vehicle into the narrow gap between the trees.

After what seemed like miles of slow, paint-scratching progress, they reached a small clearing. Across the tall grass, Savannah could see the rusted remains of an old pickup truck and a large steel gate. Lacie pulled the SUV to a stop beside the truck and parked. Savannah willed herself to open the door and get out, but she seemed frozen in place.

"We can go back to DC if you want," Lacie offered gently.

Savannah shook her head and wiped her sweating palms on her jeans. She could do anything for Caroline—even put herself at Dane's mercy. With her heart pounding, she climbed out of the SUV and walked to the gate. The gate wasn't locked, and she was able to swing it open without much effort.

"That was easy enough," Lacie said encouragingly behind Savannah.

"It will get worse," Savannah predicted as she stepped past the gate.

After a few minutes of walking through the woods, they came to a gurgling creek. Savannah would have admired it if she didn't have to cross it. A makeshift bridge consisting of mildewed pieces of plywood and haphazardly tied nylon rope spanned the waist-deep water.

"You weren't kidding," Lacie whispered when she saw the bridge. "This is definitely worse."

"It's pretty bad," Savannah agreed.

"I can't swim, so if it doesn't hold my weight, I'll drown."

Savannah peered into the distance, wondering if Dane was watching them. "I don't think he wants to kill us, so the bridge is probably safe. But I'll go first just in case. Wait until I'm all the way across before you attempt to cross it. If I fall in the creek and drown, you can drive the SUV to the police station to report my death. And be sure to press charges."

Lacie managed a little laugh.

Then, feeling like a doomed fly entering an evil spider's web, Savannah grabbed a handful of sun-damaged rope and stepped out onto the bridge. Savannah reached the end of the bridge safely and turned to wave Lacie across. Before she had time to enjoy the feeling of her feet on solid ground, it started to rain. Fat, cold drops fell silently from the sky, and she looked up, wondering if Dane had control over the elements. While waiting for Lacie, she looked around to get her bearings. She was standing at the bottom of a small hill. On the crest of the hill was a wooden A-frame house.

The design was simple, with large, square windows and a wraparound porch. The landscaping was completely natural—not a trimmed hedge or tame flower in sight. It had a friendly appearance that she knew was a dangerous illusion. Dane wouldn't allow his home to be a refuge for her.

Lacie succeeded in crossing the bridge and joined Savannah at the base of the hill. "That wasn't too bad," she claimed, but she was pale and breathing hard. "*Now* maybe the worst is behind us."

Savannah tried to laugh, but it came out more like a whimper. She pointed at the house on the hill. "The *worst* is definitely still in front of us."

They climbed the hill together, fighting for traction in the slick grass. Finally they reached the wide stairs and climbed them to stand on the wooden porch. Savannah glanced back at the bridge, which from a distance looked like a pile of scrap wood. Returning her attention to the house, Savannah summoned her courage. She wiped the rain from her face with the back of a trembling hand and knocked on the door.

A few seconds later the door was yanked open by the largest man Savannah had ever seen. He was well over six feet tall, and his bulk filled the entire doorway. Muscles rippled under his dark brown skin, stretching the fabric of his T-shirt to the limit. His hair was divided into long braids that encircled his massive head in no apparent pattern. He smiled, exposing two gold caps, and Lacie gasped.

"Hey, Hack," Savannah said.

Hack didn't return the greeting, but instead called over his shoulders to the occupants within. "They're here."

"Let them in," Dane's voice instructed.

Hack stepped back, and Savannah led Lacie inside.

The main room was large and simply furnished. Under different circumstances Savannah realized it would be comfortable and homey. But the effort to find Caroline had required that the furniture be pushed up against the walls, and computer equipment in various stages of installation filled every available space. Cables, surge protectors, and Styrofoam packing materials littered the wood plank floor.

Savannah counted three men besides Dane—all members of the old special ops team Wes and Dane had created years before. It looked as if the men had each claimed a section of the room and were now in the process of getting their new computers set up on modern, metal tables that, while serviceable, were incompatible with the rest of the decor.

Hack had chosen a spot near the large window that looked out over the creek. Doc, the medic, was seated by the bookcase and had already requisitioned an entire shelf for medications—arranging them as neatly as any pharmacist. And Cam—the body-building acquisitions clerk—was setting up shop next to the soot-stained fireplace. Savannah's eyes moved on, searching for Dane. She found him seated in a large swivel chair in front of a desk in the corner of the room, regarding her with contempt.

He pushed himself up and walked forward with an uneven gait. "Excuse the mess. I would have straightened up a little, but I've been in prison."

Savannah couldn't think of a clever response, so she just nodded.

"You're late," he said.

"Sorry," she replied without feeling.

"I see you made it across the bridge," he continued.

"Barely," she acknowledged.

"I built it myself."

"I could tell."

He seemed to consider this for a few seconds and then turned to his men. "I guess as host I should make introductions. Gentlemen, you all know Mrs. McLaughlin—the widowed wife of our old friend Westinghouse. And this is her faithful assistant, Lacie Fox."

By now Savannah wasn't surprised that Dane had researched her well enough to know Lacie's name and their professional relationship.

The men joined Dane in the center of the room, flanking him protectively as if he had something to fear from the rain-soaked women.

For Lacie's benefit, Dane gestured toward the huge door greeter. "This is Hack—nicknamed for both his computer skills and the fact that his hands are licensed as lethal weapons."

"It's nice to meet you," Lacie said.

Hack said nothing.

"Hack is an invaluable asset to us because in addition to his personal skills, he owns a security business and has a vast number of well-trained men at his disposal," Dane continued. "He's also very persuasive. No one can keep secrets from Hack."

Dane waved to the frail man near the bookcase. "And this is Doc. We call him Doc because he's a walking pharmacy. Any kind of drug you need, legal or otherwise, ask Doc and he can fix you up."

Lacie smiled at the medic, and Doc blushed crimson.

"Hey, Doc," Savannah said.

"Hey," he replied without making eye contact.

Next, Dane pointed at Cam, who was wearing combat fatigues. "And finally, we have Camouflage—nicknamed for obvious reasons. His friends call him Cam."

"Hey, Cam," Lacie said.

He gave her a curt nod.

"Cam's a master of disguise and a computer genius—a good man to have on a covert operation."

Now that the introductions were over, Savannah felt obligated to say, "I appreciate all of you coming here to help me find my daughter."

"We came here because Dane asked us to," Hack corrected her gruffly. "Not for you."

She accepted his rejection of her gratitude with a nod. There was no question of their loyalties or their feelings about her. "Of course, but I'm still grateful."

"And if she's grateful now, imagine how she'll feel if we actually find her daughter," Dane said, taking a step closer, a challenge in his eyes. "If any of you are interested in some female companionship, Mrs. McLaughlin is currently available." His eyes raked her briefly. "She assured me that she can look better than this." He gestured toward her. "But honestly, guys, I've seen no evidence to support that claim."

It had been obvious since the moment she walked in that he was determined to humiliate her, and because she needed his cooperation, she hadn't objected. But this remark could not be allowed to pass unchallenged. Savannah squared her shoulders and looked directly into Dane's dark brown eyes.

"While I am grateful, contrary to Major Dane's assertion, I am *not* available. The government is paying all of you to find my daughter, and that will have to be incentive enough."

Lacie laughed out loud. Cam grinned, Doc blushed, and even Hack looked less like he wanted to kill her.

Pleased that the tension in the room had been reduced—even if it had been at her expense—Savannah continued. "I have the information you requested in my rental car. The question is how will we carry it across that poor excuse for a bridge?"

Dane didn't answer her directly but turned to Cam and said, "Will you move her car around back and bring in the stuff?"

"I'll need the keys," Cam said more to Dane than to Savannah.

Lacie held out the keys, and Cam took them.

Savannah narrowed her eyes at Dane. "You mean there's another way to get here without having to cross that rickety bridge?"

"Sure," Dane replied. "That bridge is unsafe. I'd never set a foot on it."

Cam snickered as he walked outside.

With barely controlled anger, Savannah asked Dane, "Can I speak with you privately please?"

"I've never been one to refuse a little alone time with a lady," Dane said with a wink at his men.

Savannah just stared at him.

When he realized that he couldn't goad her into a comment, Dane sighed and said, "Follow me." He led her into a large kitchen that looked just the way it should. There was a wooden table in the middle, polished to a satiny patina by years of use. A large, black, wood-burning cook stove dominated one entire wall, and a brick fireplace took up most of another. Cast-iron skillets in various sizes hung above the fireplace, and they seemed to be arranged more for convenience than decoration. And in a far corner was an antique refrigerator. Above the handle was the word *Westinghouse.* Savannah didn't know if it was intended to be a joke or a tribute.

She pulled her eyes away from the refrigerator and addressed Dane. "That juvenile bridge-walking trick was a waste of time."

He shrugged. "It's the traditional initiation for all newcomers to the cabin."

Savannah knew if she told him she didn't want to be part of his "club," he might throw her out. So she kept her tone moderate as she said, "The special ops team isn't what I expected."

He frowned. "You've met them all before."

She wanted to point out that the good, competent men were missing. Instead she said, "But all of them aren't here."

"Some of them were unavailable, like Wes," he returned.

"I'm sure the general would give you anyone you wanted for this investigative team—to fill in the gaps. Why don't you ask him for some well-qualified men?"

Dane didn't look pleased by her suggestion. "The men I have are well qualified."

"Are you saying that the men out there," she waved toward the living room in exasperation, "are the most qualified people you could find?"

"They might not be the *most* qualified," he admitted. "But they were available and they're loyal. Besides, I owe them all favors and wanted to pay them back with six months of active duty pay."

She resisted the urge to grab the fabric of his shirt and shake him. "We're talking about my daughter's life here," she reminded him, struggling with her temper. "I can't turn that job over to a few military rejects."

Dane's expression hardened, and he leaned so close she could feel his breath on her cheek. "The only person you really need on this team is me. So relax before I change my mind about taking the job."

After a couple of calming breaths, Savannah nodded. "I guess I have no choice but to accept your terms."

"That's true," Dane agreed.

The door opened, and Cam walked in carrying the boxes Savannah and Lacie had brought with them from Washington. He seemed surprised to see Dane and Savannah alone in the kitchen. "Am I interrupting something?" he asked.

Savannah shook her head, but Dane smiled. "Not yet anyway."

Completely out of patience, Savannah moved toward the living room. "Let's get to work," she suggested. "We've wasted enough time."

When they walked back into the living room, Savannah noted that in her absence an assortment of computer and antique chairs had been arranged into a circle in the middle of the room. Dane settled himself in the most comfortable chair and then pointed to a wooden stool in a corner. "Mrs. McLaughlin, you pull that stool over here and sit by me." He moved his finger to indicate a spot right at his feet. "Doc, hand her a legal pad so she can take notes for us."

Savannah got the stool and placed it as Dane had instructed. She perched herself on it and accepted the legal pad from Doc. Then she waited with pencil poised for the meeting to begin.

"The first step is organization," Dane told them. "We'll choose a plan, divide the labor, and get busy." He glanced at Savannah before adding, "Since there's not a minute to waste." He winced as he stretched out his legs, and Savannah wondered briefly if he was in pain. "As you all know, we are here in an effort to find and retrieve Mrs. McLaughlin's daughter, the offspring of her blissful wedded relationship with our old friend Westinghouse."

Savannah ignored the jibe and removed a recent picture from her briefcase. "Her name is Caroline," she told the group as she held up the picture for them to see. "She's six years old, and she was kidnapped from her school in August."

Dane didn't even glance at the picture as he continued. "For now we'll accept the opinion of the DC police department and the FBI. They believe that the kidnapper had a personal vendetta against the McLaughlins. If necessary, we'll delve into other possibilities at a future date."

Dane rubbed the week's growth of sparse whiskers on his chin. Wes, who had needed to shave twice a day, always teased Dane about being baby faced. Dane pulled Savannah from her bittersweet reverie by saying, "For this investigation we'll use the tried and true, two-prong approach. For those of you who aren't familiar with military strategy, that means we'll attack the problem from two different directions."

"Hoping to meet in the middle?" Savannah guessed.

"Actually, no," Dane said. "Meeting is not the goal of our operation. We can do that anytime right here in my living room."

The men laughed, and Savannah gritted her teeth. *She could do anything for Caroline.*

"Only one prong—or one approach—has to be successful," Doc told her tentatively. His cheeks colored with embarrassment, and Savannah felt sure he regretted making the effort to explain. But he persevered. "The second prong of the investigation will be abandoned when our goal is reached."

Savannah nodded that she understood and gave Doc a grateful smile, but he quickly averted his eyes.

Dane didn't look pleased by Doc's intervention.

Cam asked, "So what's our first prong?"

"We'll look for someone who had reason to hate the esteemed Mr. or Mrs. Westinghouse McLaughlin," Dane replied.

"Wes has been dead for two years," Hack said with a frown. "Why would somebody be trying to get revenge on him now?"

"Maybe our kidnapper had an old grievance and a long memory," Dane murmured. "But I agree that *Mrs.* McLaughlin is the more likely hate-magnet. We'll want to keep our minds open on this prong. It could be someone who has a legitimate reason to seek revenge—like a parent who lost custody of their child thanks to Mrs. McLaughlin's interference. On the other hand, it could be some unbalanced person whose grudge is unreasonable."

"Give us an example," Cam requested.

"Like a narcissistic PTA president who lost a reelection campaign to Mrs. McLaughlin. Or maybe our kidnapper is a psychotically insecure wife who resents Mrs. McLaughlin flirting with her husband."

"I'm not a PTA officer, and I never *flirt* with anyone," Savannah defended.

Neither Dane nor any of his men seemed to notice that she'd made a comment.

Hack elaborated for the group. "The problem with this prong is that reasonable, rational people don't kidnap children as a form of revenge. Kidnappers are by nature *crazy*—or evil or selfish."

"So their motivations may be incomprehensible to us," Doc added.

"If you get hung up trying to understand their reasons for what they did, you're spinning your wheels," Hack concurred.

"True," Dane agreed. "However, this kidnapping has some distinctive elements. It shows great care in planning—the whole scheme was very clever. So while our villain may be crazy in the clinical sense, he's definitely able to function."

"So we can forget about the PTA and flirting motives?" Cam asked with a smile.

Dane nodded. "Yeah, those were long shots. Since there are so many possibilities to research on our first prong, the second prong becomes even more important."

"What other direction is there?" Savannah asked.

"We'll ignore motive completely and find out who had access to the child. We figure out who took her and worry about the *why* later." Dane looked around. "Much later."

"Some people may have helped with the kidnapping and not even known it," Doc contributed—obviously for Savannah's benefit. "So with this prong, you just look for opportunity."

Dane smiled at Savannah. "Did I tell you they were good or what?"

"You told me they were good," she confirmed.

"I'm a believer in the buddy system," Dane continued. "So we'll work in teams. When you go to do interviews or investigate, take your buddy with you—or get Hack to loan you one of his men. Share the information you find with each other."

"You know they say two heads are better than one," Hack quipped.

"Two of our heads almost adds up to one," Cam added.

Dane smiled briefly and then his expression became serious. "Kidnappers are dangerous people, and I want to be sure everyone is safe. If you have to split up, check in with each other often." He swiveled his chair to look at Cam. "Cam, you and Doc work together."

Both men nodded.

"Hack, you're with me," Dane said. Then he referred to his notes as if he'd completed the assignments.

"What about Lacie and me?" Savannah asked.

Dane raised an eyebrow. "You two fall into the category of support personnel and will just be hanging around the cabin here—at my beck and call."

Savannah sent Lacie a look of apology, but before she could actually speak, Dane shifted in his chair so that he was facing her. "Where's your list of people who had contact with you and your daughter?"

Savannah retrieved the laptop from her briefcase and extended a flash drive toward him. Dane rolled over to his computer and popped it into a USB port. Once the information was displayed on his screen, he frowned. "This isn't complete," he told her.

She stared back blankly. She and Lacie had spent hours on that list—including everyone who had even secondary access to Caroline. "Who did I leave off?"

"It's not who, it's what," Dane corrected. "You didn't give me addresses and phone numbers for everyone."

"That's because I don't know addresses and phone numbers for everyone," she explained.

"Then use your laptop to look that information up," he instructed.

She was confused. "Why don't we turn the names over to private investigators and let them find the personal information?"

Dane looked at her like she was an imbecile. "Because then we'd have to pay them, and you can do it for free. Not that money is a big issue, since General Steele and the U.S. Government are funding this operation. But the more information we give the PIs, the quicker we'll get reports back."

Savannah still thought it was a waste of time but kept her opinion to herself. "You want me to start now?"

He nodded. "Right now."

Dane and all his men were watching her, as if this assignment were a test of some kind. Unsure whether she had passed or failed, Savannah carried her laptop over to the couch. Once she was connected to the Internet, she started looking up addresses but kept most of her attention focused on the meeting that was continuing without her.

"Doc and Cam," Dane said. "Your first assignment will be to look through the McLaughlin family financial records, starting with the year before Wes died. His parents were filthy rich until they decided to join that commune in Wyoming . . ."

"It's a cooperative living farm," Savannah corrected from the couch. "And it's in Colorado."

"Whatever." Dane didn't seem overly concerned with accuracy. "They gave all their money to Wes, who was already rich because of his Grandpa Westinghouse. Sifting through his financial records will be a big job."

"We can handle it," Cam confirmed.

Dane gestured toward the boxes Savannah and Lacie had brought with them. "The financial records are there along with some personal correspondence. You two handle the boring financial stuff. I'll take care of the personal things myself." He glanced across the room at Savannah. "Maybe I'll find some love letters."

She knew he was trying to embarrass her, so she was careful not to appear bothered by Dane pawing through her private correspondence. Besides, she had the comfort of knowing that there were no love letters.

"I believe that things happen for a reason," Dane was continuing. "So we'll examine each event that transpired on the day of the kidnapping until we determine *why* it happened. The kidnapping took place at Epic School. The school has a reputation for tight security, but coincidentally on the day the kid was snatched, a substitute teacher was handling car-line. As a result, a woman who looked similar to Mrs. McLaughlin was allowed to sign for the child and leave the premises."

Hack shook his head. "Too much coincidence. The sub had to be a plant."

"That's what I think," Dane agreed. "So I'm going to ask our first team to look into it."

"Will do!" Cam answered for himself and Doc.

"In fact, you and Doc put the whole school under a microscope. That includes auxiliary personnel like school board members, the mailman, guys who deliver food to the lunchroom—everybody who works at that school or visits it regularly."

"And what are we looking for?" Doc wanted to know.

"Anything out of the ordinary." Dane counted off examples on his fingers. "An unexplained cash deposit into someone's checking account, several trips out of town over the past few weeks by someone who previously didn't travel, the purchase of size six girls' clothing by someone who doesn't have children, a move to a more expensive neighborhood, paying off a mortgage with a lump sum of cash, the purchase of a new Mercedes without an accompanying car payment. Scrutinize any change."

Doc nodded. "Okay."

"Another 'coincidental' thing that happened on the day of the kidnapping involved the director who shot the public service announcement starring the lovely Mrs. McLaughlin at Channel 7. It was just a free commercial—not something he should have been investing a lot of time in. But she says he kept insisting on needless retakes."

"You think he was stalling so they could get the kid?" Hack guessed.

"I think that is a likely possibility," Dane confirmed. "The director's name is Hilton Chastain. Find him and crack him. He's a pretty cool customer, so you might have to lean hard."

"My pleasure," the large man responded.

"Also, on the day in question there was the traffic accident that further slowed Mrs. McLaughlin's progress toward Epic School. The timing of it is too convenient. Check out all the participants, the officers who handled the accident, the tow trucks that came to pick up the disabled vehicles, etc."

"Don't forget about Lacie's flat tire," Savannah contributed.

"Flat tire?" Dane repeated.

"When I got stuck in traffic, I called Lacie and asked her to get Caroline, but she had a flat tire," Savannah explained, trying to ignore his obvious skepticism.

"I have kind of an old car, and the tires aren't new either," Lacie added. "I guess it was bound to happen eventually."

"So you don't think your tire problem was related to the kidnapping?" Dane asked her.

She shook her head. "The mechanic who plugged the hole said I ran over a nail."

"That doesn't sound like the work of a mastermind kidnapper," Dane quickly dismissed. "So we won't worry about Miss Fox's lack of regular car maintenance for now."

Hack smiled, and Cam snickered. Doc sent Savannah a look of sympathy, and she felt her cheeks turn pink with humiliation.

"I'll get to the bottom of the wreck," Hack promised, and Savannah had no doubt that he would.

"In your spare time, Hack, I want you to look over the list of cases Mrs. McLaughlin has handled since she's been at the Child

Advocacy Center and see if anything jumps out at you. The police and FBI have both thoroughly investigated them. But you know, occasionally they miss something."

Hack grinned, his gold teeth sparkling.

"After I get through scrutinizing Mrs. McLaughlin's personal life, I'll look over Wes's activities during the few months before he died—just in case he's the target."

The flippant attitude toward Wes was more difficult to take than the insults directed at her, but she didn't complain. *She could stand anything for Caroline.*

"You want me to look into the wreck first?" Hack asked.

"The list of Child Advocacy Center clients is going to take longer," Dane said. "Go ahead and put out some feelers on the director and the traffic accident. Then get busy on the case list."

Hack nodded his head, which sent his braids flying. "You're the boss."

Dane steepled his fingers and stared at the ceiling. "Statistically speaking, the vast majority of kidnapped children are taken by a relative," he continued. "Since Mrs. McLaughlin doesn't have any surviving family members, and since Wes's parents are voluntary inmates of a concentration camp, checking out that angle should be a piece of cake."

"Why would Wes's parents kidnap Caroline?" Savannah asked. "They've never made any attempt to even contact us."

"I agree that it's unlikely, but I don't like to ignore the odds," Dane said. "So we'll check out the McLaughlins as soon as someone has time."

"I could do it," Lacie volunteered.

Savannah looked up from her laptop. Lacie's teenage attire and multicolored hair didn't exactly inspire confidence. True to character, Dane gave her a look that would have withered a lesser woman, but Lacie didn't flinch.

"You?" he asked.

"Yeah, I mean, I know I'm support personnel and all," Lacie replied bravely. "But if I go, you'll still have Savannah at your beck and call. And then you won't have to tie up one of your real investigators for the job."

Dane didn't refuse the offer immediately, and after a few seconds, Savannah realized he was considering it.

"I want to help," Lacie persevered. "I'm good with computers and phones and people. I can check out the grandparents in Colorado. I can handle that."

Finally Dane nodded. "Knock yourself out." He turned back to his men. "You all know what you need to do. Now get busy."

Cam jumped to his feet and gave Dane an exaggerated salute. "Yes, *sir*!"

"Save the enthusiasm for your assignment," Dane suggested with a half smile. "Everybody's got a few hours to gather what you can. We'll meet again at eight o'clock to compare notes."

While the men returned to their computers, Lacie plopped down beside Savannah on the couch and opened her laptop. "I hope you don't mind me leaving you for a little while," she said as the American Airlines logo filled the computer screen.

"I don't mind that you need to leave." Savannah glanced around the crowded room. "Goodness knows I'm not alone!"

Lacie smiled. "Let's see what flights are available."

Savannah was watching over Lacie's shoulder when Dane called to her.

"Since you've taken a break from your assignment, bring your Christmas cards over to my desk, and we'll start going through them."

Savannah sighed in acceptance of her fate and walked toward the box.

CHAPTER 5

It didn't take long to read through the Christmas cards, but Dane made the most of every moment. He ridiculed Savannah's friends for their taste in cards, their self-serving family updates, and even their penmanship. Then they started on her personal correspondence—which he seemed to enjoy almost as much.

Savannah got a short reprieve a couple of hours later when Dane's cell phone rang. Apparently the call was too important for her to hear, since he took his phone outside. She watched him through the big windows as he repeatedly limped the length of the porch while talking in to his phone. Finally he stopped, his profile facing her. A light breeze lifted his hair and pulled it from his face. For a minute he looked like the man she had known almost eight years before. The man she had loved.

Anxious to keep sad memories at bay, Savannah looked around the cabin. Hack, who was too big for his new chair, sat pecking at the keyboard with oversized yet amazingly nimble fingers. Lacie had taken over Savannah's job of looking up addresses and phone numbers. Cam and Doc had gone into Washington to interrogate people. Savannah found the activity comforting. Surely all this effort would eventually lead them to Caroline.

Dane came back inside and reopened the file that contained invitations she had received over the past few years. "Okay," he said with a smile. "Where were we?"

Savannah reached into the box and extracted a large envelope with the Mason's Funeral Home logo printed in one corner. "These are sympathy cards I got after Wes died," she told him.

"Let's have a look," he said.

He had her make a list of everyone who sent flowers and everyone who she thought should have but didn't. He made her list flower arrangements he considered stingy sent by people with money and flower arrangements he considered lavish sent by people who were financially challenged.

When they were finished, she had a headache and writer's cramp.

He rifled through the file she had given him and pulled out a copy of the kidnapper's note. "I wonder why he didn't put it in an envelope."

She ignored the pain in her temples and flexed her fingers, trying to get some blood circulating. "I don't know."

"And it was risky delivering it to your mailbox. It would have been much safer to mail it. So far it's the only element of the kidnapping that wasn't smart."

"What do you think it means?" she asked.

"I'm not sure," he surprised her by admitting. "The use of a scripture verse indicates religious zealousness, and the verse itself raises one question—which of your daughter's wicked parents did the kidnapper want to punish."

Savannah was confused. "Wes is dead. How can you punish a corpse?"

Dane frowned. "You can deny him a legacy."

Savannah reread the last part of the verse. *And let not the sin of his mother be blotted out.* "I guess," she conceded, but she didn't believe that Wes was the kidnapper's target. She had a feeling that like everything else, the kidnapping was her fault.

* * *

By the time the group gathered that evening, Savannah was exhausted. In addition to her headache and cramped fingers, now her jaw ached since keeping her teeth clenched was the only way she could stop herself from snapping back at Dane's snide comments. As the meeting convened she tried to sit in a chair next to Lacie, but Dane pointed at the stool beside him.

"Here's your place," he reminded her.

After clenching her teeth, she crossed over to the stool and sat down with as much dignity as possible.

"I'm pleased with what's been accomplished," he announced once they were all situated. "And in just a minute I'm going to give everybody a chance to report their findings."

Savannah wondered when he'd found the time to determine their achievements, since he'd been micromanaging every move she'd made all afternoon.

He turned to Lacie. "Tell us about the Brotherly Love Cooperative Farm in Colorado."

Lacie cleared her throat and addressed the group. "I spoke with the leader of the farm. His name is Father Burnett."

"Father," Dane repeated. "Is the guy Catholic?"

"No," Lacie said.

Dane frowned. "Brotherly Love Farm sounds kind of biblical, and an obscure scripture reference was written on a card and put in Mrs. McLaughlin's mailbox on the day of the kidnapping." He passed the copy of the card around.

"The farm isn't associated with the Catholic Church," Lacie reiterated. "It's completely nondenominational."

"What about political ties?" Dane asked. "Do they back any environmental lobbyists or weirdos like that?"

"People who want to protect the environment are not weirdos," Savannah felt compelled to say.

"No ties to lobbyists that I found—environmental or otherwise," Lacie told him. "They love nature and believe in love and brotherly kindness, but they don't get involved in politics."

Dane frowned. "I'm not sure I buy that, but go on with your report about Father Burnett and his loving farm."

Lacie seemed a little annoyed as she continued. "Wes's parents have been there for ten years and have chosen to shun all contact with the outside world. They live up in a mountain compound without electricity or phone service or even transportation. Supplies are flown in by helicopter once a month. Father Burnett says that he can personally guarantee that the McLaughlins haven't left the mountain recently and wouldn't have the resources to orchestrate a kidnapping even if they were inclined to do so."

"Why should we take his word?" Dane demanded. "He might be a crazy like Jim Jones."

Lacie shook her head. "I don't think so."

Dane's expression was so explicit in conveying his contempt for her opinion that words were unnecessary.

Lacie pressed on. "The farm residents aren't very open to the press, but a few articles have been done on them, including a *60 Minutes* segment three years ago. They grow tons of organic food every year and provide for all their own needs, including medical care, there on the farm. Most residents are more open minded than the McLaughlins and have homes with running water and electricity. But there are no televisions or video games—things like that. He said it's to keep the world from influencing their young people."

"And making them want to leave the farm," Cam guessed.

Lacie ignored this and continued. "Father Burnett's been the leader there for almost twenty years and there's never been a hint of scandal. They only take married couples, and no promiscuity is allowed."

"That's what they say, anyway," Dane remarked.

Lacie didn't let his skepticism deter her. "The things I'm reporting are documented facts, but I agree that we shouldn't take anyone else's word. That's why I'm flying there tomorrow to visit Father Burnett and tour the farm. I've arranged with the local police to have someone meet me at the airport and accompany me to the farm headquarters. That way I figure Father Burnett won't be able to refuse to see me."

Dane seemed impressed by Lacie's thoroughness, but all he said was, "Ask this father guy for a copy of their membership roster from six months ago, three months ago, and the most current one. We'll compare them and see if we can find any suspicious additions. I've requested some satellite surveillance pictures, and I hope they'll be here tomorrow or the next day at the latest."

"The government keeps the Brotherly Love Farm under surveillance?" Savannah asked in surprise.

"The government keeps an eye on all kinds of organizations," Dane informed her. "You never know when one might turn out to be a terrorist training camp." Then he turned to Cam. "What did you find out?"

"That Mrs. McLaughlin is not what I'd call filthy rich," Cam replied. "She lives in a nice row house near Capitol Hill that Wes bought when they first got married. It's worth about a million—which ain't peanuts—but it's not far above average for the area." Cam glanced up for effect and then continued. "After Wes died, she sold their lake house in Lynchburg and a beach house in Key West. She used the sale proceeds, plus the money Wes inherited from his parents and Grandpa Westinghouse, to set up a scholarship fund at William and Mary commemorating her husband."

Dane looked at Savannah. "Wasn't that sweet."

Savannah felt ill with humiliation but struggled to keep from showing it.

"She makes a decent salary at the Child Advocacy Center, but she could double it if she'd take one of several job offers she's gotten from companies who don't do as much pro bono work. And she could increase the return on her investments if she'd be more aggressive."

"So, Mrs. McLaughlin had a lot of money—most of which she gave away—and now she lives modestly on an income that she could improve if she wanted to," Dane recapped.

"That's about it," Cam agreed.

Savannah kept her eyes on the legal pad. "Do you have anything else to report, Cam?" she asked.

He seemed uncomfortable with the direct question and addressed his reply to Dane. "Mrs. McLaughlin's finances are unimpressive but not suspicious. There were no unexplained deposits or withdrawals. No reason to think anyone was being blackmailed or paid off. And no one benefited from Wes's death—not even Mrs. McLaughlin since she gave the money away."

"Good work," Dane praised. "What about the woman who impersonated Mrs. McLaughlin on the day of the kidnapping?"

"I found the rental company who supplied the car. It was rented in Mrs. McLaughlin's name. The woman showed proper ID—even an insurance card that they verified. I faxed them a picture of her," Cam indicated toward Savannah, "and the guy said he'd swear it was her."

Dane looked at Savannah almost accusingly.

"It wasn't me," she assured him. "I was watching the director do retakes for the public service announcement."

Dane frowned. "Was your purse stolen or lost right before the kidnapping?"

Savannah shook her head. "No."

Dane turned to Doc. "We need to figure out how someone got access to Mrs. McLaughlin's personal information."

"Identity theft is not that complicated," Cam pointed out. "It would be easy for a decent hacker to get enough to make up a fake ID and insurance card."

Dane nodded. "I guess it doesn't make sense to waste much time there." He turned to Doc. "What did you find out at the school?"

The frail man spoke tentatively. "The principal is afraid of being sued and was nervous about talking to me without his attorney present, but I convinced him."

Dane was pleased. "Of course you did. You could talk a saint into sinning."

Savannah was surprised by Dane's confidence in the unassuming little man.

Dane explained by saying, "We can't figure out the secret to Doc's success. Maybe he has mystic powers, or maybe he's successful because people underestimate him."

Doc pushed his thick-lens glasses up more securely onto his nose and continued. "The principal claims that they followed school board procedures. On the day of the kidnapping the teacher, Mrs. Matthews, called in sick and told them she had selected a substitute from the approved list. The office staff verified the sub with the board of education."

"I presume you double-checked this?" Dane prompted.

"Yes," Doc said. "The people at the board of education were very helpful and showed me the substitute's online file. However, when I asked about the process someone has to go through to become a substitute, they found an error."

Everyone perked up at this announcement. "What kind of error?" Dane asked.

"The lady who handles the substitute list said that each prospective sub fills out a paper application, and a file is started. They require all kinds of things—references and a credit check and a fingerprint analysis. As each step is completed, it's put into the file. Once a person is approved to be a substitute, the information is transferred from the file to the computer system so it can be accessed from any school."

Dane rubbed his temples. "So, what are you saying, Doc?"

"I'm saying that the substitute," he paused to check his notes, "Mrs. Jacobs, looked legitimate on the computer, but when the substitute supervisor checked for the regular file, which should have held all the documentation from her application process, she couldn't find it."

"Which means it didn't exist," Hack interjected. "Somebody hacked into the school board's computers and put the sub in."

"She was fabricated to help with the kidnapping," Dane murmured.

Savannah was both horrified and reassured. It was unbelievable that a criminal had been able to get into Caroline's classroom so easily, but she was now positive that she'd done the right thing by getting Dane and his oddball team involved in the case. In two months of digging, the police hadn't found the file discrepancy.

"How hard would it be to hack in and alter the sub list?" Dane asked

"Pretty darn," Cam contributed. "The school board's system is top-notch, with all kinds of firewalls and intrusion protection.

"So the kidnapper has above average hacking abilities, which makes him very dangerous," Dane said thoughtfully. "What else, Doc?"

The papers in Doc's hands trembled slightly as he cleared his throat and said, "Mrs. Matthews is no longer employed by the school, and they didn't have a forwarding address for her. I'm working on that now."

"What about the sub?"

"We went to the address listed, but if she ever lived there, she's moved," Cam reported for his partner. "It's a transient apartment complex, and the landlord doesn't keep good records."

Dane frowned. "*Both* teachers are missing?"

"Well, not immediately accessible anyway," Doc confirmed.

"We'll find them," Cam sounded certain.

"If the sub was a part of the kidnapping plot, as we assume, we probably have a false name, just like the address," Doc continued.

"Then how will you find her if you don't even know her name?" Savannah asked.

Doc risked a brief, nervous glance at her before returning his gaze to the papers in his hand and saying, "The school has a picture from the security camera at the building's entrance. We're hoping we can use it to identify the sub."

Cam took up the dialogue. "The principal says the picture quality is poor, and so far no one's been able to make an accurate ID."

"The FBI ran it through their database but couldn't come up with a match," Doc said.

Dane considered this. "The fact that the sub can't be found or identified makes me even more certain that she was part of the kidnapping plot. We'll find her—we've just got to keep digging. Doc, I want you to go to the school personally and talk to the principal again. Pick up a copy of that lousy picture, and see if you can get a description of the sub from several different sources—the principal, other teachers, and lunchroom ladies."

"Okay," Doc said, and Savannah noticed that the papers in his hands were trembling more noticeably. "Will you excuse me for a few minutes?" he requested. "It's time for me to take my medication."

Dane didn't look happy, but he nodded. As Doc walked over to his medicine shelf, Dane gave additional instructions to Cam. "Collect everything you can about the sub. If anyone saw the car she drove, that would be very helpful."

Cam nodded and Dane turned to Hack. "What have you got?"

The big man leaned forward and said, "I've got a few Child Advocacy Center cases that look like possibilities, and I put some of my men to work on them. And I agree with the police that the participants in the traffic accident were not part of the kidnapping plot."

Dane frowned. "Well, that's a disappointment. I thought for sure . . ."

"However," Hack interrupted with a smile, "All the participants claim that they weren't at fault in the accident."

Dane raised an eyebrow. "And that's unusual?"

"They all say that they had a green light, and after talking to them, I think they might be right."

Now Dane was smiling too. "Our computer hacker again?"

"That's what I figure," Hack confirmed. "The guy messed up the light sequencing for a few seconds and caused the wreck."

"At just the right time to delay Mrs. McLaughlin," Cam contributed. "You got to give him credit. That was brilliant!"

"Yes, we are definitely dealing with a smart criminal," Dane concurred. "What about the director, Hack?"

The big man glowered at the mention of Hilton Chastain. "That guy won't return my phone calls. His secretary said he's in Italy, but I think she was lying."

"We'll consider that more good news," Dane said. "The fact that Chastain doesn't want to talk to you means he probably has something to hide. Stay after him."

"Don't you worry," Hack promised.

Dane turned to Lacie. "What time do you leave for Colorado?"

"Nine tomorrow morning," she replied.

Dane stood. "This is a good time to call it a night. Everybody get something to eat and at least a few hours of sleep. Tomorrow, work on your assignments and come here to report when you have something."

Surprisingly, Savannah found that being ignored was worse than being ridiculed. "What do you want me to do?" she asked as Dane pushed his chair back to his desk.

"Just keep looking up those addresses," he suggested.

Savannah was careful to keep the disappointment from her voice when she asked, "What time do you want me to be here in the morning? Right after I take Lacie to the airport?"

Dane's expression made it clear how unimportant her presence was to the success of the operation, but he nodded. "Yeah, whenever." Then he turned to Doc. "Did you guys all get hotel rooms in Fredericksburg?"

Savannah was surprised and displeased that the men were leaving the cabin. She'd assumed that based on the urgency of the situation, they'd all work through the night.

"Wouldn't it be more efficient for them to spend the night here?" she asked. "Near these expensive computers the Army is loaning you?"

Dane looked annoyed by the question. "My men need their rest, so they're staying far away from these expensive computers in the Fredericksburg Holiday Inn at General Steele's expense. You might want to see if you can cut a deal with him for yourself, unless you want to keep letting your boss, Doug Forton, pay your way."

Savannah tried to hide her embarrassment. She had come to Dane because of his uncanny ability to find out anything about anyone, but it was unnerving that he knew as much about her life as she did. "I didn't ask Doug to pay for the rental car," she defended herself. "And I'll repay him."

Dane gave her a wicked smile. "I'm sure that's what he's counting on."

Savannah turned away from him and spoke to Lacie. "Are you ready to go?"

"Just let me get my laptop," Lacie said.

Savannah was waiting impatiently by the door when Doc approached her. His pale cheeks were stained pink with embarrassment, and he kept his eyes averted as he touched the picture of Caroline that was sticking out of Savannah's briefcase.

"Your daughter is very pretty," he said softly.

Savannah was touched both by his friendly overture and his use of the present tense. "Yes, she is."

"Come on, Doc," Cam called out. "Hack's already waiting in the car."

Savannah watched the quiet man shuffle off to join his compatriots. She felt Dane's gaze on her but didn't turn to look at him.

Lacie walked over with her laptop tucked under her arm. "I'm ready." Lowering her voice, she added, "Let's get out of here."

CHAPTER 6

Lacie drove the rented SUV out of Dane's backyard, following the well-maintained gravel drive to the street.

"Leaving was much easier than arriving," Savannah commented as Lacie increased her speed.

"Much," Lacie agreed. "Your friend Dane is some piece of work."

Savannah frowned, feeling strangely defensive. "Dane's been through a lot."

Lacie appeared unimpressed by the excuse. "Haven't we all? So you married his friend instead of him. It's time to get over it and move on with his life."

Savannah couldn't bear to give a detailed explanation of the complicated relationships between herself, Wes, and Dane, so she remained silent.

As they drove past the Holiday Inn Express in Fredericksburg, Lacie said, "I'm glad Doug made us reservations at the Hampton Inn. I'm about as sick of Dane's Merry Men as I am of him."

Savannah smiled. "They are a strange group, but I'm pleased with the progress they've made so far."

"Yeah, I guess working with this bunch of misfits is better than dealing with the police, who wouldn't even take your calls," Lacie agreed.

As Lacie was turning into the Hampton Inn, Savannah couldn't stop the resentment she felt against Doug and his determination to work himself into her life by renting cars for her and booking hotel rooms. Then a thought occurred to her.

"We're only an hour from home, and you fly out of Dulles in the morning," she reminded Lacie. "Why don't we skip the hotel room and go back to Washington tonight? We can stay at my place again. Then in the morning you can take this rental to the airport, and I'll drive my own car back to Dane's."

Lacie considered this for a few seconds and then nodded. "Sounds good to me."

Once they were driving down Interstate 270 toward Washington, Savannah said, "I'm not sure I like you going off all the way to Colorado to investigate on your own. It might be dangerous."

"I'm kind of excited about it," Lacie replied cheerfully. "I feel like a real private investigator. The farm people are harmless, and I've arranged for a police escort, so I'll be more than safe."

Savannah wondered if her misgivings were based on concern for Lacie or jealousy. After all, Dane was trusting Lacie with a real job while making Savannah sit at his feet like an errant puppy. Before she could get too depressed, Lacie interrupted her thoughts.

"Tell me about Wes's parents," she requested.

"I can't really tell you much," Savannah said. "I've never met them."

Lacie's eyebrows rose. "Never? They didn't even come to your wedding?"

"The wedding was just a few minutes in the courthouse," Savannah explained, struggling to keep the melancholy from her voice. "So I didn't mind too much that they didn't come then. But when they didn't come after Caroline was born, that bothered me. And when they didn't come to Wes's funeral . . ."

Lacie glanced over at Savannah. "What's wrong with them?"

Savannah shrugged. "Wes said all that money made them crazy."

This seemed to perplex Lacie. "So why wasn't giving it away enough? Why did they have to go live in the mountains all alone like that?"

"Apparently it wasn't just the money but all the social obligations that came with being part of the Westinghouse family. Wes said his grandfather was very overbearing and pretty much directed everyone's life. Wes didn't mind because he liked the plan his grandfather made for him. But he had a younger brother who wasn't as lucky. The boy died of a drug overdose at fifteen."

"Suicide?" Lacie asked.

Savannah nodded. "It was never classified that way officially—thanks to the interfering grandfather—but Wes felt sure the boy killed himself. I guess their son's death sent his parents over the edge. They decided to cut all ties with the grandfather. That's why they gave away the money and moved to a mountain in Colorado without the ability to communicate with the outside world. Even Wes's powerful grandfather couldn't reach them there. And from what Wes said, he didn't try very hard. After all, he still had Wes."

"And their money."

"Yes." Savannah frowned. "I can see how they would have felt depressed and guilty about their fifteen-year-old son's death. I can see why they'd want to get away from the grandfather. But I can't imagine abandoning my child—under any circumstances."

"Wes wasn't a little kid anymore."

"I guess parenthood is different for everyone," Savannah said. "But when Caroline was born, it was the most profound experience of my life. I can't believe that she'll ever get too old to need me." Savannah paused to wipe at the tears that always seemed to come unbidden. "And even when she's dead, I'll still love her."

"It could be that Wes's parents left him out of love," Lacie suggested. "They had to get away to survive, but if Wes liked the grandfather's plan for his life, it would have been selfish and cruel for them to drag him along with them to the mountains."

Savannah had never thought about it that way before. "But to never see him at all . . . how did they stand it?"

"Maybe Wes was right, and the money made them crazy," Lacie said. "Or maybe they distanced themselves from Wes because they had learned that loving someone too much can be painful—even deadly."

Savannah thought about the past two months, the pain and agony she'd suffered because of Caroline's kidnapping. All of that pain would have been eliminated if she'd never become a mother at all. Finally she shook her head. "I can't accept that. No matter how much love hurts, it's worth it."

Lacie smiled, but her eyes were sad. "We can't judge them, Savannah. We just don't know what they were going through. And we don't know what we would do in the same situation. Love can make you do strange things, terrible things—like deserting your own child. We see it every day on the news and in our cases at the CAC. If living on a mountain makes them happy . . ."

"Both their children are dead," Savannah said solemnly. "I doubt happiness is really a possibility for them. Peace, maybe, but not happiness."

"Did it bother Wes that they left him?"

Savannah considered this. "He never said so, but it had to have hurt—don't you think? I mean at least his parents had each other. After his grandfather died, Wes had no one."

"He had you," Lacie reminded her. "And all that money."

"Both were mixed blessings," Savannah replied as tears threatened again.

"Really the only thing I *completely* don't understand is why Wes's parents let being rich stress them out. Now that's a problem I could deal with!"

Savannah smiled, grateful to Lacie for trying to lighten the mood.

"You just sit back and relax," Lacie suggested. "I'll have you home in no time."

Thankful for the darkness, Savannah let the tears she'd held back all day slip onto her cheeks. Then she closed her eyes and allowed the memories to fill her mind.

* * *

After their dinner together on her first day at Fort Belvoir, Savannah dated Dane and Wes simultaneously for several months. Sometimes they were a threesome, other times she would be with one or the other. She still wasn't completely sure whether they were attracted to her personally, or if they were each just trying to beat out the other in the race for her heart.

In April Dane told her that their unit would be involved in a big search and rescue operation soon. In preparation, he had to go to Miami for a few days, and Wes took advantage of his absence to woo her in earnest. He sent her flowers, wrote her poems, and took her to fancy restaurants. It was wonderful, but sometimes the conversation would lag, and she'd miss Dane.

Dane was scheduled to return on a Friday, and Savannah admitted to herself that she was anxious to see him again. Her plan was to go home after work, change clothes, and wait for him to call. But at five when she stood to leave, Wes rushed into the office. He said he'd made dinner reservations and begged her to come along. Against her better judgment and the silent advice Louise was giving her behind Wes's back, Savannah agreed to go.

His plans involved a short trip on a private plane to a restaurant called the Clam Box in Ipswich, Maine. The plane ride was a novelty, the food was delicious, and the atmosphere was wildly entertaining. But throughout the evening her thoughts kept drifting to Dane, wondering if his flight had arrived safely, if he'd tried to call her, if he'd missed her.

During the trip home she stared out the small plane window and watched the city lights pass below them. When they reached the door to her apartment, Wes pulled her into his arms and asked if she'd had fun.

"It was, well, incredible!" she told him. "I can't thank you enough."

"Yes, you can," he contradicted her. Then he leaned down and pressed his lips to hers.

The kiss was so sweet that it brought tears to her eyes.

"I think you know how I feel about you," Wes whispered when the kiss ended.

"I know, and I love you too."

He gave her a beautiful smile. "I've been waiting a long time to hear you say that."

She stepped out of his embrace, afraid he might have attached too much meaning to her words. "You're one of the best friends I've ever had," she clarified. "One of the best people I've ever known."

His smile didn't dim. "I can't believe how lucky I am," he told her.

She put her key into the doorknob. "Well, it's been a long day," she said around a yawn.

Wes wrapped his arms around her waist. "Are you going to invite me in?"

She considered this for a few seconds and then shook her head. "Not tonight. I've been wearing this same suit for nearly eighteen hours. I want to take a shower and put on my pajamas and go to sleep." She also wanted to check her answering machine to see if Dane had called, but she left that out.

Wes was obviously disappointed, but he was a gentleman. So he smiled and pressed a good-bye kiss to her forehead. "I'll see you tomorrow."

"Good night." She slipped inside and leaned against the door, listening to the sounds of Wes's car as he departed. Once she was sure he was gone, she deposited her purse on the table by the door, kicked her shoes toward the bedroom, and flipped on the light. A startled gasp escaped her lips when she saw Dane sitting on her couch.

"How did you get in here?" she demanded.

He stood and moved toward her. "Breaking and entering is one of my specialties," he told her, his tone vaguely menacing. "You'd do well to remember that."

"I-I will," she stammered, flustered by his unexpected presence in her apartment and the way he kept coming toward her like a lion on the prowl.

He didn't stop until she was backed against the wall, and he was right in front of her. "So it looks like you've been having a good time without me." His lips brushed her cheek as he spoke.

"Wes has done his best to keep me entertained in your absence," she conceded nervously.

"Good old Wes." He moved his lips so he could murmur in her ear. "I can't believe you let him kiss you first."

She tried to wriggle away, but he put his hands against the wall on each side of her so she was penned in. She swallowed hard and then pointed out, "Wes *tried* first." Then she frowned. "Just how long have you been watching me?"

This question seemed to amuse him. "Only for a few minutes. Now tell me, is Wes a good kisser?"

"That's none of your business," she replied primly.

He laughed. "That remains to be seen." He moved his hands to each side of her face and pressed his lips to hers. There was nothing sweet or comforting about his kiss, and when he released her, Savannah was breathless and unsteady on her feet.

"So," he gasped. "Who's the better kisser—me or Wes?"

"You kiss very well," she said, and her eyes strayed involuntarily to his mouth.

"You love me," he told her softly. "Go ahead and admit it."

"I love Wes too."

"Think about the kisses," he said. "That's how you can tell the difference between *loving* someone and being *in love* with someone."

She didn't even bother to argue. "Don't talk," she begged. "Just kiss me again."

He seemed happy to comply. As they kissed, he maneuvered her toward the bedroom, and when he reached for the top button of her suit jacket, she didn't object. They were in love, and spending the night together seemed like the natural progression of things. But as he pressed a kiss to her throat, she thought about their rare religious discussions. Dane was a Mormon, and he believed in abstinence before marriage. Since she wanted all their memories of each other to be good ones, she stepped back and rebuttoned her jacket with trembling fingers.

He frowned and asked, "What's wrong?"

"Mormons aren't supposed to do this," she whispered.

"You're not a Mormon," he pointed out.

"No, but you are."

He ran his fingers through his hair in a gesture of frustration. "And what made you remember that just now?"

She shrugged. "Maybe it was God."

He didn't seem pleased by this possibility, but he turned and walked out of the bedroom. She followed a few steps behind him. He picked up his uniform hat and started for the door.

"Are you mad at me?" she asked.

He turned and faced her. "No, I'm mad at myself. Will you forgive me?"

"I love you," she said simply.

He nodded and pulled her back into his arms. She rested her cheek against his chest and listened to the steady beating of his heart. Then she lifted her face to his, and he kissed her.

Finally he pulled back and said, "I've got to get out of here."

She trailed after him as he walked to the door. "I'll miss you," she said.

He settled his hat firmly on his head. "I know. I'll see you tomorrow."

And then he was gone.

As Savannah locked the door behind him, she accepted the fact that she was going to have to choose between the two men she loved. She naively thought that once she picked one, the other would continue to be her friend and things would go back to the way they were at first. She couldn't have been more wrong.

* * *

Now Savannah wished she'd chosen neither man. She should have packed her bags and left Fort Belvoir and both of them behind. But it was way too late for that. She'd failed them all—Wes, Dane, and Caroline. As tears seeped out of her eyes, she asked the Lord to forgive her.

When Savannah opened her eyes, she saw the familiar roads near her home and panic seized her. She hated to be alone anywhere, but especially there.

Lacie looked over and smiled. "You won't be by yourself. I'll sleep on your couch just like last night."

"You don't have to," Savannah tried to decline, but Lacie dismissed her.

"Your place is closer to the airport anyway."

That wasn't really true, but Savannah was too grateful to challenge the statement. "Thank you," she whispered as Lacie pulled to a stop in front of the brick row house Savannah had once loved so much. Then, gathering what was left of her courage, she climbed out of the car and walked inside.

CHAPTER 7

By the time the alarm went off the next morning, Savannah had been awake for hours. Once Lacie was ready to go, Savannah walked her to the street where the SUV was parked and wished her well.

"Call me as soon as you make it to Denver," she instructed.

"I will," Lacie promised. "Don't worry about *me*. You're the one who has to stay with Prince Charming."

Savannah had to smile. "You're right. Wish me luck."

Lacie grinned and waved. "Luck."

After Lacie was gone, Savannah felt claustrophobic in the house. It was only six-thirty, which meant if Savannah left for Fredericksburg now, she'd be at Dane's cabin before eight. That was a little early, but she figured it didn't matter if she woke him up. How much grouchier could he be?

She made it to Creekside Road without having to refer to the directions Dane had written on the index card. Driving slowly, she passed the overgrown path that led to the decrepit bridge and continued up the road until she reached the gravel drive. She parked her Mazda beside a gray sedan and leaned her head back against the car seat, intending to gather her wits and her courage before confronting Dane again. But then she glanced toward the house and realized that time was up. Dane was sitting on the back steps staring right at her.

Since she couldn't very well ignore him, she reluctantly climbed out of her car and approached the house. The morning air was cool and damp, thanks to the rain the day before. A light breeze pulled at her as she walked, and she let her eyes roam over him. His hair was mussed, as if he'd just gotten out of bed. His dark eyes were more tired than hostile, and if anything, he seemed less comfortable than she was.

As she reached the bottom of the stairs, he stood, and the unbuttoned shirt he'd apparently donned in a hurry fell open, exposing his bare chest. She stared in silent horror at the network of scars etched into his skin. Some were thin and white. Some were raised and angry red. All were monuments to excruciating pain.

Overwhelmed with emotion, she grabbed the porch railing to keep from flinging herself into his arms. Aguish and sorrow she had learned to deal with, but the sudden return of passion and tenderness was too much. She closed her eyes and breathed deeply until she felt in control. When she opened her eyes, he was regarding her with curiosity.

"My scars offend you?"

She shook her head. "No."

His look hardened. "I don't need your sympathy."

She shook her head again. Even if she could explain, she wouldn't. It would be very dangerous for her if he understood how she felt. So she averted her gaze to prevent him from being able to read too much in her eyes and said, "I know."

He pulled his shirt closed and buttoned it securely. "I didn't expect you so early."

She cleared her throat. "After Lacie left, I didn't have any reason to stay at home."

He pointed toward the door. "Come on in."

Savannah followed him up the stairs and into the house. As they passed through the cozy kitchen, she couldn't help but think that under different circumstances this could be their home—hers and Dane's. Caroline could be their daughter, safe and sound and eating breakfast at the wooden table.

Her pleasant fantasy was interrupted by Dane saying, "There's hot chocolate on the stove. Help yourself."

"Thanks," she said, but she kept walking toward the technology-crowded living room. Dane sat down at his computer and began typing. Since he didn't seem to need her at the moment, Savannah opened her laptop and settled onto the couch. She removed the picture of Caroline from her briefcase and propped it against the computer screen and then began looking up addresses.

"You didn't finish that last night?" Dane asked from across the room.

"Not quite," she replied.

Before he could reprimand her, Cam walked in, dressed in his customary jungle-print fatigues and carrying grocery bags.

"I brought supplies," he announced unnecessarily. "I thought I'd fix breakfast."

Dane shook his head. "You need to get to work. Mrs. McLaughlin can make breakfast."

He looked at her almost expectantly, as if hoping she'd refuse and give him an excuse to humiliate her further. Put firmly back in her place again, Savannah walked toward the kitchen, thankful that he hadn't told her to clean his toilets.

Cam followed her and deposited the grocery bags on the wooden table. "Once I put out a few feelers, I'll come back and help you," he surprised her by saying.

"I can handle it," she replied.

He smiled at her for the first time since her arrival. "Nobody makes gravy as good as me."

She smiled back. "I'll save the gravy for you, then."

Savannah was relieved when she saw the package of frozen biscuits in the grocery bags. It had been years since she'd attempted to make biscuits from scratch, and she didn't feel up to the task in a strange kitchen, especially with Dane a few feet away. She found an ancient-looking baking pan and arranged the biscuits on it in neat rows. She was trying to figure out how to preheat the oven and hoping that this wouldn't require her to go and chop wood, when Doc walked in.

"Do you know how to turn on this oven?" she asked him. "I can't get the knobs to work."

He walked over and flipped a switch on the side. "It can operate as a real wood-burning stove or a conventional oven," he explained. "When you want electricity, you switch it here."

She pushed *bake* again and was gratified to see the red light come on, indicating that the oven was heating.

"You're making breakfast," Doc stated the obvious.

"Yes, Cam brought the stuff, and I got the assignment." When Doc didn't go immediately into the living room, Savannah asked, "How's your part of the investigation coming?"

"Cam and I collected quite a few descriptions of the substitute teacher," he told her as Cam walked in to join them. "I have a friend who works for the CIA at Langley. He's an expert on photo enhancement, so I e-mailed him a copy of the picture we got from the security camera and the descriptions. After he puts it all together, hopefully he can come up with a composite that's pretty accurate."

"And what will we do once we have a picture?" Savannah asked.

Cam laughed. "Not much."

Doc seemed offended. "We can run it through the department of motor vehicle records and look for a match."

"There are literally millions of pictures in those databases," Cam pointed out. "I'm not trying to burst your bubble, my doctor friend. But I don't want you giving Mrs. McLaughlin false hope."

Savannah was more concerned about Doc and his fragile emotional state. "I appreciate all your hard work," she told the little man. "Dane is lucky to have such diligent team members."

Doc smiled. "Don't worry, we'll find Caroline."

Savannah was touched by his kindness. "I know," she said with more confidence than she felt.

"So, Doc, how about you get to work while I help in the kitchen?" Cam suggested.

Doc nodded and shuffled into the living room. Once he was gone, Cam said, "I'm serious about that picture thing. We might get lucky with that, but . . ."

"I understand," Savannah assured him. "You don't want me to get my hopes up." She pointed to a medium-sized skillet hanging on the wall above the fireplace and asked Cam if he'd get it down for her. He stepped up on the hearth, leaned over the mantle, retrieved the pan, and hopped back down. He placed the pan on a burner and smiled at Savannah, obviously pleased by the opportunity to demonstrate his agility.

Savannah thanked him and then fried bacon and eggs while he worked on the gravy.

"Do you think the investigation is going well?" she asked as they stood beside each other in front of the stove. She knew her question made her seem desperate, but she needed reassurance.

"We're right on track," he said with confidence. "We're zeroing in."

Savannah's heart felt lighter than it had in months. They were on track and zeroing in.

After she'd prepared enough eggs and bacon to feed a small army, Savannah watched Cam make gravy. "How's your family?"

Cam kept his eyes on the skillet as he answered the question. "My wife divorced me and took the kids to California."

"I'm sorry," Savannah told him.

"Yeah, me too." He continued to stir the gravy.

"What happened to the rest of the team?"

"Owl's in Iraq. Steamer's selling real estate in Las Vegas. Wigwam's back in Oklahoma. His wife's about to have a baby, so he couldn't be a part of this operation, but I think Dane still got him active duty pay."

Savannah had to smile. "Wes was proud of the way you guys always took care of each other."

Cam looked uncomfortable. "About Wes," he began, but Savannah held up a hand to stop him.

"I know that Wes broke the rules and that's why none of you consider him a part of the team anymore."

"Wes was an okay guy," Cam said. "Except at the end."

Which was my fault, Savannah thought to herself. To Cam she said, "I understand."

He removed the gravy from the heat. "Breakfast is ready."

As Cam placed the skillet full of gravy on the table, Savannah hurried to set out dishes and silverware. Cam helped her distribute everything into individual place settings. The others walked in during the process, and Dane gave Cam a hard look.

"Are we going to have to get you some camouflage *aprons*?" he asked finally.

Cam tucked a dishtowel into his pants. "Not necessary. I'm an expert at adapting."

The men settled around the table, and Savannah walked from one to the other, offering them a choice of milk or juice.

"What, no coffee?" Hack asked when she asked for his beverage preference.

Since these were the first words Hack had ever said directly to her, Savannah was too stunned to reply immediately. Finally she managed, "Sorry. I didn't see a coffeemaker."

Hack considered this for a few seconds and then shrugged his massive shoulders. "Milk," he decided. Savannah filled his glass and moved on down the line. When everyone had something to drink, she returned the juice and milk to the refrigerator and then stood next to the sink, watching them eat.

Finally Dane said, "Aren't you hungry?"

Actually she was starving, but since her status seemed to be more servant than guest, she hadn't been sure she was welcome at the table. Once her absence had been brought to their attention, Doc and Cam seemed determined that she join them. Doc pulled up an extra chair, and Cam got a plate from the cupboard. He placed two biscuits on it and then poured gravy on top.

"Prepare to taste the most delicious thing you've ever eaten," he said as he placed the plate before her with a flourish.

Dane watched this process and then said, "I wonder if there's such a thing as *pink* camouflage."

Hack looked up from his breakfast. "Pink?"

Dane pointed at Cam, who was scooting Savannah's chair up under the table. "I think Cam's going to need it, since he's turning into a girl."

"Women like men who are in touch with their feminine side," Cam informed them.

"But the Army likes soldiers who stay in touch with their masculine side," Dane reminded him. "So quit acting like Martha Stewart."

Hack laughed at the joke, and even Cam smiled. Doc ignored the whole conversation and walked to the refrigerator. He opened the door and asked Savannah what she'd like to drink.

"Milk," she requested, hoping Doc wouldn't get in trouble with Dane for the kind gesture. Dane rolled his eyes but didn't comment as Doc poured milk in Savannah's glass. She took a bite of the biscuits and gravy. "Delicious," she complimented Cam.

"I told you," he replied.

Dane pointed his fork at Hack and said, "To make better use of our time, why don't you give us a report on what you've found out since last night."

"I still haven't located that director," Hack informed them with his mouth full. "I've got men watching his house and his office and following his wife and his girlfriend."

"My money's on the girlfriend," Cam predicted.

"I won't bet against that," Hack agreed. "His car is wired, and his phones are tapped."

Savannah looked up from her breakfast. "Is that legal?"

"You don't want to know," Dane assured her.

Savannah addressed Hack directly. "You can break every law ever written if it helps us find Caroline. I was just curious."

Hack gave her a penetrating look and finally nodded. "If Chastain comes up for air, I'll know it."

"Sounds like you've got all the bases covered," Dane said.

Hack forked a fried egg and plopped it onto his plate. "Yeah, it's just a matter of time."

Dane reached for another biscuit. "This sure beats prison food, I'll tell you that. What about the traffic light mix-up and the wreck it caused?"

"I talked to the captain of DC's department of public safety. The light where the accident took place is controlled by computer, and there was a brief anomaly that day."

"Anomaly?" Cam repeated.

"That's code for 'mistake,'" Hack explained.

"So both lights were green and caused the crash?" Dane asked.

"The captain wouldn't admit it, but I think we can assume that's what happened."

"How many people at the department of public safety have the knowledge and opportunity to change the light sequences?"

"Several have the knowledge," Hack said. "But the captain insists that their security is so tight that if someone tried to mess with the lights, they'd be caught immediately."

"Where does that leave us?"

"The captain could be wrong," Hack pointed out. "So I convinced him to fax us an employee list, including temps who were in the building that day. We'll compare it to our other lists and look for a match. Or we could be dealing with someone who has equipment sophisticated enough to control the lights for just a few seconds from a remote location."

Dane seemed pleased with this. "Very thorough. Stay on top of both situations. Either one has the potential to break the case wide open."

Dane pushed away from the table. "Cam, when you're through with kitchen duty, I want to show you a couple of things." His eyes moved to Savannah. "And I've got some questions for you as well."

She stood and started stacking the dirty dishes, but Doc stopped her. "You cooked. Hack and I will clean up."

Savannah held her breath, waiting for Dane to verbally flail the poor man, but Dane just walked into the living room. "I don't mind, really," she assured them.

"I've washed dishes in a mud puddle," Hack told her as he moved to the sink and turned on the warm water. "This here ain't even a challenge."

* * *

Left without anything to do, Savannah returned to the living room. Cam and Dane were conferring at Dane's desk, so she walked over to the couch and sat down. A few minutes later Cam left the room, and Dane joined her on the couch.

He handed her a flash drive and asked her to download it onto her computer. She did as he asked, and seconds later she was looking at a modified version of the list she had given Dane the day before. Not only were addresses and phone numbers listed, but also credit histories, prison records, and various other types of restricted information.

Savannah pursed her lips and looked up at Dane. "Why have I been looking up addresses online if you already had them?"

Dane gave her a condescending glance. "I didn't have them until I forwarded the information you gave me to an Internet company who does wholesale background checks."

"A company that does what I've been doing faster and better," she confirmed.

He nodded.

"So why have I been wasting my time on it?" she asked through clenched teeth.

"I wanted you to feel like you were contributing."

"Thanks," she said sarcastically. "But next time you're tempted to give me busy work, just tell me you don't need me, and I'll take a nap."

He almost smiled. "I've highlighted the names of people who've made us suspicious for one reason or another. I want you to look them over and see if you can think of anything about them."

Savannah didn't even try to keep the contempt from her voice. "Like what? Their favorite color or how often they water their lawn?"

"I can't think of any reason that a favorite color could be significant," Dane replied, as if this had been a serious question. "But if you have a neighbor who always seemed to be watering his lawn when you got home from work, that could constitute surveillance. So I guess mention everything, even color preferences if you know them. Just type them into the comment section." He pointed to the edge of the screen.

"Do you promise this isn't busy work?" she asked.

This time he did smile but just briefly. "I promise. We're particularly interested in people who are associated with you in more than one aspect of your life, like neighbors whose children also attend Epic School or clients from the Child Advocacy Center who shop at your favorite grocery store."

She nodded, feeling useful. Then he told her to take her time, and she became suspicious of his motives again. Dane wasn't above lying, so maybe this was another task just to occupy her.

Lacie called at three o'clock and said she'd made it to Denver.

Savannah relayed this information to Dane, who said, "Ask her when she's going to the farm."

Savannah repeated the question to Lacie.

"I'm on my way there now," Lacie replied.

When Savannah informed Dane of this, he said, "Tell her to report back in as soon as she's done there."

"I heard him," Lacie told Savannah. "I'll call back when I'm through."

The rest of the afternoon passed by in a blur of frantic, if futile, activity. Dane had lots of wheels turning, but Savannah couldn't tell that they were really getting anywhere. Not that she'd know if they were, since she was convinced that they were withholding information from her.

Once it got dark, the men left one by one until finally it was just Savannah and Dane at the cabin waiting for Lacie to call.

"What could be taking her so long?" Savannah asked him as they sat around the kitchen table eating leftover biscuits.

"It's two hours earlier in Denver," Dane pointed out. "She'll call soon."

When the biscuits were gone, Savannah started washing their dishes. Lacie called just as she finished. After quickly wiping her hands on a dishtowel, Savannah pressed the speaker feature on her phone and asked, "Lacie, are you okay?"

"I'm great," Lacie replied. "I got a tour of the whole Brotherly Love Farm, and I was very impressed. It's so organized, and all the people seem really happy."

"Maybe they were just acting happy," Savannah suggested.

"I don't think so," Lacie said. "They weren't happy in a silly way. It was more like serenity, and it would be hard to fake that."

"I guess it would be," Savannah agreed reluctantly. Then she asked, "So did you meet the McLaughlins?"

"No, the helicopter isn't scheduled to go up there until Friday, but they told me I can come back and go with them then." After a brief pause Lacie said, "You should come too."

At this moment Savannah seriously regretted her decision to include Dane in the conversation. "No, I won't force myself on them."

Lacie didn't press the issue. "It's really beautiful here. I hate to leave."

"But you are leaving, right?" Savannah confirmed.

Lacie laughed. "My flight leaves at ten-thirty tomorrow morning. Has Dane been insufferable without me there to soften him?"

Dane raised an eyebrow, and Savannah sighed. "Dane is insufferable no matter who tries to soften him. Unfortunately, he's also sitting right here."

"Hello, Lacie," Dane greeted.

"Am I on speaker phone?" she asked.

"You are," Savannah confirmed. "I should have warned you."

"Sorry about the insufferable remark," she said to Dane.

"I've been called worse," he assured her. "Did you get the rosters we requested?"

"I did. There are a lot of children listed, but the total matches the live births exactly."

"Any infant deaths?" Dane asked.

"None," Lacie responded.

Savannah sank down into a kitchen chair. "Oh well." They'd reached another dead end.

"So did you make any progress on the investigation today?" Lacie wanted to know.

"Doc thinks he'll have a decent picture of the substitute teacher soon." Savannah tried to sound more hopeful than she felt. "Hack is hot on the heels of the director who stalled the public service commercial shoot, although his secretary still claims he's left the country. And Dane has me trying to remember how often I saw my neighbors in the grocery store."

"Nothing, huh?" Lacie summed it up.

"Nothing," Savannah agreed. "Maybe tomorrow."

"Well, I'll let you go. I talked to Doug a few minutes ago, and he said you haven't been answering his calls." Lacie's tone was mildly reproving. "He's worried about you."

"I'll call him," Savannah promised, although she was careful not to commit to a timeframe.

"Bye, Dane!" Lacie called out.

"Good-bye," he responded.

Then Savannah closed the phone. "I guess I'll go to the hotel now."

He nodded. "It's late."

She collected her laptop and briefcase from the living room and then walked back into the kitchen. Dane was gone, so she hurried out to her Mazda and drove to the Hampton Inn in Fredericksburg. During the check-in process, she was annoyed when the cheerful desk clerk informed her that Doug had prepaid for her room. But she smiled and accepted the key from the young woman without protest.

The hotel room was clean and attractive, but Savannah felt restless and uneasy. She attributed this partly to the fact that she was alone. And besides the unwelcome solitude, the effort to find Caroline wasn't progressing as quickly as she'd hoped it would. Maybe she'd built Dane up in her mind beyond the point of human capability. Maybe no one could help her.

Fighting tears, she took a hot shower. She was putting on her bathrobe when she heard her cell phone ringing. Afraid she might miss an important call, she ran to answer it. In her haste she didn't check the caller ID and regretted it when she heard Doug Forton's voice.

"Hey, Savannah." He sounded cheerful. "How do you like your hotel room?"

"Okay," she said. "I mean it's nice."

There was a brief pause, and Savannah knew Doug had expected more appreciation, but she was just too tired and discouraged to stroke his ego.

"How is the case going?"

"Slow," she admitted.

"Hey, why don't I come down and help out," he suggested. "Another pair of hands might speed the process."

And just when she had thought things couldn't get any worse. Choosing her words carefully, Savannah replied, "Dane's house is small, and it's already full of people. They've known each other forever and work well together." Doug had a short attention span and too much information would just confuse him, so she wrapped up her explanation. "While I very much appreciate your offer, I'm going to have to decline."

"You don't want me to come?" Doug asked.

"I think it would be best if you stay in Washington," she confirmed as gently as possible.

"But I want to be with you." Now he was whining. "To give you support."

"You just keep things running smoothly at the CAC. That will ease my mind immensely." She used her firmest tone. "Now I've got to go, Doug. Thanks for calling." She closed her phone and vowed to check the incoming number before answering it again.

After ordering a salad from room service, Savannah found a Dustin Hoffman marathon playing on the Movie Channel. Hoping this would distract her, she settled back on the pillows arranged against the headboard and turned up the volume on the television.

First she watched *All the President's Men,* followed by *Kramer vs. Kramer* and was watching the credits for *Tootsie* when she was startled by a loud knock on her door. She glanced at the clock on the nightstand. It was five o'clock in the morning. Thinking that Doug had driven to Fredericksburg against her wishes, she silenced the television and approached the hotel room door with angry purpose.

She pulled open the door and found not Doug but Dane standing in the hallway.

"It's very dangerous to open the door before you find out who's knocking," he told her as he stepped inside.

She couldn't imagine a guest more dangerous than him, but she kept that to herself. Her major concern was why he had come to her hotel room before dawn. "Has there been some news?" she asked tentatively.

"You could say that," he replied as he sat on the edge of her bed and picked up the television remote. "Put some clothes on. We're driving to DC."

Reminded about her state of undress, she pulled the edges of her robe more firmly together. "Now?"

"Right now," he confirmed. "Hack finally found that director, Hilton Chastain. And through his own unique form of persuasion, Hack got the guy to admit that he dragged out the filming of that public service announcement."

Savannah's heart pounded. "So he *was* involved in Caroline's kidnapping?"

Dane stared at the television screen and used the remote to surf from one channel to another. "He swears he didn't know anyone was going to snatch your kid. He was just doing a favor for a business associate."

"Do you believe him?"

"I've seen Hack in action," Dane replied. "The man wouldn't have dared hold anything back."

"Did he say who his business associate was?"

Dane nodded grimly. "I'm afraid so."

"Who was it?" Savannah forced herself to ask.

Dane glanced up. "The culprit was none other than your boyfriend, Doug Forton."

CHAPTER 8

After Dane's accusation against Doug, all the air left Savannah's lungs, and for a few seconds she was afraid she would faint. To reduce the likelihood, she dropped down onto the edge of the bed beside Dane.

"Doug?" she finally managed. "Doug kidnapped Caroline?"

"If he didn't do it himself, he helped someone else." Dane returned his attention to the television.

"Why?" she gasped.

"That's a question I can't answer," Dane said. "Which is why we're going to the Child Advocacy Center offices right now. I want to be waiting there for Mr. Forton when he arrives at work today. That way we can get his explanation first hand."

Savannah took a couple of deep breaths. "I just can't believe it."

"You're looking at this all wrong," Dane said without taking his eyes off the television. "If Forton is the kidnapper, that's a good thing, because there's no question in my mind that we can make him tell us what he did with your daughter."

She couldn't seem to get past the shock. "But he's my friend. Or I thought he was."

Dane glanced over at her. "Why aren't you getting dressed? We can talk about your friendship with Forton in the car."

Savannah's hands were trembling as she riffled through her suitcase. She pulled out a pair of jeans, a lace tank top, and a linen jacket that under normal circumstances she would never wear together. The clothes were wrinkled, but she didn't take the time to iron them. After brushing her teeth and hair, she packed her toiletry items. Then she closed her suitcase and carried it to the hotel room door.

"I'm ready," she told Dane.

He turned off the television and walked over to stand beside her.

"Do you really think Doug knows where Caroline is?" she whispered.

"Probably," he replied. "But you need to be prepared for the possibility that wherever she is, she may not be breathing." Then he opened the door and waited for her to step into the hall before closing the door firmly behind them.

The night clerk didn't seem surprised by Savannah's early-morning departure or the fact that she had a male companion. The clerk just smiled as she accepted the room key and expressed her hope that they'd had a pleasant stay. Savannah did her best to smile back and then followed Dane outside.

The same gray sedan she'd seen behind his cabin was parked by the curb outside the entrance to the hotel. He popped open the trunk for her to deposit her suitcase, then unlocked the doors with his keyless entry, and they climbed into the front seat.

They rode in silence for several minutes. Savannah leaned her head against the seat and closed her eyes, trying to come to grips with the information Dane had given her about Doug. No wonder Doug had been so willing to pay for everything. No wonder he'd wanted to come down and "help." It was all just his way of monitoring the investigation so he could protect himself. Quickly her sadness changed to anger, and her hurt solidified into determination. If Doug had stolen her daughter, she'd make sure he regretted it.

She turned her head and studied Dane's profile under her lowered lashes. There was so much she wanted to say—so much she was afraid to mention. But since she didn't know how any overture from her would be received, she decided to satisfy herself by watching him. If he felt her gaze, he gave no indication.

Once they were out of the city and headed north, Dane set the cruise control and seemed to relax a little.

"What did you do to get thrown in prison?" she asked him.

"Petersburg Correctional you mean?"

"Yes."

"I was accused of insider trading," he told her. "But I still maintain my innocence."

She smiled. "Of course." After a few minutes she asked, "Was it terrible there?"

"At Petersburg?" he verified again, and she nodded. "Having your freedom restricted is never pleasant," he prefaced. "But as prisons go, Petersburg wasn't bad, especially for a white-collar criminal like me."

"Alleged white collar criminal," she corrected.

This earned her a fleeting smile. "So why don't you tell me what form of blackmail you're using to get General Steele's cooperation," he suggested.

All traces of humor left her. "Have you ever heard of an operation called Nick at Night?"

She saw Dane's hands tense on the steering wheel. "Nicaragua, a few years ago. It was a bad one."

She nodded. "Wes had a disc with pictures and documentation of all the events."

Dane's eyes left the road and glanced over at her. "Why? He wasn't part of that operation."

"I don't know why he had the disc," she said. "But when I needed some leverage to get the general's cooperation, I decided to use it."

Dane didn't respond.

Finally the darkness gave Savannah the courage to say, "Wes loved you until the end. You know that?"

Dane still didn't answer.

Refusing to retreat, she continued. "Barely a day went by that he didn't mention your name or your team slogan—*All for one and one for all.*"

Dane glared at the road in front of him. "That wasn't an official slogan. Doc came up with it because he has romantic ideas about justice and liberty and the American way. It was so darn corny. I'm ashamed to even think about it."

She'd gone this far. She couldn't stop now. "But you lived it," she insisted. "You took care of each other. You still do. Like the way you arranged for Wigwam to get active duty pay even though he couldn't come help with the investigation."

Dane looked irritated by this statement, and she hoped Cam wouldn't be reprimanded for sharing this information with her. "You might not want to mention the fact that Wigwam isn't physically *here* to General Steele."

It was unlikely that Savannah would be saying anything to the general ever again, but rather than explain this, she just nodded. "I can be a team player, too."

He cut his eyes over at her briefly. "I believe you can."

The steady purr of the car's engine was soothing, and a few minutes later Savannah felt her eyelids start to droop. But before she could doze off, Dane said, "That disc bothers me."

She stifled a yawn and asked, "Why?"

"Because it constitutes a motive for murder," Dane told her grimly. "Wes's accident always seemed suspect to me. But like you said, the insurance company didn't contest the cause of death, and they would have if there were any suspicious circumstances."

He was full of surprises. "You know the details of Wes's death?"

"Of course. While I was healing up I had plenty of time to do research. He was leaving the practice range and ran off the road. He hit a tree and died instantly."

Savannah nodded. "I was thankful for the instant part."

"I even came to the funeral," Dane further surprised her by saying.

"I didn't see you."

"Nobody saw me. That was the idea."

"Honestly, I have worried that Wes's death wasn't an accident," she confided softly. "But I never considered murder. I figured he killed himself."

This time Dane looked at her for several seconds before returning his gaze to the road. "Why would he do that?"

"Because I wasn't enough for him," she whispered. "He needed you too, but he couldn't have us both."

"How do you know you weren't enough?" His voice was barely audible.

"Because he wasn't enough for me either," she said. Then, overcome by sadness and misery, Savannah closed her eyes and slept.

* * *

When Savannah opened her eyes, the car was filled with the soft pink light of early dawn. She pushed away from the window she'd been leaning on and squinted at the clock on the dash. It was a little after six o'clock.

She became immediately aware of the need to eat and use the bathroom. As if he'd read her mind, Dane pulled off the highway and into a truck stop.

"We'll stop here for breakfast," he announced. "And I'm sure you'll want to freshen up a little before we make our appearance at the Child Advocacy Center."

She raised her hands above her head and stretched. "Are you saying I look terrible?"

He shrugged. "Things are relative. For you, not bad."

The sleep had refreshed her, and she was feeling generous so she laughed.

Dane parked the car up close to the truck stop's restaurant entrance and asked, "What time does your boss usually get to work?"

"Never before nine o'clock," she told him. "Sometimes later."

Dane pushed open his door. "Good, then we've got plenty of time."

Savannah visited the restroom before joining Dane at a table. "I ordered for you," he told her. "French toast and orange juice."

She felt a little weak in the knees and sat down quickly. "My favorite breakfast."

"I was hoping that at least some things never change."

Savannah looked away. She'd said too much during their drive, and she'd have to be more careful in the future. "How are your parents?" she asked.

"Fine. They're on a mission for the Mormon church in Thailand, and they seem to like it."

"And your sister?"

"She's fine, I guess. Her youngest just started college, so she's dealing with the empty nest issues."

Savannah nodded. She could relate to that.

The waitress brought their food, and once they were eating, Dane asked, "So you never met Wes's parents?"

Savannah was humiliated. "No, they didn't have much interest in Wes and no interest in me or Caroline."

"It's not your fault," he said with a rare show of humanity. "Or theirs either for that matter. Life stinks."

"I don't really believe that," she said as she stared at her French toast. "I hate the situation I'm in now, but I look forward to the day when this is all a bad memory. I want to live my life and share Caroline's. I can't understand why Wes's parents would deny themselves that opportunity."

"They might think that you'd resist any efforts they made to be a part of your daughter's life," he suggested as he cut his omelet into precise little pieces. "Maybe they're afraid."

Savannah poured a generous amount of syrup on her breakfast. "I'll see what they say when Lacie goes up there on Friday. If they act interested, once I get Caroline back, I'll share."

He glanced up. "That's nice of you."

"I have my moments," she acknowledged as she put a big bite into her mouth.

Dane shook his head in mock disgust and concentrated on his food.

They finished their meal in silence and then returned to the car for the drive into Washington, DC. The traffic was heavier than before but still manageable, so they made good time. They reached the building that housed the CAC at seven-thirty. Savannah presented her ID at the security desk and signed Dane in as a guest. Then they rode the elevator up to the tenth floor.

When they reached the smoked-glass doors with Child Advocacy Center stenciled in elegant gold letters, Savannah pulled out her keys. Once they were inside, she relocked the door and flipped the light switch, illuminating the spacious and beautifully furnished lobby.

Dane looked around for a few seconds and then turned to her with a surprised expression. "These are pretty nice digs for a nonprofit organization."

"Nonprofit doesn't mean absence of income," Savannah felt obligated to explain. "We do charge fees, but they're based on our clients' ability to pay. Expenses like rental costs for our office space and staff salaries are paid out of revenues collected and patron donations." She led the way down the paneled hallway to her office.

"Do you ever wonder how many more children you could help if you had dumpy offices?" he asked as they walked past Doug's game room, dominated by an antique pool table. "And cheaper furniture?"

"The office renovation and furnishings didn't come from CAC funds," she told him. "Doug paid for it personally so that he could, well . . ."

"Be comfortable while he did his bit for the poor?" Dane provided.

"Basically," Savannah admitted.

"I like this guy more and more," Dane said, his voice dripping with sarcasm.

She lost patience with him as they reached the door to her office. Pointing a finger at his chest, she hissed, "We do good work here, so why don't you stop criticizing us."

He seemed surprised by the accusation. "I wasn't criticizing you, just Forton."

She turned away in exasperation and walked into her office. Dane was right behind her. He took himself on a tour of the room, looking at all the pictures of her receiving various awards that Doug had insisted she frame and display. Doug said the pictures would give her more credibility with clients. As Dane studied each one, she felt sure that to him the pictures just made her seem egotistical.

He didn't comment until he reached her desk. There was a picture of her and Doug taken the previous year. He glanced over and compared her with the picture. "You're right. You can look better than you do now."

She wasn't offended by this remark. Well, not much anyway. She pushed a lock of stray hair behind her ear. "I lost all interest in my appearance the day Caroline disappeared."

He replaced the picture on her desk and checked his watch. "Why don't we go on to Forton's office and wait for him there. We wouldn't want him to slip in without us seeing him."

Relieved to escape the small and intensely personal space they'd been confined in, she led the way to Doug's office. They waited in the reception area there for almost an hour before Doug's secretary, Jackie, walked in. She let out a little screech when she saw them and dropped the Starbucks cup she'd been carrying.

"That's a stain," Jackie predicted as the creamy brown liquid seeped into the light-colored carpet. Then she turned to her guests with a disapproving expression. "I didn't expect anyone to be here since the door was locked."

Savannah pulled some tissues from the box on Jackie's desk and blotted at the coffee spill. "I'm sorry," she apologized half-heartedly. "We need to talk to Doug, and we're trying to catch him first thing. But I didn't want to leave the door unlocked until there was someone sitting at the reception desk."

Jackie didn't commend Savannah for her security consciousness. Instead she reached for the phone and started punching buttons. "I need to call maintenance about the carpet." Over her shoulder Jackie added, "And Doug isn't coming in today, so catching him won't be a possibility."

After exchanging a quick glance with Dane, Savannah asked, "Why not?"

"He's gone to a technology convention in Aruba." Jackie held up a finger for silence as someone from maintenance answered on the other end. Jackie explained the carpet situation and then hung up.

Savannah stepped over to the desk. "I spoke with Doug last night, and he didn't mention a convention trip."

Jackie shrugged. "He called me this morning while I was in the drive-through at Starbucks." The secretary gave the stain on the floor a sorrowful look. "He said he'd decided at the last minute to attend the convention. I figured it was because you're out of the office. He's been moping for days."

Savannah felt Dane's gaze but steadfastly kept her eyes from his. "Do you know when he'll be back?"

"He didn't say," Jackie replied.

Now Savannah was forced to look at Dane since she didn't know what the next step was. He tilted his head toward the hallway and she nodded. It was time to go. Returning her attention to Jackie, Savannah said, "Well, if you hear from Doug, will you let me know?"

Jackie seemed annoyed. "I don't see why you can't just call him on his cell."

Dane moved toward the door and Savannah followed him. "I can, but just in case I miss him. So I won't worry," Savannah added lamely.

Jackie nodded. "I'll call you if I hear from him."

Savannah gave the secretary an appreciative smile. "Thanks." She glanced at the coffee stain one last time. "And good luck with the carpet."

Once they were in the hall, Dane leaned close and muttered, "He was tipped off."

"Who would do that?"

"Maybe you," Dane said as they hurried back to her office.

"I didn't tip Doug off!" she insisted.

"Not intentionally," Dane replied. "I just thought that while you and Forton were exchanging love words last night . . ."

"I certainly wasn't exchanging love words with Doug." They reached her office, and after they were inside she closed the door to keep Jackie or anyone else from overhearing their conversation.

"Just what *did* you and Forton talk about then?"

Savannah tried to ignore Dane's insulting insinuations and remember exactly what she and Doug had discussed. "He asked how the case was progressing and I told him it was slow. Then he wanted to come down and help us, and I told him not to."

"But you didn't mention that Hack had caught up with that commercial director—Hilton Chastain?"

"No!"

Dane frowned. "Then Forton was probably warned by Chastain personally."

Ever since Dane had appeared at her hotel room in Fredericksburg, she'd been dreading the confrontation with Doug. But now that it was apparent that the conversation couldn't take place, she was disappointed. "What now?"

"We need to find out if Forton really took that flight to Aruba, and if so, when it arrives. Then we'll arrange a greeting party for him."

"Do you want me to go ask Jackie what flight he was on?"

Dane shook his head. "No need to make her more suspicious of us. I can get all the information I need from your computer."

Savannah turned on the computer and then stepped back. "Help yourself," she invited.

She waited until he was settled into her chair and then walked over to the window. She heard his fingers striking the keys, and after a few seconds he said, "I need a password. I tried *one-man woman*, but that wasn't it."

She ignored the jibe and recited her password. In a remarkably short period of time he announced, "Doug Forton is on American Airlines Flight 4748, seat 13B. It left Dulles at six this morning, and after a plane change at Kennedy, he'll be on to Aruba for arrival just after noon. He has arranged for a limo to pick him up at the airport and take him to the Aruba Marriot, where a technology convention *is* being held. However, Mr. Forton is not registered. Not yet anyway."

Savannah couldn't hide her amazement. "You were able to find all that out so quickly?"

"Information is easy to access if you have the right skills."

Knowing that Dane had broken in to secure databases without remorse was a little unnerving. Savannah reminded herself that she was fortunate to have Dane and his incredible abilities working for her. Then General Steele's words came back to her. *"If revenge is the motive for your daughter's kidnapping, you'd be wiser to consider Dane a suspect than to ask for his help."*

Her heart pounded painfully. Someone with incredible computer skills had hacked into the school system's files and put a substitute's name on the list that didn't belong there. Then he or she had altered the sequence of traffic lights outside the school, causing a wreck. Could it have been Dane? But if Dane was the kidnapper, why was he trying so hard to help her find Caroline? Or was his helpfulness an act? After all, they hadn't found the child yet.

Dane interrupted these disturbing thoughts by saying, "I could have Forton picked up in New York, but I think I'll wait until he arrives in Aruba. The authorities down there are so much less concerned about legalities and civil rights."

Savannah cleared her throat to cover her anxiety and asked, "What are they going to do to him?"

"Scare him, mostly," Dane replied. "I'll request that some Aruban policemen meet him when he gets off the plane and take him in for questioning. If he's not immediately forthcoming with the information we need, they'll throw him in a jail cell for a while."

"How do you know they won't hurt him?"

Dane twisted the chair around so he was facing her. "I don't care if they hurt him, as long as they get us the information we need to find your daughter."

She looked away. "It's hard to stop thinking of him as a friend."

"Poor Savannah," he said without sympathy. "She still believes in fairy tales like enduring love and undying loyalty."

She squared her shoulders. "So are we done here?"

Dane regarded her for a few seconds and then nodded. "Almost. I need to make a couple of calls to Aruba, but I don't want to use my cell phone, and you probably don't want to hear what I'm going to say. Is there someplace else I can go?"

She moved toward the door. "Use the phone on my desk. I'll wait in the reception area."

"There's a beautiful irony in that," he said, "Using Forton's phone to set up his torture session."

Savannah was glad to leave Dane and his phone call behind. She knew that obtaining the information was necessary, but unlike Dane, she couldn't enjoy the thought of Doug suffering, no matter what he'd done.

Dane joined her a few minutes later. "That's all taken care of."

She nodded and led the way to the elevators. "Are we headed back to Fredericksburg?"

"I thought as long as we were here we could go by Epic School," he proposed.

"Why?" she whispered.

"I'd like to see the layout. Sometimes it helps me to get the feel of a place."

Savannah used the time it took to get on the elevator and push the LOBBY button to compose a response. She hadn't been to Epic School since the day Caroline was kidnapped. It would be painful to drive through the gates that should have kept her daughter safe, to walk up the steps she'd climbed with such confidence on that terrible day, and to see the empty bench where children sat when their parents were late.

She wanted badly to say no to the school trip. But if Dane thought it would help, she'd stand it somehow. So she nodded and pulled out her cell phone. "I'll call the director, Mr. Segars, and set up an appointment."

After arrangements had been made for Dane to tour the school, Savannah sat quietly in his car and tried to muster her courage. As they approached the intersection where the crash had been, Dane had her describe everything she could remember. She wasn't sure if he really thought it would help or if he was just trying to distract her, but she answered anyway.

"I turned here, and that's when I saw that there was a problem."

"How far was traffic backed up?"

She twisted around in her seat and looked behind them. "Not far at first, but it got bad fast."

Dane nodded. "Were there any emergency vehicles on the scene?"

"No, but I heard sirens a few minutes later."

Dane frowned. "The timing of the crash was so perfect. It makes me wonder if someone was actually tracking your movements."

That was a chilling thought. "How could they do that?"

"Lots of ways," Dane replied. "Then what happened?"

"I was moving so slowly that I realized I'd never make it in time. That's when I called Lacie and asked her to get Caroline, thinking that if she came from the other side of the intersection, she could miss the traffic."

"But her tire was flat."

"Yes," Savannah confirmed.

"The kidnapper had every base covered. He knew you'd call Lacie and made sure that her car was disabled as well."

Savannah narrowed her eyes at him. "You think the kidnapper *did* arrange Lacie's flat tire?"

He shrugged. "Probably."

Now she was mad. "So why did you act like the suggestion was unbelievably stupid when I brought it up yesterday?"

"Just for fun," he admitted. Then he waved outside the windshield toward the intersection they were passing through. "What next?"

She was still scowling at him as she continued. "I tried to call the school and let them know I was going to be late, but I couldn't get through. I asked Lacie to keep trying so I could concentrate on the traffic."

Dane shot her an irritated look. "You didn't tell me that you tried unsuccessfully to reach the school office that day." His tone was almost accusatory, as if she'd withheld important information on purpose.

"I'm sorry," she forced herself to say. "I forgot. Is it significant?"

"Maybe!" he said. "And we can't afford to ignore anything. The tied-up phone lines could be the work of our hacking kidnapper who put the fake sub on the school's computer list and messed up the traffic lights. Or maybe one of the office ladies disabled the phones." Dane ran his fingers through his hair in frustration. "Now we'll need to go back and check out all the office personnel more closely."

Savannah was so preoccupied by her failure to report the jammed phone lines that they were parked in front of the school before she realized it. Dane looked across at her and said, "You can wait here if you'd rather."

His unexpected sensitivity took her by surprise and made her more emotional. She swatted at the tears leaking from her eyes and said, "I want to go in." This wasn't precisely true, but she sure didn't want to wait alone in the car.

"We'll keep this short," he promised, and she realized that he was trying to apologize for the necessity.

"I can do it," she said, hoping she could.

CHAPTER 9

Mr. Segars was waiting for them at the main entrance of Epic School. He seemed nervous, and Savannah would have reassured him that they weren't there to collect ammunition for a lawsuit if she hadn't been so busy trying to hold herself together.

Dane asked for a general tour of the school, and with a nod the director led them through the quiet halls. When they reached the first grade wing, Mr. Segars pointed out Caroline's classroom. Savannah expected to be overcome with painful memories, but Dane started asking questions about the nearest exit and the closest parking lot, and soon her thoughts were diverted from the emotional to the analytical. She tried to look at things through a stranger's eyes, to see how the building might have looked to a kidnapper.

Dane walked up and down the hall, looking in classrooms, looking out doors, and checking the view from each window. When he was satisfied, he asked Mr. Segars to show them how car-line was set up each day.

The principal led them out to the circular drive in front and pointed to the yellow line painted across both lanes. "The cars line up here, two abreast. Each teacher leads her car-riders out and stays with them until the last one is picked up."

"How many car-riders does each teacher have?"

"It varies," Mr. Segars said. "I'd estimate an average of about five or six."

"How do the rest of the children get home?"

"They are picked up from our daycare facility later."

"How do you make sure that a child isn't picked up by someone other than a parent?"

"Parents are always required to sign for their children, and for the first two weeks we require the parents to show identification in car-line. After two weeks, the teachers know the parents well enough to skip that step."

"What happens when a substitute teacher brings the children to car-line?" Dane asked.

"Another teacher or an assistant principal is supposed to help them."

"Was this procedure followed on the day of the kidnapping?"

Mr. Segars nodded. "The lead teacher for the first grade was helping the substitute."

"And she thought the woman in the car was Mrs. McLaughlin."

"Yes."

"But it was early in the year, and the lead teacher only knew vaguely what Mrs. McLaughlin looked like," Dane continued.

Mr. Segars dropped his gaze to the sidewalk. "Yes."

"The kidnapper waited until the third week of school, when he or she knew IDs wouldn't be required and the other teachers wouldn't know me well," Savannah said, and Dane looked at her with something approaching pride.

"Yes," Dane confirmed. "That's exactly what our kidnapper did." Dane turned and addressed Mr. Segars. "Your system seems thorough, but no system is foolproof. The kidnapper found a weakness and took advantage of it. In the future, anytime a substitute handles car-line, you should have them check parent identification. And as an added precaution, make sure the child can see the person driving the car. If it's an imposter, the child will know."

"We will implement the changes you suggest immediately." Mr. Segars shot Savannah a remorseful look. "I wish we had done so sooner, but the procedures we're using have worked without exception for decades."

"Using the same procedures for decades was your biggest mistake," Dane told him. "Predictability makes you vulnerable. You need to alter your procedures regularly so that a criminal can't use them against you."

Then Dane asked to see where deliveries were made, where garbage was disposed of, and where visitors were allowed to park. Once the tour was complete, he thanked Mr. Segars and led Savannah back to the car. While they walked she considered all she had learned. It surprised her how much she hadn't known about the school and its procedures. She'd thought she had been very thorough in her investigation of Epic School and its security. Dane had taught her otherwise.

After putting on her seat belt, Savannah leaned her head against the seat, drained emotionally and physically. But the ordeal was over, and she comforted herself with that fact. Then Dane asked if she'd be willing to let him look around her house as well.

Knowing that a home tour would be worse than visiting the school, she turned to stare at him. "Why?"

"Same reason," he responded. "I'd like to get a feel of your house too."

This didn't sound like a compelling enough reason, but rather than argue, she nodded. "Turn left at the next light and drive until you reach Pennsylvania Avenue. It's two blocks down on the right."

Minutes later they pulled up in front of the row house she had lived in since her marriage to Wes. Savannah watched as Dane took in the brick bowfront with tall, narrow windows that faced the street. His eyes moved to the small, neatly landscaped lawn surrounded by a three-foot wrought iron fence.

"Unless that fence is equipped with motion detectors and laser sensors, it's useless as a security measure."

"It was never intended to provide security," Savannah said. "It's just for decoration."

He didn't comment on this but instead asked, "Do you always park on the street?"

"Usually," she confirmed. "There's a covered parking area in back, but it's crowded and inconvenient."

He climbed out of the car and continued his inspection. "Your neighbors are very close."

She joined him on the sidewalk in front of her house. "That's true of most houses in the historical district. They were built in rows like this to conserve the valuable property near the capitol."

"You have a corner lot, which gives you a little more space," he noted as he walked to the edge of her property. "But that extra exposure means an intruder would have numerous points of access."

Savannah frowned. "Caroline wasn't kidnapped from home."

"No, but I'd be willing to bet that the kidnapper watched you both for weeks before he actually took your daughter."

Savannah shivered as Dane studied the upstairs windows of the houses across the street.

"Are any of these houses empty?"

"I don't think so."

"Have any new neighbors moved in recently?"

"If so, I didn't notice."

"Any construction in the area?" He continued his staccato questions.

"Not that I remember."

"Do you know your immediate neighbors well?"

"I'm on a speaking basis with most of them. I don't have time to really socialize," she offered as an excuse.

"The kidnapper would have had a good view of your house from any of those places across the street. He could determine your regular schedule and make his plans accordingly. We'll need to come up with the names of your neighbors and add them to our list of suspects." Dane pushed open the gate and waved toward the front door. "I'm ready to see the inside now."

Savannah followed him to the door and unlocked it. The alarm immediately started to hum, and she entered the code into the keypad by the door.

"How often do you change your code?" he asked.

"Never," she told him.

He shook his head. "Then your alarm system is worthless. Since there's no perimeter system outside, and you never change the alarm code, I'll guarantee you that the kidnapper has been in your house."

"Inside?" she whispered.

"It's what I would do if I was planning to kidnap a kid," he told her. "I'd come inside the home while the family was away."

She stared at him. "And get a *feel* of the place."

He nodded. "Exactly."

Savannah gritted her teeth as they walked through the entryway. Dane glanced into the small living room and dining room combination to their right before continuing on into the family room. The house felt strange to Savannah. She wasn't sure if it was because she'd just been informed that Caroline's kidnapper had visited there or if it was Dane's presence that was making her uneasy.

Her eyes followed his as he took in the soothing, sage green paint, the brick fireplace, the comfortable earth-tone furniture, and the wall of windows that provided a breathtaking view of Washington, DC. She expected him to comment on her good fortune in finding a house with such a feature. Instead he frowned.

"Don't you have curtains?"

"That would defeat the purpose of the windows."

He seemed annoyed. "You realize that glass works both ways? Since you can see *out,* every pervert within miles of here can see right into your house? All they need is a good pair of binoculars."

"It never occurred to me that anyone would want to look in at us," Savannah admitted.

He shook his head in a gesture of hopeless frustration as he walked over to the French doors that led out onto the deck. Leaves in various colors had accumulated there during the months of neglect. He pointed at the six-foot wooden fence that surrounded her small backyard. "Please tell me you keep that gate locked."

She nodded.

"But there are no motion detectors back here either?"

"No." She was beginning to feel responsible for Caroline's kidnapping since obviously he thought she'd been negligent in terms of home security. "I should have gotten a better system and changed the code frequently." She glanced up at the windows. "And I should have bought some curtains."

"Your house is no worse than other places I've seen," he offered as meager comfort. "Most homes are grossly underprotected." He turned and started up the stairs.

With deep reluctance, Savannah followed him. He glanced in the room that the realtor had called a bonus space, which had become Wes's office. It looked much the way it had when he died—as if it were waiting patiently for Wes to return.

Dane walked past the office and stopped in front of the closed door that led into Caroline's bedroom. Savannah's heart pounded painfully. She'd only been to the house a few times since the kidnapping, and she always carefully avoided Caroline's room—as if seeing it empty would make the child's absence more real.

She remained in the doorway as he walked inside. He ignored the toys scattered on the floor, the tea set arranged neatly on the table in the corner, and the books lined up on the nightstand waiting to be read. In a few strides he was across the room and pulled back the pink gingham curtains to look out the window.

"Did your daughter play with any children in the neighborhood?"

Savannah shook her head. "No, there aren't many children on this street. The area is popular with professional people, mostly staff members who work for politicians on Capitol Hill. When they start families, they move to the suburbs."

Dane took a small notebook from his pocket and made a few notations, presumably the addresses of the houses directly across the street. Then he asked, "What was your regular daily routine?"

Savannah took a deep breath and forced herself to remember. "We left the house at seven-thirty. I dropped Caroline off at seven forty-five and then drove to the CAC. I picked her up at two-fifty every afternoon."

"What would the two of you do after school?"

"Sometimes we'd go back to the CAC and Caroline would watch TV while I worked. If I was done for the day, I'd give Caroline the choice. We would either go to the park or shopping or to her favorite pizza parlor for dinner." Savannah wiped an inevitable tear away.

"What about the nights you went out by yourself—for business or pleasure. Who watched Caroline then?"

"I didn't go out much, unless it was a mandatory CAC function. On those occasions Lacie babysat for me."

"You attended these functions with Forton?"

"Yes," she admitted.

"And he picked you up here?"

"Yes."

"Did he come inside?"

Savannah put a hand to her temple and tried to think. "Yes."

"Was he a guest here on other, nonmandatory occasions?"

"He was here a couple of other times, yes."

Dane allowed the curtain to fall back in place and crossed the room. She stepped aside so he could pass into the hallway and followed him around to the stair landing. After glancing into the bathroom, he walked to her bedroom and flipped on the light switch. Dust particles danced in the sudden illumination.

He looked out both windows, and then his eyes settled on a portrait of Caroline that hung above the bed.

"Your daughter looks like Wes," he said.

Savannah smiled at the picture, tears gathering in her eyes. Caroline was a delicate duplicate of her father. "Yes."

Apparently finished with his inspection, Dane moved toward the door. She stepped in front of him, blocking his path.

"Why don't you ever say her name, or mine?" she asked.

His gaze met hers, and after a few seconds he said, "First names make it too personal. It's important to remember that this is strictly business."

She closed her eyes briefly, absorbing the pain and loss and longing. Then she opened her eyes and nodded. "Business."

He pulled out his cell phone. "And speaking of business, I need to check in with the others to see if they've made any progress."

Savannah trailed behind him as he walked down to the family room and sprawled out on her couch. She curled up in a chair by the windows and watched leaves fall while listening to Dane's side of the phone conversations. From what she could gather, nobody had anything earthshaking to report. He had just finished talking with Hack when his phone rang. He answered it and then covered the tiny receiver while whispering to Savannah, "It's the Aruban authorities. They've got Forton."

Savannah walked over to stand behind the couch. He turned on speaker phone, and she could hear a man in accented English explaining that they had questioned Doug. He had admitted to arranging for the commercial shoot to be delayed. She gripped the back of the couch. Despite the evidence to the contrary, she'd clung to the irrational hope that Doug was innocent.

"Would it be possible for me to speak to Mr. Forton?" Dane was asking the Aruban policeman.

After assuring Dane that this was possible, the man put him on hold. Afraid that she wouldn't be able to stand during Doug's confession, Savannah circled the couch and sat on the opposite end. He placed the phone on the coffee table between them and put his fingers to his lips indicating that Savannah should be quiet. She nodded wordlessly.

A few seconds later, Doug's frantic voice burst from the cell phone and echoed around the room. "Hello! Who is this? Can you help me, please? I have been arrested on false charges, and they won't allow me to call my lawyer!"

"You've been detained by the Aruban police because of your role in the kidnapping of a child," Dane informed Doug coldly.

"But I had no role in that!" Doug insisted. "I was horrified when I found out. I would have done anything to help Savannah and Caroline."

"Anything except come forward and tell the police about your involvement," Dane said.

"I didn't see how it could help!" Doug cried. "Since I didn't know who wanted to delay Savannah on the day of the kidnapping or why. My reputation would have been damaged for nothing."

"And your hopes of starting a romantic relationship with Mrs. McLaughlin would have been severely damaged as well."

"I'll admit I didn't want Savannah to know." Doug's voice took on a whiny quality, and she was ashamed for him. "But you have to believe me! I didn't withhold any information that could help her find Caroline."

"The thing about information is that a piece by itself seems worthless," Dane said. "But if you'd given it to the police and allowed them to put it with other pieces of information they had collected, the child might be home with her mother right now."

After a short silence, Doug asked, "Who is this? Are you her friend Dane?"

"That's not important," Dane snapped back. "Who wanted the filming of that public service announcement to run long?"

"I don't know," Doug said.

"That's a lie," Dane accused.

"I want to help," Doug insisted. "But . . ."

Dane pounded a clenched fist on the coffee table in a rare display of emotion. The cell phone skittered to the edge and would have fallen if Dane hadn't reached out to retrieve it. Dane pressed the phone to his ear and said, "You *will* tell me immediately. Otherwise the time you've spent with the Aruban authorities so far will seem like a vacation compared to your next few hours in their custody."

"I can't," Doug said in a whisper. "He's very powerful, and if I give you his name, I'm a dead man."

"If you don't give me his name, by the time someone finds you, there will be nothing left to kill!" Dane threatened with chilling sincerity. Then his tone became less scary and more persuasive. "Think of it this way. If you tell me what I want to know, you'll be released from jail, and you'll have a few hours to disappear. If you wait until he hears you're in jail, he won't even have to look for you to kill you."

There was a long pause, and Savannah thought she could hear the sounds of Doug weeping. She was about to tell Dane to stop when Doug said one word. "Ferrante."

"Mario Ferrante?" Dane demanded.

"Yes." Doug spoke so softly they could barely hear him.

"Give the phone back to the policeman," Dane commanded. Once the phone had been transferred, Dane expressed his appreciation to the Aruban authorities and asked that Doug be released immediately.

When he ended that call, Savannah asked, "Who is Mario Ferrante?"

"One of the most dangerous crime bosses in the DC area."

"The Mafia?" Savannah put a hand to her throbbing temple, trying to assimilate this information. "Why would Doug be involved with the Mafia? And why would the Mafia want to kidnap Caroline?"

"People go to someone like Ferrante when they need dirty work done, so he may have just arranged the kidnapping for someone else. But the Mafia's involvement would explain the efficient execution of the kidnapping. Ferrante has a lot of people working for him, plenty of money, and unlimited experience in committing crime. I have no problem believing that he could pull off something like your daughter's kidnapping."

Savannah wasn't sure that this new development was good news. "How will you find out for sure?"

"I know an FBI agent who specializes in organized crime," Dane replied. "I'll see what he can do for us." Dane opened his phone and placed another call. He spoke to an Agent Gray and explained his interest in Mario Ferrante. When he closed the phone, he looked over at Savannah.

"Well?" she prompted.

"Agent Gray agreed to bring Ferrante in for questioning. He's under indictment on several other charges, so depending on what he knows, we might be able to cut a deal with him. I'd like to watch the interrogation so I can be sure the right questions get asked. Agent Gray said he'd call when they have Ferrante."

"Is there anything you can do to protect Doug Forton?"

He cut his eyes over at her, the old hostility back in full force. "You really like the guy that much?"

She shook her head emphatically. "Of course not. I just don't want him to die."

"He helped arrange for the kidnapping of your daughter," Dane reminded her. "And then he stood by for over two months and watched you grieve and search without saying anything about his role or Ferrante's involvement. You should be ready to kill him yourself."

She shrugged. "If I thought it would help find Caroline, maybe I would. But useless death helps no one."

He expelled an exasperated breath and said, "The best thing that can happen to Forton is for the FBI to arrest Ferrante. I've set that in motion. There's nothing more anyone can do."

Accepting that she had fulfilled any obligation she might have to Doug, she forced herself to ask, "If Ferrante kidnapped Caroline, do you think he killed her?"

"It depends on why," Dane told her. "If it was just a job, the child is probably dead. If he kidnapped her for a client, like your friend Forton, she might still be alive."

"Doug?" Savannah whispered. "You think he was lying, even though you threatened his life?"

"A good liar can be very convincing."

She thought about this for a few seconds then shook her head. "I don't believe that Doug would kidnap Caroline, and if he helped someone else, it was because he felt he had no choice."

Dane scowled. "Right now Forton's the only connection I have between you and Ferrante. Until I find another one, I'm keeping him on the top of my suspect list."

She was confused and hurt and terribly lonely. She turned toward the window, hoping he couldn't see the tears in her eyes.

He walked into the kitchen, and she followed reluctantly. Once he was settled on one of the barstools, he propped his elbows on the granite countertop and asked, "Can I borrow your laptop?"

Wordlessly, Savannah retrieved it from the family room and handed it to him. She watched as he signed on and then asked, "What are you doing?"

"Checking out your neighbors," he replied. "One of them might be employed by Ferrante to spy on you."

Savannah considered this almost as depressing as the idea that Doug Forton was the kidnapper. "I'll be in the family room if you need me." Without waiting for him to reply, she left the kitchen. To distract herself, she picked up the stack of accumulated mail and settled in a chair by the wall of windows.

She had almost an hour of peace. Then Dane walked in and sat in the chair across from her.

"So, did you find a spying neighbor?" she forced herself to ask.

"No," he replied. "They all seem legitimate, but that doesn't mean they are." After a brief pause, he added, "Ferrante's involvement in this changes everything."

"You mean it makes things worse, right?"

His eyes strayed to the windows. "Much worse."

A knot of anxiety formed in her stomach. "You've found something, haven't you?"

He lifted a shoulder in a casual shrug. "Maybe."

"Well," she prompted. "What is it?"

"It's kind of a good news and bad news discovery," he said. "The good news is that if I'm right, your friend Doug Forton didn't orchestrate the kidnapping. I know how important that is to you."

"What's the bad news?"

"I think your daughter was kidnapped because of that disc you found about the operation in Nicaragua."

"The disc?" Savannah repeated stupidly.

"If the information on the disc is as damaging as you say, and it must be since you used it to wrap General Steele around your finger . . ."

She winced at this reference. "It is pretty terrible just from what I saw, and I didn't watch all of it."

"A lot of people would want to keep the information on that disc from surfacing."

"You mean the participants?" Savannah asked. "There weren't many, and I didn't recognize any of their names."

"Not just the participants," Dane corrected. "The Army, the Defense Department—even the White House has a stake in this."

She could barely breathe. "Are you saying the United States Government kidnapped my daughter?"

He shook his head. "I'm just saying the possibilities are broader than we originally thought."

Savannah shuddered. Mario Ferrante was a formidable opponent, but how could she hope to win against the government? She pushed this thought away and asked, "If the disc was the motive, why did I get that note with the scripture about punishing the father and mother?"

"The note always bothered me," Dane admitted. "All other aspects of the kidnapping were perfectly planned and executed. But the hand delivery of an obscure scripture reference was a senseless risk, which made it suspicious."

"What purpose could it serve besides the obvious one?" Savannah asked.

"It may have been a decoy," Dane replied, "Intended to make sure that the investigators limited their search."

"Which they did."

He nodded. "If that was the card's purpose, it worked very well."

The revenge motive had been the working theory since the beginning, and Savannah wasn't ready to let go of it yet. "Do you have any proof, or are you just guessing?"

He gave her a smile that resembled a smirk. "I don't have proof, but I know how I can get it. Tell me more about the disc."

"Like what?"

"Where you found it, for starters."

Savannah was reluctant to answer because she wasn't sure that she could trust Dane, and because the memories surrounding the disc were painful.

"The photographer who has taken pictures of Caroline for us since she was born sent me a postcard a few months ago. He was going out of business and said I needed to make other arrangements for the negatives and proofs he was storing. When I went by his studio to pick them up, I asked him if he could make one more print for me." She paused, wanting to choose her words carefully.

Dane watched her, his expression was expectant. "What did you want him to print?"

"We had some pictures made right before Wes died. The one you saw of Caroline upstairs was from that photo session. The photographer also insisted on taking some family group shots." The memory hurt as much as she had suspected it would. She forced herself to continue. "When the proofs were ready, Wes and I met at the studio. The photographer removed the proofs from an expandable file and spread them out on a table. All the ones of Caroline were beautiful, but I couldn't make myself look at the others. Wes and I were, well, barely speaking to each other by then, and the pictures just seemed like a lie."

She risked a glance up at Dane, and he nodded for her to continue. "I pointed out the one I liked best of Caroline and told the photographer to have it printed on canvas. He asked if we wanted copies of the other proofs, and I said no. Then I saw that Wes was holding one of the family shots in his hand." Savannah cleared her throat, pushing back the guilty emotions. "I told Wes he could add anything he wanted to our order, but he just shook his head and started collecting up the proofs. He put them all into the envelope and gave it back to the photographer."

"So when you found out the photographer was closing up shop, you decided to get a print of the family picture Wes showed an interest in?"

She nodded. "I thought Caroline would like to have it, and even though it was too late, it was the only way I knew to apologize to Wes for not wanting it earlier."

"And what does all this have to do with the disc?" Dane asked. His tone was unusually gentle.

"The photographer said he would do a print for me and told me to look through the envelope and pick out the proof I wanted. When I opened the envelope, along with the negatives and proofs was a disc. I thought it was just some additional shots of Caroline, so I put it into my laptop. But, well, the pictures on the disc weren't of Caroline."

"Wes put it there on that day right before he died?"

"Yes," Savannah confirmed. "That's the only way it could have gotten into the envelope with the proofs."

"When you saw the information on the disc, didn't you realize Wes had put it there to hide it and that keeping it would be very dangerous?"

She shook her head. "Honestly, when I realized that Wes must have left it there, I assumed he wanted to protect the disc by leaving it in the photographer's temperature-controlled safe. I planned to give it to General Steele, but then a few days later, Caroline was kidnapped, and I forgot all about the family picture and the disc—until I needed leverage with the general."

"Did you tell anyone that you had the disc?"

Savannah considered this. "No," she reported finally. "I did e-mail myself a reminder about it."

Dane gave her a blank look. "Why would you do that?"

"I have a lot of things to remember," Savannah explained, "So I often e-mail myself."

"What did you say in your e-mail?"

She could tell he considered this practice ridiculous and tried not to care. "I just said I needed to find a day when Caroline and I could make a trip to Fort Belvoir so I could give the disc to General Steele."

"But you never contacted the General to make an appointment?"

She shook her head. "No."

"Does anyone else have access to your e-mail?"

"No," Savannah replied. "It's password protected."

Dane smiled grimly. "That wouldn't stop our computer-savvy kidnapper. So where is the disc now?"

The disc was her only bargaining chip, and Savannah was reluctant to disclose its location. "Why do you want to know?"

"If I can see exactly what's on that disc, it might help me narrow the field of possible suspects."

With deep trepidation, she said, "The photographer still has it."

Dane frowned. "I thought you said he was going out of business."

"He was," she confirmed. "I mean he did. But when he called to tell me that the print of our family picture was ready, I explained about Caroline's kidnapping and he said he'd hold on to our file until things were settled."

Dane stood and waved for her to follow. By the time she reached the kitchen, he was entering commands into her laptop. "What's the photographer's name?"

She extracted a business card from her wallet and handed it to Dane. "There's a cell phone number listed that should still be in service even though the business is closed."

He dialed the number into his cell phone. Then he extended it toward her.

"When he answers, tell him you want to meet him and get your file. Tonight if possible."

She pressed the small phone to her ear. Finally voicemail picked up. "He's not there," she told Dane. "Should I leave a message?"

"Just your name and phone number," Dane said. "Don't mention the disc."

She rolled her eyes at this unnecessary advice and left a brief message. Then she closed the phone and returned it to Dane. "He said he was going out of the country. It might be a while before we can get the disc."

Dane frowned. "In the meantime I need you to write down everything you can remember about the contents of the disc. Names would be particularly helpful."

She waited for him to say more, but he had returned his attention to the laptop. So she walked into the family room and began her list.

It didn't take Savannah long to complete the list of everything she could remember about the disc. She took it to Dane, who glanced at the scant information and frowned.

"That's it?"

She nodded, eliciting a displeased sigh from Dane.

Savannah returned to the relative tranquility of the family room and settled back into her favorite chair. As she watched leaves fall into her neglected backyard, she could hear Dane in the kitchen, alternately talking on his cell phone and typing on her laptop. It was a relief to be a safe distance from him and his depressing theories. But finally curiosity and hunger drove her to join him.

"Are you hungry?" she asked as she walked into the kitchen.

"I could eat," he said.

"I haven't been to the store in a while, so all I have is soup."

"Soup is fine," he returned without looking up from her computer screen.

She opened a cabinet and removed a can of chicken noodle and some crackers. Then she faced him bravely. "So have you found out anything interesting about my neighbors?"

"No," he muttered. "They're all as dull as you told me they'd be."

She opened the can of soup and poured it into a pan. While filling the can with water, she asked, "None of them are suspects, then?"

He shrugged. "I guess not."

She took a few steps toward him, abandoning the soup. "Were you able to confirm your theory about the disc?"

He gave her his full attention. "I don't have what would qualify as proof in a court of law, but I'm satisfied that we've found the reason behind the kidnapping. This will help us look for the culprit in the right places."

"So the kidnapper knew Wes had the disc?"

"Yes," Dane agreed. "In fact, I think the kidnapper killed Wes to get it."

"Then his death was murder?"

"I'm just about positive," Dane confirmed.

"I'm glad he didn't commit suicide," she whispered. Then she looked up at Dane as the implications of Wes's death became clear. "If the kidnapper killed Wes, then Caroline . . ." She couldn't make herself say the words.

"I think they'll keep her alive until they have the disc," he surprised her by saying.

Her heart swelled with hope. "So ever since Wes died the kidnapper has been looking for the disc?"

Dane nodded. "He's been searching your house, checking your e-mails, monitoring your phone calls, and following your movements."

Savannah chewed her lip, trying to get things straight in her mind. "Hoping I'd lead him to the disc?"

"Yes."

"Which I did," she realized bitterly. "And I endangered Caroline in the process."

"You didn't know," he offered as lame comfort.

Savannah clinched her fists in frustration. "But if they kidnapped Caroline to get the disc, why didn't they demand it from me as a ransom?"

"Ferrante didn't want the disc. He wanted to be sure that no one knew it ever existed," Dane hypothesized. "So he couldn't ask about it openly. He has FBI agents and DC policemen on his payroll. I'm sure he set it up so that some of his guys were assigned to your case." Savannah was horrified by this thought. "The agents and policemen who were supposed to be finding Caroline were working for Ferrante?"

"At least some of them probably were. Of course you gave them access to everything."

She nodded. "Of course."

"But they still couldn't find Wes's hiding place," Dane said grimly. "So Ferrante instructed his inside men to shut down the investigation. Then he could approach you without risk of exposure and propose a trade."

"But before Ferrante could approach me, I involved you in the search for Caroline."

Dane nodded. "Which inadvertently thwarted his plan."

Savannah pressed a finger to her temple, trying to think. "Maybe we should contact Ferrante ourselves and offer to trade the disc for Caroline."

"If he realizes that we understand the significance of the disc, he might decide to eliminate us all—including Caroline. Assuming he hasn't killed her already."

Savannah refused to be goaded. "Yes, assuming that." She walked back over to the stove and heated the soup. Once it was ready, she divided it into two bowls. She put his on the counter beside him and carried hers back into the family room. She was eating the last spoonful when he walked in.

"Agent Gray just called."

The pounding in her heart returned. "And?"

"And they can't find Mario Ferrante. They've checked all the usual places, but he's not in any of them. They'll keep looking, but Gray thinks it's possible that Ferrante was tipped off and left the country. In which case it could be days before they locate him, if ever."

"Doug warned him?" she guessed.

Dane nodded. "Probably. I should have left the weasel in jail until we had Ferrante."

Savannah knew Dane had been relatively lenient with Doug because of her, so she was partially responsible for Doug's release. She didn't even try to hide her disappointment. "I'm sorry."

He handed her the laptop. "Don't blame yourself. I'm in charge of this operation so all mistakes belong to me." He gestured toward the phone. "No calls from the photographer?"

She shook her head absently, still thinking about Doug's latest betrayal.

"Since there's not going to be an interrogation of Ferrante anytime soon, we might as well go back to the cabin."

As they drove, Dane glared out the windshield at the snarled downtown traffic. Savannah wasn't sure if he was annoyed by the delay or mad at her for being concerned about Doug or angry that Ferrante had escaped their grasp. But the silence wasn't companionable the way it had been on the drive down that morning.

Hurt and confused, she closed her eyes to separate herself from him. At some point the gentle jostling of the car lulled her to sleep. She startled awake to the sound of gravel crunching under the tires. She was surprised to see that they were turning on to the drive that led to the back of Dane's cabin.

She sat up, stretched, and said, "You didn't take me to my hotel."

He parked the car and stared straight ahead. "Lacie called and said her flight from Chicago was cancelled because of bad weather, so she won't be back until tomorrow. I can drive you back to the hotel if you want, or you can sleep on the couch here."

She wondered briefly if Lacie might have told him about her fear of being alone, prompting this extraordinary offer. But since that would require a level of sensitivity she didn't believe he possessed, she abandoned the thought.

He looked steadfastly ahead at the light fog that hovered around the steps to his cabin. "I don't usually let anyone stay overnight."

"But you're willing to make an exception for the world's most undesirable woman?" she suggested.

He made a face. "I just don't want you to die from sleep deprivation."

"Sleep deprivation?"

"When I got to your hotel room last night, you were wide awake and watching dumb movies."

"They weren't dumb," she objected.

"You should have been asleep."

"I don't sleep much, especially when I'm alone."

He nodded. "When you're with me, all you do is sleep."

"It's nothing personal," she assured him. "It's just that I'd rather sleep than fight."

He opened his door. "All the more reason to stay."

They got out of the car, and he retrieved her suitcase from the trunk. The temperature had dropped since their departure from Washington, and this combined with the continuously high Virginia humidity made the evening air uncomfortably cold. Savannah clutched her jacket more tightly around her and shivered.

Dane led the way inside and put her bag on the couch before arranging a couple of logs in the fireplace. The damp chill evaporated slowly as heat from the fire permeated the room. She held her hands out to the warmth while Dane climbed the stairs. She thought he'd retired for the night, but he returned a few minutes later with some quilts and a pillow.

"If the fire starts to go out, you can throw an extra log on."

She nodded.

"There's stuff to make sandwiches in the refrigerator if you're hungry."

She nodded again.

"And hot chocolate mix in the cupboard."

"I'll be fine," she assured him.

He gave her a critical once-over. "You don't eat enough, and you always look exhausted. If you don't sleep or eat, you'll die."

"Lacie reminds me of that often enough. I'll make a sandwich," she said, anxious to be rid of him. Her nerves were taut with sensory overload, and she needed time to relax without his disruptive presence.

She was relieved when he turned toward the stairs again. He seemed reluctant to go and finally said, "If you hear anything tonight . . ." his voice trailed off and he tried again. "I sometimes have nightmares . . ." He paused to run his fingers through his longish hair. "Just don't come upstairs under any circumstances."

"I won't," Savannah promised with conviction.

He nodded. "Then I'll see you in the morning."

Savannah watched until he was out of sight before going to the kitchen. She made a sandwich and ate it standing up. Then she changed into her nightgown and robe in the bathroom and hurried back to the warmth of the fire. After spreading a quilt out on the couch, she lay down and covered herself with the other one. The pillow smelled faintly like Dane, and she wondered if it was his. Comforted by this thought, she burrowed her face deeper into the pillow and closed her eyes.

CHAPTER 10

The next morning when Savannah woke up, rays of sunlight were pouring through the windows of Dane's cabin. The fire was still burning brightly, even though she hadn't gotten up one time during the night to add fresh wood. She assumed Dane had come down occasionally to tend the fire. The idea of him keeping her safe and warm was strange yet intriguing.

Savannah checked her watch and was amazed to see that it was almost eight o'clock. She couldn't remember the last time she'd slept so long or so well. She knew she should be up and dressed by the time Dane's team arrived, but the warmth was seductive. So she burrowed down under the quilts and turned her face toward the fire.

A few minutes later, Hack burst in through the front door. As surprised as she was to see him, he seemed even more astounded to find her on Dane's couch, bundled in quilts and enjoying a warm fire.

"We got back late last night," she explained vaguely as Hack stared. She sat up straight and clutched her robe closed at the neck. She pointed to the Krispy Kreme bags in his hands. "Looks like you brought breakfast today."

Hack seemed to remember belatedly where he was and why. "Oh, yeah," he confirmed. "I got doughnuts and *coffee*."

She smiled. "I love doughnuts. I've never been all that fond of coffee, but Dane makes great hot chocolate."

The bewildered expression returned to Hack's face. Before he was able to formulate a comment, Dane descended the stairs. He was wearing the usual jeans and a flannel shirt, but today it was buttoned, his damaged chest hidden from view.

"Where are the rest of the guys?" he asked Hack, as if having a woman snuggled on his couch was no rare thing.

Hack's eyes swung slowly from Dane to Savannah and then back to Dane again. "Uh, Doc and Cam are meeting with the first grade teacher."

"Mrs. Matthews?" Savannah confirmed.

Hack shrugged his massive shoulders. "I guess. They should be here soon."

Dane eyed the doughnut bags in Hack's hands. "Follow me and I'll get some hot chocolate going." Dane led the way to the kitchen, politely leaving Savannah in relative privacy. She stood and folded the quilts. After stacking the quilts and placing Dane's pillow neatly on top, she carried her suitcase to the bathroom and took a fast shower.

Energized by her first full night's sleep in months, she dug through her cosmetic case and pulled out some long-neglected makeup. Once her face was done, she dried her hair and briefly considered styling it, but she decided that would be too much too soon. She did leave her hair loose instead of pulling it into the ponytail that had become her trademark hairstyle since Caroline was kidnapped.

By the time she emerged from the bathroom, Cam and Doc had arrived, and a meeting seemed to be taking place around the kitchen table. In addition to making her feel energetic, the sleep had given Savannah an appetite. So she poured a mug of hot chocolate before approaching the table. After claiming an empty chair between Doc and Cam, she helped herself to a doughnut. She ate it in three bites and reached for another. Then she realized that all conversation had stopped and everyone was staring at her.

"What?" she asked with her mouth full.

Doc gave her a shy smile. "You look nice."

She remembered about the makeup. "Oh, thanks."

"Very nice," Cam elaborated. As he leaned forward and flexed his biceps, Savannah had to hide her amusement. Poor Cam—little did he know that she was immune to male charms. Well, the charms of most males anyway.

"Not bad," Hack offered as an endorsement.

Savannah looked over at Dane. Unlike the other men, his expression was not complimentary. She was wondering what she'd done to earn his disfavor this time when he pointed at her chin. "You've got chocolate glaze on your face."

She swiped her chin with the back of her hand, and Cam laughed. "You got it."

"So what are you talking about?" she asked Dane.

"I was filling the team in on my disc theory," he replied.

"I looked at the list of things you can remember about the disc, and it's pretty sketchy," Hack said. "Any chance you'll be able to remember more if you apply yourself?"

"My daughter has been kidnapped," she reminded him unnecessarily. "So I don't need more motivation. I wrote down everything I can remember."

"When do you think we can get our hands on the disc itself?" Cam asked between bites of doughnut.

"The photographer's out of the country," Dane reported. "He closed up his photo studio, and the space has been converted into a video arcade. The company who rents the space has no idea where he is or where he put his equipment. He's not answering his cell phone, and I haven't been able to come up with the name of a relative, but I'll keep working on it."

Savannah was pleased that Dane had already investigated the photographer thoroughly. "Maybe he'll call me soon."

"We might be able to approach this from another direction," Dane said thoughtfully. "Cam, will you take some time this morning to drive over to Fort Belvoir and see if General Steele can help you locate the file on the Nick at Night operation? Even if it's been sanitized, we might be able to get a few useful details from it."

Cam nodded. "Will do."

"In the meantime the investigation continues as before?" Doc asked.

Dane nodded. "Until I tell you otherwise." He glanced at Savannah. "Lacie called a few minutes ago. She flew into the airport in Fredericksburg instead of Dulles and should be here soon."

"So Lacie's calling you now instead of me?" Savannah reached for another doughnut.

Dane watched as she brought the doughnut to her mouth. "Yeah, pretty soon I'll have to add her to the Army's payroll."

Savannah laughed. "That won't be necessary. I'm willing to share Lacie with you."

The men were all watching them closely. They seemed to know that a shift in the relationship between Dane and Savannah had occurred, but no one was sure exactly what or why.

Dane said, "I also told the team about your friend Doug Forton and his connection to Mario Ferrante. We need to take a deeper look." He turned to Hack. "Will you handle that?"

The big man nodded, sending his braids dancing. "Sure."

Dane swung his eyes to Doc, who was meticulously dividing the day's medications into the appropriate sections of his pill organizer. "So Doc, can you take a break from your pharmaceutical duties and give us a report on your meeting this morning with the first grade teacher?"

Doc placed the pill bottle he was holding on the table and faced the others. His pupils were dilated and Savannah wondered if he'd taken too much of something. "Cam and I interviewed Caroline's teacher this morning."

"What was her story?" Dane prompted patiently.

"Claims she really was sick the day of the kidnapping," Cam answered. "She ate out the night before. We confirmed that."

"Afterward she became violently ill," Doc contributed.

"Intentional food poisoning?" Dane guessed.

Doc nodded. "That's what she thinks, although for some unfathomable reason, she never went to the doctor."

Dane addressed his next question to Cam. "What else did she have to say?"

"When she realized she wasn't going to be able to go to work, she called a woman who has substituted for her many times. The woman agreed to cover her class, and the Matthews woman didn't know anything about the kidnapping until she saw it on the evening news."

"I presume you got the regular sub's name?" Dane asked.

"We did better than that," Doc reported proudly. "She lives near Mrs. Matthews, so we dropped in on her." Doc's gaze returned to the pill bottles in front of him.

Cam explained. "Sub confirms that Mrs. Matthews did call her that morning and arranged for her to substitute. But a few minutes later a woman claiming to be from the school called and said they wouldn't need her after all."

Dane frowned. "So at this point our kidnapper stepped in and replaced the regular sub with his own."

"Mrs. Matthews is very upset about Caroline," Doc told them. "I tried to convince her that none of what happened was her fault, but she feels responsible. She quit her job and says she'll never teach kids again."

"It doesn't sound like the real teacher or the regular sub was part of the kidnapping plot," Dane remarked.

"No, probably the only teacher involved in the kidnapping was the fake sub who we can't even identify, let alone locate," Hack said.

"But eliminating suspects is a good thing," Doc pointed out.

Savannah took a sip of hot chocolate. "Not as good as finding the kidnapper."

"No, not that good," Doc agreed.

"Another dead end," Hack growled.

"Maybe not," Doc said. "I got an e-mail from my friend at Langley who is trying to enhance the picture from the school's security camera. He's putting the finishing touches on it and should be sending me the finished product soon."

"When you get it, I want to be the first to see it," Dane said. Then he turned to Hack. "What about the traffic light anomaly?"

"The best we can tell, the sequence interruption was entered from a remote computer," Hack replied. "Then the kidnapper must have used the same computer to jam the school's phone lines and put the false entries into the school board's sub list. A wireless card is difficult to trace, but I'm working on it. One thing I do know," Hack paused for emphasis, and once he was sure everyone was listening, he continued. "The equipment this guy has is so good, it makes the stuff General Steele gave us look like kiddie toys. Just any laptop wouldn't do."

Savannah frowned. "General Steele gave you state-of-the-art equipment though."

Hack nodded. "That's what I mean. The kidnapper was able to do things that *nobody* can do. It makes me wonder if we're dealing with a rogue CIA agent or somebody like that."

"A Mafia connection might explain the phenomenal hardware," Dane said. "They have access to stuff before it's available to the general public."

Cam laughed. "Yeah, and they have access to CIA agents too."

Dane smiled. "True."

Savannah waited for Dane to mention the possibility that the government or the Army could be involved because of the disc, but he didn't. She hoped that meant he'd decided that they were only dealing with the Mafia.

"I'll keep digging and let you know what I find out," Hack promised as Lacie breezed into the kitchen. Her multicolored hair was windblown, her cheeks pink from the cold. She was smiling, and her eyes were shining with excitement.

After they filled Lacie in on the events that had transpired since she left, Savannah asked, "Did you find out anything?"

"No," Lacie said as she took the one remaining seat. "But I had a great time. I love the mountains. I can hardly wait to go back."

Dane asked to see the rosters.

Lacie pulled a sheaf of papers from her huge purse. She placed them on the table in front of Dane. "Like I said, the number of children living at the farm matches the live births that occurred there. The roster is divided by families, so you can see where the kids are distributed. Father Burnett says that they don't send kids up to the compound in the mountains where the McLaughlins live because the conditions are too primitive."

Dane skimmed the roster and then nodded. "The McLaughlins can be moved down toward the bottom of our suspect list. But just to be sure, I'd like you to take that helicopter trip on Friday. I don't want the farm people to have advance notice that you're coming in case they do have something to hide. And since the kidnapper seems to know every step we take, we'll have to figure out a way to get you there without advertising our plans."

"That rules out plane reservations," Cam remarked.

"Maybe we can get her on a military transport plane," Doc suggested. "The passenger list would be classified and hard to access."

"Not for a talented computer hacker like our kidnapper," Hack pointed out. "Especially if he has a contact in the CIA or FBI."

"Especially if the kidnapper is *in* the CIA or FBI," Cam added with a smile.

"If I start driving now, I could be there by Friday," Lacie said.

"I suggest a compromise," Hack interjected. "She could fly to someplace close to Denver—but not too close—and then drive the rest of the way in a rental car."

Dane nodded. "I've got a contact in Laramie. I'll call and tell him we have a lead from his area, and Lacie's coming to check it out. Fly in there tomorrow, get a hotel room, and rent a car. You'll meet with my contact to establish that you're investigating there. Then you can drive down early Friday morning and be at the farm before the helicopter leaves."

"Okay." Lacie stood. "I'll go ahead and make my airline reservations for Laramie."

"When you're through with that, I'd like you to go to the Child Advocacy Center. Things should be in an uproar with the boss gone."

"Without Savannah or Doug there, things will be at a standstill," Lacie corrected.

"See what you can get out of the secretary. And then I want you to look through Forton's office. Check his computer, calendar, etc. I want to know who he talked to, who he ate lunch with, and the phone calls he received for the past three months."

Lacie nodded. "I'll try, but Jackie is very protective of Doug and his office."

Dane looked at his men. "We need to get rid of the secretary for a few hours."

"I can have the secretary taken into police headquarters for questioning," Cam volunteered.

"Perfect," Dane said before turning to Doc. "I'd like to see copies of the Brotherly Love Farm's rosters from another source, like the Homeland Security people who sent me the satellite photos."

Savannah was surprised by this. "Why? Do you think the farm people fixed their rosters?"

"No, but I want to be sure," Dane replied. "So Doc, will you handle that?"

Doc nodded.

"My contact's information is inside this file." Dane extended a folder toward Doc. The edges of several black and white photographs were sticking out of the folder, and Savannah intercepted it. "Can I see the satellite surveillance photos?"

Dane passed it to her. "Give it to Doc when you're through."

Lacie stepped back into the kitchen and announced, "My plane to Laramie leaves tomorrow morning at six."

"Good." Dane's cell phone rang, and he opened it absently. "Hello." As he listened, his expression went from its normal grim to extremely grim, and Savannah knew before he told them that it wasn't good news. "Forton is dead," he informed them all. "They found his body stuffed in a dumpster behind a hotel in Haiti."

Savannah fought back the sadness she felt at this announcement. "He tried to run."

"But Ferrante killed him?" Lacie whispered.

Dane shrugged. "Probably. And if Forton knew any more than what he'd already told us, he took it with him to the grave—or to the dumpster at least."

Hack cursed under his breath.

Cam slapped his palm against the table. "Every lead slips away the minute we find it."

"It does seem like the kidnapper is always a step ahead of us," Doc agreed morosely.

"Another way to look at it is that we are getting some response from the feelers we're putting out," Dane told them. "So we must be headed in the right direction." He turned to Lacie. "The Haitian authorities are going to wait to notify the Washington, DC police of Forton's demise. That gives you time to get to the Child Advocacy Center and see what you can find before the police take over."

Lacie grabbed her huge bag and headed toward the door. "I'm on my way."

Dane looked at Cam. "Go ahead and arrange to have the secretary picked up for questioning so she won't get in Lacie's way."

"Yes, *sir*!" Cam stood and moved into the living room to make his call. "Then I'll head on over to Fort Belvoir."

Dane nodded. "And the rest of us will spend the day trying to find out what connection Forton had to Ferrante."

Savannah was afraid for Caroline and sad about Doug and irritated by all the seemingly futile effort that was being expended.

"What difference does that connection make now?" she asked Dane. "Doug's dead!"

Dane gave her a narrow look. "I told you I like to be thorough." He turned toward Cam, who was returning from the living room. "Is the secretary taken care of?"

Cam nodded. "A squad car's on the way to pick her up now."

"Good. When you get back from Fort Belvoir I'd like you to canvass the McLaughlins' neighborhood. Talk to the folks who live there and see if any of them noticed anything suspicious during the week or so before the kidnapping."

Another canvass, too, seemed unnecessary, and Savannah couldn't stop herself from pointing it out. "I didn't notice anything. Why should they?" she asked Dane. "Most of my neighbors work eighty hours a week and are rarely home. Why would they remember some small detail from a normal day over two months ago? If anyone has incentive to remember, it's me. After all, I'm the one whose child has been kidnapped. And I don't remember a thing."

Savannah saw all eyes turn to Dane to see how he would handle her challenge.

"Maybe your neighbors are more observant that you are," he said tersely. Then he returned his attention to Cam. "You'll probably increase your chances of finding people at home if you start after five-thirty."

Cam nodded, but Savannah was exasperated.

"It's a waste of time," she insisted. "Like everything else we've done."

The silence in the room was almost tangible as Dane turned angry eyes toward her. "Maybe you'd like to take back the investigation since you made so much headway during the two months before I got involved."

She shook her head. "I just feel like we're chasing around in circles."

Doc reached over and patted her shoulder gently. "Don't worry. Dane will find Caroline."

Savannah did the best she could to smile at him. "Thanks."

Dane looked annoyed by both her rebellion and Doc's compassion. "Let's get busy." He glanced at Savannah. "Unless you have any more *helpful* comments."

"Actually," she said, "I do. I think we should move to the CAC offices. Doug's gone, so his presence isn't an issue anymore. There's more room, and we could all quit wasting time driving back and forth to Washington."

Dane surprised her by saying, "It's true that working in the city would be more convenient. And more space would be nice, but moving the computers would be a lot of trouble. Besides, I think better here. And you definitely want me at my best." He stood. "But if you inflict many more of these emotional outbursts on me, I may have to quit."

Savannah stood as well and looked him in the eyes. "That doesn't scare me anymore. I know you won't quit until we find Caroline."

His eyebrows rose. "And what brought you to this astounding conclusion?"

"I know you won't quit because that would be letting the kidnapper beat you. And you'll never do that."

They stared at each other for a few seconds until finally Dane said, "You're right. I won't quit, but it has nothing to do with winning or losing. I just don't want to give up all this nice computer equipment and six months' active duty pay."

She knew he was lying and conveyed that with her eyes.

Finally he said, "Since you don't want to waste time, let's get busy."

"What do you want me to do?" she asked.

"We're running kind of low on supplies. Why don't you go grocery shopping?"

It was an insult, and they all knew it. But rather than argue, Savannah just said, "Okay, I'll get groceries." She turned to Cam. "I'd like to go with you this evening when you talk to my neighbors. They might be more willing to cooperate if I'm there."

Savannah was galled to see Cam glance at Dane for permission before nodding at her. "That's fine," he agreed. "We'll leave about four."

Savannah collected the file that contained the satellite surveillance photos and moved toward the kitchen door. "I'm going to study these in the living room where the light is better. After I've looked at them, I'll put them by Doc's computer, and then I'll head to the store. If anyone has special requests, you'd better tell me now."

She waited for someone to speak up, but no one did. "Time's up." Savannah turned her back on them and carried the pictures into the living room.

* * *

Savannah sat down by a window to scrutinize the surveillance photographs. She held them up to the light and turned them so she could examine them from different angles. But after a few minutes, she accepted that she couldn't make out anything. She was about to give up when Cam walked in.

He moved into position behind her and pointed at the photo she held in her hand. "Discover anything interesting?"

"There are trees on the mountain," she said. "That's about all I can say for positively sure."

He pointed to a large blob. "That's the house where the McLaughlins live." Cam's finger moved to a gray mass near what he claimed was a house. "This is a barn, and these little specks are animals. That's a cow, this is a horse, and these are chickens."

Savannah was impressed. "How can you tell all that from this awful picture?"

He turned the photograph over and pointed at an index taped to the back. Each blob or speck in the photo was numbered and identified.

She looked up at him. "You cheated."

He laughed. "I wouldn't call it cheating. I used the resources available to me."

She compared the index to the photograph. "What does *M-1* mean?"

"Male 1," Cam explained. "That's Wes's dad. *F-1* is his mom."

Savannah felt a strange longing as she looked at the indiscernible pictures of the in-laws she'd never met. "And they're up on the mountain by themselves?"

Cam nodded.

"What's this?" Savannah pointed at a blurry spot near the house.

Cam squinted at the picture and then checked the list. "It says *miscellaneous livestock*. Probably a goat."

Savannah frowned. "It doesn't look like a goat."

Cam laughed. "A minute ago you could barely distinguish a tree."

"What's so funny?" Dane wanted to know as he walked into the living room, followed closely by the others.

"Savannah is becoming a surveillance photo expert," Cam teased, and Dane raised an eyebrow in her direction.

"We're having a disagreement over the species of some *miscellaneous livestock,*" Savannah explained. "Cam thinks it's a goat, but it looks more like a dog to me."

"I'm not sure dogs qualify as livestock," Cam said thoughtfully.

"Why waste time trying to guess?" Dane asked. "If you really want to know, request a blow-up of that section."

"I'll do it for you," Doc offered as he joined them. "All I need is the number off the back of the picture and the section you want enlarged."

"It's not really that important," Savannah said as Doc took the picture and wrote down the number he needed.

"It is to me!" Cam claimed. "I want to prove that I'm a better judge of miscellaneous livestock than you!"

Savannah smiled as she returned the rest of the photos to the file and handed them to Doc. "I'm willing to concede that." She stood. "I'll head to the store now. Where's the closest one?"

"There's a Wal-Mart in Fredericksburg or a small store in Tylerton."

"The small store will probably do, and it has the advantage of being closer," Savannah said. "How do I get there?"

"I'll take you," Cam offered.

"You're headed to Fort Belvoir," Dane pointed out curtly. "In case you've forgotten, we're trying to solve a case."

"I haven't forgotten," Cam assured him. "Savannah can ride with me to Fort Belvoir, and then we'll stop by the store on our way back here."

Savannah had no desire to return to Fort Belvoir, but she didn't want to reject his friendly overture, so she nodded. "That's fine with me."

"Don't be gone long," Dane said with a scowl.

"We won't," Cam promised. Then he turned to Savannah and pointed at the door with a flourish. "Ladies first."

CHAPTER 11

As they walked down the stairs off the back porch, Savannah studied the cars parked in the yard. It wasn't hard to match each with its owner. The huge, bright yellow Hummer obviously belonged to Hack. A well-preserved Bonneville may have belonged to Doc's grandmother originally, but Savannah had no doubt that he drove it now. Then there was the unremarkable gray sedan that Dane had driven the day before, which she decided made sense for Dane. It gave away nothing—not his income bracket, his style preferences, or even his favorite color.

The last car, besides her own sensible Mazda, was a new, red Chrysler 300. The car was flashy and ostentatious, just like Cam, so she wasn't the least bit surprised when he led her to the passenger door. He entered a code into the recessed pad and then opened the door for her.

"Nice car," she said.

He grinned. "I've always wanted one of these, but my wife said we couldn't afford it. When Dane told me I was back on active duty, I figured my wife didn't have anything to say about what I buy anymore, so I went straight to the dealership and got one."

Savannah slid into the soft leather seat and took a deep breath of the "new car" smell. "How will you pay for it in six months when your active duty status ends?"

He shrugged as he climbed behind the wheel. "I'll worry about that in six months."

After showing her how to control both her seat's temperature and reclining position, Cam asked if she'd like to watch a DVD or listen to the stereo. She chose the stereo, and soon mellow jazz notes filled the car via surround sound. Savannah settled into the seat, closed her eyes, and luxuriated in the extravagant comfort.

They arrived at Fort Belvoir in less than thirty minutes, so Savannah was glad she hadn't been watching the speedometer. Once they were parked in front of the administration building, Cam considerately suggested that she wait in the car. "I shouldn't be long," he said. "And if you get bored you can always watch a DVD."

She smiled. "Thanks. I'll be fine."

Cam took the steps two, sometimes three at a time and then disappeared into the building that had once been almost home for her. She rested her head on the window of Cam's expensive car and watched the wind rustle through the autumn leaves that covered the grass in front of General Steele's office. The memories came unbidden.

* * *

Everything about that day was engraved on Savannah's mind with crystal clarity. When she'd returned from lunch, Louise had been waiting for her. The secretary had pulled her into General Steele's office and closed the door.

"You're in trouble," Louise announced grimly.

Savannah assumed the "trouble" was work related and wondered if she was about to be fired.

Then Louise continued. "Major McLaughlin was here earlier, looking for you."

Savannah was intensely relieved. "Is that all?"

"He didn't come to *see* you," Louise continued in her doomsday voice. "But he wanted to speak with the general *about* you."

"What about me?" Savannah demanded.

Louise was suddenly reluctant to talk. "I'm not sure I should tell you . . ."

Savannah resisted the urge to grab the secretary by her stiffly starched lapels. "Yes, you should!"

After a quick glance at the door, as if she expected Wes and General Steele to be standing there, Louise divulged, "He asked if you could have the rest of the week off—unpaid leave."

For a few seconds Savannah was too astonished to speak, but finally she managed to ask, "Why?"

"So that you can go with him to Paris for a brief honeymoon before the big overseas operation starts next week," Louise said. "He's already got the ring and is planning to ask you tonight."

Savannah collapsed into one of the chairs arranged in front of General Steele's desk as waves of nausea assailed her. "I can't marry Wes," she whispered.

"Of course you can't," Louise agreed. "Not when you're head over heels about Major Dane."

"I'm an idiot."

Louise shook her head. "I can't argue with you there. I tried to warn you . . ."

Savannah held up a hand to stop the secretary. "I know. I know. The question is what am I going to do now?"

"My advice is you go see Major Dane right away and tell him the situation." Louise raised an eyebrow. "And maybe this time you'll listen to me."

Savannah pushed herself upright and prayed she wouldn't lose her lunch. "You'll explain to the general for me?"

Louise nodded.

"Do you know where Dane is?"

"He's at the practice range training his men for next week's operation."

"Great," Savannah muttered. They would be running maneuvers until dark, and then Wes would be on his way over to propose. Somehow she had to find a way to stop him. She rubbed her temples and tried to think. She couldn't go running out to the practice range unless she wanted to get shot, which at the moment didn't seem like the worst solution to her problem. Finally she looked up at Louise. "Will you call Dane and tell him to meet me in the clubhouse at the practice range?"

"He doesn't like being interrupted," Louise reminded her.

Savannah nodded. "I know, but this is an emergency."

Louise reached for the phone. "And you're not calling him yourself because . . ."

"Because if I call, he'll try to make me explain, and this is a conversation we need to have face to face."

Louise didn't argue this. Instead she made the call and then nodded at Savannah. "He said he'll be there in thirty minutes."

Savannah took a deep breath. "Thanks. And now I need one more thing."

"More?" Louise demanded.

"I need to borrow your engagement ring."

Louise stared at the solitaire nestled against her wedding band. "I've worn this ring for nearly forty years and never planned to take it off."

"How do you expect me to get engaged without a ring?"

"I'd expect you to plan ahead a little more for something important like that." Louise removed the ring and passed it to Savannah. "If you lose that ring, I'll kill you."

Savannah put the ring in her pocket and hurried toward the elevator.

Dane was already in the equipment shed that the men affectionately called "the clubhouse" when Savannah arrived at the practice range. Instead of the perfectly starched uniform he normally wore, Dane had on battle fatigues. He looked stressed and a little annoyed and unbelievably cute.

"What's wrong?" he demanded.

"I have to talk to you." She locked the door and turned back to face him.

"Do I need to remind you that I'm taking my men into a hostile foreign country in a few days, and wasting time could cost someone their *life*?"

"You don't need to remind me," she assured him. "This is a matter of life and death too."

He didn't look convinced, but he walked toward her until they were just a few inches apart.

Their time was short and the situation grave, but she couldn't resist kissing him. When she finally pulled away, he smiled.

"You're right," he murmured. "That was more important than national security." He reclaimed her lips, and it was several more minutes before she breathlessly insisted that she really had come there to talk.

"Then talk," he invited as he pressed a series of little kisses along her jawline.

"Wes is planning to take me to Paris tonight. On our honeymoon!"

The kissing stopped, and Dane gave her his full attention.

"He asked the general to give me the rest of the week off, and Louise said she heard him say he already had the ring!"

Dane's eyes, which moments before had been so full of passion, now regarded her with serious solemnity. "Well," Dane said. "That is unexpected. Will you have enough time to pack, or will you just buy a new wardrobe in Paris?"

Savannah was irritated by his offhand attitude. "I'm not going to Paris, and I'm certainly not marrying Wes."

Dane raised an eyebrow in challenge. "Because you don't love him?"

"I love Wes," she conceded. "But I'm *in* love with someone else. The kisses showed me the difference."

Dane smiled, but he didn't look particularly relieved. "So what are we going to do?"

"The only way I can keep Wes from humiliating himself without marrying him is for us to announce our engagement before Wes can propose."

"But we're not engaged."

Savannah dug Louise's ring out of her pocket. She slipped it on her left ring finger and then said, "Now we are."

If anything, Dane's expression became graver. "Marriage is a serious commitment," he pointed out.

"I know that," Savannah agreed.

"My job is dangerous," he continued. "When I go out on an assignment, there's no guarantee that I'll come home."

She swallowed hard and nodded. "I know that too."

"It could take months for us to get post housing."

"Until then I'll live in my apartment, and you'll come when you can."

Finally he got to the heart of the matter. "I'm not sure I'm ready for marriage."

She had been prepared for several different reactions from him but not reluctance. She stepped back, putting a small but significant distance between them.

"Fine. I'll just give the general my resignation and leave immediately." She turned toward the supply room door, anxious to hide her tears of humiliation and grief. "It's been nice knowing you."

Dane grabbed her arm and spun her around. "Okay, I'll marry you."

Savannah pulled herself free. "Don't do me any favors."

He backed her against the cinderblock wall of the clubhouse, and the kissing began again. After a few seconds, she felt herself mellowing. After a minute, she couldn't remember ever being mad.

"Come on, Savannah," he whispered. "Do you want to marry me or not?"

"I want to marry you," she admitted shamelessly.

"Did you know that Mormons believe marriage should last forever?"

"Forever," she whispered, trying to imagine how it would feel to belong to someone that completely.

He smiled. "I'll tell you all about it when I get back from the operation next week." He kissed her nose then stood up straight and took her hand in his. "But for now we've got to go announce our engagement to the men."

"Don't you think we should tell Wes first?"

Dane frowned. "I thought we were trying *not* to humiliate him."

"We are," Savannah confirmed.

"Well, in order to do that we'll have to treat him just like one of the guys."

"Even though he's much more than that." She fingered the collar of Dane's fatigue shirt. Then she sighed. "I guess he's going to be hurt no matter how we handle it."

"Yes," Dane agreed.

She looked up at him, miserable. "I'm so sorry that I've come between the two of you like this."

Dane stroked her hair in a comforting way but didn't dispute the truthfulness of her words. He leaned down and gave her a quick, hard kiss. "That's for courage," he explained. Then he opened the clubhouse door and led her to the shady spot where his men were waiting.

Savannah had met all the men in Dane's elite unit. There was Hack, who considered himself Dane's bodyguard. Doc, the nervous medic who treated mostly blisters and hangovers. Cam, the body-builder who always wore combat fatigues. There were a few others with familiar faces whose names she couldn't remember. And there was Wes, who was leaning against a tree. He stood up straight when he saw her, surprise and confusion registering on his face.

Dane came to a stop in front of the group. He was holding her hand so tightly that she was afraid he might break a bone. Then with the poise of an Academy Award nominee, he announced, "I asked Savannah to come here this afternoon so we could let you guys be the first to know that we are engaged to be married." He lifted her left hand so they could see the ring glittering in the afternoon sun.

There were whistles and catcalls from the group. Dane smiled and accepted the soldier version of congratulations. But Savannah couldn't take her eyes off Wes's face. His expression went from shock to anger and finally settled on embarrassment. She was thankful that they had been able to spare him worse.

"So what do you think, Wes?" Dane called out to his old friend.

Wes walked over to them. "I say, I hope you'll let me be your best man, since I certainly *am* the best man." The words were right, but there was no life in them.

Wes stuck out his hand, and Dane clasped it. "I'll accept that offer, even though I dispute your claim."

"So does this mean we get the afternoon off?" a soldier called from the back.

Dane smiled and shook his head. "Not a chance. We've got work to do, and the wedding won't be for several weeks."

Savannah had been hoping that they'd follow through with Wes's plan and get married right away. Then they could have spent the weekend together as husband and wife before Dane had to leave on his operation. But she was careful to hide her disappointment.

"Can I kiss the bride?" another man yelled, and Dane fixed him with a stern look.

"Not a chance," he said to the group. Then he leaned over and whispered to her, "Time to get you out of here before I lose what little control I have over them." He turned to Wes. "While I walk Savannah back to her car, will you show these guys a few survival tricks so they don't get killed next week?"

"It will be my pleasure," Wes replied.

* * *

As Savannah saw Cam emerge from the administration building, she allowed the memories to fade with a feeling of deep regret. On that day she'd felt like her life was full of hope and destined for happiness. Many things had happened since then to convince her otherwise.

"So did you get the file?" she asked Cam as he swung into the seat beside her.

"Naw, it wasn't where it should have been, but the general says they'll keep looking."

Savannah was disappointed. No file meant that the only record they had of the disc was her faulty memory.

Cam seemed to understand how she felt. "Don't worry. That file will turn up eventually. And we've got plenty of other leads to follow in the meantime."

"That's true," she admitted.

"Now just sit back and relax again. I'll have you at the grocery store near Dane's cabin in no time."

Surprisingly, Savannah found that she was able to relax during the drive back to Tylerton. Cam parked and then ushered her into a small but well-stocked grocery store. As they walked up and down the aisles, Savannah found she was enjoying herself.

"I haven't been grocery shopping since Caroline was kidnapped," she told Cam. "It just seemed too sad."

"You have to eat," Cam said.

Savannah selected some perfectly ripe bananas. "So everyone keeps telling me."

Cam helped her select breakfast foods and sandwich makings. "We need to keep the meals simple so you don't spend all your time in the kitchen," he said to her with a smile.

"I don't know," she returned. "If Dane puts his mind to it, he'll find plenty of worse things than cooking for me to do."

On the drive back to the cabin Savannah admired the beautiful houses built on generous lots. "This is a very nice area," she mentioned.

"Yeah, it's really growing, and developers are always after Dane to sell his land. They could chop up his property, build a bunch of houses, and make millions."

"He ought to sell a few acres so he could afford to build a decent bridge."

Cam laughed. "He can afford that now, but he keeps the old one for the entertainment value."

Savannah frowned at the thought of the men watching her and Lacie teeter across the homemade bridge. "Very funny," she told him.

Once they were parked behind the cabin, they unloaded the groceries and carried them inside. Then Cam helped her put everything away. It seemed like he took every opportunity to flex his muscular arms, and finally she realized he was trying to impress her. Wondering if putting on makeup that morning had been a mistake, she closed the cupboard and said, "You'd better get to work before Dane fires you."

He didn't argue and led the way into the living room where the others were hard at work. After reporting on his trip to Fort Belvoir, Cam turned back to Savannah. "Maybe you could give me a hand," he suggested as he sat in front of his computer.

She was surprised. "How?"

He grinned. "Well, since you have a knack for identifying miscellaneous livestock . . ."

She smiled back.

". . . I thought you could help me make a list of your neighbors and everything you know about them. That will give me a way to prioritize our canvass this afternoon."

Savannah was pleased with what seemed like a constructive approach and retrieved the extra chair from beside Dane's computer. He glanced up briefly as she carried it over to Cam's workspace. "It's worth a shot," she said.

Cam pointed to the first name on his list. "The Wilsons live in the row house next door. Do you know them?"

"We've talked a few times," she said. "The wife is a lawyer for the Public Defender Service in DC. I think the husband works for a lobbyist."

"How long have they lived there?"

"Since before we moved in," Savannah replied.

They went down the list, and Savannah told Cam what she knew about each resident. One man down the street walked his German shepherd every day, and when Savannah commented on that, Cam laughed. "You probably noticed him because you have a thing about animals."

"Just miscellaneous livestock," she corrected.

"Could you two keep it down?" Dane finally requested, his voice louder and more aggressive than Savannah considered appropriate.

Savannah blinked at him. "I beg your pardon?"

"You and Cam are being so loud, the rest of us can't concentrate."

Savannah wanted to point out that nobody else was complaining, but she saw Cam's jaw tense and decided to apologize quickly in hopes of avoiding further conflict. "Sorry."

Instead of graciously accepting her apology, Dane said, "Why don't you head into the kitchen and make some sandwiches for lunch. That way maybe Cam can get something done."

This remark forced Cam to engage in the conflict. He rolled his chair away from his computer and walked to the center of the room. He waited until Dane looked up and then said, "Make your own sandwich. She's helping me."

Dane stood and limped toward Cam. "She's *flirting* with you," he corrected.

"I am not," Savannah denied indignantly.

The well-developed muscles in Cam's arms stiffened, and his jaw jutted forward belligerently. "And what if she is?" he demanded. "You've made it clear that you don't want her. Why can't you let another guy take a shot?"

Despite her humiliation, Savannah was extremely curious to hear Dane's response. But she was more anxious to defuse the potentially explosive situation. She stepped between the men. Since there was no question about which one was most likely to listen to her, she put a hand on Cam's arm.

"We all know how grouchy Dane can be when he's hungry," she said, in what she hoped sounded like a light, teasing tone. "So it would probably be best if I go ahead and make sandwiches. We can go through the rest of your list after lunch."

Cam pulled his eyes away from Dane and looked down at her. "You're not the maid here," he said. "You don't have to do everything Dane says."

She nodded. "I know. I just want to find my daughter."

Cam considered this for a few seconds and then sighed. "I'll help you make lunch." He shot Dane one last angry glance before following her into the kitchen.

In order to avoid a possible confrontation at the table, Savannah decided to serve lunch to the men at their workstations. With Cam's help, she made each man a plate with a sandwich, chips, and a dill pickle spear. Then she delivered the plates one at a time along with a canned soft drink. Just as she and Cam sat down at the kitchen table to eat their lunch together, her phone rang. It was Doug's secretary, Jackie, and she was beyond distraught.

"Doug's dead!" she wailed into Savannah's ear.

With an apologetic look in Cam's direction, Savannah walked out onto the back porch and sat on the top step. "I know, Jackie. It's a tragedy." She decided not to tell Jackie about Doug's involvement in Caroline's kidnapping. Not yet anyway.

"And I guess the police think I killed him!" Jackie was saying. "They've had me down at their headquarters all morning."

"I'm sure they don't think you killed Doug," Savannah said, trying to sound reassuring.

"I don't know how I would have since he was in Haiti and I was in Washington!" Jackie continued stridently. "Oh, Savannah, what was Doug doing in Haiti, and why would someone want to kill him?"

"It's a mess," Savannah replied vaguely.

"Doug was the major stockholder in the CAC," Jackie informed her unnecessarily. "What will become of our jobs and our insurance and our pensions?"

"That will be up to the board of directors."

"They've called an emergency meeting for seven o'clock this evening. Do you think they'll close down the center?"

"I don't know," Savannah replied honestly. "It's a possibility."

"Will you come to the meeting and represent all the employees?" Jackie begged. "The directors like you. They might listen if you plead our case."

"I'm sorry. I can't come tonight." At least half of that statement was true. "But I'm sure the directors will deal fairly with everyone."

"I'm not sure of anything anymore," Jackie said between sniffles. "It could be weeks before we're even able to have Doug's funeral! According to the police, the Haitian officials won't give them a definite date about releasing the body." A sniffle-filled pause. "Doug's sister is coming in from Seattle. I guess she'll handle it."

"It's all very sad," Savannah agreed. Then she forced herself to listen to the other woman vent for a few more minutes before ending the call.

As she stared out at the woods that separated Dane's cabin from the rest of civilization, she wondered if Doug Forton had been the mastermind behind Caroline's kidnapping. Was it possible that Doug had purposely caused her so much pain? Was it possible that she was such an incredibly bad judge of character? Had Wes really been murdered? Could it all be over a computer disc?

She walked down to the edge of the creek and sat on a large rock. The cool autumn breeze lifted her hair as her mind raced from one unanswerable question to the next.

At four o'clock she left the peace of the creek and went into the living room. She walked directly to Cam's workstation and asked if he was ready to leave. He glanced at Dane, who stared steadfastly at his computer screen and nodded.

During the drive into Washington, Savannah asked Cam about his children. Away from the watchful and disapproving gaze of Dane, Cam was almost chatty.

"I've got two great boys. My oldest is six, and the little one is four," he told her. His expression darkened a little as he added, "They live in Santa Barbara right by the ocean. My wife's boyfriend has a boat, and he takes them sailing all the time."

Savannah knew this must be a painful subject, but she'd learned from experience that talking helped. So she said, "I'm sorry your marriage didn't work out."

"Me too," Cam said. "But a military career is tough on a family. I think she's going to marry him." Cam glanced over at Savannah. "The boyfriend, I mean."

"It's hard to let go," Savannah said. "But you have to move on." Then she smiled. "Or at least that's what people say."

When they reached the Capitol Hill Historical District, Cam parked in front of her row house, and they spent two hours walking the streets and talking to her neighbors. Nobody remembered seeing anything unusual on the days leading up to Caroline's kidnapping. Most of them didn't even remember that a neighbor had been kidnapped. Savannah was relieved when Cam said they'd done enough and led her toward his car.

The traffic was relatively light, and they made it back to Fredericksburg in less than an hour. Cam offered to drop her off at the Hampton Inn, but she shook her head. "My suitcase is at Dane's cabin."

Cam didn't comment on this, but his expression made it clear that he disapproved of her spending the previous night on Dane's couch. "Well, how about dinner then?"

"I won't turn down food," she said with a smile.

They ate barbecue sandwiches and drank chocolate milkshakes. The food was good and her mood mellow when they returned to the car.

"You want to go see a movie?" Cam offered, obviously enjoying himself.

"I'll have to take a rain check on that," Savannah replied. "I'm exhausted."

Cam looked disappointed, but he led her around to the passenger side door without complaint. When he pulled up to the back of the cabin, he said, "You want me to wait while you get your suitcase?"

She shook her head. "My car's here. Hack brought it back from the hotel for me earlier today."

"So you're going back to the hotel?"

"I'm not sure," she replied vaguely. "I don't sleep much, and if I wake up during the night, I'd like to have something constructive to work on."

"You could take some files with you to the hotel," he suggested.

She opened the door and nodded. "I might do that. See you tomorrow."

Savannah wasn't sure what to expect from Dane as she climbed the back stairs of the cabin. Would he be the thoughtful host who had kept logs on the fire for her last night or the relentless critic who had complained about everything that morning?

The back door was unlocked, so Savannah let herself in. She found Dane alone, working at his desk in the living room. It was a peaceful scene, with a fire blazing in the big stone fireplace, the hot yellow flames licking at moss-covered logs.

Dane looked up from his computer screen. In the soft light he seemed younger and less bitter. "Where's Cam?" he asked.

She pulled up a chair and sat down. "He's gone back to the hotel in Fredericksburg."

"Did you find out anything while you were in Washington?"

"I found out that I don't ever want to be a door-to-door salesman."

He smirked. "Anything *else*?"

"No, it was a complete waste of time, just as I predicted."

"I'll be the judge of whether time is well spent during this investigation," Dane said, but he didn't sound angry.

She nodded. "It's just frustrating to see everyone go in all these different directions without any results." She kicked off her shoes and rubbed an aching foot.

His eyes followed this action, and finally he asked, "Are you planning to stay here again tonight?"

"My stuff is here," she began. "But if you'd prefer, I can go to the hotel . . ."

"No," he dismissed. "That would be senseless."

He picked up a pencil and drummed it against his desk. She continued to rub her feet. Finally he said, "I guess I owe you an apology for what I said earlier about you and Cam."

This enormous concession left Savannah momentarily speechless, which was probably for the best since she could think of several adjectives that better described his behavior, like boorish and rude and insufferable.

"But it seemed like you were getting pretty chummy with Cam and, well, he doesn't have a good track record when it comes to relationships with women."

She wasn't sure what astounded her more—that he thought she wanted to be "chums" with Cam or that he cared. "I'm not planning to have a *relationship* with Cam."

Dane had made his point, but he didn't seem to be able to leave it alone. "Cam has some emotional issues stemming from his divorce. His wife got total custody of his children and . . ."

Savannah frowned. "What are you saying?"

"Just that Cam's not exactly what I'd call mentally sound."

She raised an eyebrow. "And the rest of you are?"

"Even in this group Cam stands out," Dane said grimly. "In the future I'd appreciate it if you wouldn't go off with him by yourself."

If it was a safety issue, she couldn't object, so she nodded. "Okay."

"Just until the end of this investigation," he added. "After that you can date whomever you want."

"Thanks," she acknowledged sarcastically. Then she couldn't stop a yawn.

He logged off his computer and stood up stiffly. "We'd better get some rest and start fresh tomorrow." He paused to put several logs on the fire before limping toward the stairs.

"Good night," she said.

He waved before trudging up the stairs and into the murky darkness of the cabin's second floor.

CHAPTER 12

Savannah changed into her pajamas, and when she returned to the living room she saw the quilts and pillow from the night before still on the couch. She made up her bed and then snuggled down under the quilts and looked around the room. If you took away the computers and printers and fax machine, it was a really nice place. The high ceilings with the rough-hewn, exposed beams were simple yet dramatic. The big windows brought in plenty of light during the day and gave a stunning view of the moonlit creek at night. Even the odd assortment of furnishings was kind of charming.

She squinted at the pictures that lined the mantle, presumably Dane's ancestors. The women wore old-fashioned gowns, and the men stood stiffly and stared at the camera with stern expressions. Maybe crabbiness was a family trait. She had to smile.

Bringing her knees up under her chin, Savannah wondered what it would be like to be part of a big family with an extensive, if crabby, history. She'd never known her father. Not even his name. Her mother had been very sensitive about the subject, as if telling her his identity would be an admission of error. So Savannah had allowed her mother her privacy and lived with the curiosity. It had been worse when she was a teenager. Once she was grown, she had more pressing issues to worry about.

Savannah dozed off while studying the picture of a man wearing a military uniform with a sword strapped to his side. Later, she blamed the picture for the nightmare that followed. She dreamed she was being chased by a solider with a sword. She ran screaming down long, dark halls that never seemed to end with the certain knowledge that the soldier was right behind her and meant her harm.

Finally she saw an open door in the distance. She ran inside just as the soldier reached her and slammed the door in his malevolent face. Feeling safe and exhausted, she turned and saw that she was in a hospital room. Dane was lying on the mechanical bed, covered with bandages. Wes was alive and standing beside him.

She looked into Dane's eyes, which regarded her with such anger. Or was it anguish? She wanted to run to him, to kiss him and soothe his wounds. But she couldn't, because she was Wes's wife. She tried to explain—to tell Dane she still loved him and that she'd only married Wes because she thought Dane was dead.

Now both men were staring at her with accusation. She turned and ran. Even the psychotic soldier in the hall was preferable to the atmosphere inside the hospital room. As she rushed into the hall, she heard the sound of someone screaming. She knew it was Dane and turned to go back to him, but the hospital room was gone and only darkness remained—darkness and screaming. With a start, she realized she was awake. The darkness and the screaming were real.

She jumped from the couch and ran up the stairs. She'd never been in this part of the house before. It was unfamiliar territory, and she had only the pale illumination provided by the moon to light her way. She was trying to decide which of the two doors to try when Dane screamed again. She grabbed the doorknob to her left and wrenched it open.

The room was darker than the hall, and it took her eyes a few seconds to adjust. Then she saw him thrashing around on a bed that was pushed against the wall. Her only thought was the need to put a stop to his pain, so she stepped to the side of the bed and reached out a hand to shake him.

"Dane!" she cried.

Without warning, his arm shot out and grabbed her around the neck, cutting off her ability to speak or even breathe. He slung her down onto the bed beside him. His eyes were open but vacant, and she knew he was still asleep. Her fingers clawed at his arm, desperate to clear her air passages.

He blinked, and then his expression changed. Whether it was recognition or resignation, she couldn't tell. Maybe it was both.

"Dane?" she mouthed soundlessly, pushing with her last ounce of strength against the arm that was strangling her. He relaxed his arm, allowing some air to pass into her lungs. She was lying weakly against his pillow, waiting for the oxygen to revive her, when she saw his face begin a slow descent.

It seemed like an eternity before his lips finally pressed against hers. Then she clung to him as tears of loneliness and longing spilled onto her cheeks. Of their own volition, her fingers gently traced the scars on his chest in a futile effort to remove the pain he'd suffered.

He caught her hand in his and looked into her eyes. Then he kissed her again. After pulling away the second time, he whispered fiercely, "Am I still a better kisser than Wes?"

She tried to laugh, but it sounded more like a whimper. "Are you going to require me to be a disloyal wife as part of my penance?"

"I guess that answers my question."

"You always knew the answer," she said as more tears gathered in her eyes.

He pushed himself into a sitting position and swung his legs over the side of the bed. Then he placed her back on her feet in front of him. "I told you not to come in here . . . no matter what."

She sniffled. "I guess I forgot, what with all the screaming and everything."

He winced, and she knew he was embarrassed.

"You have nightmares."

"A legacy bestowed upon me by the Russian prison system."

She didn't know what to say, so she just stared miserably at him.

"I'm not my usual charming self when I'm having a nightmare," he told her, his voice unsteady. "I might even be dangerous. If you hear me again, don't come back in."

She nodded. "I won't."

He stood and pulled on a shirt. "I doubt if I'll be able to sleep anymore tonight. Can I interest you in a cup of hot chocolate?"

"Your specialty."

"That and kissing," he agreed with a rare smile that was heartbreakingly reminiscent of happier days.

They walked to the kitchen, and she sat at the table while he heated the water and added the hot chocolate mix. As he placed a mug before her, their eyes met, and for a second she was back in time.

They were in her little apartment near Fort Belvoir, they were young, they were in love.

"Dane," she whispered.

He broke his own rule about calling clients by their first names and said, "Savannah."

Ignoring the hot chocolate, she held his eyes with hers. "I'm so sorry for what I did to you and to Wes. Will you forgive me, and let it be like it was?"

He shook his head. "No."

She grabbed his hands in hers. "You're going to punish me forever?"

"For a while I needed my hatred to survive. But now that I'm home and all healed up, I find that maintaining so much emotion takes too much energy. But it can never be like it was."

"Why?" she demanded desperately. "Because of Wes?"

He stared at their joined hands. "No, because of me. I'm not who I used to be."

She was relieved by this answer. It gave her hope. "Dane, what happened in Russia?"

"You don't want to know."

"I do," she insisted. "I want to understand you."

Finally he shook his head and said, "I don't even understand myself."

"If I could go back . . ." she began.

"But you can't," he interrupted.

"No," she agreed as he pulled his hands from hers.

"You married our friend Westinghouse." This time she didn't detect any rancor in his tone. "And the two of you have a child who is now missing."

She nodded. That was the important thing. "Caroline is a really great kid."

"I have no doubt," he replied. "Since she's a combination of you and Wes."

Tears threatened again, but she managed to hold them back. "I can hardly wait for you to meet her."

He raised his eyes to meet hers. "Me too."

The moment was broken by the sound of a phone ringing in the distance.

"I think that's mine," he said. He stood and walked out of the kitchen.

While he was gone, Savannah sipped her hot chocolate and thought about the progress they'd made since she'd arrived at Dane's cabin. Maybe they weren't any closer to locating Caroline, but Dane was no longer her enemy. And that was something she had been sure she could never achieve. She was musing at the wonder of this new state of truce when Dane walked back in.

"It was Doc," he said. "I got there too late, but he left a message. He said he has a picture to show us, and he's on his way here."

Savannah's heart started to pound. "He must have gotten that computer-enhanced picture of the substitute teacher from his friend at the CIA. Did he say he was coming from Langley?"

"He didn't say."

Dane didn't seem very excited, and Savannah frowned. "What's wrong?"

"Nothing," he claimed.

"Something is," she refuted. "If Doc has a good picture of the sub . . ." Then a terrible thought occurred to her. "You don't think he really has a picture, do you?"

He shrugged. "I'm not even sure he has a friend at Langley who can enhance pictures."

"You know everything about me," she whispered. "Why don't you find out about Doc?"

"Doc deserves some privacy," he said.

"But what if he doesn't have a friend at Langley, and we aren't going to get an enhanced picture?"

"Since Doc is a little . . . unpredictable, I always duplicate his assignments," he explained. "Cam's got a guy at the Washington Police Department working on the picture. He doesn't think there's much hope, but I didn't leave it up to Doc and his friend at Langley."

Savannah felt relieved and sad at the same time. "Poor Doc."

"Yeah," Dane agreed.

"It's kind of late for Doc to be meeting with someone at Langley."

"I guess they work round the clock there, but it does seem like his friend would have scheduled a more normal meeting time."

"How long will it take him to get here?"

"If he's really coming from Langley, a couple of hours. If he's somewhere else, it's anybody's guess." Dane picked up his cup of hot chocolate. "Let's wait for him in the living room where it's warm."

She followed close behind him and settled onto the couch while he put more logs on the fire. Just as he sat down beside her, they heard the sound of the fax machine humming. She looked at Dane. "Maybe it's not anything important."

He frowned. "But then again, maybe it is." He shoved himself up and removed the fax from the tray. "It's from my contact at the Department of Homeland Security," he announced.

"So Doc did fulfill that assignment."

"Maybe. Or Cam might have requested it."

"I doesn't really matter who requested it," Savannah said. "What does it *say*?"

"It's the last four quarterly rosters supplied to them by the Brotherly Love Cooperative Farm." Dane shuffled through the papers, scanning each quickly. She knew the instant he found the discrepancy. His body went still, as if he were concentrating his entire being on the few words that interested him.

"What is it?" She jumped from the couch to look over his shoulder.

He pointed at a column in the middle of the page. "On June 30 of this year the Brotherly Love Farm had forty-four children." He extracted a different page and pointed out another number. "On September 30 they had forty-five children with no live births."

Savannah's mouth went dry. "The rosters Lacie brought back didn't show a discrepancy."

"No," Dane agreed. "Because the rosters Lacie brought back were doctored."

Savannah almost hated to say the words out loud, but she knew she had to. "Then Caroline is alive and living on the mountain with her grandparents?"

"She might be," Dane replied cautiously.

"She is!" Savannah wiped impatiently at the tears that spilled onto her cheeks. "That's the only logical reason for the discrepancy."

"I agree that it's a good possibility," Dane conceded.

"But why would Wes's parents kidnap her?"

"That I don't know," Dane admitted. "And honestly I don't care."

"So now what?" Savannah asked, her voice trembling with excitement.

"Now we go up there and find out if they have her. But we've got to do it carefully so they don't know we're coming. Otherwise, if Caroline is the extra child on that roster, she'll be gone before we can get there." He opened a cabinet and took out a box. The box contained a cell phone. "This is a disposable, prepaid cell phone. The range isn't great and the voice quality is worse, but they are untraceable. So from now on we make calls only on this."

He dialed a number and Savannah listened long enough to realize he was making arrangements for a private plane before she grabbed her suitcase and headed for the bathroom. Her hands were shaking so badly it took forever to change from her pajamas into a pair of jeans and a sweatshirt. After pulling her hair into a no-nonsense ponytail, she packed overnight essentials into her canvas makeup bag. Then she zipped the suitcase closed and pushed it into a corner where it could be retrieved when she returned—with Caroline.

Savannah smiled as she hooked the makeup bag over her shoulder. For months she'd been dividing time into things that happened before Caroline was kidnapped and after. It felt so good to think of the future in terms of having her daughter back.

When she returned to the living room, she found Hack and Cam waiting. They both looked like they had just rolled out of bed. Dane was filling them in on the big discovery.

Hack grinned when he saw her. "So there's a good chance we've found your little girl."

"Yes!" Savannah was so happy that she hugged the man.

He patted her back with a hand the size of a small ham. "I knew we could do it!"

When Hack released her, she felt obligated to hug Cam as well. She glanced at Dane out of the corner of her eye during this process and saw him scowling at her. Hysterical laughter bubbled up in her throat as she gave Cam's shoulders a quick squeeze.

"It's too early to celebrate," Dane warned with a meaningful look in her direction.

She broke contact with Cam and quickly put as much distance as possible between them.

"The extra child might not be Caroline," Dane said.

"It is," Savannah assured them all. "I can feel it."

"That last roster of farm residents is over a month old," Dane pointed out.

"A lot can happen in a month," Hack agreed with a sympathetic look at Savannah.

Dane's words tempered her exuberance but couldn't extinguish it completely. "I'm sure it's Caroline."

Dane put the untraceable, disposable phone in his pocket and said, "Doc is on his way here with a picture he supposedly got from his friend at Langley."

A look was exchanged between the men, and Savannah's concern for Doc increased. Apparently his presence on the team was a result of their duty toward him and not because of any contribution they thought he could make. They gave him busy work to make him feel important and keep him out of the way, just like her.

"He says he has a picture," Dane was continuing. "I presume of the substitute teacher who might have helped with the kidnapping. If we retrieve Caroline tomorrow, the picture won't make that much difference . . ."

"Except that it might help us nail whoever did it," Hack pointed out.

"True," Dane acknowledged. "Anyway, when Doc gets here, regardless of what he has, make sure he knows I'm pleased with his work, and tell him that I'll examine the picture at length when I get back."

Hack nodded. "I know how to handle the little man."

"Should I call and tell Lacie?" Savannah asked.

Dane shook his head. "If we call Lacie's cell phone, we might tip off the kidnapper. She's already in Laramie, so we can't save her the trip. We'll just explain things when we see her at the helicopter." He pulled the disposable phone out of his pocket briefly. "Contact me only on this until further notice. The number's printed on a card I left on my desk."

Hack and Cam nodded in unison.

"I've called General Steele, and he's making arrangements with the commander at Fort Carson for a large military presence to accompany us into the farm."

"Is that legal?" Savannah asked.

"We're using the doctored rosters to invoke authority under the Homeland Security Act," Dane explained briefly.

"And the Homeland Security Act gives the military pretty broad powers," Cam said.

"If there's suspicion of terrorist activities, national security supersedes the law," Hack added.

Savannah frowned. "But we know the farm people aren't harboring terrorists."

"We don't know anything of the kind," Dane contradicted her. "People who will kidnap a six-year-old might do anything."

Savannah was slightly uncomfortable with the idea of ignoring the Constitution, but getting Caroline off the farm was her highest priority. So she stopped arguing and touched Dane's arm to get his attention. "When do we go?"

Dane looked at her hand on his arm for a few seconds and then replied, "*We're* not going anywhere. I arranged for a pilot who owns a small plane to take me and Cam to Colorado. We're supposed to meet him at the airstrip in Fredericksburg in thirty minutes."

Savannah stepped in front of them. "You're not leaving here without me!"

Dane raised an eyebrow. "The last time I checked, I was in charge of this operation."

"She's my daughter," Savannah reminded him unnecessarily. "If Caroline is on that mountain, I want to be there when you find her."

He moved closer and lowered his voice. "People who kidnap children are serious—maybe deadly serious—about keeping who they kidnap. Doug Forton is already dead, and a Mafia boss is unaccounted for. This trip could be very dangerous."

Savannah nodded. "I understand that."

Dane didn't even try to hide his annoyance. "There will be hundreds of armed men under hostile circumstances. The chances of someone getting killed are good. If I let you go with me, I won't be able to guarantee your safety."

"I trust you," she said simply.

"Savannah," he tried again, but she shook her head.

"You're risking your life. I will too."

"My life has no value," he whispered. "Yours does. Don't ask me to endanger you."

"I'm sorry." And she was. But she had to go.

Dane ran his fingers through his hair in frustration. "It might not even be your daughter!"

"It's Caroline," Savannah insisted.

"She can feel it," Hack reminded him.

"Let her go in my spot," Cam offered. "I'll stay here."

"Yeah, let her go," Hack seconded the suggestion.

Dane looked between his men and Savannah. Then he shook his head. "Hack and Cam are some of the best friends I've ever had," he told her. "We've risked our lives for each other, stood together through thick and thin. Yet in just three short days you've turned them against me."

She sensed he was weakening and smiled with relief. "They aren't turning against you. It's just that they recognize a reasonable argument when they hear one."

He sighed and nodded. "Okay, I don't have time to argue anymore. You can come. But you can't say that I didn't warn you."

"No," she agreed. "I can never say that."

"Are you ready?"

She patted the canvas bag on her shoulder. "All packed."

Dane took a step toward the door. "You guys keep busy while I'm gone," he told his men. "Hack, keep working on finding Ferrante, and Cam, we really need that Nicaraguan file from General Steele."

Both men nodded. "We'll work as hard as we would if you were here," Hack promised.

"Well, almost," Cam amended with a smile.

Dane shook his head in mock disgust and walked through the door. After a slight hesitation, Savannah followed him outside.

CHAPTER 13

When they reached the airstrip, Dane led Savannah up to the smallest plane she'd ever seen. She was a little terrified, but she took courage from the fact that the contraption was going to take her to Caroline. She climbed inside and allowed Dane to help her strap in. Then he settled into the seat beside the pilot.

After a harrowing takeoff, the flight was surprisingly smooth. It was too dark to see the ground, and Savannah considered that a good thing. Dane and the pilot talked about their military experiences as Savannah dozed. They landed at a small airstrip in Kansas long enough to refuel. Savannah made use of the time to visit the restroom in a hangar that doubled as the terminal. There was a vending machine with a limited selection outside the bathroom door. She bought a pack of cheese crackers and walked back out to the airstrip.

Dane was standing by the plane, looking up at the clear, dark sky.

"Are you expecting bad weather?" she asked him.

"No, the forecast calls for unseasonably warm temperatures. But I'm always watching for an unexpected disaster. And I'm rarely disappointed."

She held out the pack of crackers. "Have one," she offered. "Then you can mark starving to death off your possible disaster list."

He reached out and took a cracker from the pack and popped it into his mouth.

She watched him chew and swallow. Then she said, "I can't believe that in just a few hours I might be with Caroline."

Dane's eyes urged caution, but Savannah shook her head.

"If she's not there, I'll deal with that then," she told him. "But for now, I'm going to believe."

He nodded in acceptance as the pilot called for them to board.

They landed at a little airport northwest of Denver at five o'clock in the morning The pilot dropped them off at the edge of a runway where a black sedan was conveniently parked. Dane helped Savannah out of the plane and thanked the pilot.

"You owe me," the pilot replied. Then he turned the plane and taxied toward the refueling station.

Dane waited until the plane was far enough away to make communication easier, and then he pointed at the car. "This is for us."

She followed him to the vehicle and watched as he opened the passenger door.

"How did this get here?" Savannah asked as she climbed inside.

"A friend left it for me."

Savannah examined the sleek interior of the late-model vehicle. "Nice gift."

"You can thank General Steele the next time you see him," Dane replied, and Savannah blushed, remembering why the general was financing this operation.

Dane closed her door and walked around to the back of the vehicle. He opened the trunk and checked through the supplies that were stacked there. Finally he opened the driver's door and slid in under the wheel. He handed her a sack and said, "See what you can find in there that looks good to eat."

She glanced through the assortment of beef jerky, bottled water, and trail mix. "None of it is particularly appealing."

He smiled as the plane passed them on the runway and then lifted off, presumably returning to Virginia.

"Will he come back for us?" she asked.

Dane shrugged. "When we leave, the need for secrecy will be over, so we can use a commercial airliner."

He started the car, and she asked, "Which way is the farm?"

"It's about a hundred miles northwest of here, but our first stop is a Cracker Barrel on Highway 27," he told her. "I don't want you keeling over on me before we rescue your daughter."

They arrived at the Cracker Barrel and were seated promptly. Savannah reviewed the menu and was eyeing the French toast when Dane said, "Don't order French toast."

She glanced over the menu at him. "It's really annoying the way you can read my mind."

"I can't read it *all* the time," he said with a knowing smile, and her heart started to pound.

She scowled back at him, hoping that his mind-reading powers didn't really exist. "And why can't I have French toast?"

"Because you need more protein," he replied. "Get scrambled eggs or an omelet."

The waitress returned and asked for their order. Savannah chose a sausage biscuit since it was neither of the options Dane had recommended. Once the waitress was gone, she asked, "Have you talked to Cam and Hack? Has Doc made it to the cabin yet?"

"I talked to Hack, and Doc's not there yet. He's sent Cam to look for him."

"What happened to Doc?" Savannah asked. "I mean he used to be pretty normal."

"He's seen too much death, been too helpless to stop it. That's taken its toll too."

"Is he mentally ill?"

Dane shrugged. "Who isn't?"

"I'm serious."

"Doc's okay as long as he takes his meds. He just needs supervision."

"And the team provides that?"

Dane nodded. "What's *left* of the team does its best."

"Cam told me that Owl's been reassigned to another unit, Steamer's selling desert real estate, and Wigwam's becoming a family man."

Dane nodded. "The whole team kind of fell apart while I was presumed dead. I was looking for a chance to reassemble it when you came to me with your offer I couldn't refuse."

"You did refuse," she reminded him.

"I'm here," he pointed out.

Savannah decided not to pursue that sensitive subject and returned to the original topic. "Why was Hack discharged from the Army?"

"He was up for reenlistment when I was rescued. He opted out so he could take care of me," Dane said. "When I opened my eyes in Walter Reed, his ugly face was the first thing I saw."

"He's a good friend."

"Yes," Dane agreed. "And leaving the Army was the smartest thing he's ever done. He makes more money in one month with his security firm than he would have in a couple of years as a soldier."

"But it never was about the money," Savannah said with certainty. "It was about you."

Dane glanced up. "And the other guys," he agreed. "We were a good team at one time."

"Because of you."

"You're giving me too much credit again," he said, refusing to accept a compliment. "Everyone played his part."

"Where was Doc while you were in the Russian prison?"

"He was a patient in a private mental institution."

Savannah was upset until Dane added, "It was a real nice place. Wes arranged it."

"But you got him out."

"There wasn't any reason for him to stay there once I was home," Dane said simply.

Savannah understood. Wes cared enough to pay for Doc to be hospitalized. Dane cared enough to look after him personally.

The food arrived, and Savannah found that she was starving. In between bites she asked, "So how long have your parents been in Thailand?"

"About six months," Dane replied.

"How long do they have to stay?"

"Another year."

"How often do they get to come home?"

"They don't. They're gone for the whole eighteen months."

Savannah looked up from her breakfast. "That's a long time to be away from your family."

He shrugged. "The young men who go at nineteen are away for two years."

"You didn't go on a mission for your church?"

He shook his head. "I joined the Army instead."

She'd been hoping for an opportunity to bring up the subject and decided this might be the best one she'd get. "My mother wasn't big on going to church. She taught me to pray and told me Bible stories, but we weren't members of any organized religion."

Dane nodded. This wasn't news to him.

"Since Caroline's been gone, I've felt closer to God."

He glanced up from his food. "That's strange. It seems like you'd be mad at Him for letting something so terrible happen."

"It may not be logical, but it's true," she told him. "I pray all the time, and when I get Caroline back . . ."

"*If* you get Caroline back," he interrupted.

She frowned at him and then continued. "When I get her back, I think I'd like to take her to church. Since I don't have one, I thought I might try yours."

Dane put down his fork and gave her his full attention. "Religion is an area where I can't help you."

She was disappointed but not surprised. "Okay. I'll figure it out for myself." She pushed back from the table and said, "I've eaten all I can."

Dane wadded up his napkin and put it on top of his half-eaten meal. "Me too. Let's go."

Once they were settled back in the car, Savannah asked, "Do you know where you're going?"

"Basically," he replied. "But there's a map in my bag if we need it."

Savannah pulled the map out, deciding it was better to be prepared. But Dane never asked for any directions. They drove for nearly two hours before he finally pulled off the highway and parked under a large tree.

"The main entrance to the farm is about two miles ahead. We'll wait here for our military escort," he told her.

"What time do you expect them?"

He checked his watch. "It will be light in an hour or so. The general promised to have his covert teams in place around the perimeter by dawn. The helicopter is scheduled to leave at 10:00 AM, so I figure we'll want to approach the gate about nine o'clock."

Savannah had hoped they would go in sooner. It was hard to be so close and still have to wait. With the car off, there was no heat being generated, and the air started to cool. She rubbed her hands up her arms.

"Are you cold?"

"A little," she admitted.

"There are some blankets in the trunk," he said. "I'll get them."

He returned with a blanket for each of them. She pulled the one he gave her up under her chin. Dane's phone rang and he answered it. Savannah leaned closer in an attempt to identify the caller. As it turned out, moving closer was unnecessary. The call was from Hack, and he was talking loud enough to be heard from several feet away.

"We've got a problem!" he hollered.

"What?" Dane demanded.

"Doc's overdosed."

She saw Dane close his eyes briefly. Then he asked, "Is he alive?"

"Barely!" Hack replied with uncharacteristic panic in his voice. "He never showed here, so I had Cam go look for him. He got to Doc's apartment just as they were loading him into an ambulance. A neighbor found him and called 9-1-1."

"Is he going to be okay?"

"Too soon to tell," Hack replied. "Me and Cam are in the waiting room at the hospital now. They won't let us see him. The doctor said it looked like he had taken a week's worth of all his medicine at once."

"Call me when you know more," Dane requested. Then he closed his phone.

"Doc was always so meticulous about his medicine," Savannah said. "I can't believe he would take a whole week of pills at one time."

"He would if he was trying to kill himself."

"But why would he do that?"

"He's tried before," Dane told her. "Maybe I should have left him in the hospital where Wes put him. At least there he was supervised."

"Doc was well supervised as a member of your team," Savannah reassured him. "And while he might have had suicidal moments in the past, it doesn't make sense for him to kill himself now! He had a picture to show us. He was excited about finding Caroline and had every reason to live!"

"What if there was no picture and he couldn't face us?"

Savannah bit her lip. "Poor Doc." She thought about his kindness to her when she first arrived at the cabin, calling Savannah by name when no one else would. Finally she frowned at Dane. "Doc wasn't crazy, and he didn't lie. He wasn't even confused all the time. If he said he had a picture, I believe that he did."

Dane seemed to consider this for a few seconds. Then he flipped open his phone and dialed a number. "Hack!" he demanded when the other man answered. "Did Cam find a picture at Doc's apartment? He was supposed to be bringing us an enhanced photograph of the substitute teacher."

Savannah could barely make out the sounds of a muffled conversation, presumably between Hack and Cam. Finally Hack reported, "There was no picture."

Savannah wasn't willing to give up so easily. "If the kidnapper knew Doc had the picture and that it could help to identify him, he could have followed Doc to his apartment, forced him to take too much medication, and then he would have taken the incriminating picture with him when he left!"

Dane put his finger over the small phone receiver and whispered, "I think you're wrong, but I pride myself on being thorough." He removed his finger and told Hack, "Savannah is insisting that Doc's in danger, and I don't want to have to listen to her go on about it anymore. So have one of your men guard his hospital room around the clock until further notice." Then he closed the phone.

"Why did you blame that on me?" Savannah asked.

He cut his eyes over at her. "So if you're wrong, I don't look like a fool."

"I'm willing to look like a fool if it saves Doc's life," she told him.

He shrugged. "Me too."

She wasn't sure if he meant her or him, but she didn't challenge him. They sat in silence for a few minutes, watching the sun light up a beautiful mountain morning. Finally she said, "I really do want to know about Russia."

He didn't reply for a few seconds, and she thought he was going to ignore the comment. But then he turned to her and said, "I was in pretty bad shape when they captured me."

"Why did they capture you?" she asked. "I thought we were on good terms with Russia."

"Better than when it was the USSR," Dane conceded. "But our relationship still isn't what I'd call trusting. And we were inside their country uninvited, trying to extract a scientist who didn't want to leave."

"Did you get the scientist out?"

He nodded. "Yes, the mission was a success."

"But not for you."

"They took me to a secret prison, similar to the ones the CIA runs for our government. My left leg was useless—broken in several places, crushed in others. They didn't set it. Just made me drag it around." He spoke in a dull, steady cadence.

She kept her expression carefully blank, but it didn't matter since he wasn't looking at her anyway. He was staring at a place over her shoulder or maybe even farther away.

"At first they kept me in a concrete cell about the size of a large dog house. There was no light, so I couldn't tell if it was day or night, and it was freezing cold. They came every few hours to pull me out and torture me. I'd get so cold that I would actually pray for the guards to come since it was warm in the interrogation room. Then the pain would be so bad that I'd long for the cold. Whatever I wasn't enduring at the time always seemed better."

"You should have just told them anything you knew," Savannah whispered.

"I did," Dane told her. "That was the instruction we were given. If you're captured, you tell them what you know. The folks who are safe back home can change codes and protect themselves. But even after I'd answered their questions, they kept on torturing me just for the fun of it. The days all ran together, a blur of hopeless agony."

"I guess finding you presented a real challenge to the Army since their best rescuer was also the captive."

He shook his head. "The Army has other guys who are almost as good as me." He gave her a ghost of a smile. "But I knew they wouldn't find me because they weren't even looking. They thought I was dead."

"How did you eventually get out?"

"The Russians offered me as a trade for a U.S.-held Russian prisoner."

"That was fortunate," she murmured. "I guess God was looking out for you after all."

He lifted one shoulder in a casual shrug. "I guess."

Dissatisfied with his response, she twisted around in her seat so she could face him. "What you went through was terrible . . ."

"You have no idea," he interrupted.

"I have an idea," she insisted. "I've seen your chest."

He shrugged again.

"You've been through a terrible experience, but I think instead of concentrating on the suffering you endured, you should be thankful that you survived."

"At what cost?" he whispered. His eyes reflected his inner pain. "The Russians finally got bored with torturing me and transferred me to a cell. I didn't think anything could be worse than the doghouse, but the new place was infinitely more terrible. There were hundreds of poor creatures there in various stages of dying. The prison didn't provide even the most basic medical care or feed us enough to keep a cat alive. There were no sanitary provisions and our 'beds' consisted of filthy mats on the floor."

She wanted to reach across the small distance that separated them and offer comfort, but instinctively she knew that any attempt at consolation would not be appreciated.

"There were two other men in the cell with me, and both were sick. One died a couple of days after I got there, but I didn't tell anyone. I just ate his rations until his stench led the guards to his body. The other guy was burning up with fever and delirious half the time. One day he was too weak to reach his food and collapsed back on his mat. I stared at his food for a long time. Then I ate it. From that point on I ate his food every day until he died."

Savannah blotted her tears on the blanket, unsure if she was crying for Dane or the dead cellmate or both. "There was no point in letting the food go to waste," she said finally. "If he was too sick to eat . . ."

"I should have fed it to him!" Dane cried in anguish. "That's what a Christlike person would have done. That's what I was *taught* to do!"

He calmed himself with an effort and continued. "Instead, I ate it, day after day while he lay there and died."

No longer able to restrain herself, she leaned across the seat and grabbed his hands in hers. "The other man was sick and weak. He would have died anyway."

"Probably," Dane agreed. "But that doesn't make it right. That doesn't make it any easier for me to live with myself."

"I'm sorry that man died," Savannah told him. "But I'm thankful that you're alive. I wouldn't want to trade his life for yours. That may not be a Christlike attitude, but it's the truth."

He seemed relieved for a second, but then he pulled his hands away and looked out the window. "That man's wife wouldn't have wanted to trade him for me either."

"It's something that happened in the past," she said to the back of his head. "You can't change it, so you just have to deal with it."

He turned around. "That's easy for you to say. You haven't killed anyone!"

"You didn't kill that man! The inhumane conditions in the prison killed him!"

"I killed several soldiers during my capture."

"That was self-defense!"

He leaned down until his face was close to hers. "But I'm not sorry. My only regret is that I didn't kill more of them."

"Dane," she whispered. "I wish . . ."

"Wishing doesn't make it go away," he told her. "Believe me, I've tried."

She felt confused and sad. "I thought faith in Jesus was supposed to make it easier to deal with the mistakes we make."

"My knowledge that someday I'm going to have to face the Savior and account to Him for all the things I've done makes me so sick I can barely stand it."

She wanted to give Dane some form of encouragement or comfort but felt terribly inadequate. Her mother's simple prayers and the rare religious discussions with Dane back in the early days had not prepared her to offer counsel on such a large scale.

Finally he leaned back. "That's enough talking. Try to sleep until our escort gets here."

She settled down under her blanket, but she didn't sleep. Instead she bowed her head and prayed for Dane's soul.

CHAPTER 14

Savannah was awakened by an insistent shake from Dane. He waited until her eyes were open and focused before he said, "The cavalry is here."

She looked out the windshield of their borrowed car at the road. An impressive number of military vehicles were approaching from the south. One by one they turned off the road and lined up in neat rows in the field behind the car where Savannah and Dane sat watching. "I wasn't expecting quite so *many,*" she whispered.

Dane smiled. "General Steele wanted to be sure the farm people know we mean business." He pocketed the car keys and opened his door. "Let's go."

The brisk wind caught Savannah in the face as she climbed from the car, effectively chasing away the last vestiges of sleep. She followed Dane to a group of men who had gathered near the lead Jeep.

"I'm Dane," he said.

The men all saluted and Dane looked mildly uncomfortable. He touched his forehead in half-hearted return.

One man stepped forward. "Major, I'm Captain Findley with the 4th Infantry out of Fort Carson. I'm the commanding officer on this operation, although I welcome any input you might have."

The men shook hands. "We appreciate your help," Dane said.

"Glad to do what we can." Captain Findley glanced at Savannah.

Dane remembered his manners. "Oh, and this is the girl's mother, Mrs. McLaughlin."

Captain Findley touched the brim of his hat. "Ma'am."

Dane reclaimed his attention by asking, "So what's the plan?"

"I've got teams in place all around the perimeter fence to make sure no one leaves on foot. If possible, General Steele would like for us to slip in, get the child, and slip out without anyone the wiser. So we'll try a covert approach first."

"And if that doesn't work?" Dane asked.

"Then we'll come in openly with full force." He motioned for a man behind him to step forward. "This is Lieutenant Kimbrell, and he's going to escort you in."

Savannah gave Lieutenant Kimbrell a quick once-over. She was relieved to see that he looked very competent and severely serious.

"When the helicopter pilot arrives, Kimbrell will try to convince him to take you along on his ride to the mountains," the captain continued.

"And if he refuses?" Dane asked.

This possibility didn't seem to concern Captain Findley in the least. "Then Kimbrell will disable the pilot and fly the helicopter himself."

Dane nodded, obviously satisfied.

"And if the covert plan doesn't work, we'll storm the gate," the captain said. "We'll search every square inch of the farm property. The administration building where all the personnel and resident files are kept. The warehouses where they're storing last year's harvest. Even individual homes. The helicopters will be hovering around, taking photographs and blowing up dust. After a few minutes I'll pull the good father aside and explain that I can make the whole nightmare go away if he hands over the little girl."

Dane nodded. "I like it. Simple yet brutal."

"I don't do things any other way," the captain said to Dane. Savannah was glad he was on their side.

"When do we go in?" Savannah asked.

Captain Findley checked his watch. "About now." He handed Dane what looked like a small, black iPod. "That's an emergency transmitter. Kimbrell has one too. If something goes wrong, all you have to do is push the red button, and we'll come barreling in."

Dane glanced down at the device and then tucked it into his coat pocket.

Captain Findley waved at Dane. "Lieutenant Kimbrell, follow me."

The captain seemed surprised when Savannah fell into step behind them. He gave Dane a questioning look, and Dane shrugged. "She's determined to come along."

"Taking a civilian on an operation like this is against regulations," the captain said.

"General Steele approved her participation," Dane said, and Savannah wondered if this was true. "You can call and check it out with him if you want."

"I'll take your word for it," Captain Findley replied with a scowl in Savannah's direction. "But I still don't like it."

"Me either," Dane assured him. "But believe me, she's impossible to reason with."

Savannah opened her mouth to defend herself, but Dane silenced her with a quick head shake.

With a grunt that clearly expressed his displeasure, the captain turned to Lieutenant Kimbrell. "You know what to do."

The lieutenant nodded. "Yes, sir!" He turned to Dane and Savannah and tipped his head toward the woods. Dane had made his objection to her involvement in the recovery operation very clear during his conversation with the captain, so Savannah was surprised when he reached for her hand. Any tender feelings she had for him disappeared as he pulled her, less than gently, and whispered, "If you can't keep up, he'll leave you behind."

Savannah bit back a scathing reply and increased her speed to a slow trot. Soon they were encompassed by trees. It took all her concentration to keep her balance as Dane dragged her swiftly over damp pine needles and fallen limbs that littered the forest floor. After a few minutes, she was winded and desperate for a chance to catch her breath. Just as she was about to beg Lieutenant Kimbrell for a short break, he came to an abrupt stop. Savannah looked up to see that they were standing beside a tall, chain-link fence.

"This is the perimeter fence for the farm," the lieutenant told them. Then he proceeded to cut a hole in the crisscrossing metal with what looked like a small set of pliers.

"Is the fence wired?" Dane asked.

The lieutenant shook his head. “Naw, they don’t really have much trouble with people breaking in or out. The fence is just to keep their livestock rounded up.”

Lieutenant Kimbrell held the fence open, and Dane climbed through. After checking the fence line, he waved for Savannah and the lieutenant to follow. They continued through the woods at a more sedate pace, which gave Savannah a chance to admire her surroundings. If she hadn’t been so anxious to see Caroline, she would have enjoyed the scenery. Like Lacie said, the farm was a lovely place.

They walked for nearly an hour with the lieutenant stopping to check his compass often. Finally they reached a large field, and across the wide expanse of brown grass Savannah could see a modern three-story building encircled by a parking lot. To the far right, the land was dissected into brown squares that undoubtedly yielded crops during the growing season. Between the fields and the brick building were rows of white houses. Savannah swung her eyes back to the left and focused them on a small shed and a raised cement slab. Perched on the slab was a big, black helicopter.

“Now what?” Savannah whispered.

“I’ll go first and secure the area,” Lieutenant Kimbrell said to Dane. “When I give you the all-clear signal, bring her and come on.”

Dane nodded, and the lieutenant moved stealthily toward the helicopter pad. Savannah had to remind herself to breathe as she watched Lieutenant Kimbrell cross the open space. Once he reached the helicopter pad, he circled the large vehicle twice and then checked inside the cinderblock building. Finally satisfied that it was safe, the lieutenant stepped out and waved for them to join him.

Dane pulled a gun from his coat pocket, and Savannah shrank back instinctively. “I don’t plan to use it on you,” he said.

“I didn’t think you would,” she scoffed, trying to cover her alarm. “I was just surprised you had it.”

He seemed amazed by this comment. “How did you think we were going to convince the pilot to take us up the mountain? By asking real nice?”

She shrugged, still uneasy. “I didn’t think about it.”

He started toward the helicopter where the lieutenant was waiting and then paused. “Why don’t you wait here until after we’re through negotiating with the pilot? And if there's trouble, you run back the way we came in and find Captain Findley." He pressed the prepaid cell phone into her hand.

She looked up into his eyes and whispered, "You're not leaving me here. 'One for all and all for one.' Remember?"

He stuffed the gun into the waistband of his pants and grabbed her shoulders. Then he shook her gently. "When I took this job it was with the understanding that you would do exactly what I said. You promised!"

"I take it back."

"Savannah!" The sound of her name on his lips was intoxicating, and she leaned toward him. His hands on her shoulders became almost an embrace as he demanded, "Think of your daughter!"

"I'm going with you," she said, fighting the nearly uncontrollable urge to press her lips to his. "I have to."

With a sigh of resignation, he nodded. "You can come with me, but just because Lieutenant Kimbrell has already checked the area out. The helicopter isn't scheduled to leave until ten, so the pilot probably won't be here for another half hour. We should be able to wait safely for him in that shed."

"I understand," she told him. "You aren't giving in to me. You're just changing your mind based on hard, cold facts."

He made a noise in his throat and grabbed her hand. "You'd better hope I don't come to my senses."

"I'm not really concerned about that," she muttered as he pulled her out into the open. During the crossing, his eyes were moving constantly, searching everywhere for signs of danger. They reached the helicopter pad, and he left her at the front of the large vehicle with the lieutenant while he circled it twice. He checked the locked doors and then returned.

"It's not that I don't trust you," he told the lieutenant. "I just believe in being thorough."

"I understand, sir," Kimbrell responded without offense.

"If you'll stand guard here, I'll double-check the shed," Dane said, and the lieutenant nodded.

"Yes, sir!" Lieutenant Kimbrell pressed his back against the nose of the helicopter and faced the empty field with vigilance.

Dane reclaimed Savannah's hand and pulled her toward the equipment shed. When they reached the door, he addressed her firmly. "You stay right here. Once I'm sure it's clear, we'll wait inside for the pilot."

Savannah would have preferred to accompany him but didn't want to push her luck too far, so she just nodded. Lieutenant Kimbrell had already forced the lock on the door during his original search, so Dane was able to enter the shed easily. With a glance back at her, he stepped inside and was swallowed up by darkness. For several minutes Savannah followed Dane's instructions and waited impatiently by the door. But eventually curiosity drove her to peek inside.

The interior of the shed was dim, lighted only by the few rays of sun that trickled in through a small window. She saw Dane's shadow moving along the far wall. Deciding that she had waited long enough, she placed a foot on the door landing, intending to step inside. But before she could complete the action, a hand covered her mouth and jerked her backward.

Savannah screamed, but the hand at her mouth prevented any sound from escaping. She kicked her feet—hoping to hit her captor or even the doorframe—anything to warn Dane. But her legs encountered only air. Her unseen assailant carried her a few feet back from the door and positioned her firmly in front of him. She continued to struggle for a few seconds until he pressed the cool metal of a gun muzzle to her forehead, effectively ending her resistance.

She watched miserably as Dane emerged from the shed. When he saw her situation, he dropped instantly into a defensive stance, his gun raised. The man who held her laughed.

"Unless you want one of us to shoot *her,* I suggest you drop the gun."

Dane considered his options for a few seconds and then threw his gun to the ground. Savannah stared in despair at the discarded weapon.

"It's a good thing I'm in the habit of coming early to get the copter ready for my supply trips," the man said. "Otherwise I wouldn't have been here to see you folks come out of the woods. That was quite a surprise, I can tell you."

"What did you do to Lieutenant Kimbrell?" Dane asked.

"Poor fellow is out cold," the man replied in a conversational tone. "He was so busy looking into the field for trouble, he never suspected that it was right behind him."

Dane said, "We're here on official business for the U.S. Army."

The man laughed again. "I'm an Air Force man myself, but surely even the Army can run an operation better than this." He waved the gun to encompass the immediate area.

Dane didn't try to dispute with him. "We just found out that Mrs. McLaughlin's daughter, who has been missing for over two months, is up on the mountain with her grandparents. We didn't have a lot of time to put together a plan but hoped you'd let us ride up there with you."

"I won't be taking any of you anywhere until we talk with Father Burnett. I called him while I was watching you folks sneak up, so he should be here soon."

As if to punctuate the pilot's words, several men emerged from the three-story building across the field and started toward them at a trot. Another man followed behind them at a more dignified pace. The men were all dressed in coveralls, and most of the ones in front held menacing rifles. Once they reached the shed, they formed a semicircle behind Savannah, and one stepped up to Dane. He pulled a pair of handcuffs from the pocket of his coveralls and motioned for Dane to turn.

Savannah watched in misery as Dane's hands were roughly secured behind him. She knew that he would never have submitted to such treatment so docilely if her safety weren't in jeopardy. The pilot moved his hand from her mouth but kept the gun to her head.

She couldn't bear to see Dane in restraints, so she turned to watch the last man make his approach. He was dressed in the same coveralls as the other men, but he had an air of authority that distinguished him from the rest. When he reached them, he stood between Dane and Savannah. He was tall and broad shouldered with shaggy blond hair and penetrating blue eyes.

"I'm Father Burnett," he introduced himself.

"I'm sorry for our unconventional entry," Dane said. "But we had a good reason."

"And I'd like to hear it," Father Burnett assured him. "Why don't we go in the shed where we can be more comfortable?"

One of armed men pointed to the shed with his rifle, and Dane shuffled inside. His limp seemed more pronounced than usual, and Savannah's guilt grew exponentially. Another man retrieved the unconscious form of Lieutenant Kimbrell and dumped him on the shed's cement floor.

Savannah and Dane were told to sit in two metal folding chairs, and the armed farmers took strategic positions around the small room. Savannah risked a glance at Dane. He was staring straight ahead, his hands clenched in fury. She knew he blamed himself for the situation they found themselves in. He didn't have much patience for other people's mistakes and none for his own.

She wanted to make him feel better and knew that, as usual, sympathy would not accomplish that. So she leaned close and said, "I'm probably going to have to dock your pay for this."

He glanced over, and she saw first surprise and then amusement in his eyes. "You'd be within your rights. I've made a mess of things."

She shrugged as if she didn't care. "It's just a job, remember. Don't take a little mistake personally."

His expression softened. "Lean a little closer," he whispered.

She obeyed.

"Closer," he whispered again.

Now their lips were almost touching and she could smell maple syrup from breakfast on his breath. She was so overwhelmed by his nearness, so touched that he would want to draw comfort from her, that she had to fight back tears.

Then he said, "Reach into my coat pocket."

She blinked. "Huh?"

She felt more than saw his lips curve into a smile. "It's time for plan B. The transmitter is in my pocket. Push the red button, and notify Captain Findley that we need him."

So his invitation to come nearer had been a tactical move, not a romantic one. She felt foolish and embarrassed but reached into his pocket and pressed the button just as Father Burnett came inside the shed and stood in front of them.

"Will you please explain your uninvited presence on our property?" Father Burnett requested.

"My name is Major Dane of the U.S. Army."

Savannah was surprised by the way Dane kept bringing up the Army since they'd been caught trespassing on private property. He indicated toward her while keeping his eyes on the religious leader.

"And this is Savannah McLaughlin."

"I understand that you've damaged our fence." Father Burnett's tone was pleasant, but his eyes were wary, especially as he examined Savannah.

"Send the repair bill to General Steele at Fort Belvoir in Virginia," Dane said. "It will be taken care of promptly."

Father Burnett gave Dane a narrowed look, but before the interrogation could continue, they heard the distant whir of rotors, and everyone looked out the small window to see Captain Findley's helicopters approaching from the south. While the farm's leader was processing this turn of events, a thin young man with a freckled face and drooping overalls appeared in the shed's doorway.

He braced both hands against the door frame and cried, "Father! A tank just drove straight through the gate. Busted it clean off the hinges, and now a whole bunch of Army trucks are heading this way."

"That would be our backup," Dane said smugly.

Father Burnett put a hand on the boy's shoulder. "Thanks for getting here so quick to let me know. Now go wait with your family."

As the boy ran back out, Father Burnett motioned toward the door. "I guess we might as well go meet your friends." He stepped through the door and into the morning sunlight, followed closely by his guards. One of them stopped to pick up Lieutenant Kimbrell and dragged the wounded man along.

Savannah was annoyed that they hadn't removed the handcuffs that bound Dane's arms but was relieved that help had arrived. She stood and waited for Dane to do the same. Then they joined the others outside.

They watched as Lieutenant Kimbrell was placed in an Army Jeep and driven away. "Will he be okay?" Savannah whispered to Dane.

"He let an air force pilot get the drop on him, so his pride will hurt more than anything else." Dane didn't sound particularly concerned.

People started emerging from the white houses in the distance. They stood on their front porches staring at the military might arrayed before them. Father Burnett stepped up to the captain. "I demand an explanation for this illegal intrusion."

"Before we explain anything, maybe you could have someone remove these handcuffs," Dane suggested. Then he looked at Captain Findley. "I told him I was a major in the Army, but he didn't seem too impressed."

Captain Findley's expression darkened as he addressed Father Burnett. "This farm has come under scrutiny because of a discrepancy in your residency roster. I've been sent here to clarify things."

"I don't know what you're talking about," Father Burnett blustered. "We send accurate records to the government. We're law-abiding, peaceful people."

"There's nothing peaceful about kidnapping," Dane interjected sharply.

Now Father Burnett looked offended. "We would never kidnap anyone."

Dane smiled, but his eyes were cold. "And yet you have Caroline McLaughlin up on your mountain with her grandparents. The child was taken from her school two months ago without her mother's permission. That sounds like kidnapping to me."

"I don't know what you're talking about," Father Burnett said, but he was a bad liar.

"Well, if you aren't involved in the kidnapping of Mrs. McLaughlin's little girl, I'm sure you won't mind us riding up to the mountain with your pilot here." The handcuffs were removed, and Dane flexed his hands to restore circulation.

"And Major Dane, while you're checking out the mountain, we'll do a little research down here," Captain Findley said. "I'll have one team start in the farm's offices going through personnel records and resident applications. The rest of my men can start searching houses." He pointed to the rows of white homes. "No telling what we might find here if we look hard enough."

"This is illegal," Father Burnett tried again. "You don't have a search warrant."

Captain Findley shrugged. "Thanks to the Homeland Security Act, we don't need one." He signaled his men to proceed.

Father Burnett stood in silence as he watched the first team reach the administration building. Once they had disappeared inside, he turned his gaze to the vehicles driving across the dormant fields, headed to the houses full of confused, frightened people.

Savannah couldn't stand by silently any longer. She stepped forward and claimed Father Burnett's attention. "Please help us. I know my daughter is up on that mountain. I'm not angry at Wes's parents." She paused and then amended this statement. "Well, of course I'm angry. They've put me through a nightmare no parent should ever have to experience. But I understand that they wanted to be a part of Caroline's life, and that can still be arranged. But she belongs with me." Savannah pressed a hand to her chest. "I'm her mother, and I love her with all my heart."

Father Burnett looked uncertain for the first time. His eyes returned briefly to the search team that was approaching the first house. Finally he turned to Captain Findley and said, "Please, stop them."

"You'll cooperate with us then?" the captain clarified.

Father Burnett nodded. "I need to talk to you before anyone goes up on that mountain. There are extenuating circumstances you should know about."

"Extenuating circumstances!" Dane yelled. "Nothing justifies kidnapping a little girl!"

But the captain was of a mind to be more conciliatory. "It might be better if we hear his side of the story first."

"And while we talk, he can have the child moved!" Dane objected, and Savannah felt all the blood drain from her face. How could they be so close and still fail?

"Nobody's moving anyone anywhere," Captain Findley reassured them. "My team has control of the administrative offices where the only communication equipment is located. We've got helicopters patrolling the air space and teams around the perimeter. This place is sealed tight." He assigned several men to guard the helicopter and its pilot and then waved for everyone to follow Father Burnett to the administrative offices. While they walked, Findley radioed his search teams, ordering a suspension of activities for the moment.

Once they reached the building, Father Burnett asked if he could speak to Dane and Captain Findley alone. Savannah was surprised by the request but not really alarmed. The man lived on a primitive farm as if he was trying to turn back the hands of time, so antiquated feelings toward women were to be expected. She sat on a wooden bench near the door and watched as Dane and Captain Findley followed Father Burnett into an office at the back of the room. She tried not to be offended when they closed the door. *Anything for Caroline.*

A few minutes later the door opened, and Dane came out alone. He was holding a piece of paper and extended it to Savannah. "What can you tell me about this?" he asked.

Savannah unfolded the paper. It was a photocopy of a newspaper clipping, and the headline proclaimed, "Abusive Mother Receives Suspended Sentence." Savannah's eyes moved to the picture of a woman standing in front of the federal courthouse in Washington, DC. She gasped when she realized that the face in the photograph was her own.

"I would never hurt Caroline," she whispered. "This is a lie."

Dane rolled his eyes. "I know that. I've investigated you thoroughly. But what about the case mentioned in the article? Does it sound familiar? Did you work on it?"

She squinted at the picture, trying to remember. Finally she said, "Maybe the Wilcox case. The mother in it was found guilty of abuse." She looked up at Dane. "But how did my picture get here, and how did Father Burnett get it?" She pointed at the article.

"The kidnapper must have had the article expertly adjusted. The face of the actual abusive parent was removed and yours was inserted. Then they changed the names and other information to gain Father Burnett's cooperation."

"He thought he was protecting Caroline from me," Savannah said. "He was giving her asylum?"

Dane nodded. "That's the way he sees it. The kidnapper was smart. He hacked into the newspaper's website too, so when Father Burnett checked to be sure the photocopy was legitimate, he read the same thing there."

"But you've convinced him that it was a lie?"

Dane glanced at the closed door to Father Burnett's office. "He's talking to General Steele now. They're faxing over some things, and I think it will all be cleared up soon."

After what seemed like hours, the office door opened. Father Burnett and Captain Findley rejoined Savannah and Dane. She could tell from the devastated expression on Father Burnett's face that he now accepted her innocence.

"I don't know what to say to you," he said.

Savannah couldn't bring herself to absolve him of responsibility for all the misery she'd been through over the past two months, so she just asked, "Is Caroline okay?"

"She's fine," Father Burnett replied. "Thriving even."

Savannah's anger evaporated, and tears welled in her eyes.

"Can you have your pilot take me to her? Right away?" Savannah wanted to be insistent but knew her request sounded like a plea.

"Of course," Father Burnett agreed. "I'll arrange it immediately." He reached for his phone and spoke with the pilot. Then he turned back to them. "He says he can be ready in fifteen minutes."

Dane nodded. "Good, that gives you a few minutes to explain how you became involved in a kidnapping, which I don't have to tell you is a felony."

Father Burnett wrung his hands. "I'm not sure if I should say anything without a lawyer present."

"We're not trying to build a case against you or the farm," Savannah assured the man impatiently. "Just tell us what happened."

Father Burnett took a deep breath and began. "A couple of months ago a woman arrived at our gates late at night. She said that she was Caroline's foster mother and showed me several legal documents confirming this. She also showed me the newspaper articles and claimed that Mrs. McLaughlin was an abusive mother. She said that a good lawyer had gotten the charges against Mrs. McLaughlin dropped, and the child was supposed to be returned the next day. She was afraid for Caroline's life and begged us to allow the child to stay here with her grandparents until permanent arrangements could be made."

"Didn't Caroline contradict what the woman said?" Savannah demanded as the tears slipped onto her cheeks.

"Caroline was asleep in the backseat of the car," Father Burnett explained in obvious agitation. "The woman said she was exhausted from her trip across the country."

Savannah glanced at Dane. "They probably drugged her," he said.

At that point, Savannah lost all sympathy for Father Burnett and didn't even try to keep the anger from her voice when she asked,

"Didn't you question Caroline later? She would have told you the truth."

"I did meet with her," he said. "I wanted her to feel safe and welcome here, so I avoided questions about the abuse. Besides, children from abusive homes often repress their experiences, so I didn't see what I could accomplish by trying to make her discuss it."

Before Savannah could say more, Dane took over the questioning.

"Surely you realize this was not the legal way to handle the situation," he said.

"Of course," Father Burnett acknowledged. "But when the safety of a child is involved, legalities don't seem so important. The foster mother promised to make other arrangements soon. This was just to be a temporary safe harbor for the child. I know there's nothing I can say to take away your pain, but I am sorry."

Savannah nodded. "I just want to see my daughter."

"We'd better get on out to the helicopter." Dane stood. "Can you give us the name of the woman who pretended to be Caroline's foster mother?"

"She said her name was Mary Jacobs. She's about 5'4" tall, 140 pounds, short dark hair, and green eyes."

"The substitute teacher from Epic School?" Savannah asked Dane.

"Apparently." He stood and led her toward the door.

As they were about to leave, Savannah remembered Lacie. "My assistant, Lacie Fox, should be arriving here any minute. She was planning to ride the helicopter up to see the McLaughlins. Will you tell her that Dane and I have already taken care of things?"

Father Burnett nodded.

Captain Findley led the way outside while Dane and Savannah trailed a few feet behind. As they walked across the grass toward the helicopter pad, Dane whispered, "I think the good father is terrified that you're going to sue him and the farm."

"He might be right," she muttered.

"If you got a big settlement from the farm folks, you could repay General Steele for this operation."

Savannah shook her head. "There's no way I can repay General Steele. Ever."

Captain Findley motioned to one of his men guarding the helicopter and then told Dane and Savannah, "Corporal Knox will accompany you. He can keep an eye on the pilot, and if there's any trouble, he can fly the helicopter back."

Dane nodded. "Thanks."

The helicopter rotors roared into motion, sending gusts of dusty air billowing toward them and making conversation impossible. When they reached the door, the pilot leaned down to help Savannah climb in, and Captain Findley informed him about the additional passenger. The pilot didn't look pleased, but he didn't object, so Corporal Knox climbed in and took the copilot's seat. Dane swung up without assistance and secured the door. Then he took the seat beside Savannah.

"Fasten your seatbelts, and I'll have you there in no time," the pilot yelled over the sound of the motor.

And then the helicopter lifted off the ground.

CHAPTER 15

The helicopter ride was short and the view of the Rocky Mountains spectacular, but Savannah couldn't focus on anything except the hope that she was about to see her child again. The separation had been so long and grueling that it almost seemed like a malignant presence in her life. It was hard to imagine being free of it.

When the helicopter began its descent, Savannah peered through the thick windows and tried to catch sight of her daughter. The compound looked much as it had in the surveillance photographs, vague and out of focus. The pilot parked the helicopter on a concrete pad identical to the one at the farm headquarters. Then he turned and spoke to his passengers.

"I'll unload the supplies while you get your kid. I don't like to stay up here long because the winds are unpredictable, and we could get stranded."

Savannah nodded. She had no desire to spend much time on the mountain.

Dane looked at Corporal Knox. "You stay here with the helicopter, and don't trust the pilot. He's already gotten the best of one of your teammates."

"Yes, sir," Corporal Knox responded with a scowl in the pilot's direction. The pilot cut the engine and climbed out of the cockpit. After opening the door, he jumped to the ground, and Savannah looked outside.

Few moments in her life had been so profound that she knew the instant they happened that she'd never forget them. There was the moment she heard that Dane had died in Russia and the moment she learned that he was alive after all. And the moment Caroline was placed in her arms for the first time and the moment she realized that her child had been kidnapped. As Savannah looked through the helicopter's open door, she knew that this moment, too, was one she would never forget.

A few yards away, clutching the hand of a middle-aged woman who looked very much like Wes, stood Caroline. She seemed taller. Her hair was longer, and she was wearing an old-fashioned Amish-style dress. But her smile was just the same.

"Mama," she said, and Savannah thought her heart would break in to a million pieces.

"Don't cry," Dane warned sternly. "You'll scare her."

Savannah nodded and scrambled from the helicopter. Mrs. McLaughlin released Caroline's hand, and the little girl met her mother with open arms. Savannah knelt and caught Caroline to her chest. She wrapped her arms tightly around the child's warm body. It was the most exquisitely wonderful feeling she had ever experienced.

"You finally came!" Caroline's tone was mildly reproachful. "You were supposed to come here right after me!"

"About when you came here . . ." Savannah began, but Dane put a hand on her shoulder.

"Later," he said.

Savannah knew that Dane was right. Pressuring Caroline to answer questions now was unwise. They had been living completely separate lives for the past two months. Caroline would need time to incorporate Savannah into the present.

"I'm sorry I was late," Savannah said carefully. "But I'm here now, and I'm so anxious to hear all about what you've been doing."

"I've been helping Grandma and Grandpa," Caroline informed her proudly. "We had a garden, and we picked tomatoes and green beans and squash. Then we put them in jars and we eat them for dinner. Now the garden is over, but I help take care of the cows and pigs and chickens. Grandpa taught me how to fish, and Grandma lets me get the eggs from the henhouse every day. Our cat just had new kittens. When they're big enough, I'll get to hold them and pick out their names."

Savannah stared at her daughter in amazement. Caroline was happy and healthy. As a result of the imposed separation from her mother, Caroline had expanded her circle of loved ones to include the grandparents she'd never met. Only Savannah had suffered during the ordeal, and she was more convinced than ever that disc or no disc, the kidnapper's wrath was directed at her. While she was thankful that Caroline had been spared any ill effects, the thought that she had such a determined enemy was chilling.

Caroline looked up over her mother's shoulder at Dane. After studying him carefully for a few seconds, she asked, "Are you my father?"

The question took Savannah by surprise. Caroline had been young when her father died, but she had a few memories, and she'd seen pictures. "You know your father is dead," Savannah said gently. Then she glanced back at Dane, who didn't resemble Wes in any way. "And you know what he looked like."

Caroline continued her examination of Dane. "They are sort of the same though," she insisted.

Dane smiled at her. "Your father was my best friend. In fact, he was like my brother."

Caroline seemed pleased by this answer. Savannah's reaction was more conflicted. Happiness and sadness and regret combined and then threatened to overcome her with emotion. Tears spilled onto her cheeks, and Caroline pointed at them. "You're crying," she said.

"Happy tears," Savannah promised. And it was mostly true.

Caroline grabbed her hand and pulled. "Come on and meet Grandma and Grandpa."

Savannah stood and allowed herself to be led to the spot where Wes's parents waited. They watched her approach with suspicion and obvious animosity.

"This is my mom," Caroline introduced. "This is my grandma and grandpa."

Savannah nodded. "It's nice to meet you."

The McLaughlins just stared.

Dane stepped in front of Savannah and spoke to Wes's mother. "Hey, Mrs. McLaughlin."

"Hello, Christopher," she replied. She was tall and solemn. Her dress was similar to Caroline's, devoid of ornamentation or color.

Dane turned to Wes's father and extended his hand. "It's been awhile."

Like the other farm men, Wes's father was wearing coveralls. Like his wife and son, Mr. McLaughlin was tall and blond. When he was younger, before sadness had etched itself on his face, he had probably been very handsome. He didn't return Dane's greeting or shake his hand. He was too busy giving Savannah a look that could kill.

"There's been a misunderstanding," Dane told them as he allowed his hand to fall back to his side. "The information Father Burnett received was wrong. Savannah is a devoted mother and has never been accused of anything illegal. Since August she has been . . ." He paused to choose his words carefully. "Frantic."

The McLaughlins both looked equally unconvinced. For over two months they had thought the worst of her, and Savannah knew it would take some time for them to adjust their opinions. So she tried not to take their animosity personally.

Dane showed them the information that General Steele had faxed to the farm's administrative offices. "This is a copy of the original newspaper article that was doctored to make Savannah look guilty. I also have statements from the DC police department and the FBI showing that there have never been any charges against Savannah."

Wes's father accepted the copies, but he didn't even glance at them.

"I don't blame you for any of this," Savannah said, hoping to ease the tension and reassure them. But her words had the opposite affect. If possible, Wes's parents now looked less friendly.

"Blame them for what?" Caroline asked.

"Caroline," Dane addressed the child. "Why don't you show me your kittens while your mother talks to your grandparents?"

Caroline smiled up at him. "Okay." Then she turned to Savannah. "Don't you want to come too? We can look at them, but we can't hold them until they get their eyes open."

"I really want to see your kittens," Savannah said. And she really didn't want Caroline out of her sight, but she knew she had to talk privately with Wes's parents. And oddly, there was no one in the world she would have trusted with her daughter at that moment except Dane. "I'll join you in a minute," she promised.

This seemed to satisfy Caroline. She took Dane by the hand and pulled him toward the barn. As they walked away she heard Caroline ask, "Is Grandpa mad at Mama?"

Dane's voice rumbled in reply, but they were too far away for Savannah to make out the words. As they disappeared into the barn, Savannah squared her shoulders and addressed her in-laws. "I'm not an abusive mother. Caroline was kidnapped, and whoever took her made that story up to gain your cooperation. I understand that you were trying to protect Caroline." Savannah thought she was being very generous and expected Wes's parents to reciprocate.

Instead, Mrs. McLaughlin said, "But if she has nothing to fear from you, why would someone kidnap her and give her to us?"

"I don't know," Savannah admitted. "Apparently someone hates me. A lot. I'm just thankful to have her back."

Mr. McLaughlin obviously didn't believe a word she'd said. But his wife nodded. "Caroline is a darling girl. Having her here . . ." She had to pause and compose herself. "Well, it has been like heaven."

Mr. McLaughlin spoke for the first time, and Savannah was surprised by how much he sounded like Wes. "We love her."

Savannah nodded. "I can see that you do. And she loves you too."

"It's not right for you to just come and take her," he continued.

At this point Savannah lost her patience. "It wasn't right that someone took her from me in the first place. You've had two months with her that should have been mine. You'll have to be satisfied with that."

Savannah and Wes's father stared at each other for what seemed like a long time, neither one willing to break eye contact first. Finally Mrs. McLaughlin pointed toward the barn. "The helicopter will be ready to leave soon. She'll be disappointed if you don't meet her kittens. So you'd better go now."

Savannah was anxious to end this awkward conversation and more anxious to be with Caroline. So she accepted the opportunity of escape that Wes's mother had provided and hurried over to the barn. Caroline and Dane were sitting on the hay-covered floor, observing a cat and her four kittens. When Caroline saw her mother, she put a finger to her lips.

Savannah settled quietly beside them, drinking in the sight of her daughter and savoring every whispered word. "We don't know if they are boys or girls yet," Caroline explained. "Grandpa says we have to wait to tell until they are older. So I can't pick names."

"They're beautiful," Savannah said. "You'll have to be thinking of some really great names, so you'll be ready when you find out about the boys and girls."

"I'll be thinking," Caroline promised.

Dane stood and brushed the hay from his jeans. Then he waved for Savannah and Caroline to follow him. "It's time to go."

Caroline looked confused. "But I thought we were going to live here now."

"No," Savannah said gently as they walked toward the helicopter pad. "We have to go back to our house in Washington."

Caroline turned stricken eyes to Savannah. "But who will take care of the cows and pigs and chickens?" She ran ahead and grabbed her grandmother by the hand. "Who will name my kittens?"

Savannah glanced at Dane. She hadn't expected resistance from Caroline. "I thought she'd want to go home."

He put a hand on the small of Savannah's back and guided her forward. "This has been her home for the past two months," he reminded her unnecessarily. "Be glad she likes it."

When they were all assembled in an unfriendly little group, he said to Caroline, "Your grandparents will take care of your animals, just like they did before you came."

"You can send them a letter with names for the kittens," Savannah proposed. "And if your grandparents come to visit us in Washington, maybe they'll bring a kitten with them."

Caroline's face lit up. "Can I keep it in my room?"

Savannah laughed. "We'll have to see about that." Then she turned to Wes's parents. "You'll come soon, won't you?"

Mrs. McLaughlin shook her head. "That's impossible. We can't leave the mountain."

Savannah didn't know whether this inability to leave, even for a short time, was a rule imposed by the Brotherly Love Farm or if emotional scars kept them imprisoned. But she nodded, accepting that the McLaughlins were destined to be permanent residents of the mountain compound.

She saw how they watched every move Caroline made, and Savannah's happiness at having her daughter back was clouded by the knowledge that Wes's parents were going to grieve when the child left.

With love came pain, a lesson the McLaughlins had been taught many times over.

Savannah reached a decision suddenly and spoke before she could talk herself out of it. "If you can't come to us, we'll visit you."

Dane looked surprised, but Caroline was thrilled. "Can we come back tomorrow?"

"Not tomorrow, but before too long." Savannah was beset by doubt. "That is, if your grandparents will have us."

Mrs. McLaughlin actually smiled. "We'd love to have you."

"Thanksgiving is coming up soon. That's a good holiday to spend with family," Savannah suggested.

"Yes," Wes's mother said. "Please come then."

The pilot started the motor of the helicopter, and Dane waved toward it. "Time to go."

Caroline's eyes filled with panic. "I won't have time to pack my stuff?"

"Why don't you just leave it here," Savannah suggested. "You'll need it when we come in a few weeks. Now hug your grandparents before the helicopter leaves without us."

Caroline embraced each of her grandparents enthusiastically. "I'll be back soon!" she promised. "Take good care of my kittens!"

Then she allowed Savannah to put her into the helicopter. Dane took the seat near the far window, and Savannah strapped Caroline into the seat between them. As the helicopter lifted off the ground, Savannah looked down and saw Wes's parents. Two broken people saying good-bye to another child.

Savannah turned away from the window, refusing to let this moment be a sad one. She smoothed back several blonde strands from her daughter's face. "Your hair is so long," she said.

Caroline shrugged. "Grandma never worried about haircuts or clothes or stuff like that. When it was warmer, I didn't even have to wear shoes, and she let me take a bath in the lake."

Savannah smiled. "That sounds fun." She looked up and saw Dane watching her. "I still can't believe it's real," she told him. "I keep thinking I'm going to wake up and find out it was all a dream."

"Do you want me to pinch you?" he offered.

"Thanks anyway." She leaned down and pressed a kiss to the child's cheek.

"I hope Grandma and Grandpa will be okay," Caroline said as a frown creased her brow. "They need me pretty much."

"I'm sure they'll be fine," Savannah said.

"And I'll be coming back soon," Caroline reminded her.

"Yes, for Thanksgiving," Savannah promised, trying to fight the jealousy she felt.

"You've had her to yourself for too long," Dane said softly. "Most parents have to share their child's affection with at least another parent. This is healthier."

She raised an eyebrow. "Now you're an expert on parenting?"

He shrugged. "I've talked to enough psychiatrists. I think I'm qualified to give advice."

She looked down at Caroline, who was watching the mountain disappear below them. "I just wanted her to be as happy to see me as I am to see her."

He shook his head. "You always did have impossible expectations."

She smiled. "Who can look at Caroline and *not* believe in fairy tales."

Dane studied the child for a few seconds and then said, "She is pretty miraculous. You've dealt with enough kidnapping cases to know how fortunate you are."

She stroked Caroline's soft velvet cheek. "Yes," she whispered. "I'm very fortunate."

When they approached the field near the farm's administrative building, Savannah shuddered at the sight of the shed where they had been held captive. Even though the farm people had been much more cooperative since Dane convinced them of her innocence, she knew she wouldn't feel completely safe until they were off the property.

The helicopter hovered momentarily over the small concrete pad and then descended with caution. Savannah watched as the strong wind created by the propellers flattened the brown grass and pulled at the clothes of their welcoming party. Most of the Army vehicles were gone. Captain Findley and a few of his men were waiting with Father Burnett by the shed, but Lacie was nowhere in sight.

Father Burnett waited until the pilot cut the engine and then moved forward to greet them as they climbed out of the helicopter. Caroline seemed happy to see him.

"I'm leaving with my mom," she told him. "But I'll be back soon."

"You're welcome here anytime," Father Burnett assured her.

Captain Findley introduced himself to Caroline and then raised an eyebrow at Dane. "Mission accomplished?"

Dane nodded. "We can't thank you enough for your help."

Captain Findley looked down at Caroline. "It was a pleasure. Now we'll drive you folks back to your car and let you get on your way."

"Thank you," Dane replied.

"Did Lacie leave already?" Savannah asked Father Burnett, although this seemed unfathomable. Surely Lacie would want to be here for the happy reunion.

"We haven't seen your friend," Father Burnett replied.

Savannah checked her watch. It was ten-thirty, a half-hour past the scheduled time for the helicopter to depart, and Lacie had said she'd be there early. "Are you sure?" she pressed Father Burnett. "Lacie's short, with," she had to stop and think, "orange hair. She was here a couple of days ago. She took a tour of the farm, and you offered to let her ride the helicopter up to the mountain today."

Father Burnett shook his head. "We don't give tours of the farm, and I haven't met with anyone from the outside in more than a week."

Savannah was so stunned by the information that she couldn't process it. She turned to Dane and managed, "If Lacie didn't come here, where did she go? And why did she lie to us?"

"Lacie lied to me, too," Caroline informed them, and all eyes turned to the child.

"When did Lacie lie to you?" Dane asked. Both his expression and his tone were grave.

"When she picked me up at school that last day," Caroline reported as a matter-of-fact.

All the air left Savannah's lungs, and she was afraid she would collapse. Dane's arm reached out automatically to steady her. "Lacie picked you up at school that last day?" she gasped.

Caroline nodded. "Her and another lady who looked just like you. Lacie said she was an actress who was helping you with a commercial."

Dane knelt down in front of Caroline. "What else did Lacie say?"

"She said we were going to visit my grandparents in the mountains, but my mom couldn't come right now. She said for me to go, and she'd bring my mom later, but she didn't."

Savannah tried to keep her voice even as she said, "Caroline, I would never send you on a trip with someone else. We'd wait and leave together."

A frown creased Caroline's forehead. "I thought that," she admitted. "But Lacie said it was okay, and since my teacher was taking me, I decided I could go. Since you always tell me to mind my teacher."

"Your substitute teacher?" Dane asked.

"Yes. Her name was Miss Jacobs. She was our teacher because Mrs. Matthews was sick that day. Miss Jacobs brought me to my grandparents."

"I can't believe it." Savannah looked at Dane, numb with shock. "Lacie betrayed me, *too*?"

"I'm sorry we don't live in a fairy tale world," Dane replied.

This made her mad, as she was sure he intended. "I don't think it's unreasonable to believe that you can trust your friends."

Dane shrugged one shoulder. "Then you need to look back over the past few days. Trusting people is foolish, Savannah, and there's no such thing as a friend."

They stared angrily at each other for a few seconds, and then Caroline asked, "Did I do something wrong?"

Savannah dragged her gaze from Dane. "No. But Lacie and Miss Jacobs did. They took you away from me without permission. I haven't been able to find you."

Caroline's eyes widened. "I've been lost?"

Savannah smiled. "Well, sort of. But I've found you now, and I'm going to take you home." She wanted to lift the child into her arms but knew Caroline would resist the baby treatment. So she settled for taking one soft little hand in hers.

Dane turned to Captain Findley, who had been watching everything from a polite distance, and said, "We're ready for that ride now."

CHAPTER 16

Dane waited until they had transferred from the Army Jeep into their borrowed car before calling Hack. Savannah was grateful for Hack's booming voice, which allowed her to listen to both sides of the conversation. After reporting that Caroline had been successfully rescued, Dane asked about Doc, whose condition was unchanged. Then he told Hack about Lacie's perfidy and asked him to investigate her.

"What kind of information are you looking for?" Hack wanted to know.

"Ideally her whereabouts," Dane replied with a touch of sarcasm. "But anything will be helpful. Where's Cam?"

"He went in to Fredericksburg to get us some food. Without Savannah here to cook for us, we're starving."

Dane asked Hack to notify the police and FBI that Caroline had been located. "Call General Steele and anyone else you can think of who should be told before the press gets wind of it."

"So did the rescue go smooth?" Hack asked.

Dane glanced into the seat where Caroline was nestled beside Savannah. "We've got her, and that's what counts."

A few miles outside of Denver, Dane stopped for gas. Then he parked in front of a department store and suggested that Savannah might want to buy Caroline some new clothes. Savannah looked at the child dressed for a different time and place, and she nodded. "I think that would be a good idea."

Caroline seemed confused by the suggestion. "But this is my favorite dress."

Savannah reached down and tucked a lock of blonde hair behind Caroline's ear. "It's a very nice dress, and we want to take good care of it so you can wear it again when we visit your grandparents. But when you're off the farm you need to wear the things you used to wear at home, like jeans and T-shirts."

Caroline considered this for a few seconds and finally nodded. "But we'll save my dress?"

"Yes," Savannah promised.

Once they got in the store, Caroline enjoyed the shopping process. After they made their purchases, Savannah helped her change in the dressing room. When they walked out, with the farm dress folded neatly in a sack, Savannah felt like she really had her daughter back.

By the time they arrived at the airport, everyone was starving. They purchased three nonstop tickets to Dulles International that left in an hour, and then Dane led them into a restaurant near their departing gate. When the waitress came and gave them menus, Savannah started to order for Caroline. She realized that she wasn't sure what her daughter would like to eat. It was unnerving not knowing her own child.

She showed Caroline her choices, and she picked chicken fingers. After the waitress left to turn in their orders, Caroline frowned. "Are chicken fingers made from real chickens like mine?"

"Yes," Dane confirmed.

"I wouldn't want to eat any of my chickens," Caroline said.

"No," Dane agreed. "Anonymous donors are much better."

While they waited for their food, Dane asked Caroline if she could tell him about the day she left school with Lacie.

Caroline looked at her mother. "I'm sorry about that. I didn't know I wasn't supposed to."

"I know," Savannah assured her. "But we're going to be extra careful from now on."

"Okay."

"So Lacie and the lady who looked just like your mom picked you up at the school," Dane prompted.

"Yes," Caroline confirmed. "Lacie said we were taking a trip to see my grandparents in Colorado. I was glad about that." She looked at

Savannah. "But I thought you were coming with us. Then the car stopped and Lacie got out. She said she had to go back to work, but Miss Jacobs was going to take me to my grandparents. I was a little scared that you weren't there but not much because it was my teacher."

"Of course," Savannah agreed.

"I don't remember too much more. Grandma said I flew on an airplane, but I was asleep."

"Your grandparents took very good care of you," Savannah commended.

"Yes. At first they were real quiet. Father Burnett said they were scared that they didn't know how to take care of a little girl. But they learned."

Savannah smiled.

"I missed you, though," Caroline confided. "I wanted to call you, but they didn't have a phone."

Savannah's heart ached, but she simply said, "I missed you more than I can ever say."

Caroline frowned. "I wonder why Lacie tricked us. I thought she was our friend."

"I don't know why she tricked us." Savannah glanced at Dane. "But sometimes even friends make mistakes."

"It makes me sad," Caroline said.

Savannah nodded. "It makes me sad too."

The waitress arrived and distributed their food. All conversation was suspended for a few minutes while they ate. When their flight was called, Dane asked for the check and hurried them to the gate. Since their seats were in first class they boarded first. Caroline took the window seat, and Savannah sat beside her. Dane was across the aisle from Savannah.

The stewardess made a fuss over Caroline, telling her how pretty she was and offering to give her a tour of the cockpit. Two months before, Savannah would have agreed without a second thought. Now she didn't trust other people or her own judgment. She looked to Dane, silently requesting his opinion.

"I think that would be fine," he said softly. "She'll only be a few feet away."

Savannah nodded her permission to the stewardess but added a condition. "Please just make sure we can see her at all times."

The stewardess looked mildly offended, but Savannah didn't care.

"Overprotective mother," Dane whispered to the stewardess with a charming smile.

She smiled back and took Caroline by the hand.

Once they were out of earshot, Dane pulled out his cell phone. "I'm going to check in with Cam to see if he's making any progress on his assignments."

"Why are you continuing the investigation?" Savannah asked. "I've got Caroline. That's enough for me."

Dane leaned across the aisle so that his face was almost touching hers. "Well, it's not enough for me. Somebody used the people closest to you to steal your daughter. If it's the disc they want, your daughter is still in danger. You too for that matter."

"Do you think I'll ever let Caroline out of my sight?" she hissed back, keeping her eyes glued to her daughter and the stewardess. "And I can take care of myself!"

"That's no way to live!" he countered. "Always looking over your shoulder. And it's not fair to Caroline. Don't you want her to be able to go to school and birthday parties and ball games and college?"

Savannah had to admit that even though Caroline was back in her possession, the threat to her safety still existed. "I'll just mail Ferrante the disc, and then maybe he'll leave us alone."

"You can't do that," Dane returned. "That disc is proof of criminal activity. It has to be turned over to the Army so the guilty parties can be prosecuted."

"I'm more concerned with Caroline's safety than with justice," she admitted.

Dane looked disappointed. "Giving the disc to Ferrante wouldn't work anyway. You know what's on the disc, so if he's trying to keep its contents secret, he'd be forced to kill you. The only way to protect you is to make secrecy impossible."

"So if we can get the disc and give it to General Steele, Ferrante will leave me alone?"

"You'll need to be very careful for a while," Dane insisted. "But I think so."

"If you find Lacie, will you turn her over to the authorities?"

"Of course," Dane replied. "She's a criminal."

"I don't want to help the police hunt down Lacie," Savannah said. "No matter what you think, friendship does exist. I don't know how Lacie got involved with the kidnapper, but I feel sure that she did all she could to safeguard Caroline. Like you said, most kidnap victims aren't nearly as lucky."

Dane shook his head in frustration. "I don't understand you."

She accepted this. She didn't understand him either.

"The investigation continues," he decreed. "It's not up to you."

"It began with me," she pointed out.

"But General Steele pays the bills," he reminded her. "You don't have to work with the team, but we won't abandon the search until we find the disc and identify everyone involved in the kidnapping."

Savannah nodded in acceptance, since it was obvious she couldn't change his mind. And in one way, Dane's insistence that they continue their investigation was a relief. She was dreading the day she had to leave his cabin, because she knew that the chances of seeing him again were negligible. And she knew saying good-bye was going to be painful.

"Okay," she said. "What do we do now?"

"We go back to the cabin," Dane said. "We keep trying to find the photographer and secure the disc. Once we have it, we review its contents and figure out who was behind all this."

While Dane made his phone call, the stewardess returned Caroline, and Savannah belted her securely to the seat.

During takeoff, Caroline giggled. "It kind of feels like riding in an elevator."

Savannah smiled. "It kind of does."

"How long will it be before we're home?"

"Actually, we're not going home right away." Savannah had to control a shudder at the thought of the row house that had been invaded by their enemy. "Dane has invited us to stay at his cabin for a while. It's pretty nice. I think you'll like it."

Caroline leaned around her mother and asked Dane, "Do you have kittens?"

He shook his head. "No, but there's a creek and a really great bridge that I built myself."

"It's a terrible bridge!" Savannah corrected. "And my daughter isn't going anywhere near it."

Caroline seemed delighted by this exchange. "Oh please, Mom, can I walk on it? I love bridges."

Savannah couldn't deny Caroline anything, so she relented. "Okay, but only when I'm with you."

"Does your creek have fish?" Caroline wanted to know.

Dane nodded.

"Will you take me fishing like my grandpa?"

"Yes, I like to fish, but I have to warn you, I'm not very good."

Savannah was amazed. "You're admitting a flaw?"

"It's more of a time allocation deficit," he corrected. "All my specialized training didn't leave room for hobbies."

"Well, it's a good thing Caroline had a grandfather who took the time to be a good fisherman."

Caroline laughed. "Grandpa's not a good fisherman! I'm the one who always catches the fish. Then he trades me fishing poles because he says mine is luckier!"

Savannah felt a new pang of sorrow for the McLaughlins as she ruffled Caroline's hair.

"How long are we going to stay at Mr. Dane's cabin? Am I going back to school?"

"It's Major Dane," Savannah corrected. "And I'm not sure how long we'll stay there."

Caroline leaned around Savannah again. "Are you going to marry my mother?" she asked inexplicably.

This caught Savannah by surprise, and she couldn't think of an appropriately lighthearted response. So she let Dane field the question. Apparently he couldn't come up with a sarcastic quip either, because he answered with a single, emphatic word. "No."

Tears burned Savannah's eyes. It wasn't his answer that hurt her. She knew Dane didn't want to marry her. But his tone was so cold, so final.

The stewardess stepped between them at that moment, and Savannah was grateful for the temporary separation that prevented Dane from seeing the distress his response had caused her.

Caroline watched intently as the stewardess demonstrated how to use the oxygen masks and how to turn the seat cushion into a flotation device. Then the stewardess gave Caroline a blanket, a pillow, and a set of headphones in preparation for the in-flight movie.

Savannah thanked the stewardess and adjusted the earphones to fit Caroline's small head. While she was tucking the blanket carefully around Caroline's shoulders, she heard Dane's cell phone ring. He answered it in flagrant violation of airline regulations but ended the conversation quickly.

"Who called?" she asked.

He glanced over irritably as if she had interrupted some deep thought. "Hack."

"And?" she prompted.

"Doc's the same. Lacie's disappeared, but they found her sick mother in a pricey assisted-living facility in Maryland. It has round-the-clock nursing care, and she's receiving biweekly treatments for her leukemia that Medicare considers experimental and won't pay for."

"How is Lacie's mother paying for them?"

Dane shrugged. "Money just materialized in Lacie's checking account a couple of months ago."

"About the time Caroline was kidnapped?"

"Exactly that time."

"Lacie told me her mother was doing better, that they were trying some new treatments. But it never occurred to me . . ."

"Of course not, because you believe in friendship."

She nodded. "And fairy tales." After a few minutes of consideration, she said, "If Lacie's mother was sick, dying even, she must have been desperate. Then the kidnapper offered her the money she needed to save her mother's life, and she did what she thought she had to do."

"It was still wrong," Dane pointed out.

"Of course it was," Savannah agreed impatiently. "I'm not arguing in favor of crime as a way to supplement income! I'm just saying that sometimes people are forced to choose between those they love, and it's a terrible thing."

He looked at her for several painful seconds. Then he said, "I guess I'll have to defer to you there, since you're the one with all the experience."

She sighed, determined not to fight. "Does our knowledge that Lacie was involved help us identify the kidnapper?"

Dane rubbed the stubble on his jaw. "I'm not sure. We now know that our kidnapper has large amounts of money at his disposal, in addition to a connection with organized crime and access to the latest technology. Forton and Ferrante both fit the criteria."

"So you still think it was Doug?"

Dane shrugged. "He would have known about Lacie's mother and her medical problems. He knew your schedule and would have been able to manipulate circumstances to facilitate the kidnapping."

Savannah sensed his lack of conviction. "You're not convinced it was him. You know Doug wasn't mean enough for a scheme like this."

Dane looked a little surprised by her remark. "I know Forton wasn't *smart* enough for a scheme like this. He isn't a computer genius, and while he could have hired someone who was, the whole plan was hinged on the ability to break into various secure computer systems. That points to a kidnapper who is a hacker at heart. Another annoying problem with Forton is motive. He was in love with you and hadn't been able to interest you in a romantic relationship. Kidnapping your daughter wouldn't help him there."

"No," Savannah agreed. "Unless . . ."

"What?"

"Well, I told you that when Doug asked me out, I frequently used Caroline as an excuse."

Dane frowned. "You think he removed Caroline from the picture so you'd go out with him."

"I know it sounds crazy."

"I find it hard to believe that a successful businessman like Forton, with money and prestige and even a fair amount of political power, would risk it all for a date with you—even back when you used to look better than you do now."

"That's an old joke."

"Who's kidding?"

She smirked. "What I'm saying is that whoever kidnapped Caroline was very careful to arrange a safe, healthy environment for her." Savannah glanced at her daughter. "She didn't really suffer at all."

"We've established that," Dane acknowledged.

"Many aspects of the kidnapping show cold calculation," she said. "But when it came to Caroline, the kidnapper was more than careful. He was *kind!*"

"Which means . . . ?"

"He could have hurt her, but he didn't. In fact, he went to great lengths to protect not only her safety, but also her happiness."

"You're repeating yourself but not making a point."

"I know you're very attached to your theory about the Nicaraguan disc." She took a deep breath and forced herself to continue. "And maybe you're right. But to me the whole thing feels *personal*." She met his eyes bravely. "I think that the kidnapper is someone who both loves *and* hates me."

She expected Dane to scoff, but instead he asked, "Did Forton hate you?"

"He hated rejection."

Dane nodded. "And you rejected him frequently."

"He was used to getting what he wanted," she added.

"Which you denied him," Dane said. "You make a convincing argument." He examined her through narrowed eyes. "I guess it's not inconceivable that a man would break the law for you."

She gave him a bland look. "Was that a compliment?"

"Yes," he said. And then he smiled.

Her heart constricted, and her face felt hot. She turned away, hoping he wouldn't be able to see the effect he had on her. "So you think it was Doug?"

"No." He waited until she turned back to face him before saying, "The final and most compelling problem I have with Forton as the kidnapper is that he's dead. That indicates to me that there's somebody else running the show. When Forton was no longer useful, he was killed and put in a dumpster in Haiti."

Savannah was disappointed. As bad as it was to think that Doug had inflicted this misery on her, not knowing who did it was worse.

"I think Forton was a pawn, like Lacie and the substitute teacher and Father Burnett and the McLaughlins. I think you were probably right when you gave Lacie credit for protecting Caroline. Forton might have aided in that area as well. Or as he claimed, he might not have known he was helping a 'friend' commit a heinous crime against you."

"Ferrante," Savannah whispered. "You think he was behind the whole thing?"

Dane sighed. "I know Ferrante orchestrated most of the kidnapping, but since I can't find any reason he'd be interested in the disc or you or Wes, I have to think that he was acting on behalf of a client."

She twisted toward him in her relatively spacious airplane seat. "So you're saying we're right back at square one? We don't know any more than we did before?"

"We know a lot more," Dane disagreed.

"Just not who arranged to have my daughter kidnapped," she said in frustration.

"Let's focus on the things we do know," Dane suggested. "On the day of the kidnapping, Lacie left the television studio right after you and went to Epic School."

"Riding in a car like mine driven by my identical twin," Savannah contributed.

"Since she knew there was going to be a crash at the intersection right in front of the school, she approached from the other direction. And by the way, the look-alike didn't have to be as close to you in appearance as we previously believed, since the sub was part of the plot and Lacie was in the car to entice Caroline inside."

Savannah nodded. "She just had to be blonde."

"And beautiful," he added.

She cut her eyes over at him.

"No compliment intended this time. I was just stating facts."

"And during the kidnapping, Doug was at the CAC," Savannah said. "He knew that I was driving to the school to get my daughter and what it would do to me when I found out she'd been kidnapped."

Dane nodded. "And thinking about all the opportunities he would have to comfort and console you."

Savannah was hurt by Lacie's betrayal, but she knew how it felt to be desperate about a loved one. So she could excuse Lacie's actions to some extent. Doug was another matter. He'd been her friend, he'd been her mentor, and he had claimed to love her. The thought that he would destroy her life for selfish reasons was very painful.

"You've made some good points," he conceded. "And you could even be right. The disc may not be the reason behind Caroline's kidnapping."

Savannah felt warm with happiness. Having Dane's respect was almost as good as having his affection. Almost. "So where do we go from here?"

"We continue the investigation following all possibilities rather than limiting ourselves to my pet theory."

"The disc could be the motive," she offered in an effort to be fair. "In which case *you* would be right."

He smiled. "I often am."

She turned to look at Caroline, who was snuggled under the airline blanket watching the movie. It was hard to dwell on the negative with her child beside her safe and sound.

"Honestly, I don't care who is right or who is wrong or if we ever figure it all out," she admitted. "I'm just glad to have Caroline back."

* * *

When they arrived at Dulles, Hack was there to meet them. He bent down so that he was on Caroline's eye level and said, "Hello, little lady. It's nice to finally meet you."

"You have gold teeth," Caroline replied.

Hack stretched his lips into a grin so she could get a better look. "Just two," he said. "I got them for my birthday. Do you like them?"

"They're very shiny." Caroline looked up at Savannah. "Can I have gold teeth for my birthday?"

Savannah smiled. "We'll have to see about that."

Caroline seemed satisfied with this and turned back to Hack. "My name is Caroline."

"My name is Harold," he reciprocated. "But my friends call me Hack."

"Am I your friend?" Caroline asked.

Hack nodded. "You are if you want to be."

"Okay." Apparently the subject was settled in Caroline's mind as well. She reached out and took one of Hack's huge hands in hers.

"My mom says we're going to Major Dane's house, and he's going to take me fishing, but he doesn't have any kittens."

Hack glanced up at Dane and then said, "No, he's not much of a kitten kind of guy."

Dane smirked at Hack. "When you're through playing Romper Room, we need to get back to the cabin. We still have a kidnapper to catch."

Hack stood and led them outside where his bright yellow Hummer was parked illegally against the curb. He helped Caroline into the backseat and then held the door for Savannah while Dane settled himself in the front passenger seat. Once they were moving, Dane asked, "Where's Cam?"

"He's with Doc," Hack reported.

Dane secured his seat belt. "I thought you were going to use your men to guard him."

"I've got a guard on his door round the clock," Hack replied. "Cam's just there visiting."

Savannah leaned over the seat and asked, "Can we go by and see Doc?"

Hack glanced at Dane, who nodded his permission. "Hold on to your hats," the big man advised. "This thing can really fly."

CHAPTER 17

As they drove at breakneck speed toward the hospital, Savannah entertained Caroline by pointing out Washington, DC landmarks. The men were talking in hushed tones, which Savannah knew was intended to keep Caroline from knowing the more disturbing aspects of the past few hours. But she hated being left out of the loop herself.

When they arrived, Hack double-parked the huge vehicle in the emergency parking zone and then opened the door for the ladies. "Was that the quickest, smoothest ride you've ever had?" he asked.

"It was the most terrifying," Savannah managed.

Hack smiled, flashing his gold teeth. "That's even better."

Savannah gestured toward the illegally parked Hummer. "Doesn't anyone ever give you a ticket?"

Hack seemed astonished by the question. "Who would dare?" he demanded.

"You've got a point," Savannah had to admit.

They walked into the hospital, and once they were on the elevator, Caroline asked, "Why are we visiting a doctor at the hospital?"

"We're visiting a man called 'Doc,' but he's not really a doctor," Savannah explained. "He's a friend of Major Dane's and Hack's."

"Was he my daddy's friend too?" Caroline asked.

Savannah carefully kept her eyes averted from the others as she answered with a firm, "Yes."

"Is he sick or does he work here?" Caroline further inquired.

"He's sick," Savannah told her.

Cam was in the visitor's waiting room when they arrived. After he was introduced to Caroline, Dane asked, "What's the story on Doc?"

"The doctors don't know why he's not waking up," Cam reported. "The drugs have had time to work out of his system, and they said he should be showing some improvement by now. It may be brain damage. Or it could be emotional trauma." Cam shrugged. "They said we'll just have to wait and see."

"Since Doc was so fragile to begin with, his reaction to the drugs was probably worse," Savannah remarked. "So it might take longer for him to recover."

"I hate waiting." Dane scowled. "Is he allowed to have visitors?"

"They've been letting me go in every half hour for a short visit." Cam checked his watch. "It's time now."

Dane started down the hall with Savannah and Caroline right behind him. "What's his room number?" he called out.

Cam grinned. "You can't miss it. It's the room with a *giant* standing guard."

When they reached Doc's room, Savannah realized that Hack had very specific employment requirements. All his men had to be huge, strong, and scary.

Caroline shrunk against her mother as they passed the guard. "Why is that man mean?"

"He's not really mean," Dane explained. "It's just his job to look mean."

"I wouldn't want to have that job," Caroline said as she peeked anxiously back at the guard.

Savannah led her daughter up to the hospital bed where Doc lay looking pale and ill.

"Hey, Doc," Savannah greeted, fighting tears. "I've come to visit you, and I brought my daughter, Caroline." Savannah lifted the little girl up and sat her on the edge of the bed. "We got her back safe and sound—just like you promised."

Caroline reached over and patted Doc's limp hand. "I'm sorry you're sick," she said. "I hope you feel better soon so you can go fishing with me and Major Dane. We're friends now, and Hack and Cam too. You can be my friend if you want, when you wake up. I have kittens, but they don't have names yet or their eyes open."

Cam stepped into the room and motioned for Dane to join him by the door. Savannah didn't want to be excluded from the exchange of more information, so she whispered to Caroline. "Come stand over here with me for a minute."

Caroline frowned. "Can't I stay right here by Doc so he won't be lonely? Please. Just until it's time for us to go?"

Savannah was torn between Caroline's concern for Doc and the need to know what was going on in the investigation. Finally she compromised by lifting Caroline and placing her on the floor. "Stand here so I don't have to worry about you falling off the bed." Then she walked over to the door where the conversation was already in progress.

"Did the police come up with any prints from Doc's apartment?" Dane was asking.

Cam shook his head. "Nothing."

"Did they check his car?" Dane asked.

"Yeah," Cam confirmed. "No unexplained fingerprints there either, but they did find a picture."

Savannah moved a little closer to the men, but kept her eyes on Caroline. "Was it a picture of the substitute teacher?"

Cam shook his head. "Naw, it was a blowup of a section of that surveillance photo. The description on the back had been updated from *miscellaneous livestock* to *unidentified child*." Cam smiled at her. "You were right. It wasn't a goat."

Savannah couldn't share in his joke. She shifted her gaze to study Doc. He had risked his life to bring them a picture that told them something they'd already discovered. Her heart was heavy with sadness and guilt. When she'd asked Dane to help her, she hadn't realized how much she was asking. "I've put you all in danger," she said.

"Don't worry," Cam consoled her. "Doc was our weakest link. The rest of us can take care of ourselves."

Dane grimaced, and Savannah guessed that he felt partially responsible for Doc's condition as well.

"Have you heard from General Steele about the file on Nick at Night?" Dane asked Cam.

The other man shook his head. "No, the general says he's beginning to wonder if it's been shredded."

"Who would do that?" Savannah asked.

"Someone on Ferrante's payroll," Dane replied grimly.

"He's got people in the Army too?" Savannah was aghast.

Cam nodded. "He's got people everywhere."

"Well, it's been a very long day. We'd better get Caroline on out to the cabin," Dane said. "Are you staying here, Cam?"

"I'm going to do a couple of follow-up visits on some of Savannah's former Child Advocacy Center clients," he said. "I don't think they were involved in the kidnapping, but I know how you like to eliminate every possibility."

Dane nodded. "For Savannah's peace of mind, take Hack with you. I'll drive his Hummer and see you both back at the cabin later."

Cam glanced at Savannah and then did his exaggerated salute, "Yes, *sir*!"

Savannah held out her hand to Caroline. "Major Dane is ready to go."

Caroline smiled and joined them by the door. "Don't worry about Doc," she said to Dane. "He's going to be okay."

Dane raised an eyebrow. "How do you know?"

"Because he squeezed my hand," Caroline informed them.

"Probably a muscle spasm," Cam contributed. "Happens sometimes even with people who are brain-dead."

"Doc's brain isn't dead," Caroline was positive.

Dane didn't look nearly so optimistic, but he smiled at Caroline and said, "Then we'll consider the hand squeeze a good sign."

Dane stopped by the waiting room to get Hack's keys and then led the way out to the Hummer. When they reached the cabin, Dane insisted that the girls wait in the vehicle with the doors locked while he checked out things inside.

"If I don't come back, you drive out of here quick."

Savannah nodded but prayed she wouldn't have to choose between his safety and Caroline's. Then she watched him climb the steps onto the back porch and disappear inside. A few minutes later he came out and waved for them to come in.

"All safe and sound?" Savannah asked as they entered the kitchen.

"As far as I can tell," he confirmed. Then he addressed Caroline. "Do you like hot chocolate?"

The child nodded.

"It's my specialty," Dane informed her. Then he glanced up at Savannah. "Among other things."

Savannah ignored him.

Caroline looked perplexed. "Is it hard to make good hot chocolate? Don't you just heat up water and mix in the chocolate?"

He raised his eyebrows. "Sit, watch, and learn."

Caroline climbed into a kitchen chair and scrutinized every move Dane made as if there really was a right way to make good hot chocolate. When he placed the three matching mugs on the table, Caroline pulled one toward her and sipped from it carefully. "Delicious," she pronounced, and Savannah could see that Dane was pleased. Then Caroline asked, "Do you have doughnuts?"

Dane frowned. "I don't think so."

This seemed to puzzle Caroline. "How can you have hot chocolate and not doughnuts? They go together."

Savannah opened the ancient refrigerator and pulled out a bakery sack. "One doughnut!" she announced. Then she handed it to her daughter. Caroline immediately tore the doughnut into three equal pieces and then extended a portion to Dane and Savannah. Dane hesitated, and Savannah wasn't sure if he was concerned about the unhygienic nature of the transaction or if he was afraid that by accepting the gift he would be obligating himself in some way. Finally, he reached out and took the doughnut fragment from Caroline's sticky fingers.

Caroline tossed the small piece she'd kept for herself into her mouth and then took another sip of hot chocolate. "Try it together," she said with her mouth full. "It's so good!"

Laughing, Savannah ate her own doughnut bit and took a sip of hot chocolate from one of the mugs Dane had placed on the table. "It *is* good," she assured him.

With a sigh, he put the doughnut into his mouth and swigged some hot chocolate. Then a smile lit his face. "It's delicious," he admitted.

The child nodded in satisfaction. "I told you."

They sat around the table, sipping hot chocolate and discussing their plans for the next day almost like a family. Almost.

Caroline said she wanted to write her grandparents a letter and ask how the kittens were doing.

"And we need to go to our house," Savannah said. "Since Caroline doesn't have any clothes."

"Or toys," Caroline pointed out.

Savannah smiled. "That too."

Dane stood. "The first order of business is to get the two of you settled in the guest room."

Savannah was surprised, both that he had a guest room and that he was willing to let them use it.

He led them to a closed door on the second floor directly across from his room. He opened the door, and Caroline ran inside. Savannah paused beside him in the doorway. They were very close as she whispered, "What if you have a nightmare?"

His breath stirred the hair around her ear when he replied, "I'll have to make sure that doesn't happen."

She forced herself to concentrate on his words and ignore his proximity. "How?"

"I won't sleep."

She glanced up quickly and caught a small smile on his lips. Then he walked around her and joined Caroline in the bedroom.

Savannah surveyed the room from the doorway. It was bigger than she had expected, with two twin beds, a mirrored dresser, and a rocking chair. There were lace curtains on the windows and antique-looking quilts on the beds.

"This is the best room in the house," Dane informed them. "It has a great view of the creek."

"If it's the best, why don't you sleep here?" Caroline asked logically.

Dane gave her a quizzical look. "That's a good question. You must have inherited your father's analytical personality."

Caroline plopped down on the twin bed closest to the window. "My mom says I inherited my dad's eyes."

"You look just like him," Dane confirmed.

"He was handsome," Caroline notified him.

"That's what he always told me."

"And he was almost your brother," Caroline added.

Dane nodded solemnly. "Yes."

Seeing them together, talking about Wes was almost too much. Savannah pressed a finger to her lips to keep them from trembling.

"So why do you?" Caroline asked.

Dane frowned. "Do what?"

"Sleep somewhere else if this is the best room?"

Dane glanced at the window. "Because it catches the morning sunlight, and I like to sleep late."

This seemed unlikely to Savannah, but she didn't think it wise to contradict him.

Caroline accepted the explanation readily. "Me and my mom get up early, so it will be okay." She twisted to look out the window. "Is that your bridge?" She pointed to the collection of scrap wood that spanned the creek.

"It is," he confirmed.

Caroline frowned. "I thought you said it was a good bridge."

"It's better than nothing," was his defense.

Caroline considered this for a few seconds and then proposed, "Maybe me and my mom could help you fix it while we're here."

Dane smiled at this suggestion. "Maybe you can."

"When are we going to fish?" Caroline wanted to know.

"Tomorrow," Dane promised. "Right now we need to start a fire, and then we'll eat dinner if you're not too full from our doughnut and hot chocolate snack."

"I'm not too full." Caroline jumped off the bed. "And I can help you make the fire."

"You know how to start a fire?" he asked.

"Sure," Caroline replied. "My grandpa taught me."

Dane held out his hand. "Then let's go get some wood."

Savannah watched them walk out together with mixed emotions. She was glad that Dane seemed to like Caroline, but she wasn't sure why he'd bonded with her so quickly. Maybe it was the child's resemblance and relationship to Wes that attracted him. Or maybe it was just that Caroline was an irresistible child. But Dane had made it very clear that once this was over, their contact with each other would end. She hated for Caroline to make another new friend she was destined to lose.

Savannah transferred her suitcase upstairs along with the plastic sack containing Caroline's new articles of clothing. By the time she returned to the living room, Dane and Caroline had a fire blazing. Savannah settled on the couch and commended them for their accomplishment.

"Major Dane did most of it," Caroline told her modestly. "I just helped a little."

Savannah pulled the child beside her on the couch and pressed a kiss on her soft, smooth forehead. Caroline sat patiently in her mother's embrace for a few minutes. Then she leaned forward and pointed at the mantel.

"Who are all those people?" she asked.

Dane glanced up from the wood he was stacking on the hearth. "I'm not sure."

Caroline frowned. "Why do you want to have pictures of people you don't know on your fireplace?"

Dane laughed. "I don't really want them, but my mother put them there, and I'm afraid to move them."

Caroline considered this and then nodded. "You have to mind your mother."

"In my experience, it's usually wise," Dane agreed.

"Where is your mother?" Caroline asked.

"She's in Thailand serving a church mission with my dad."

"Is that far away?" Caroline wanted to know.

"Pretty far," Dane confirmed.

"Are you lonely?"

Dane's eyes met Savannah's briefly. Then he said, "How could I be lonely with Cam and Hack and Doc to keep me company?"

Caroline laughed. "That's good."

As if on cue, Hack and Cam walked through the door.

"Well?" Dane asked.

"Nothing," Cam reported.

"What about Ferrante?" Dane asked. "Has the FBI been able to find him yet?"

Hack shook his head.

Anxious to cheer them up, Savannah said, "Can I interest anyone in a sandwich for dinner?"

"I'm interested," Hack said. Then he gave her a gold-toothed grin. "It sure is good to have you back."

Smiling, Savannah walked into the kitchen.

They ate sandwiches for dinner, and then Savannah took Caroline upstairs to change into pajamas while what was left of the investigative team met in the living room. Caroline was thrilled with her recently purchased sleepwear and insisted that she be allowed to model for her new friends. So Savannah trailed behind her daughter as they descended the stairs.

The men were sitting in their computer chairs, facing each other in an ever-shrinking circle. After the fashion show, Savannah told Caroline it was time for bed.

"I'm not sleepy!" Caroline insisted, although her eyes were drooping with fatigue. "Please let me stay up for just a few more minutes."

Since it was their first night back together, Savannah couldn't bring herself to deny such a simple request. So she led Caroline over to the couch. Within minutes Caroline was asleep and Savannah pulled the child onto her lap, drawing comfort from the warm little body while she eavesdropped on the meeting taking place behind her.

"Now that we've got Caroline back, keeping her secure is a major concern," Dane said. "Hack, I'd like you to add a few more men to the group you've got watching the cabin. I don't want anyone to surprise us here."

Savannah hadn't realized that the cabin had been guarded up to this point, but it was a reassuring thought.

"No problem," Hack agreed. "Is Ferrante still a threat?"

"Ferrante will be a threat as long as he's breathing," Dane confirmed.

"I ain't scared of him," Cam insisted disparagingly.

"Well I am," Dane returned. "So far we haven't been able to link Ferrante to any of the other people involved in the kidnapping—not Savannah, not Wes, not Lacie, not even Forton—except that commercial delay thing. Until we determine whether Ferrante himself has a grudge against Savannah and Wes or if someone who hired him does, we'll have to be very careful. So from this point out, nobody goes anywhere alone."

"I work better solo," Cam argued.

"I'm not willing to negotiate on this, Cam," Dane said with unusual firmness. "There's safety in numbers."

"What are we going to do about Doc?" Hack asked on a related but slightly different subject.

Dane's countenance darkened. "The hospital will keep him for a few more days and then if he's still unconscious, we're going to have to make some more permanent arrangements. Our basic options are to put him in a long-term care facility or to take him back to his apartment and hire a nursing service to provide round-the-clock care."

Both options were depressing, and nobody answered immediately.

Finally Hack said, "The long-term care facility would be easier to secure."

"I don't see security as a big deal for Doc," Cam interjected. "I don't think anybody drugged him. He just got mixed up and took too much of something."

Savannah twisted around and claimed their attention by commenting from her position on the couch. "I don't believe he tried to kill himself, and he was too careful with his medications to overdose by mistake. You can't take a chance someone did try to kill him and might try again."

Dane sighed. "She's right, so security is an important consideration. If he doesn't wake up before the hospital discharges him, we'll put him in a long-term care facility." Dane looked at Hack. "I want you to keep pressure on the Haitian officials, and maybe we'll find out who killed Forton."

"If it was a mob hit, there won't be any evidence," Hack pointed out.

"Probably not, but try anyway." Dane looked at Cam. "And we'll all keep looking for a connection between Ferrante and someone who has a connection to Savannah or Wes." He paused to glance at Savannah. "Or that disc. I have a feeling that when we find that link, we will also find our kidnapper."

"And our murderer," Savannah said.

"Yes," Dane agreed. Then he looked at Cam. "If you have to go anywhere, take Hack with you."

"What about Lacie?" Savannah asked.

"What about her?" Dane seemed distracted.

Savannah frowned. "Who's going to be looking for her?"

"Hack's men have the assisted-living place where the mother is staying staked out," Dane replied absently.

"For what good that will do," Cam muttered.

Savannah turned to address him. "You don't think Lacie will visit her mother?"

"I don't think she *can* visit her mother," Cam returned.

"You think she's left the country?"

"I think she's left the *earth*," Cam clarified. "Ferrante killed Forton. Why not Lacie? I figure the missing substitute teacher is probably dead too. It makes going to trial safer if all the witnesses against you are dead."

Savannah returned her stricken gaze to Dane. "Do you think Lacie's dead?"

Dane shrugged. "Like Cam said, it's likely." He didn't seem concerned about Lacie's possible demise. "Cam, I want you to follow the money trail Doug Forton left before he died. You might be able to come up with something interesting."

This time Cam gave him a half-hearted salute, obviously displeased with his assignments and the restrictions to his movements.

Dane referred to his notes and said, "So everybody get to work trying to find a connection between someone and Ferrante."

"What are we hoping for there?" Savannah asked.

"The best case scenario would be that someone wanted to suppress the information on the disc and hired Ferrante to kidnap Caroline to that end."

"Why is that the best case scenario?" she asked Dane. "Because it's *your* scenario?"

"Because if that was the reason for Caroline's kidnapping, once we get the disc and give it to General Steele, it becomes public knowledge. Well, so to speak."

Savannah had to smile. If they were successful in retrieving the disc, the Army would make sure that the information on the disc was never seen by most of the public.

Dane continued. "Once the information on the disc is no longer a secret, there won't be a reason to kill you." He gave her a pointed look. "Since Forton's dead, he's no longer a threat regardless of his motivations."

"But if I'm right, and someone has a personal vendetta against me?" Savannah asked, even though she wasn't sure she wanted to hear the answer.

Dane didn't look happy as he replied. "If Ferrante or one of his clients wants revenge against you, then the threat to your safety and Caroline's will continue no matter what happens with the disc."

"So we're hoping that the disc is the motive, but we're still looking at other options," Cam summed up.

"That's the way I see it," Dane agreed. "If any of you have a good working relationship with God, I suggest you pray that the disc is the motive. Because if Savannah has somehow attracted Ferrante as an enemy . . ."

"Then your troubles are just beginning," Cam said as he looked at Savannah.

"On a happier note," Dane said as he lifted his arms over his head and stretched, "I've got a construction crew coming tomorrow to build a decent bridge across the creek, so I'd like a little extra security. Can you handle that, Hack?"

Cam and Hack stared back at Dane, obviously shocked.

"You're going to replace the old bridge?" Cam managed finally.

"We've got a child here now, and it's a safety hazard," Dane confirmed.

Cam glanced at Savannah and then whispered, "Well what do you know about that?"

Savannah was too surprised to respond.

"I know it's about time," Hack contributed.

"Way past time," Cam agreed.

Dane ignored all the jibes and said, "The crew is using a prefabricated bridge kit, so they should be able to get it done in a day. But having strangers roaming around the place would make it easy for someone to infiltrate us if they're looking for an opportunity."

Hack nodded. "I'll have extra men here and tell them all to be on their toes."

Dane stood. "That's it for tonight then. See you guys in the morning."

Cam and Hack left through the kitchen, and Dane walked them to the door, presumably to lock it behind them. Savannah lifted Caroline and started toward the stairs. Dane met her at the landing.

"I'll take her," he offered. Without giving Savannah a chance to accept or reject, he slipped his arms under the sleeping child.

The incidental contact with Savannah herself was sweet torture, over too soon and not likely to be repeated. She followed him upstairs and watched as he gently put Caroline on the bed closest to the window. "She'll love it when she sees the sun rise over the creek in the morning," he predicted.

Savannah smiled. "It's a good thing Caroline doesn't sleep in."

He tucked the patchwork quilt around Caroline's shoulders and then stood up beside Savannah. They looked into each other's eyes for what seemed like a long time. With only moonlight for illumination, she couldn't see his face well enough to read his expression. She thought he might say something nice or even kiss her again like he had after his nightmare. But finally he turned toward the door.

"Good night," he said over his shoulder, and then he disappeared down the stairs.

CHAPTER 18

The next morning Savannah was awakened by a child's scream. Disoriented and terrified, she looked around the unfamiliar room and suddenly remembered the events of the day before. "Caroline," she whispered.

"Look, Mama," her daughter cried from a few feet away. "The sun is shining on the creek!"

Savannah sat up and saw her daughter kneeling on the other twin bed, looking out the window at the beginning of a spectacular sunrise. But before she could answer, the door crashed open and Dane burst into the room.

"Are you okay?" he demanded. There were circles of fatigue under his eyes, an indication that he really had been awake most of the night.

"Caroline was just excited by the sunrise." Savannah pulled the quilt up to cover her nightgown. Dane's tired eyes followed the movement and remained fixated on the spot where the worn edge of the quilt touched the skin of her neck. She hoped he couldn't hear the pounding of her heart, which was only partially a result of Caroline's early-morning scream.

Dane pulled his gaze from Savannah and directed it toward Caroline. As he looked at the child, his expression softened. "I told you it was nice," he reminded her.

"It's the best thing I've ever seen," Caroline amended with reverence.

Dane walked over and sat on the edge of the bed so he could enjoy the sunrise with Caroline. After a few minutes he said, "Today some men are coming to install a new bridge across the creek. By tonight we should be able to sit on it and fish."

Caroline smiled. "We could have a fishing contest. Me and Grandpa did that sometimes."

"I'll bet you usually won," Dane predicted.

"Yep," she confirmed. "Did you used to swim in the creek when you were six like me?"

"I didn't live here when I was six," he told her.

She looked wistfully at the sun-kissed water. "I think it would be fun."

Dane smiled as he stood. "I'd better get downstairs and start making hot chocolate."

Caroline climbed off the bed. "Can I help you?"

He glanced at Savannah. "If it's okay with your mom."

Savannah didn't trust her voice, so she just nodded.

"Okay, then." Dane led Caroline out into the hallway.

As they started down the steps, Savannah heard Caroline ask, "What about doughnuts?"

"I've already called Hack and told him to bring some," Dane's fading voice replied.

After making the beds and returning the room to order, Savannah went downstairs and took a shower. She dressed in what had become her typical daily attire: jeans and a long-sleeved T-shirt. When she left the bathroom, she heard voices coming from the kitchen and guessed, correctly, that Cam and Hack had arrived.

"Good morning everyone," she greeted.

"Good morning yourself," Hack returned.

"We have doughnuts!" Caroline announced. "And hot chocolate."

Savannah sat down in the chair Cam was holding out for her and picked up the one remaining mug. "So I see."

Dane was scowling as usual. "Eat fast," he instructed her. "We're going to your house this morning, but I want to get back here as soon as possible so I can supervise the installation of the new bridge."

"I'm done eating," Caroline announced. "So we can go."

"You gonna wear your new pajamas?" Hack asked with a golden smile.

"I do like them a lot," Caroline said. "But I guess I should put on some jeans."

"That would be best," Savannah agreed. She took a few quick gulps of hot chocolate and picked a jelly-filled doughnut from the bakery bag. "Come on. I'll help you change."

The bridge builders arrived while Savannah was getting Caroline ready. When they walked outside, they found the backyard transformed into a construction site. Crowding the space were several trucks, a backhoe, and a cement mixer. Caroline stared at the men in hard hats and tool belts with fascination.

"I wish we could stay and watch," she told her mother.

"We'll be back soon," Savannah promised.

Dane ended a conversation with one of the construction workers and joined them by his car. "Let's go," he said, more irritable than usual.

While they drove, Caroline entertained them with stories about Colorado. But once they entered the Capitol Hill neighborhood that had been home to the McLaughlins for years, Caroline stopped reminiscing and looked out the window.

"I didn't think I missed my house and stuff," Caroline explained. "But I guess I did."

"We're almost there," Dane replied with a smile.

But when they were just a few blocks away, Caroline pointed through the windshield and asked, "Who are all those people at our house?"

Savannah looked up to see television vans parked at the curb in front of their house and numerous reporters milling around waiting for their arrival.

"Word must have gotten out that Caroline has been found," Dane said grimly.

Savannah frowned at the strangers trampling the shrubbery in her yard. "What are we going to do?"

Dane pulled his car in behind a Suburban parked a few houses down and took out his cell phone. "I have an idea," he told them. Then he called the NBC affiliate and told them that Savannah was holding a press conference in the CAC offices at noon. He dialed another number and repeated the message. As he ended the second call the reporters started climbing into vehicles and speeding away.

Once the coast was clear, Dane drove around behind the house and parked his car. Then Savannah unlocked the back gate, and they entered the house through the French doors that opened onto the deck.

To Savannah the house seemed cold and unwelcoming, as if she no longer belonged there. But Caroline displayed no hesitation. She ran from one thing to the next, showing Dane items of interest, comfortable being home.

"Here's a picture I drew of an apple when I was in kindergarten." She showed him a piece of construction paper held to the refrigerator by a smiley-face magnet. Then she ran into the family room. "And this is the chair where I sit when I watch TV."

Savannah hated to spoil Caroline's fun, but she was afraid the reporters would return. So she headed toward the stairs and called for Caroline to follow. "We have to get you some clothes packed."

"Come on, Caroline," Dane concurred. "I'll help you while your mother gets dressed for the press conference."

Savannah stared at him in horrified astonishment. "I thought that was just a trick."

"It was a trick," Dane agreed. "But it's one we'll have to follow through with. Otherwise I'll lose my credibility."

This was a sacrifice Savannah was willing to make, but before she could say so, Caroline ran up between them and asked, "Did Major Dane tell a lie?"

Savannah sighed and said, "No." Then she turned to Dane. "What exactly am I supposed to say at this unplanned press conference?"

"You'll tell them that your daughter has been rescued and that you appreciate all the efforts of local law enforcement, the FBI, and the U.S. Army. Then you'll explain that you can't take questions because you've been separated from your daughter for a long time and she needs your attention. At that point you'll walk out, and nobody will fault you under the circumstances."

Savannah glanced at her watch. "You told them the press conference was at noon. That gives me barely an hour to get ready."

"Actually you only have about thirty minutes," Dane corrected. "We'll need a little time to get to the Child Advocacy Center." He smiled then, and all Savannah's reasonable objections evaporated. She enjoyed the moment, but it ended when Caroline pulled on Dane's hand.

"You said you were going to help me pack," she reminded him.

"Run on to your room. I'll be there in a minute," he promised. Once the child was gone, he said to Savannah, "You need to transform yourself back into the composed, beautiful widow of the late, great Major Westinghouse McLaughlin before you face the cameras. No one would recognize you the way you look right now."

Savannah narrowed her eyes at him. "I'll do my best."

He climbed the stairs, and Savannah trailed behind him. Then he joined Caroline in the pink bedroom with cheerful, gingham curtains. Left alone, Savannah crossed her bedroom and stepped into her walk-in closet. For a few seconds she just stared at the rows of business suits, overwhelmed by the task of choosing the right one. Finally she picked a blue wool Anne Klein for no particular reason. Once she had the suit on, she stared into the full-length mirror and frowned. It felt wrong, as if the Savannah McLaughlin who had worked at the CAC and worn designer clothes and done public service commercials ceased to exist when Caroline was kidnapped. The new woman who had taken her place wore jeans and rarely put on makeup and never visited a hairdresser. She had learned to be scared of strangers and to doubt her friends. She had been forced to face the fact that she loved a man who wouldn't or couldn't return her affection.

Refusing to cry, Savannah applied some makeup and did what she could with her hair. She suffered a pang of regret when she thought of how Lacie used to do a final inspection of her appearance before she stepped in front of the camera. Once she was ready, she put some more jeans and T-shirts into what used to serve as her gym bag and stepped into the hall.

Dane and Caroline were standing by the stairs, their arms overflowing with toys.

"Did you pack any clothes or just toys?" she asked them.

Caroline laughed as she started down the stairs. "We packed clothes and toys."

Left alone with Dane and feeling insecure, Savannah extended her hands and said, "So will I do?"

Dane's eyes examined her from head to toe and then back again. Finally he nodded but he didn't smile. "Let's get Caroline's stuff in the car. If we don't leave soon, you'll be late for the press conference."

* * *

Savannah was nervous when they left the row house, and her anxiety level increased with every mile they traveled toward the downtown high-rise that housed the offices of the Child Advocacy Center. Once she could see the building, she was filled with full-fledged dread.

A few blocks before they reached the entrance, Dane pulled his car to the side of the road. Thinking that he had decided to spare her the ordeal, Savannah turned toward him with gratitude. But her hopes were dashed when he said, "I'm going to drop you off here. Then Caroline and I will circle the block until the press conference ends."

Savannah hated to show weakness, but the thought of dealing with the reporters alone was too much. "I can't do it without you," she whispered.

He didn't take advantage of the opportunity to ridicule her but pointed out the window at a massive figure that could only be one man. "Hack is going to take you in. He won't let them bully you. Cam's around here somewhere, too, providing additional security."

There was no question of anyone bullying Hack, but she still wanted Dane by her side when she faced the cameras and the questions. Since she'd already sacrificed most of her pride, she decided the rest could go too. "Please."

He leaned close, his lips grazing her cheek. "We can't give the media access to Caroline," he said softly.

Savannah bowed her head in defeat. Of course Caroline couldn't go to the press conference, and there was no one she could leave the child with besides Dane. "Okay," she said, although terror was still threatening to squeeze every ounce of air from her lungs.

Dane reached over the seat and grasped her shoulders with his hands. "You can do this."

She could feel the warm imprint of each finger through the thin fabric of her suit jacket. For a moment she concentrated on the comforting sensation instead of her fear. Then she nodded. "I know."

He removed his hands, leaving her bereft. She put her selfishness aside and turned to Caroline. "You're going to stay with Major Dane while I go inside for the press conference."

Caroline nodded, unconcerned by the thought of a temporary separation. "When you come back, can we get ice cream?"

Savannah smiled stiffly. "Of course."

With one last look at Dane, she pulled the door handle and stepped out. Hack met her at the corner. "Stand close and don't make eye contact with anyone," he instructed. "Maybe we can make it inside before anyone figures out who you are."

They only made it ten yards before she was recognized, and from that point until they reached the entrance to the CAC offices, the press dogged them. Savannah was grateful for Hack, whose imposing presence kept even the most aggressive reporters and photographers at bay.

Jackie was waiting inside the lobby and unlocked the door when she saw Savannah. "What's going on?" she demanded. "Those reporters say you have a press conference here in just a few minutes!"

"I do," Savannah confirmed.

"This will be a good place to set up," Hack said after surveying the lobby. "You'll stand right here. That way after you get through saying what Dane told you to, we can get out quick."

Savannah didn't like the assumption that Dane was calling all the shots, but she knew it was senseless to waste energy arguing small points, so she nodded.

"I'm not sure about this," Jackie said, trying to wield some authority. "I should call the board of directors."

"Go ahead," Savannah suggested. "Although I don't know what you'll do if they object, since by then the press conference will be over."

Jackie considered this and then her shoulders slumped in defeat. "I may not be able to stop you, but I don't have to be a party to this." With what dignity she could muster, Jackie walked down the hall toward Doug's office.

Savannah felt a twinge of sympathy for the woman, who had lost her boss and probably her job. But mostly she was just glad to be rid of her.

"Are you ready?" Hack asked.

Savannah positioned herself in front of the receptionist's desk and nodded.

Hack opened the door and representatives from all segments of the media surged in. Under the intense lights of the cameras, Savannah made her statement, almost word for word as Dane had suggested. Then Hack led her out of the room, ignoring the questions that were called after them.

Dane's car was waiting at the curb right outside the entrance. Hack opened the door for her and while she climbed inside, Hack reported to his boss. "Went just like you wanted."

Dane pointed at the laptop set up on the front seat. "I saw it."

"She was a real trooper," Hack added.

This was high praise from Hack, and Savannah was touched. "Thanks for protecting me," she told him.

"Anytime." He looked up and scanned the crowd. "I guess I'd better go find Cam and get back to work." He closed the door and blended into the throng of people on the sidewalk as well as a man the size of a mountain could.

Dane closed the laptop and eased the car into traffic. Savannah leaned over to kiss Caroline. "So how did you two do without me?"

"We did good," Caroline reported. "Major Dane said I could help the men making the bridge when we get back to his cabin. Then when they're finished, he's going to take me fishing. But he's scared of worms, so he said I have to load the hooks."

Savannah met Dane's gaze in the rearview mirror. "Another defect?" she murmured.

"Not much of one," he pointed out. "Anyone with sense is scared of worms."

"Don't forget about the ice cream!" Caroline reminded them.

Dane negotiated a deal that included waiting until they were outside the Washington metropolitan area before they stopped, and lunch before they ate ice cream.

"Impressive," Savannah complimented him afterward.

He dismissed his skills with a shrug. "It comes from all those years of Army training."

They stopped at a strip mall near Dale City for lunch. There were several restaurant choices, but Caroline wanted to get a hot dog from a street vendor. And when it was time for dessert they walked down to a Baskin Robbins and ordered cones. Savannah got vanilla.

"Boring," Dane whispered in her ear.

She did her best to ignore his warm breath on her neck as she replied, "I prefer to call it *safe*."

"I want double chocolate," Caroline declared. "That's not boring!"

"It's not as boring as vanilla," Dane conceded. "But it's not as interesting as dill pickle."

Caroline's eyes widened in amazement. "There's dill pickle ice cream?"

Dane tapped on the label taped to the glass partition that separated the ice cream from potential customers. "Dill Pickle," he read aloud. "I'd like a triple please," he told their server.

Caroline accepted her double chocolate cone and then watched as the teenage employee piled three mounds of dill pickle ice cream onto a cone for Dane.

"You're not really going to eat that!" Savannah whispered as they walked back outside.

"If you could have seen some of the things I've eaten, you'd realize this is no challenge." He took a big bite of ice cream, shuddered, and then said, "Delicious!"

"It is not!" Caroline contested his claim. "You hate it!"

He tossed the ice cream cone in a nearby garbage can. "You're right. It's awful."

Caroline held up her untouched cone. "You can have mine."

Savannah's heart swelled with love for her daughter. Dane ruffled Caroline's hair and said, "Thanks anyway, but I don't really like chocolate either."

"How about vanilla? Mama will share hers," Caroline said with confidence.

Mutely, Savannah extended her cone to Dane. Their eyes met and held. He took the cone, licked a drip that was trickling down the side and then returned it to her. "Thanks," he said.

She nodded. "You're welcome."

Caroline only made it halfway through her ice cream, but Savannah ate every delicious, boring bite of hers. Dane threw away the remains of Caroline's soggy cone and then suggested they leave.

"Your Savannah McLaughlin Television Personality uniform is attracting attention."

Savannah looked down at her blue woolen suit. “Sorry.”

He shrugged. “It’s the price of fame.”

Savannah rolled her eyes as they walked to the car.

CHAPTER 19

On the way back to Tylerton, Savannah quietly reflected on the events of the past few days and tried to determine what the future might hold. Dane liked Caroline. She was sure of that. And he wasn't indifferent to her either. But whether this new softening was enough to convince him that they should be a part of his life, she didn't know.

When they arrived at the cabin, Caroline weaved through the construction equipment that still cluttered the yard and ran down to the edge of the creek. Savannah and Dane were right behind her. Spanning the creek was a simple, yet graceful, arched bridge. It was so lovely that tears came to Savannah's eyes.

"Isn't it pretty, Mama?" Caroline asked.

"It is," Savannah managed.

A man wearing a hard hat and a tool belt stepped up to speak to Dane. "We're basically through," he said. "The cement landings on each side are still wet, so you need to keep everyone off of them. I'll send a few guys over tomorrow to take off the framing."

Dane nodded. "You did a good job. I appreciate the quick service."

The man touched his hat. "I hope you'll remember us if you need anything else done here."

"I will," Dane promised.

Caroline watched the men pack up their equipment. Then she finagled a ride on a backhoe and salvaged several pieces of wood that she insisted were too nice to throw away. Once the construction crew had gone, she reminded Dane of his promise to take her fishing.

"It's hard to find worms in the afternoon," Dane pointed out. "We might have to wait until tomorrow."

"We can use bread crumbs if we don't have worms," Caroline informed him. "Me and Grandpa did sometimes."

"Major Dane has important things to do," Savannah told Caroline gently. "Fishing can wait."

Caroline's disappointment was obvious, but she didn't argue.

Dane knelt down in front of the child so they could talk eye to eye. "How about we make a deal?"

Savannah could tell that Caroline was intrigued. "What kind of deal?"

"How about I work for a couple of hours and then we'll go fishing this evening. The fish always bite good right about sunset."

Caroline smiled. "Okay. Do you want me to look for some worms while you work?"

Dane sent Savannah a speculative look. "That's a great idea. I'll bet your mother will help you with that project."

"No problem," Savannah responded. "*I'm* not scared of worms."

"Your bravery is impressive," Dane said, although he didn't sound like he meant it. "But you might want to change out of that fancy suit first." Then he turned and walked into the cabin. Savannah and Caroline followed behind him.

Savannah let Caroline sit on the couch to wait while she went upstairs and took off the suit. As she hung it in the closet of Dane's guest room she wondered if she'd ever have cause to wear it again. The future of the CAC was uncertain, and even if she did keep her job there, it was hard to imagine going back after all that had happened.

Savannah dedicated an hour to the futile search for worms before she finally convinced Caroline to abandon the effort and take a short nap in preparation for the evening of fishing with Dane. At sunset Dane collected Caroline, insisted that she put on a coat, and then got a loaf of bread from the kitchen before heading down to the new bridge. Savannah stayed on the porch steps, content just to watch them.

Dane lifted the child over the wet cement and then jumped past it himself. They settled on the edge of the bridge with their legs dangling through the railings. Caroline loaded one of the hooks carefully and then passed the pole to Dane. He supervised while she loaded the other hook, and they sat beside each other in companionable silence, waiting for the fish to bite.

Occasionally Caroline or Dane would make a comment. Savannah couldn't hear the words, but she would see the dark head lean down toward the blonde one, or vice versa. The sunset was as spectacular as the sunrise had been, coloring the sky with shades of red and orange. Savannah rested her chin on her knees, unable to imagine being more content than she was at that moment.

Then Cam came outside. "Hack's back from Fredericksburg with pizza," he told her. "You need to get some while it's hot and before Hack eats it all."

Savannah smiled. "Thanks for letting me know. It's almost dark, so I'm sure Dane and Caroline will be ready to come in soon."

Cam pointed at the fishermen. "Are they catching anything?"

"It looks like their bucket is almost full."

He sat on the opposite edge of the steps. After a few minutes, he said, "It's good that Dane has been able to get past his feelings toward Wes and make friends with Caroline."

Savannah smiled. "Yes, I'm glad about that too, although Dane's hard feelings are mostly directed toward me and not at Wes."

Cam frowned. "How do you figure?"

"I'm the one who promised to marry him and then married his best friend," Savannah explained, grateful for the near darkness that hid her shame.

Cam laughed without humor. "You marrying Wes is nothing compared to Wes leaving Dane behind in Russia to be captured and tortured and almost killed."

Savannah felt obligated to defend her deceased husband. "Wes couldn't risk his men to retrieve what he thought was a dead body from a burning building."

Cam stiffened but didn't comment, and a feeling of dread started to build inside Savannah. She narrowed her eyes at him.

"Cam, talk to me," she commanded, but he stared straight ahead in terrible silence. "Are you saying that when Wes left Russia, he knew that Dane was still *alive*?"

"I'm not saying nothing," Cam insisted, still refusing to meet her gaze.

Savannah grabbed his arm and shook him. "You can't stop now. You have to tell me what you know."

When Cam faced her, his eyes were full of regret. "I'm so sorry. I thought Dane had already told you." He glanced nervously down at the water's edge where Dane and Caroline were fishing in the glow of the setting sun.

Savannah forced her voice to remain calm as she said, "What happened in Russia?"

Cam answered with obvious reluctance. "We were pulling out when Dane went down. We never leave a man behind, so we all stopped, but Wes sent us on to the helicopter. He said he'd get Dane."

Savannah nodded. She'd heard this part before.

"I was running with the others, but then I got to worrying that if Dane was hurt bad, Wes might not be able to handle him alone. I turned back, and when I got to the building, the fire was worse. Flames were everywhere, and it was hard to breathe because of the smoke. I saw Dane just where we'd left him, lying on the road right in front of the building. Dane was holding his hand up to Wes, but Wes was just standing there. Staring."

Savannah tried to ignore the pain in her chest. "You're sure? Maybe Wes was trying to think of a way to lift Dane."

Cam shook his head resolutely. "No, ma'am. He didn't help Dane. Instead he started to back away. I can still hear Dane's voice calling out for Wes to help him."

Tears filled Savannah's eyes as she demanded, "What happened next?"

"I started running toward Dane. I was thinking if Wes wasn't going to save him, then I would. We had a team motto . . ."

Savannah nodded. "All for one and one for all."

Cam smiled. "Dane always made fun of it, but it was true. We were there for each other, you know?"

"I know."

Cam's expression darkened. "At least until that night when Wes left Dane to die."

"You tried to rescue Dane, but you couldn't?" Savannah prompted.

"I reached Dane, and he lifted up his hand to me, but he didn't say my name. Instead he said, 'Wes.' Then I was hit from behind—knocked out cold. I didn't come to until we were in the helicopter."

"What hit you?"

"Wes told me that I got hit by debris from the burning building. He said Dane had stopped breathing right after I went down. He said it took too long to get me to the helicopter, and he couldn't risk going back for a dead body."

Savannah felt better. "Then Wes had to choose between a wounded man and one he thought was dead. We can't fault his decision."

"But Dane wasn't dead," Cam said.

"But if Wes thought he was . . ."

"No." Cam's hands were clutched together tightly. "When I went to see Dane in the hospital after he came back, he asked if I'd told anyone what Wes did in Russia. I wasn't sure what he meant, but I could see it hurt for him to talk, and I didn't want to make him explain, so I just nodded. He said that was good—that I understood about loyalty. He said Wes would have to live with himself and what he'd done but that we couldn't be the ones to turn him in. That's when I knew."

The feeling of dread was back in full force. "Knew what?"

"That Wes left Dane in Russia on purpose." Cam's head dropped into his hands. "Wes hit me in the head, and then he left Dane to die."

"That's impossible!" Savannah tried to argue against the facts. "Nothing would make Wes betray Dane like that!"

This time when Cam turned his eyes to her, they were full of pity. "Nothing except you."

For several seconds Savannah fought a combination of shock, horror, and intense guilt. When the accompanying nausea faded, Cam was gone. She sat there and stared at Dane and Caroline, still sitting side by side on the edge of the nice, new bridge as if nothing had changed. But in an instant, everything had.

There was no question in her mind that what Cam said was true. It explained a great deal. Now she understood why Wes was so depressed that he couldn't enjoy anything—not his career, his wife, or even his daughter. It explained General Steele's reluctance to involve Dane in her life and his suggestion that Dane might be her enemy, or an enemy to Wes's daughter anyway. It explained the animosity she'd felt from the other men in the special ops team. It explained the look in Dane's eyes when they had visited him in the hospital. She had thought Dane was angry with her, but all along it was Wes. In fact, her presence in that room had been incidental. Both Wes and Dane had been concentrating only on each other.

She shook her head, trying to clear it. Did Wes really think that Dane would forgive him? Since Dane survived the ordeal that followed Wes's betrayal, did Wes believe that they could resume their friendship as if all was well that ended well? Or did he hope that Dane wouldn't remember his treachery?

For a few minutes she wished she were dead. Then she just wished she'd never met Dane or Wes. But slowly, a more important and disturbing truth dawned on her.

She was still trying to decide what to do with this newfound, and not entirely welcome, knowledge when Dane and Caroline started up from the creek. They were a breathtaking sight as they walked toward the cabin holding the day's catch in a bucket between them, the last vermillion rays of sunset providing a backdrop.

When they reached the porch, Savannah gave Caroline a hug and then sent her in to eat pizza with Hack and Cam. Dane moved to follow Caroline, but Savannah put a hand on his arm.

"I need to speak to you," she said.

He frowned. "It's getting chilly, and I smell like fish. Maybe we could talk a little later, after I've had a chance to clean up."

She shook her head. "No, this conversation can't wait, and it has to take place outside where we'll have some privacy." She moved away from the house and walked down toward the woods that lined the creek, confident that he would follow. Once she was sure they couldn't be seen from the house, she turned on him.

"You are a liar!" she hissed.

If he was surprised by this accusation, he didn't show it. Instead he nodded and said, "Unquestionably."

"You don't hate me and you never did!" she flung at him. "All this time you let me think that you despised me, but really you don't!"

"Savannah," he tried a soothing tone, but she was having none of it.

She closed the distance between them and grabbed fistfuls of his flannel shirt. "I know the truth, and at this moment I could kill you!"

A look somewhere between fear and pain crossed his face. He covered her hands with his. "What is this all about?"

"Cam thought I knew what *really* happened in Russia," she said, tears spilling onto her cheeks. "He thought you'd told me that Wes knew you were alive and left you there to die so he could marry me." Saying the words hurt so much she thought her heart would break, and she wondered how Dane had dealt with it for years. How did he stand the anguish? "Wes was like your brother, and yet he left you to an unspeakably awful fate." She shook him. "You had so many opportunities to tell me, but you didn't."

"What was the point?" he whispered. "I survived, in a manner of speaking. And knowing wouldn't have changed anything except the respect you had for your husband. You still would have been married to him instead of me. You still would have been the mother of his child instead of mine."

The crippling pain returned, and she had to press her face against his chest to keep from crying out loud. He extracted his hands from her grasp and pulled her close. He held her while she wept, occasionally stroking her hair. She listened to the steady beat of his heart and grieved for all of them.

Finally she cried herself out and lifted her eyes to his. "Why did you pretend to hate me?"

"I *tried* to hate you," he said. "It would have been so much easier that way. But I couldn't. I couldn't even hate Wes."

"He tried to *kill* you."

"He chose to leave me," Dane corrected, as if this made a difference. "I was hurt, and he didn't know for sure that he could save me."

For some reason this made Savannah even more furious. "Don't defend what he did!"

"Wes was my friend," Dane said. "So I have to defend him. And things are rarely black and white, Savannah. There are so many shades of gray."

The tears began again. "I thought you didn't believe in friendship."

"I lied about that, too."

She returned her cheek to his already damp shirt. "It's all my fault. You and Wes were friends, almost brothers, and I came between you. I should have left Fort Belvoir on the day we all met."

"Then there would be no Caroline," he pointed out.

This gave her pause.

"Surely your daughter is worth any amount of pain."

"It wasn't worth it for Wes," she said. "He regretted every day of his life after he left you for dead. I thought he was just missing you. We'd always been a threesome."

He nodded.

"Even though Wes never said so, I knew he regretted our marriage. I did too, of course, but by the time I found out you were still alive, I was pregnant with Caroline. I didn't love Wes the same way I loved you, but I believed that we could build a happy life together if we tried. Only Wes wouldn't try. He became so withdrawn and depressed. When they told me he had died, I was terrified that he'd killed himself because without you life just wasn't worth living." She lifted her eyes to his. "I knew how that felt."

"Wes loved you more than anything on earth," Dane told her. "That's why I couldn't hate him—because I understood that his betrayal was just an indication of how much he loved you."

"Is that supposed to make me feel better?" she wailed.

He gave her a sad smile. "I guess not. But if my disc theory is right, then you'll know that Wes didn't kill himself because he was unhappy in your marriage."

"Whether he killed himself of not, I still made him miserable," she whispered.

"Wes made himself miserable," Dane countered. "But dwelling on the past is a senseless waste of time. Our focus now needs to be keeping you and Caroline safe."

Savannah sniffled back the last of her tears and said, "You like Caroline."

"She's a great kid."

Savannah smiled. "So where do we go from here?"

He stood a little straighter, and his expression became terrifyingly serious. "We find the kidnapper. Then we go back to our lives. You and Caroline in Washington. Me here."

"But," Savannah began in confusion. "You don't hate me. In fact, you . . ."

"It means nothing!" he interrupted. "I told you. I'm not the man you knew in Fort Belvoir. The things I've been through have changed me, ruined me. We have no future together."

"I'll never accept that," she told him. "Whatever you've done, you can be forgiven."

"You've got to stop absolving me of my crimes against humanity." The sarcastic tone was back in his voice. "You don't have the power to forgive me."

"I don't, but Jesus does," she said.

"How many times do I have to tell you that everything is different now?" he demanded.

"Is Jesus different?" she asked. "Are your sins so great and horrible that He can't forgive them?"

Dane shook his head. "My great and horrible sins aside, you can't stay here. You've seen how the nightmares affect me. If we were marr—" he broke off as if he couldn't bring himself to say the word. "Well, if you were there with me while I was asleep, and I had a nightmare, I could mistake you for a prison guard and snap your neck. Or I could hurt Caroline." He shuddered at the thought.

"You'll get counseling," she suggested. "And . . ."

"No!" He pushed her away from him. "No." His tone was final. "I've already got enough on my conscience."

She understood that he was trying to protect her and Caroline. But she couldn't bear the thought of living the rest of her life without him. "Dane," she pleaded. "Don't do this."

"You promised if I'd help you, we'd do it my way," he reminded her. "You agreed that it wasn't personal, just a job. You have to stick to our agreement."

"But I love you," she whispered. "And I think that you . . ."

"Forget about all that," he insisted.

"How can I?"

"It takes practice," he assured her grimly.

She blinked back a fresh wave of tears. "Okay, we'll do it your way for now." She moved up and put her arms around him. "But first you have to kiss me, just once, like you used to."

"Savannah," he tried to object, but she leaned forward and pressed her lips to his.

The kiss started out sweet and tender and poignant. Then the old passion flared between them, and it became desperate and frantic and more than even she had bargained for. His fingers tangled in her hair, and she wrapped her arms tightly around his neck. When they finally pulled apart, they were both shaken and breathless.

"Dane," she tried, but he shook his head.

"You promised," he reminded her.

She stood up straight. "You're right. I did. Nothing personal, you said." She took a step toward the cabin and then looked back over her shoulder at him. "I guess I can stand it if you can."

CHAPTER 20

Savannah was in such a hurry to put some distance between herself and Dane that she rushed straight into the cabin. Caroline was sitting on the couch, flanked by Hack and Cam. They all looked up when she stormed in.

Caroline asked, "Is something wrong, Mama?"

Savannah regretted not taking some time to compose herself outside. But it was too late for that now. Too late for many things. She smoothed her hair and smiled at her daughter. "I'm fine, just starving. Where's that pizza?"

Hack pointed toward the kitchen, a quizzical expression on his face. She went into the kitchen, thankful for the reprieve from curious eyes. However, it wasn't destined to last long. Caroline and her bodyguards walked in seconds later.

"Where's Major Dane?" Caroline wanted to know. "He said he'd let me watch him clean our fish."

"I'm here," Dane said from the back door.

Savannah didn't want to look at him, but her eyes had a will of their own. She saw the rumpled flannel shirt that had recently received her tears, the arms that had held her while she cried. Then she looked into the dark, gray eyes that had been filled with passion. They were now dull and hopeless.

She pulled her gaze away and addressed her daughter. "Maybe the fish cleaning can wait until tomorrow."

Caroline seemed horrified by this suggestion. "We can't wait until tomorrow. If we do, the fish will spoil, and then killing them will be a waste. Grandma said that's like a sin."

"I'm ready to clean the fish now," Dane interjected. "Come to the back porch. I have a table out here that I use."

"I could give you a hand," Hack offered.

Dane nodded. "Thanks."

Savannah followed them outside but stationed herself on the opposite side of the porch from the table. Once Hack and Dane were busy filleting fish, Cam came out and sat by Savannah.

"I wanted to apologize again," he began.

Savannah saw Dane glance their way. "It's okay," she said quietly. "I don't want to talk about it."

He reached into the pocket of his coat and extracted a wristwatch. "I have something for you," he whispered. Then he placed the watch in her hand and folded her fingers securely over it. "This belonged to Wes," he continued in hushed tones. "It was a gift from his parents when he graduated from high school, back before they gave away all their money. Dane gave it to me, but since it belonged to Wes, I wanted you to have it so you can give it to Caroline."

Savannah reluctantly accepted it. "Thank you."

Cam nodded. "You're welcome."

After a few minutes of silence, Cam stood and walked over to the table where the fish were being cleaned. "I'm ready to head back to the hotel," he told Hack. "You coming?"

"Can you handle the rest of these without me?" Hack asked Dane.

"I've got it," Dane assured him.

"Then I guess it's good night, Miss Caroline," Hack said. "I'll see you in the morning."

"Bring more doughnuts," Caroline requested. "I like the kind with jelly inside."

"Please bring more doughnuts," Savannah corrected.

"Please," Caroline echoed.

Cam and Hack waved good-bye as they descended the steps and climbed into the Hummer. Savannah took advantage of the distraction caused by their departure to tell Caroline that it was time to take a shower in preparation for bed.

"Do I have to?" Caroline whined.

"Mind your mother," Dane said firmly. "I'm almost done here."

Savannah led her daughter to the bathroom and supervised as Caroline bathed, brushed her teeth, and changed into the same pair of pajamas she'd worn the night before. Savannah had hoped they'd get upstairs before Dane finished with the fish, but he was waiting for them at the bottom of the stairs.

"Are you going to come up and help tuck me in again?" Caroline asked.

"Your mom can probably handle that tonight." He tried to decline further, but Caroline wouldn't accept no for an answer.

"I want you to." She put her arms around his neck. "Carry me."

Dane lifted the child and carried her up the stairs. When they reached the guest room, Caroline jumped down and ran to the bed by the window. "Now it's time for me to say my prayers. Mama, you kneel down here." She pointed to the space to her right. "And Major Dane can come here."

Dane was staring at the kneeling child with something like horror, and Savannah would have been tempted to laugh if she hadn't been so upset with him.

"Major Dane has a hurt leg, so he'd better just stand there while you pray," Savannah suggested.

Caroline readily accepted this excuse. She pressed her hands together the way Savannah had taught her, tilted her face toward the ceiling, and began to pray. She thanked the Lord for everything, including the new bridge and the fish they'd caught that evening. Then she mentioned all her loved ones by name, including Lacie and her grandparents and her daddy in heaven.

When the prayer ended, Caroline scrambled up into bed. "Now you tuck the quilt under my neck," Caroline instructed Dane, and he complied.

Once his task was done, he brushed his hand briefly across her hair. "I'll see you in the morning."

Savannah waited until Dane was gone before telling Caroline that she was going downstairs to take a shower. "I'll be back soon."

"Promise?" Caroline asked with a yawn.

Savannah smiled. "I promise."

She hurried to the bathroom, and while undressing for her shower, she found the watch Cam had given her stuffed in her jeans pocket.

She made a mental note to ask Dane if he had any objection to her keeping it as she stepped into the steady stream of warm water. Feeling better after her shower, she put on her gown and robe before gathering her dirty clothes and leaving the bathroom. When she reached the stairs, a figure stepped out of the shadows. Startled, she screamed and nearly lost her balance.

Dane moved quickly to catch her. The embrace was short lived. Once he was sure she'd regained her balance, he released her and bent down to pick up the clothes she'd dropped. On the bottom of the pile was Wes's watch. Dane studied it in the dim light.

"This looks amazingly like the one I gave Cam," he said.

"Since it originally belonged to Wes, Cam thought I should save it for Caroline."

"Did he tell you how the watch came into my possession?"

Savannah shook her head.

"Wes lost it to me in a bet."

"A bet?" she repeated.

Dane's eyes met hers. "We both met this fascinating woman, and we made a bet with each other that whoever could get her to fall in love with him would give up their most valuable possession. Mine was a rifle my grandfather gave me. Wes's was this watch. It's Swiss and has all kinds of gadgets, including a compass, a GPS signal, and even a fork in case of true emergencies."

She knew he was being cruel to push her away, so she did her best to hide the pain caused by his words. "I can see how a watch with a fork could come in handy," she said. "It's a good thing you won that bet."

His eyes were unfathomable. "Lucky me."

She turned away and started up the stairs.

"Savannah." The rare use of her name stopped her.

She turned back. "Yes."

He placed the watch in her hand. "Keep it for Caroline."

With a solemn nod, she slipped the watch onto her wrist. In a way it was a gift from Wes and something that Caroline could treasure. But it was also a gift from Dane, and it made her feel strangely connected to them both. Unwilling to explore these dangerous emotions, she hurried upstairs. Caroline was sleeping soundly when she walked into the guest room. Savannah kissed her daughter's forehead and then knelt beside the other bed and prayed for Wes's soul.

* * *

The next morning Caroline and Savannah awakened early enough to watch the sunrise. Then they dressed for the day and went downstairs to find Cam, Hack, and Dane already seated around the kitchen table.

"Did you bring doughnuts?" Caroline asked.

Hack pointed at the big white bag in the middle of the table. "The kind with jelly inside."

Caroline took a seat beside Hack, which left Savannah to sit on either side of Dane. Trying to act like she didn't mind, she took the chair to his left. While eating doughnuts and drinking hot chocolate, they went over their plan for the day.

"Hack, Caroline needs some new clothes and shoes. The stuff we picked up yesterday is too small," Dane said. "Will you take her and her mother into Fredericksburg this morning to shop?"

"Sure," Hack agreed.

"Cam, I'll go with you to check on Doc, and then we can visit Ferrante's office downtown and try to ruffle some feathers."

"Fine by me," Cam said. "I enjoy feather ruffling."

Savannah reached across the table for a doughnut, and Wes's watch fell down to dangle around her wrist. The men stared at it, as if its presence around her arm reminded them all that she had been Wes's wife. She could sense their disapproval and pushed the watch back up around her forearm, out of sight.

At first she felt embarrassed, as if she'd been caught in an act of disloyalty. But then she started to feel defensive. After all, Wes was her husband, and she had loved him. If the others had a problem with that, then there was nothing she could do about it.

The shopping trip to Fredericksburg was quick and successful. They returned to the cabin with bags full of clothes and shoes and Subway sandwiches for lunch. They were again seated around the kitchen table, eating sandwiches this time, when Dane got the call.

Savannah knew him well enough to realize instantly that he had received bad news. After closing the phone, he motioned for her to follow him. By the time they reached the living room, her heart was pounding.

"What?" she demanded.

"It's Lacie," he said. "The police found her body."

Savannah had known that this was a possibility, but facing the reality was difficult. She wanted nothing more than to lean into Dane's arms and obtain the comfort that she knew awaited her there. But she leaned against the wall instead. "Poor Lacie," she whispered. "How?"

"A single bullet wound to the head," Dane replied. "Execution style."

Savannah pressed a finger to her temple, where a dull headache was beginning to form.

"I need to tell Caroline."

"I wouldn't give her any details," Dane advised.

Savannah gave him a bland look. "Thanks. If you hadn't said something, I probably would have described the bloody bullet wound."

A ghost of a smile played across Dane's lips. "I meant that you should just say she died, not that she was killed. Caroline's had enough trauma lately."

They returned to the kitchen, and Savannah asked Caroline to come upstairs. Once they were alone she explained briefly about Lacie and fielded the inevitable questions. To cheer Caroline up, Savannah suggested that she try on some of her new clothes and model them for the guys. When Caroline was dressed in the first outfit, they went back to the kitchen.

"I'm wearing some new clothes," Caroline announced as she entered. Then she noticed Hack's absence and asked, "Where's Hack?"

"He's headed to the airport for a flight to Miami," Dane replied.

Savannah waited until Caroline had gone upstairs to change into another new outfit before asking, "Does Hack's sudden trip to Miami have anything to do with Lacie?"

Dane shook his head. "It has to do with Mario Ferrante. While you were upstairs we got a call from the FBI. Ferrante tried to reenter the United States at the Miami International Airport. He was arrested, and they're going to wait to question him until Hack arrives. I'll be in contact with Hack by cell phone, so I can make sure our questions get asked."

Savannah sat down with a feeling of relief. "Do you think the FBI can get Ferrante to explain his role in Caroline's kidnapping?

Dane shrugged. "It depends on how good a deal they offer him. He usually takes his chances with a jury."

"Maybe that has something to do with the fact that he can intimidate people, including jury members and judges," Cam suggested.

"That could be it," Dane agreed. "We'll just have to wait and see."

Caroline returned and modeled more new clothes. Then she asked Dane if he would take her fishing.

Savannah decided to spare him and answered, "Major Dane is very busy at the moment, but I can take you."

Caroline looked surprised. "Do you know how to fish?"

Savannah smiled. "No, but you could teach me."

Dane interrupted by saying, "I am busy, but if you can be patient for a couple of hours, I'll take a break for some fishing. Is that a deal?"

"It's a deal!" Caroline confirmed. "And while we're fishing maybe we can both teach my mom how."

He glanced at Savannah. "Maybe."

Savannah held out her hand to Caroline. "Let's go into the living room, and I'll let you play games on my laptop."

Caroline played games for a while and then took a nap. Savannah dozed beside her daughter and tried not to think about Lacie.

It was considerably longer than two hours when Dane finally came into the living room and announced that he was ready to go fishing. Caroline was already headed toward the door when his cell phone started ringing.

"Surely no one else has died," Savannah murmured as he checked his caller ID. "There are barely any suspects left alive."

Cam smiled at the joke, but Dane was frowning. "This is the hospital calling."

Savannah sobered and sat up straight. They all waited anxiously while Dane spoke to a nurse at the hospital. He closed his phone and reported that Doc was showing signs of improvement.

Caroline smiled. "I told you he was going to be okay!"

"He's conscious?" Savannah asked Dane, hugely relieved.

"Well, not yet," Dane replied. "But the nurse thinks he will be soon."

Savannah stood. "Well, let's go see him. Maybe some verbal stimulation will speed up the awakening process."

"I'll go with her," Cam volunteered. "Safety in numbers and all that."

Dane didn't look happy about the arrangement. "I'll go with you to see Doc, and Savannah can stay here with Caroline," he suggested as an alternative.

Savannah shook her head. "I want to see Doc. We can all go."

"No," Cam pointed out. "We can't, because Dane's expecting a call from Hack, and you aren't allowed to keep cell phones on in the hospital."

"And me and Major Dane are supposed to go fishing," Caroline reminded him.

"Okay," Dane agreed with obvious reluctance. "I'll stay here with Caroline while the two of you go see Doc. But don't be gone too long. Without Hack I feel a little shorthanded."

Cam laughed at this. "I can protect Savannah as well as Hack." He put a muscular arm around Savannah's shoulders, and she saw Dane's frown deepen. "And besides," Cam continued, "the FBI has Ferrante."

"That doesn't make him any less dangerous," Dane said grimly.

"I'll be in the car," Cam said and headed out through the kitchen.

Savannah turned to Caroline. "Will you be okay while I'm gone?"

"Sure, I'll be with Major Dane," the child replied.

Savannah kissed her daughter good-bye and then looked at Dane. He nodded, accepting responsibility for Caroline. Confident that the child was safe, she hurried out after Cam.

Once Savannah and Cam were settled in his car, she sighed. "I didn't know if we were ever going to be able to convince Dane to let us go."

"He's good at giving the third degree," Cam agreed. "And he doesn't trust anybody to protect you except Hack."

"Actually, I don't think it has anything to do with your ability to protect me," Savannah told him. "Dane's afraid that if we spend too much time together, we might become interested in each other."

Cam glanced over at her. "He said that?"

Savannah nodded. "Pretty much."

The idea seemed to please Cam. "I'm in if you are."

Savannah laughed. "Thanks for the offer, but the last thing I need at the moment is romantic involvement."

"Well, if you ever change your mind, you know where to find me."

"Yes, I do," Savannah replied.

They drove in silence for a few minutes, and then Savannah's cell phone rang.

"Hello," she said into the phone.

"Mrs. McLaughlin?" a voice asked.

"Yes," she confirmed.

"This is Max Lowe," the photographer said. "I just got back into the country, and I had a message on my answering machine to call you."

Savannah felt weak with relief. "Mr. Lowe! It's so good to hear from you. I need to get my proofs and negatives from you as soon as possible."

"We can set up an appointment next week," he offered.

"I need them pretty urgently," she pressed. "Could I come and get them tonight?"

She knew it was impolite for her to be so insistent and wasn't surprised by the annoyance in his voice when he replied. "I suppose. Can you meet me in front of my old studio in thirty minutes?"

She covered the mouthpiece and relayed the request to Cam. "We'll be there," he promised. Then he stepped on the gas, and his expensive car surged forward.

"I'll see you in thirty minutes," Savannah told the photographer. She disconnected the call and dialed Dane's cell number.

"Yes?" he answered curtly.

She ignored the feeling of contentment that blossomed the second she heard his voice and said, "The photographer just called. He's meeting us in front of his old studio in thirty minutes. Once we have the disc, we'll go on to the hospital to check on Doc."

"Good." Dane sounded pleased. "Get back here with the disc as soon as you can."

"We will," she assured him. "How's Caroline?"

"She's fine."

Savannah hated to end the call but felt awkward talking in front of Cam. "I guess I'll see you soon."

"Hurry," he said.

She closed her phone and returned it to her purse.

"So was Dane excited about the disc?" Cam wanted to know.

Savannah made a face. "As excited as he gets about anything."

Cam laughed. "He was excited whether he let you know it or not."

* * *

Cam pulled his car in front of the video arcade that used to be Mr. Lowe's photography studio two minutes early. The photographer was there waiting for them. Cam accompanied her to the sidewalk, although that meant leaving his car illegally parked.

"If I get a ticket, I'll let Hack handle it for me," he told her with a smile.

Savannah accepted the brown expandable envelope from Mr. Lowe and thanked him for his cooperation.

"No problem," he said with a cool tone. "I'm glad you got your daughter back."

"Me too," she assured him. "If you'll tell me what I owe you, I'll write you a check."

He waved the offer aside. "I'll bill you."

She hated for Mr. Lowe to leave empty handed and opened her mouth to argue, but Cam took her by the elbow and pulled her to the car.

"Sorry," he said once they were settled inside. "But he said he'd bill you, and we need to check on Doc. Besides, standing on a street with that disc is dangerous."

Savannah nodded. "I should have realized that."

He smiled. "You wouldn't make a good criminal."

"Or a good investigator," she added. Then she opened the envelope and checked the contents. It was just as she remembered—proofs, negatives, and one disc.

"You got it?" Cam confirmed.

"Yes, it's here."

With this reassurance, Cam pulled back out into the traffic and left the video arcade behind them while Savannah used the disc as an excuse to call Dane again.

* * *

When they arrived at the hospital, Cam led Savannah in through the main lobby to a bank of elevators.

"It looks like you know your way around here," she teased.

"I've spent enough time here over the past few days." He pushed the button for the sixth floor.

When the elevator door opened, they stepped off and were almost trampled by a security guard running past. Cam grabbed Savannah and pulled her against the wall as two male nurses followed the security guard at a trot.

Savannah looked down the congested hallway. "I wonder what's happening?"

"Nothing good," Cam predicted with a frown. Then he stiffened. "They're going in Doc's room!" Cam pushed into the crowd. "Come on!"

Savannah held on to the back of Cam's shirt and stayed in his wake as they made their way.

"No guard," Cam pointed out as they reached the door to Doc's room.

A stressed woman wearing a lab coat blocked their way. "I'm sorry, but you can't come in here," she said.

Cam ignored her and pushed the door open. "Where's Doc?" he demanded.

"Are you members of Mr. Moser's family?" the woman asked.

"Mr. Moser?" Savannah repeated.

"That's Doc's real name," Cam explained briefly. Then he returned his attention to the woman. "I'm the closest thing to family that he's got. I checked him into the hospital a couple of days ago!"

The woman still seemed hesitant, but Cam didn't really give her much choice. He walked past her into the room and dragged Savannah with him. Her eyes went first to the empty bed, registering that Doc was gone. Then her eyes moved to a large man sprawled on the industrial-tile floor. He fit the physical description of one of Hack's men.

"The guard?" she whispered.

Cam nodded and then asked one of the several hospital employees loitering around the room to explain what had happened.

"We aren't sure," the woman in the lab coat answered from behind them. They turned to face her as she continued. "Mr. Moser was checked for vital signs at four o'clock, and nothing was amiss. The nurse returned an hour later to replace his IV fluid bag, and she found, well, this." The woman waved to encompass the room.

The security guard stepped forward at this point, presumably to take charge of the situation and protect the woman from Cam's wrath. "I just reviewed the security camera tapes, and the patient left the hospital through the south entrance. The nurse was with him, against her will, of course."

Savannah tried to process this information. "So Doc is conscious, and he left the hospital under his own power, and he made a nurse go with him?"

The guard nodded.

Savannah resisted the urge to laugh. "That's ridiculous!"

Contradiction came from an unexpected source. "Maybe not," Cam said from behind her.

She spun around. "Are you kidding me? Doc wouldn't hurt a fly."

Cam pulled her into a relatively private corner and whispered, "There are things you don't know about Doc."

"You think Doc got up from a coma, knocked out Hack's guard, grabbed a nurse, and escaped the hospital?" she whispered back.

"Sometimes he gets confused and thinks he's on an operation," Cam explained. "There's a name for it. It's called post-traumatic stress disorder."

"But Doc's so frail," she said, struggling to understand. "How could he have been strong enough to overpower the guard?"

"He's small but strong. I've seen him take out guys twice his size lots of times. And if he's still got some dope in his system . . ." Cam paused to run his hand across his military-short hair. "Yeah, it could happen."

The guard stepped over to them. "We've called the police, and they should be here any minute. They'll want to talk to both of you."

"Sure," Cam agreed. "We'll wait in the hall." He took Savannah's arm and led her out of the room.

"We have to call Dane," Savannah whispered once they were out of hearing range.

Cam pulled out his phone and kept walking down the hall to the elevators. "I'm on it."

They reached the elevators, and Cam pushed the button for the lobby. "The guard said the police would want to talk to us," Savannah reminded him.

"Let's just say we don't have time for that now." The elevator door opened and Cam waved for her to get on first. Then he followed.

Dane answered while they were riding to the lobby. She listened to Cam's concise explanation of what they'd found at the hospital. As they stepped off the elevator, Cam closed his phone and put it back in his pocket.

They reached Cam's car without being challenged, and Savannah waited until they were headed out of Washington on Highway 1 before asking, "So what did Dane say?"

"We think we might know where Doc went."

"The practice range?" Savannah guessed. It was the unit's meeting spot whether for training purposes, recreation, or solace in times of trial. It was where she had proposed to Dane. It was where Wes had been the night he died.

"Yes," Cam confirmed. "Dane said to go there and see if we can find Doc. He's on his way, but from Fredericksburg it will take him longer."

Savannah clenched her hands together. She was worried about Doc and unhappy about the necessity of visiting the practice range. It held many memories for her—some good, some bad, and all painful. Since she dreaded the moment of arrival, the time passed quickly. When they pulled up outside the "clubhouse," they saw a late model sedan parked near the door.

"Is that the nurse's car?" she asked.

"Probably," Cam replied. "Commandeering her vehicle would be the logical thing for Doc to do."

"He wouldn't hurt her, would he?"

"I hope not." Cam's anxiety was evidenced by the way his hands were clutching the steering wheel. He parked the car and hurried around to open the door for her. Once she was standing beside him, he reached into the glove compartment and removed a revolver.

"Surely that won't be necessary," she whispered.

"It's best to be prepared," he returned. Then he put a finger to his lips, requesting silence and led her toward the clubhouse.

The setting sun cast the building into sinister shadow, and Savannah's heart beat fast with fear as Cam reached for the doorknob. He turned the knob and pushed the door open while staying safely outside. Savannah peeked around him into the dark interior of the clubhouse. She was intensely relieved to see Doc sitting in a chair on the far side of the room.

"It's okay," Cam whispered and stepped back to allow her to precede him into the building.

Tucking the envelope that contained the disc firmly under her arm, she stepped inside. Doc didn't stand or speak or acknowledge their presence in any way. Surprised, Savannah squinted in his direction. As her eyes adjusted to the dim light, she saw the silver tape that sealed Doc's mouth and bound his wrists firmly to his chair. She turned to Cam in surprise and was about to demand an explanation when he raised the gun and pointed it directly at her.

"Cam?" she whispered.

"Don't make this worse than it has to be," he said. His eyes were sad but his tone firm.

"What are you doing?" she cried.

"I'm afraid I'm going to have to ask you for that disc. Mr. Ferrante is very anxious to get it."

Savannah stared at him incredulously. "*You* work for Mario Ferrante?"

"Yes. I'm sorry." He seemed sincere.

"You helped with the kidnapping?"

"I *planned* the kidnapping," Cam sounded almost proud. "I arranged for the substitute to come to Epic School. I fixed the traffic lights and convinced Lacie and Doug to betray you. I sent Caroline to live with her grandparents."

She waited for him to say it was all a joke, but he just stood there with the gun pointed at her chest. And finally she had to accept the unacceptable. Cam was her enemy. Her knees buckled, and his arm shot out to catch her before she fell.

CHAPTER 21

Savannah opened her eyes, and for a few seconds she was too stupefied to be afraid. She saw the corrugated metal roof over her head. She felt the cold, hard cinderblock wall against her back. But she couldn't remember where she was or why. Then her eyes focused on Cam, who was still holding the gun. Beside Cam stood a woman who looked very much like him. Cam with long hair. Under other circumstances Savannah would have laughed.

As it was, she whimpered and scrambled away from him. She moved over to the chair where Doc was taped. Doc looked down at her with sad eyes.

"I don't think you've met my twin sister, Mary," Cam said as if they were making polite conversation.

"Mary Jacobs," Savannah whispered. "You're the substitute teacher who kidnapped Caroline."

The woman remained silent, but Cam answered for her. "Jacobs is an alias. Her real name would have led investigators to me."

"Her face too." Savannah glanced at the medic taped to the chair. "And that's why you couldn't let anyone see the picture that Doc's friend at Langley enhanced. So you drugged him and stole the picture."

Cam nodded. "Yeah, if anybody saw a clear shot of Mary's face, they wouldn't be able to miss the resemblance."

"Using her was a risk," Savannah said weakly, still recovering from the shock.

"I needed someone I could trust completely," Cam explained. "And keeping the police and FBI from finding out Mary's true identity was easy since most of them were on Mr. Ferrante's payroll."

"But you didn't count on my involving Dane."

Cam frowned. "He was the last person you should have turned to."

Savannah glanced at Mary, who stood mutely by the door. "She brought Doc here?"

"When we got the word that Doc was waking up, I knew I had to act fast."

"Because he'd tell everyone that you drugged him."

Cam didn't deny it. "I called her from my car right before we left Dane's cabin and told her to dress up as a nurse and get him out of the hospital before he woke up and said something incriminating. That little detour to meet the photographer not only gave me access to the disc—it gave Mary more time to get Doc relocated."

Savannah forced herself to ask a question, even though she wasn't sure she wanted to know the answer. "What now?"

"First, give me the disc."

Savannah surrendered it without argument. Cam tucked the disc into the pocket of his jacket and walked over to a chemical drum. He opened a laptop that was set up on it. After studying the screen for a few seconds, he said, "Mr. Ferrante is anxious to meet you, Savannah. So we'd better get out of here before Dane arrives."

Savannah fought against despair. Dane was probably the only person who could save her, but based on Cam's behavior over the past few minutes, she was certain that Dane would be putting his own life at risk if he tried. And she wanted Dane to live.

Cam addressed his sister. "Mary, you go first. Tuck your hair up under that hat." He pointed at a baseball cap hanging on a nail by the door. "And take my car. Hopefully the goon Hack had tailing Savannah will think you're me and follow you. Lose him as quick as you can, and then meet me at my apartment." He tossed her his keys.

Once Mary's hair was hidden underneath the cap, the resemblance to her twin brother was startling. Without a word she slipped outside, closing the door softly behind her.

"Hack had someone following me?" Savannah asked.

"Since the minute we got involved in the case," Cam confirmed as he watched the computer screen. "Dane insisted on it."

She appreciated Dane's concern for her safety, for what good it had done. She looked up at Doc. "Are you okay?" she asked, and he nodded. She turned her attention back to Cam. "Can I take the tape off Doc's mouth?"

"No," was his brief reply. Talking more to himself than her, he added, "Mary's gone, and Hack's goon left right behind her. Now just a few minor adjustments . . ." His fingers tapped the keyboard for a minute or two. Then he stepped away from the makeshift computer desk and moved toward Savannah. When he reached her, he held out a hand. "Time for us to go."

She ignored his hand but rose to her feet. "How can you take me to Mario Ferrante? He's in FBI custody."

"Actually, he's not. That was just a scam to get rid of Hack," he informed her. "I needed to even the odds a little before I made my move."

"Please," she begged. "Whatever he's paying you, I'll give you more."

Cam smiled without amusement. "It *was* about money at first—me working for Mr. Ferrante I mean. I just did a couple of jobs a year to supplement my income. I thought I could quit at any time. I didn't realize that once he gets you—he never lets you go. Mario Ferrante owns my soul."

She was searching for something to say when her thoughts were interrupted by the series of beeps from the laptop. Frowning, Cam walked back to the laptop and studied it. "It looks like a new regiment of Hack's men have arrived much sooner than I was expecting. They've spread out to cover strategic positions around the practice range." He glanced over at Savannah. "Which means Dane can't be far behind."

Savannah was torn between elation and terror. Dane didn't know what he was walking into, and there was no way for her to warn him without putting Doc's life at risk.

"I had hoped to avoid a confrontation, but now it's inevitable." The light from the laptop's screen gave Cam's face an evil glow.

The only thing she could think of was to try and distract Cam. So she asked, "Please, at least let me give Doc some water. He's been sick, and he's so pale . . ."

"He'll be fine," Cam dismissed her concern for Doc. Then he looked up. "Dane's here."

Savannah's heart pounded, and her eyes moved of their own volition toward the door.

"Don't even think about it," Cam said softly. "Come over here by me."

She shook her head and tried to move out of his reach. But that was impossible in the small confines of the clubhouse. He grabbed her by the arm.

"I don't want to hurt you or Doc," he said. "But I will if I have to."

Cam dragged her into position in front of the door just as Dane burst in. Dane's eyes locked with Savannah's briefly, and she gave him a teary smile.

"I'm okay."

Cam interrupted the tender exchange. "And she'll stay that way as long as you cooperate. Come in and close the door."

Dane did as he was told. Then he turned back to face Cam. "Hack's men have the whole area sealed off. You can't escape."

Cam laughed. "I've gotten out of tougher situations than this lots of times."

Dane didn't contradict him, and Savannah wasn't sure if it was because this was true or just because he didn't want to antagonize the man with a gun.

"Stay back and keep your hands where I can see them," Cam commanded.

"Okay." Dane held his hands out. "Now what do you want?"

"It has nothing to do with what I want. It's what Mr. Ferrante wants."

"He's been working for Mario Ferrante for years," Savannah explained.

Dane nodded. "We figured Cam was the connection with Ferrante when we saw his name listed on the Nick at Night disc."

Savannah saw the shock she felt reflected on Cam's face. "You couldn't have seen the information on the disc! We just got it from the photographer!"

"The disc you got from the photographer is a copy," Dane contradicted him. "General Steele sent a team to get the original yesterday. It's been carefully reviewed. We know everything."

"Mr. Lowe wasn't really out of the country?" Savannah asked in astonishment.

Dane shook his head. "No. He cooperated with us so we'd have time to analyze the disc." He returned his gaze to Cam. "The disc that implicated Cam."

Savannah was confused. "But Cam's name wasn't on the disc. I'm sure I would have remembered."

"His real name isn't Cam," Dane pointed out, and Savannah felt foolish.

"Of course it's not," she whispered.

Surprisingly, Cam laughed. "I'm not going to fall for that trick," he told Dane. "You don't have the original disc."

"Then how do I know you were involved?"

Cam shrugged. "Wes did a good job of sanitizing the records to protect me, but it's possible you found some evidence. Or maybe you're just guessing."

"Are you willing to bet your life on that?" Dane asked.

"I don't have to," Cam replied. "The information on the disc is as damaging to the Army as it is for me. If the general has the disc, he has no intention of making it public. He just wants to use the disc to prosecute me. But as long as Savannah is under Mr. Ferrante's "protection," the Army will leave me alone and the team will keep silent."

"You have no honor," Dane accused.

"I use my training to make a living just like you do," Cam used as his defense. "And I still have honor. Mr. Ferrante told me to take you out permanently, but I won't do that unless you give me no choice."

"All for one and one for all," Dane taunted.

Cam nodded. "We take care of each other whether we want to or not."

"That motto didn't stop you from killing Wes," Dane pointed out, and Savannah couldn't control a gasp.

She twisted her head so she could see Cam. "Is that true?" she demanded.

"Cam ran him off the road just a few miles from here," Dane answered instead.

"I am responsible for his death, but I didn't kill him," Cam said stubbornly. "And besides, Wes didn't deserve to be a member of the team. He proved that when he left you behind in Russia."

"That was between me and Wes," Dane said. "I didn't need you to fight my battles for me."

"Obviously you *did!*" Cam contradicted. "Since you didn't do a thing. You let Wes take your place as commander of the special ops unit. You let him live with the woman who was supposed to be your wife. You just pretended like Russia never happened."

"You don't care about what happened in Russia," Dane accused. "You were just trying to protect yourself."

Savannah remembered the horrific images on the disc. "You killed all those innocent women and children?"

"There was nothing innocent about them!" Cam yelled. "They would have killed us if we gave them the chance!"

"Wes sanitized the records that related to Operation Nick at Night," Dane said for Savannah's benefit. "But he held on to the original disc that contained the accurate information. Probably to keep Cam in line."

"If Wes saved you from prosecution, why did you kill him?" Savannah asked Cam.

"I told you I didn't kill Wes," Cam responded wearily. "Mr. Ferrante had some of his goons do it."

"Why?" Savannah whispered.

Cam faced Dane and answered, "Wes threatened to come clean about everything. He said the guilt was eating him alive. He felt like his only hope for happiness was to confess. He was going to tell Savannah what he did in Russia and let her choose between the two of you. He was going to tell General Steele that he took my name out of the records of the operation in Nicaragua and let the general decide whether to court martial us both. He promised that it would all be for the best."

Dane raised an eyebrow. "But you didn't agree."

"No!" Cam cried emphatically. "I begged him not to do it. My ex-wife barely lets me see my boys as it is. There's no chance that she'd bring them to visit me in military prison! I explained to Wes that confessing might save his marriage, but it would ruin my life!"

"Wes didn't care?" Dane guessed.

"He said he was sorry, but it was something he had to do," Cam replied. "It was so unfair! His soul cleansing was going to cost me my *family*!"

"So you asked Ferrante for help," Dane guessed.

Cam nodded. "He told me to arrange a meeting with Wes at the practice range and to be sure he brought the disc. He said they were going to teach Wes a lesson about ratting out his friends."

"I presume that Wes didn't bring the disc?"

"No," Cam confirmed. "And he wouldn't tell them where it was. That's what got him killed." Cam looked at Dane with pleading eyes. "I swear I didn't know they were going to run him off the road. I thought they were just going to follow him until he led them to the disc."

"After Wes died, Ferrante continued to look for the disc?" Dane pressed.

"Yeah, the search was pretty intense for a while," Cam said with a sigh. "After a few months of nothing he told me to relax. He'd keep an eye on Savannah, monitor her phone calls, e-mails, visitors. If the disc turned up, we'd get it."

"And finally, two years later, Savannah did find the disc," Dane said.

"Yeah," Cam confirmed. "Ferrante called me and said we needed to figure out a way to get it without making any waves."

"Which is how the kidnapping plot was born." Dane made no effort to hide his contempt.

Cam didn't deny it. "Yeah."

Savannah blinked back tears and asked, "If you love your boys so much, how could you take Caroline from me?"

Cam's expression hardened. "I didn't want to, but like I told you, Mr. Ferrante owns me."

"And a great asset like Cam wouldn't do Ferrante much good in jail," Dane added.

Cam continued to appeal to Savannah. "Mr. Ferrante knows where my boys live. I couldn't refuse without endangering them. So I did everything I could to protect Caroline. I even involved my own sister, which like you said was a significant personal risk."

"Do you expect me to thank you for kidnapping my daughter nicely?" Savannah was incredulous.

"Of course not." Cam's tone was dull, hopeless. "Although you probably should. If Mr. Ferrante had assigned someone else to grab

Caroline, they would have killed her immediately. I knew I could protect your child. But if he went after my boys, there would be no one there to save them."

Savannah felt an unwelcome kinship with Cam. She knew how terrible it was to fear for the safety of a child.

"And didn't you think Caroline's 'rescue' was accomplished pretty easily?" Cam continued.

"What are you saying?" Dane demanded.

"There was no rescue," Cam claimed. "I *gave* Caroline to you." Cam waited for this announcement to sink in before adding, "When you figured out that Caroline was on the mountain with her grandparents, I delayed telling Mr. Ferrante to avoid a confrontation with the Army."

"I suppose you expect Savannah to thank you for that too?" Dane said with derision.

"I do thank you for that," she said.

Cam looked relieved. "I took every precaution," he told her. "My honor demanded it."

"If you're so honorable and dedicated to our old code, what's your excuse for Doc?" Dane asked, and he didn't sound even slightly sympathetic. "How did his attempted murder fit into your dedication to 'All for one and one for all?'"

"Doc." Savannah looked at the man taped to the chair. He nodded briefly, confirming Dane's accusation.

"I wasn't trying to kill him!" Cam claimed. "I just wanted to give him enough meds to confuse him so I could convince him he'd been wrong about the picture. I was real careful about the amounts I gave him, but the next thing I knew, he was in a coma."

"He was going to show me the picture of your sister," Dane said.

Cam nodded. "I couldn't let Mary get into trouble."

"The whole kidnapping operation was brilliantly planned," Dane said. "But what now? Ferrante leaves no witnesses behind, but your 'honor' code won't allow you to kill us."

"I'll deliver Savannah and the disc to Mr. Ferrante," Cam replied. "As long as you and Doc keep quiet about Operation Nick at Night, she'll be safe."

Dane smirked. "Once you turn her over to Ferrante, you relinquish control. If he kills her, your honor is history."

Cam looked shaken, but he said, “I won’t let him kill her.”

Dane laughed. “Like you could stop him!”

Cam pulled Savannah toward the door. “Enough talk. We’re leaving.”

Savannah couldn’t control a whimper. “Don’t separate me from my daughter again.”

“I’m sorry,” Cam replied, and he really did seem to be. “I’m sure Dane will take good care of Caroline.”

“How do you plan to get past Hack’s men outside?” Dane asked.

“With Mr. Ferrante’s help, I was able to obtain a large quantity of a biological weapon currently being developed in several countries,” Cam said. “It’s a mixture of halothane and fentanyl, similar to the cocktail that was used in Moscow in 2002.”

“Knockout gas?” Dane asked, and for the first time since he’d walked into the clubhouse, he looked worried.

Cam nodded. “Our scientists have been perfecting it to be used in hostage situations.” He glanced down at Savannah. “It causes instant unconsciousness but not death, so it can be pumped into a room full of hostages and their captors. Over the past few weeks, I altered the sprinkler system here at the practice range. Now the hoses that were intended to release water have released knockout gas instead.”

“Released?” Savannah repeated.

Cam nodded toward the chemical drum where the computer was set up. “I used the laptop to start the process a few minutes ago. Dane engaged me in this long, soul-searching conversation to give the other members of his assault squad time to surround me. Instead, he gave the gas time to work. Now all of Hack’s men are unconscious.”

Savannah felt almost as desperate as she had on the day Caroline was kidnapped. She looked to Dane, hoping he had a backup plan.

“You know, Cam, a court martial isn’t the worst thing that can happen to you. With our testimonies and some help from the general, you might get off pretty easy.” Dane’s tone was earnest, almost pleading, and Savannah’s hopes died. If Dane had resorted to begging, there was no backup plan.

Cam pulled Savannah closer to the door. “Move out of the way.”

“You know I can’t let you take her without a fight,” Dane said softly.

Cam smiled at Dane. "I know you can't win. There was a day when it might have been a good contest, but after Russia . . ."

Instead of moving out of the way, Dane planted his feet firmly on the concrete floor in obvious challenge.

Cam sighed. "Why do you always have to do everything the hard way?"

He pushed Savannah against the wall and yanked a set of handcuffs from his belt. He clipped one end to Savannah's wrist and the other to one of the security bars on the window, all without taking his eyes off Dane. Then he leaned down and whispered, "This is going to be very bad for Dane. He is forcing me to hurt him, but I won't kill him if you stay still. Do you understand?"

She nodded, her heart pounding with fear.

Cam tucked the gun in the waistband of his pants in an obvious gesture of disrespect and then stepped out into the small, open space. He waved both hands at Dane. "Come on."

Dane moved quickly, and the two men clashed together with a sickening thud. Savannah watched in horror as they fought savagely for an advantage. They crashed against the walls and knocked over boxes as first one, then the other, gained temporary control. They spun, and she could see Dane's face taut with effort. They spun again as Cam seemed to gain the upper hand, and Savannah despaired. Then she heard the ominous sound of a bone cracking, and Cam cried out. Her relief was short lived as he used his good hand to pull the gun from his waistband.

With sweat glistening on his face and his eyes focused firmly on Dane, Cam stepped over to Savannah. He extended the handcuff key toward her and said, "Unlock it and come on."

"Don't do it, Savannah," Dane instructed. "He won't kill us."

"My sons are worth more than my honor, and I will kill *anyone* to protect them!" Cam's voice was shrill.

Afraid Cam was beyond reason, she unlocked the cuff from around her wrist and walked to Cam. Dane stared at her with unconcealed fury.

"Take a deep breath right before we go outside," Cam instructed Savannah. "The knockout gas should have dissipated into the air by now, but just in case, we don't want to breathe until we are inside the car."

Savannah nodded numbly.

Cam addressed Dane. "Don't make me kill you." Then he put his right arm around Savannah's neck and she could see the injured wrist dangling uselessly. He held the gun to her head with his good hand and kicked open the door. As he pushed Savannah toward it, Dane lunged at them. Cam spun, pulling Savannah with him, and shot Dane squarely in the chest. The deafening sound reverberated off the metal ceiling while Savannah stared at the hole that formed in the fabric of Dane's jacket as he fell backward. Their eyes locked for a second, and she whispered, "I'm sorry."

Then Cam forced her out into the night.

Savannah stumbled as Cam dragged her, but he didn't seem to notice. He just kept moving toward his sister's car. Tears blurred her vision as she thought about the bullet hole in Dane's chest. How would she go on through life without him? And who would take care of Caroline? She wiped angrily at her eyes and then scanned the trees that lined the practice range, hoping that some of Hack's men hadn't been affected by the gas, but no friendly giants appeared.

Just before they reached the car, he turned suddenly and ducked behind the clubhouse. He returned the gun to his waistband and reached down to yank open what looked like a cellar door. "Get in quick," he instructed.

Savannah wasn't particularly claustrophobic, but the idea of going into the dark, damp hole was terrifying, and she shrunk back. "Please don't ask me to go in there."

"I'm not asking you," he growled. "I'm telling you!"

She put a foot hesitantly onto the first rung of a mildew-stained ladder.

"Hurry or I'll push you down," he said.

Left with no choice, Savannah obeyed. She reached the end of the ladder and put her feet on a moist dirt floor. The air was stale and the earthen walls were too close. When Cam shut the trap door above, she felt panic rising inside her. Then he turned on a small flashlight and pointed the beam of light down a narrow corridor. "This way," he told her.

In spite of her determination to displace herself from her current surroundings and the events in the shed, Savannah couldn't seem to stop her tears. She would wipe them away, but they were immediately replaced by new ones. Each time she raised her hand to clear away the fresh wave of tears, Wes's watch would slide from her wrist to her elbow and then back again. It was heavy and annoying, and she briefly considered dropping it on the dirt floor of the tunnel. If she survived this, she could always come back for it later. If not, it wouldn't matter.

Then she remembered that Dane had said the watch had special features, including GPS. She felt a momentary burst of hope. Maybe someone was tracking them through the dark tunnel. But only a few people knew she had the watch. Hack was in Miami, Doc was taped to a chair, Cam had betrayed them, and Dane was bleeding to death on the clubhouse floor. A small sob escaped her lips.

"Keep up!" Cam demanded, jerking her attention back.

She increased her pace while casually pushing the watch up past her elbow where it clamped firmly to her upper arm. She didn't want Cam to notice the watch, just in case.

They walked for what seemed like miles through the dark, musty tunnel. Cobwebs brushed her face, and crawling creatures crunched under her feet. She tried not to think about anything except putting one foot in front of the other.

Finally they reached the end of the tunnel and Cam led her up another ladder similar to the one they used to get in. At the top of the ladder, Cam extinguished the flashlight and pushed open the door with his good arm. He climbed out and pulled her after him. Once they were standing, he hooked his bad arm through hers and handed her the flashlight so he could hold the gun in his good hand. Then he pulled her toward a line of trees.

Suddenly the darkness of the night was pierced by two headlights. Cam cursed as a familiar form stepped into the intersecting beams of light.

"It's over, Cam," Dane said, pointing a gun at her captor.

"How did you get out of the clubhouse?" Cam seemed mostly curious.

"Hack didn't really go to Miami on that wild goose chase you set up for him. He was parked at the end of the road—close to the spot where Wes died—as my last line of defense. I had my cell phone on the whole time, so he heard your announcement about the gas. He waited for it to dissipate before he came up to the clubhouse."

Cam laughed. "So I made a mistake, and you have nine lives. But I have Savannah, and we all know how much she *really* means to you!"

"Let her go and drop the gun," Dane said gently. "We have your children in protective custody. We'll help you safeguard them from Ferrante."

"No one can help me," Cam's voice was filled with despair. "Ferrante is like you—invincible. I have to deliver Savannah to him or my kids will die. Maybe not today or tomorrow, but he'll get to them eventually."

Savannah understood some of Cam's terror for his children and felt sure that Dane wasn't going to talk him into surrender. Besides, she was tired of playing the part of a damsel in distress. It was time she did something to save herself. She considered her options quickly and came up with a plan. The stakes were painfully high. Failure meant death. Success meant freedom.

Slowly she eased her hand up her arm until her fingers closed around the watch that had belonged to both Wes and Dane. Refusing to think about the sentimental value and concentrating only on practicality, she pulled off the watched and slipped it into the outside pocket of Cam's jacket. One way or the other she hoped Cam would lead Dane to Ferrante. Then Caroline would be truly safe.

Once she was sure Cam would be easy to track, she laced her fingers together and brought her combined fists down onto Cam's broken wrist with all her might. He screamed in pain and released her abruptly. She flung herself away from Cam and ran toward Dane.

Dane moved remarkably fast for a man who had just been shot in the chest, and seconds later he was wrapping his arms around her. Her fingers went straight to the hole in his jacket.

"I thought you were dead!" she whispered.

"Bulletproof vest," he replied, keeping his eyes on Cam. Dane's free hand circled her waist and kept her pressed against him. Then he said, "Don't make me hurt you, Cam."

"You won't shoot me," Cam said with breathless confidence. "All for one and one for all." Then he turned and staggered toward the woods, cradling his injured hand against his chest.

As he disappeared into the night, Dane whispered, "He's right. I can't shoot him."

"Well, as long has he's wearing his jacket you *can* track him," Savannah said. "I put Wes's watch with the GPS signal into his pocket. I'm hoping he'll lead you to Mario Ferrante."

There was rare approval in Dane's eyes. "That was good thinking." He pulled his cell phone from his pocket and spoke into the receiver. "Hack, did you get that? The same GPS signal you've been tracking to help us find Savannah will now lead you to Cam."

"Roger," Hack's voice replied. "Do you want me to call the police?"

"You'd better call General Steele and let him send some men to handle it," Dane replied.

"Where are you and Doc?" Dane asked.

"On our way to you," Hack responded.

Apparently satisfied with that answer, Dane closed his phone and returned it to his pocket. Then he ran his hands down her arms as his eyes did a visual inventory. "Are you okay?"

She was afraid that once she admitted she was fine, his semi-embrace would end, so she asked another question instead of answering his. "You didn't send Hack to Miami because you knew the FBI didn't really have Ferrante?"

He nodded. "I let Cam think that I had fallen for that trick, but I hadn't."

She looked up at him. "Why didn't you let me in on your little secrets, like the fact that Hack wasn't in Miami, and the disc had already been recovered?"

"Because I couldn't risk your safety. If you'd have known, you might have made a slip. Besides, Cam was right about the disc. You picked up the original from the photographer."

She sighed. "How will I ever know when you're telling the truth?"

He smiled. "It's probably safer to assume that I'm not."

Since he'd just saved her life, she decided to let this pass. "Where's Caroline?"

"In General Steele's office."

Savannah's eyes widened. "General Steele is babysitting?"

Dane shrugged. "I couldn't think of anyone else I was sure we could trust."

She thought her heart would burst. Savannah reached up and touched his cheek. "Thank you."

He squeezed her shoulders and then set her back from him as Hack joined them, followed closely by Doc. "I'll call and tell General Steele to bring Caroline and meet us at the cabin."

* * *

Savannah watched Doc in amazement as he climbed out of Hack's Hummer and walked toward them. It was hard to believe that just a few hours before the little man had been in a drug-induced coma.

"Someone should call an ambulance," she told Dane. "Doc needs to be taken back to the hospital."

There was an awkward silence, and finally Doc said, "I don't need to go back to the hospital. I'm fine, really."

Savannah turned to Dane. "I know you won't be irresponsible with Doc's life. You have to be sure that he doesn't have permanent neurological damage."

Doc looked abashed as he admitted, "I wasn't in a coma."

Savannah stared at him in confusion. "What?"

Doc glanced at Dane before continuing. "I kind of exaggerated my condition to fool Cam."

Savannah frowned at Dane. "So for the past few days you've let me worry myself sick about Doc when there's absolutely nothing wrong with him?" Her voice rose dangerously on the last word, and Hack took a step backward. "Doc's illness was all a lie *too*?"

"Savannah," Dane began. "There are things you don't understand."

"Caroline really did feel Doc squeeze her hand, because the whole time we were there encouraging him to live, he was just fine!"

Doc sent Dane an apologetic look. "Sorry."

Dane waved this aside and addressed Savannah. "I can explain."

She planted her hands firmly on her hips. "Then I suggest you get started."

"Why don't we wait until we get back to the cabin . . ." Dane tried, but Savannah was not in the mood to be placated.

"Now."

Dane ran his fingers through his hair in a gesture of frustration. "Ever since Wes died, I've been suspicious about the circumstances, and I had a feeling that Cam was involved. But I thought it was just revenge for what happened in Russia. Then General Steele called and told me about your visit to his office and the disc you claimed to have. He'd done some checking and knew that Cam was a part of the Nick at Night operation. So now I had a suspect and a motive. All I needed was the disc."

She stared at him in astonished horror. "The only reason you took the case was to recover the disc?"

"The official reason I took the case, and the official reason General Steele cooperated, was to recover the disc," Dane admitted.

Now Savannah was almost as angry with Dane as she was with Cam. "When I came to the prison, you let me grovel!" she yelled. "You treated me like a servant and an imbecile and . . . worse! And the whole time you *wanted* to take the case so you could trick me into giving you the stupid disc!"

"I'm sorry," he said, but he didn't look it.

"Your behavior was despicable!"

Dane shrugged. "No worse than blackmail."

Savannah couldn't dispute this, and some of her anger receded. "I can't believe that General Steele would lie to me."

"He didn't lie," Dane pointed out. "He accepted your terms and lived up to every promise he made. He just didn't tell you everything he knew."

She had been betrayed so many times over the past few days that she was beginning to believe that no one could be trusted. "Why?"

"To protect the Army," Dane said.

"All for one and one for all," she whispered.

Dane ran his fingers through his hair. "Most of what I've just told you is classified. If the general finds I divulged Army secrets to a civilian, he'll probably shoot me."

Savannah was in no mood for his morbid humor. "So it was always a trap you and the general were setting for Cam, and I was just there as the bait?"

"More like the catalyst," he amended.

"How could you do that to me?" she demanded. "How could you have so little regard for my feelings and Caroline's safety?"

"You were never in any danger," he assured her. "And we found Caroline."

"But that wasn't your first priority," Savannah countered. "That's why you wasted so much time. You weren't looking for Caroline. You were ambushing Cam."

Dane leaned close and whispered. "The disc may have been the official objective of the operation, but finding Caroline was always my personal priority."

"And why should I believe that?" she hissed back.

His expression hardened, and he took her by the arm. "Come on, Savannah. You can rant and rave all you want on the ride back to the cabin, but I'm through watching you make a spectacle of yourself here."

She jerked her arm away. All the pain and loneliness and guilt that she'd been dealing with seemed to overwhelm her, and she just couldn't be reasonable anymore. "I'm not riding with you! You are a liar and a cheat, and I'll never believe anything you say, ever!"

Dane's lips formed a hard, angry line. "I won't deny your assessment of my character, and you don't have to believe me, but at least this one last time you *are* going to ride with me." Then he reached down and lifted her off her feet. He slung her over his shoulder and pinned her legs firmly to his chest. Savannah found herself hanging upside down in a very undignified position.

"Put me down this minute!" she demanded.

He ignored her. "Doc, you and Hack see about his men. I don't know how long it takes for that knockout gas to wear off, but they should all probably be checked by a doctor."

"Don't worry, we'll take care of things here," Hack assured him. "You've got your hands full already."

Savannah beat on Dane's back with her fists. "I'm not kidding. If you take me to your cabin against my will, I'll call the police and file kidnapping charges against you."

Dane ignored the threat and continued toward the headlights. Savannah lifted her head and yelled at Hack and Doc. "Are you two just going to stand there and let him treat me this way?"

Doc looked apologetic. Hack looked amused. Neither man made any attempt to help her. Dane carried her the last few feet to his car. Then he swung her down and pinned her to the side with his body.

She had never felt such rage toward another person. She lifted her hand to slap him, but he caught her by the wrist, denying her even this minor satisfaction. Her chest was heaving with indignation, and her eyes were burning with unshed tears.

"If I let you go, will you behave yourself?" he asked with infuriating composure.

She kicked at him but missed.

"I'll take that as a no." He opened the passenger door and dumped her unceremoniously inside. As soon as she could right herself, she grabbed the door handle, but it wouldn't budge. He slid in under the wheel and explained, "Child locks. It's a very nice safety feature for children and childish adults."

Dane shrugged off his jacket and then reached for the hem of his T-shirt. He pulled it over his head, exposing the damaged vest. He ripped open the Velcro fastenings, pulled off the vest, and threw it into the backseat. It took him a few seconds to turn his shirt right side out and put it back on. During that time Savannah stared at the beginnings of a terrible bruise on his chest, surrounded by old scars. How could she hate someone who had suffered so much because of her? She leaned her head against the seat in defeat.

He started the car and stepped on the accelerator. The tires spun in a futile attempt to find traction. She put on her seatbelt and watched anxiously as he careened down a dirt path. By the time they reached the highway, she was almost calm.

"Did you know that Lacie had betrayed me?"

"Not at first."

"But before we went to the farm?"

"I had one of Hack's men follow her, so we knew she didn't tour the farm like she claimed," he admitted. "A review of her financial records told the rest of the story."

"But you didn't warn me."

"I separated you from her, and I had you followed everywhere," he said. "That was the best I could do without risking the operation."

Savannah let her mind drift back. When he'd given Lacie an assignment, she'd been jealous, thinking that Dane had more confidence in

Lacie than he did in her. But really he was trying to separate Lacie from the investigation in general and Savannah in particular. When he'd allowed Savannah to stay overnight at the cabin, she'd thought it was because he knew she was afraid of being alone. Now she saw that it was a safety precaution. Strictly business. Nothing personal.

"And Doug really didn't have a major role in the kidnapping?"

Dane shook his head. "It was just like he said. He did a favor for a dangerous friend, unaware that he was facilitating Caroline's kidnapping."

"And Cam sold his soul to the devil?"

"Yes."

"And Doc's not as confused as he seemed to be?"

"No," Dane admitted. "He did go through a bad time after the operation in Russia, but the hospital Wes put him in found the right medications for him. He's been fine for a couple of years now. I told him to act confused so I'd have a reason to double-team him with Cam."

"It looked like Cam was keeping an eye on Doc, but really it was the other way around."

"Right," Dane acknowledged.

"And he didn't overdose on drugs?" she asked.

"Cam did force Doc to take a whole bunch of his pills, but they were placebos."

"And Doc's obsession with taking pills at exact times throughout the day was just part of his crazy act," Savannah guessed.

He nodded.

"I'm mad that you tricked me," she told him. "But I'm glad Doc's okay."

"That's the way to look at it." He flashed her an annoying grin. "And you got your daughter back, which is what you hired me to do."

She scowled at him. "So I was right? All the running around in circles and checking things that had already been checked—it was just for show?"

"You agreed to let me run the operation the way I wanted to," he reminded her. "And it was important for Cam to think we didn't have a clue about his involvement."

"You did a wonderful job of looking clueless."

He didn't seem offended. "Thanks."

Savannah took a deep breath and forced herself to ask, "How long did you know Caroline was at the farm?"

"Not until you did. But once I found out, I arranged for General Steele to secure the area to be sure she couldn't be moved before we got there." He paused for emphasis and then continued, "I wanted to prove Cam's guilt, but finding Caroline was more important to me."

Their eyes met for a few seconds, and she nodded. "Thank you."

His expression was solemn as he replied, "You're welcome."

CHAPTER 22

When Dane pulled his car up to the back door of the cabin, Caroline and the general walked out to greet them. Savannah desperately needed comfort and reassurance. Since she had no one else to provide either, she knelt on the damp grass and hugged her daughter.

"Are you okay, Mama?" Caroline asked when the embrace lasted longer than usual.

Savannah forced herself to release the child and stand. "I'm okay," she said.

"You're dirty." Caroline pointed at the grime from the underground tunnel that still clung to Savannah's clothes.

"It will wash out," Savannah promised. She took Caroline's hand and turned to face the general. He and Dane stood together, regarding her with grim expressions.

"I believe I owe you an apology," the general said.

"You helped me get my daughter back even though I tried to blackmail you," Savannah told him, "If you can forgive me, I'll forgive you."

He smiled. "Then we're friends again."

"Have you heard from Hack?" Dane asked.

"Yes," General Steele confirmed. "His men that were gassed are groggy but fine, and the police have arrested Cam's sister at his apartment."

Dane glanced at Caroline. "What about Cam?"

"He's in jail at Fort Belvoir, and the disc is secure."

"Hack was able to track Cam thanks to Savannah's quick thinking," Dane said.

The general nodded. "And because Dane insisted that his entire special ops unit be returned to active duty, we can court martial Cam instead of using civil courts. That way we can keep a lot of sensitive details about the Nicaraguan operation out of the press."

Savannah couldn't muster much enthusiasm for Army public relations problems, but she was glad things had worked out to the general's satisfaction.

"General Steele knew my daddy," Caroline announced suddenly. "He's been telling me stories while we were driving."

Savannah smiled at her daughter. "You were lucky to have General Steele for a babysitter. He's a very important man."

Caroline's eyes widened. "He didn't tell me that."

General Steele laughed. "What are your plans, Savannah?"

She glanced at Dane before answering, but he looked away.

"I'm not sure," she said honestly. "Now that you have the disc, I guess Mario Ferrante will leave us alone. But in an effort to be more safety conscious I should probably sell my row house since it has too many windows and is impossible to secure." She saw the corners of Dane's mouth curl up at this remark.

"Will you return to your job at the Child Advocacy Center?" General Steele asked.

"The future of the CAC is yet to be determined," she told him. "So I'm not sure that I'll have a job to go back to."

"Why don't you come and work with me at Fort Belvoir?" the general surprised her by suggesting. "I could arrange for you to get post housing, which would be very secure, just in case Ferrante holds a grudge."

Savannah smiled at him. "Thank you. It's good to know I have options."

"Well." The general rubbed his hands together briskly. "I guess I should get going." He took a few steps toward his car and then turned back. "Whatever you decide about the future, I hope you'll bring Caroline to visit me."

"I will," Savannah promised.

After the general drove away, Dane led them into his cabin.

"Are Hack and Cam coming home?" Caroline asked.

Savannah couldn't think of a response, so she let Dane handle the question.

"No," he said. "Not tonight."

"Is Doc better?"

"He is," Dane said.

Caroline smiled. "I told you."

He smiled back. "Yes you did."

Once Caroline was asleep, Savannah went downstairs and took a long, hot shower. She wrapped her hair in a towel and put on her thick robe. Then she went into the living room, where Dane was sitting on the couch staring at the fire.

She sat beside him, close but not touching. She pulled off the towel and let her damp hair fall around her shoulders. Then she said, "I guess I should thank you."

He answered without taking his eyes off the blazing fire. "No thanks are necessary. We both got what we wanted out of the deal."

"Did we?"

He turned to her. "What is it that you want that you haven't gotten yet?"

She took a deep breath and prayed for the courage to express her feelings. "I want for you to be a part of my life and Caroline's. I've never felt as safe and happy as I do here at your cabin. You offered me forever once and . . ."

"This is sounding familiar," he said, retreating into the sarcastic humor that she now recognized as a defense mechanism. "Are you asking me to marry you, *again*?"

"I love you," she said simply. "I always will."

He turned back to the fire. "I know."

"I can't leave you again."

"Yes you can, and you will," he replied firmly. "Because that's what's best for you and your daughter."

"You're determined to push me away?" she said. "Caroline too?"

He stared at the flames, his expression sullen. "It's for your own good."

"You can keep telling yourself that, but I know it was cowardice and not a desire to protect us that led you to that decision."

This got his attention. He turned to face her. "I'm a lot of things, but I'm not a *coward*."

He was angry now, but she didn't care. As long as she knew she was getting through to him.

"You're afraid to love again, and that's understandable," she said. "Love can be painful. I can't promise that if you let me and Caroline into your life we won't ever hurt you. But I know that the love is worth the pain."

He didn't speak for a few minutes, as if he was considering her words, weighing his options, and reaching a sensible conclusion. But when he answered her, she realized that he'd just been stalling. He'd already made up his mind. "Stop begging, Savannah," he said. "You've asked me to marry you. I've said no. Don't make this any more humiliating than it has to be."

Her pain was eclipsed only marginally by her anger. "Okay," she bit the words out. "You win. We'll leave."

Dane looked relieved, which only infuriated her more.

"But this time *I* have a condition," she added and was pleased to see his relief change to wariness.

"What?"

She leaned closer and said, "You have to tell me that you don't love me."

They faced each other for what seemed like a very long time. In the cozy room with the fire crackling happily beside them, she felt removed from the rest of the world. She looked into his warm, brown eyes and was certain that he would be willing to take a leap of faith and risk his heart just one more time.

And then he whispered, "I don't love you."

She knew he was lying, but the words cut deeply just the same. She blinked back tears and said, "Kiss me first and then say it."

She thought he was going to refuse the challenge, but then he took her face into his hands and pulled her gently toward him. He kissed first her forehead, then each of her closed eyes. He kissed her nose, her chin, and pressed several quick kisses along her jaw. Then his lips claimed hers, and she lost all sense of time.

When he moved away, she whimpered in grief at the separation. Then she opened her eyes and saw him watching her with terrible determination. "I don't love you," he said.

The tears spilled onto her cheeks. "Yes you do."

He shook his head. "You promised."

She took a deep, shuddering breath and nodded. "Okay. We'll leave first thing in the morning."

She stood and moved toward the stairs.

"Savannah," he said.

She turned back, her heart pounding with hope. "Yes?"

"You should take the general up on his offer. It will be safe on the base at Fort Belvoir."

She stared at him for a few seconds and then shook her head. "You can't have it both ways. If you're a part of our lives, you get to give me advice. If not, then I make my own decisions."

She held her breath, waiting to see how he would respond.

"Okay," he said with a sigh. "Make your own decision."

Savannah turned away. She walked upstairs and into the guest room with its spectacular view of the creek. She curled up beside Caroline in the twin bed by the window. She lay awake all night, waiting for him to come and admit he loved her and wanted to be a part of their lives. He never did.

* * *

When the first rays of sunlight filtered through the window, Savannah climbed out of bed. She packed their things, woke Caroline, and led the sleepy child down the stairs for the last time. They got into the Mazda that had been parked in Dane's backyard for almost a week. In that short time so much had changed. Caroline was back. Doug and Lacie were dead. Cam was in jail. But one thing had remained the same. Dane was still unreachable.

As she pulled down the gravel road, she looked in the rearview mirror, hoping to see Dane on the porch. She saw only a charming, A-frame cabin nestled along a creek spanned by a new wooden bridge. He might be sending them away, but they had left their mark. She doubted that Dane would ever look at his guest room or that bridge without thinking of them. Determined to be satisfied with that, she drove the car toward the road that led back to Washington, DC.

EPILOGUE
TWO MONTHS LATER

Savannah stood at the window of the lawyer's office, staring at the lights of Washington, DC below. They were waiting for the attorney who was currently handling another closing in the office next door. Savannah tried to tune out the excited chatter of the young couple seated at the table. She liked them, so she had sold the house for what they could afford, even though the price was below the market value. But they were expecting a baby in March, and all the talk of nursery wallpaper and redecorating made her sad.

She studied her own face, reflected in the dark glass. During the past few weeks she'd gained a little weight and visited the hairdresser. She'd accepted General Steele's offer of employment and was now a research assistant for his staff. She and Caroline had a nice apartment at Fort Belvoir, and as an additional safety measure, she'd hired Hack's firm to provide round-the-clock protection.

Since she wasn't ready to let Caroline go to school yet, she'd found a tutor who came to her office every day. The general had arranged for a supply closet to be converted into a schoolroom/playroom for Caroline. Savannah felt settled into her new life, and things were basically back to normal, except for her freshly broken heart. Maybe Dane had been right to keep his true feelings from her for so long. It was certainly harder now than it had been before when she'd thought he hated her. She now had to live with the knowledge that he loved her and just couldn't live with her.

The real estate attorney rushed in and apologized for the delay. Savannah said something polite and took her place at the table. Fifteen minutes later, she left the lawyer's office. Her bodyguard, one of Hack's seemingly endless supply of huge, grim-faced, heavily armed men stepped up beside her. He opened the glass door and accompanied her into the cool December night. The new black Yukon Hack had insisted she purchase was parked at the curb. When her escort opened the backseat door, she saw that Hack himself was behind the wheel.

"Evening," he said with a smile.

Savannah smiled back. "What brings you here personally? Did Dane send you to spy on me?"

"Dane didn't send me," Hack replied.

Savannah turned away so he wouldn't see the disappointment on her face. Because of their business relationship, Savannah saw Hack frequently, and Doc stopped by often, but she hadn't seen Dane since they left his cabin two months before. Sometimes she felt his presence or thought she saw his face in a crowd. She smiled sadly and wondered if she was going crazy like the rest of his associates.

"I call him every day," she told Hack. "I leave him messages, but he doesn't return my calls."

Apparently Hack didn't have an explanation or an excuse because he didn't comment.

"I guess if he really wants me to quit calling, he'll change his number."

Hack remained silent, and Savannah decided to drop the subject.

"Would you take me by the house before we go back to the base?" she asked. "Just one last time?"

Hack glanced at her in the rearview mirror. "That might not be such a good idea."

"Please," she said, knowing he wouldn't be able to refuse her.

When they reached the Victorian row house with the bow front and long, narrow windows, Hack pulled to the curb. She wiped the condensation from the interior of the Yukon's window so she could see more clearly. Light from the windows spilled out onto the small courtyard with the decorative, wrought-iron fence.

She thought about the first day she'd come there with Wes as a new bride, before they knew that Dane was alive, before guilt and despair had overwhelmed their lives. She thought of the day they'd brought Caroline home from the hospital, hoping that the baby could make them a family. Then she thought of the day she and Caroline had come home after Wes's funeral when she'd finally accepted that they'd never be a real family. Finally she remembered how much she'd dreaded coming here alone after Caroline was kidnapped.

Now the house belonged to someone else, and they would make new memories here. She hoped theirs would be happier. It started to rain, and drops of water clung to the glass, further distorting her view and separating her more completely from the only real home she had ever known. That chapter of her life was over. She had to move forward.

"Thanks, Hack," she said to the man, who was staring straight ahead in disapproval. "I'm ready to go to the apartment now. Doc's babysitting for me, and Caroline is probably driving him crazy."

"Short trip," Hack teased, happier now that they were leaving the row house behind.

Savannah smiled. "I won't fall for that again. Doc's saner than the rest of us."

"Can't argue with you there," Hack replied.

During the ride to Fort Belvoir, Hack asked questions about Caroline and the events of the past week. Savannah knew the man was trying to distract her from painful thoughts about Dane, and he was mostly successful.

"Almost home," Hack said, slowing the vehicle as they approached the Tulley Gate entrance to the base. One of the MPs stepped out of the guard shack and held a flashlight to the DOD decal displayed on the front windshield of the Yukon. After a cursory examination, he waved Hack through and retreated into the booth.

Just as Hack began to accelerate, a specter moved in front of the vehicle, and he slammed on the brakes amid a flurry of curses.

Savannah leaned over the backseat and stared at the figure swaying in the illumination provided by the headlights. It was a young, rain-drenched woman. Her hair was wet and a brassy blonde thanks to a terrible dye job that was sadly reminiscent of Lacie. The girl's clothes clung to her thin body, emphasizing the bulge at her midsection that indicated impending motherhood. Her round, frightened eyes were fixed on the Yukon with determination.

Hack opened his door and stepped out into the rain. "Stay inside," he ordered Savannah. "This could be a trick."

Savannah did as she was told, but lowered her window a crack so she could hear what was being said. Three MPs and Hack all approached the girl.

"Help me," she cried toward the Yukon. "Please."

"I'll take care of her," one of the MPs told Hack. "She's just a vagrant who's been hanging around the entrance all day. I warned her that if she didn't leave, I'd have to call the police. Apparently she didn't believe I'd keep my word."

He pulled the girl roughly toward the guard shack, and Hack headed back for the Yukon.

Savannah watched in morbid fascination as the girl twisted away from her captor and called out, "Please, Mrs. McLaughlin! I'm here to see you! I've waited all day!"

"Hack," Savannah began as the big man opened his door.

"No, no, no!" the giant said, anticipating her request. "There's no way you're talking to her. She may be working for Ferrante."

Savannah studied the girl again. "I don't see how she could possibly be a threat."

"She could have a bomb or a hidden weapon," Hack disagreed.

"You can search her. If she isn't carrying a bomb or a weapon, I'll listen to what she has to say. Then we'll decide whether or not to call the police."

"I don't like it," Hack continued to argue.

"But you'll do it," Savannah said with a smile. Then she appealed to his softer side. "She's been waiting all day in the rain, Hack."

He glanced back at the girl, and Savannah knew he was weakening.

"Please," she coaxed him.

Hack was still frowning, but he nodded. "Okay, but you stay here until I've checked her out." He walked to the guard shack and talked to the MPs. Then the men conducted a thorough search with the young woman's cooperation. Finally Hack returned to the Yukon.

Savannah lowered the window, ignoring the rain that pelted her face. "No weapons or bombs?"

"None that we found," Hack admitted.

"So you're ready for me to talk to her?

"Yeah," Hack confirmed. "But I've got a feeling I'm going to regret this."

Savannah laughed. "Don't tell me you're afraid of a half-drowned girl."

"No," Hack agreed. "But I am afraid of Mario Ferrante, and he's smart enough to send a helpless-looking girl to lure you away from safety."

"I'll be careful, Hack," Savannah promised as she climbed out. The last thing she wanted was to put herself or her daughter back in danger. "But I have to be sure."

"I know," he said.

"The girl probably needs medical attention," Savannah remarked.

Hack nodded. "I already called Doc and told him to come."

"Who is watching Caroline?"

"The men I had posted on the outside will go in until we get there. And I sent over a couple of MPs for good measure."

Caroline had gotten used to Hack's large, mean-looking guards, but she wouldn't be particularly comfortable in their care. Savannah wondered if this was Hack's way of ensuring that her interview with the girl was completed in a timely manner.

She followed Hack to the MP station. When they reached the door, he stepped back, allowing her to precede him inside. The girl was seated in one of several wooden chairs lined up along the far wall. The three MPs standing guard all moved back when Hack entered the room. There was no question about who was in charge of this interrogation.

Hack removed his coat and settled it around the girl's thin shoulders.

"Thank you," she whispered through chattering teeth.

Before Savannah could ask any questions, a well-preserved old Bonneville pulled up outside. Savannah watched through the rain-splattered windows of the MP station as Doc climbed out carrying a large cardboard box.

When the small man appeared in the doorway, Savannah announced, "We've got a patient for you."

"So I heard." Doc examined their guest from his position by the door.

"What do you think?" Savannah asked.

"Malnourished, dehydrated, exhausted, and on the verge of hypothermia," Doc diagnosed.

Savannah was impressed. "You can tell all that just by looking?"

Doc nodded. "And she's about seven months pregnant."

"Eight," the girl provided.

Doc crossed the room and put the box on the floor by the girl's feet. He removed Hack's wet coat from her shoulders and replaced it with a blanket. Then he used a towel to dab her damp hair.

Finally Hack seemed to lose patience with Doc's ministrations and stepped forward. "We need to ask her some questions."

"Not until she's had something to eat," Doc replied with surprising authority. He drew a microwaveable container of tomato soup out of his box and handed it to the girl. He watched while she took a few sips and then nodded. "Okay, you can ask your questions now."

Savannah sat in a chair beside the girl. "Let's begin with the basics. What's your name?"

"Rosemary Allen."

"And how old are you, Rosemary?"

"Twenty," the girl replied.

Savannah was pleasantly surprised. She would have guessed fifteen. "And what brings you here?"

"I'm in trouble," the girl stated. Savannah's eyes dipped to her distended abdomen, but Rosemary shook her head. "I don't mean the baby." Rosemary clutched the sides of the blanket with clawlike fingers. "It's something worse. Much worse."

Savannah leaned closer. "Tell me about it."

Rosemary took another sip of soup and then faced Savannah. "My mother died when I was very young. I barely remember her."

This seemed like an odd place to begin an explanation of why the girl found herself in her current circumstances, but Savannah just nodded encouragingly.

"My father was gone a lot, so I was raised by a series of nannies and housekeepers. I never thought Father was neglectful," Rosemary added. "Just busy."

Hack sighed impatiently, and Savannah gave him a cross look. "I understand," she assured the girl.

"My father was protective—obsessive even—about my safety, so I didn't have a lot of freedom. I thought when I started college that would change, but it didn't. He enrolled me at George Washington University, just a few miles from our house. If I was ten minutes late getting home, he'd send someone to look for me." Rosemary's face brightened. "Then I met Chad."

"He's the father of your baby?" Savannah guessed.

Rosemary nodded. "And my husband. My father was furious when he found out we got married behind his back. But when I told him about the baby, he calmed down. He remodeled part of the house to make us our own apartment and even gave Chad a job at his company. I thought everything was going to be fine. But then Chad said they were trying to get him to do things at work that were wrong. Things that were *illegal.*"

Savannah felt a prickling of uneasiness.

"Chad was desperate to get away from my father and arranged for us to live with his parents until he could find another job. But when we told my father, he laughed. He said we weren't going anywhere. He took away our cell phones and our car keys. He withdrew me from school and made Chad ride to work with him every day. We were prisoners."

"Who is your father?" Savannah forced herself to ask.

Rosemary answered with obvious reluctance. "My father is Mario Ferrante."

Hack stopped pacing, and Doc was no longer fidgeting.

"That's it," Hack bellowed. "I'm calling the police."

Savannah held up a hand to stop him. "Not yet." Then she addressed Rosemary. "Do you know that your father helped kidnap my daughter a few months ago?"

Tears seeped out of the girl's eyes. "Yes, Chad told me. I'm sorry."

Savannah patted Rosemary's cold hand. "It certainly wasn't your fault."

Rosemary looked nervously toward the windows of the MP station. "Yesterday I ran away. Chad was supposed to come too. We were going to change our names and make a new life for ourselves where my father couldn't find us."

"But something went wrong?" Savannah guessed.

Rosemary fixed Savannah with a bleak look. "I had a routine doctor's appointment scheduled, and we decided that was our best opportunity to escape. While I was supposed to be waiting to see the doctor, we'd slip out the back door and be gone before my father's driver got suspicious. But when the driver came to pick me up, he said Chad had been delayed at work."

Savannah frowned. "But you escaped anyway? Alone?"

"Yes!" Rosemary sobbed. "Chad made me promise to go on alone if I had to, for the baby's sake. But I didn't really have a plan. Chad was supposed to be there to help me!"

"I imagine you were terrified."

Rosemary nodded. "I walked for hours, trying to stay in large crowds. Then I realized that I needed to change my description, so I found a drugstore and bought a bottle of Sun-In. I sprayed it on in the bathroom at a McDonald's. I guess I used too much, because my hair keeps getting lighter." She lifted a damp, yellow lock. "I hope it doesn't fall out."

Savannah studied the splotchy mess thinking that starting over fresh might not be the worst that could happen to Rosemary's hair. "I'm sure it will be fine," she lied.

"Then I walked some more trying to figure out how to help Chad and my baby." Her lips quivered. "Finally I decided to come to you. You defeated my father once, and you know how it feels to be separated from someone you love. So I hope you'll help me."

Hack shook his massive head. "Mrs. McLaughlin can't help you find your husband. Nobody is crazy enough to take on the mob."

Rosemary kept her eyes steadfastly on Savannah. "I don't have anyone else to turn to."

Later Savannah wasn't sure what tipped the scales in Rosemary's favor. Was it empathy for the girl and her situation? Was it a desire to get some revenge against Mario Ferrante for the pain he'd caused her? Or was the excuse to see Dane again just more than she could resist? Smiling at Rosemary, she said, "I can think of one person crazy enough to take on *anyone*."

Hack and Doc both stared back at her with amusingly horrified expressions.

"Hack, will you take us to my apartment? Rosemary needs a shower and some dry clothes. Caroline and I need to pack. Then we'll head to Tylerton."

"No," Doc whispered.

Hack kicked a chair.

"I strongly discourage you from this course of action," Doc tried.

Hack was less tactful. "Are you *crazy*?"

"Yes," Savannah admitted, too happy to be offended. She was going to see Dane, and under the circumstances, she knew he wouldn't turn them away. "Will you drive us, Hack?"

"What, you think I'm crazy too?" the big man demanded.

"I think craziness is a prerequisite for working with Dane." She turned to Doc. "You're invited too."

The frail man wrung his hands. "Savannah," he said sternly. "This is a mistake."

She laughed. "I've made so many mistakes. What's one more?" Then she took Rosemary by the hand and led her to the waiting Yukon, confident that Doc and Hack would follow. They didn't really have much choice. All for one and one for all.

ABOUT THE AUTHOR

BETSY BRANNON GREEN currently lives in Bessemer, Alabama, which is a suburb of Birmingham. She has been married to her husband, Butch, for twenty-eight years, and they have eight children, two sons-in-law, one daughter-in-law, and three grandchildren. She loves to read—when she can find the time—and watch sporting events—if they involve her children. She is a Primary teacher and family history center volunteer in the Bessemer Ward. She also works in the office at the Birmingham Temple. Although born in Salt Lake City, Betsy has spent most of her life in the South. Her writing has been strongly influenced by the town of Headland, Alabama, and the many gracious people who live there. Her first book, *Hearts in Hiding,* was published in 2001, followed by *Never Look Back* (2002), *Until Proven Guilty* (2002), *Don't Close Your Eyes* (2003), *Above Suspicion* (2003), *Foul Play* (2004), *Silenced* (2004), *Copycat* (2005), *Poison* (2005), *Double Cross* (2006), *Christmas in Haggerty* (2006), and *Backtrack* (2007).

If you would like to be updated on Betsy's newest releases or correspond with her, please send an e-mail to info@covenant-lds.com, or visit her website at http://betsybrannongreen.net. You may also write to her in care of Covenant Communications, P.O. Box 416, American Fork, UT 84003-0416.